WHITE CITY

Also by Dominic Nolan:

Past Life
After Dark
Vine Street

WHITE CITY

Dominic Nolan

HEADLINE

First published in 2024 by
HEADLINE PUBLISHING GROUP

1

Cataloguing in Publication Data is available from the British Library

ISBN 978 1 0354 1675 2

Typeset in 12.32/16.24 pt Adobe Garamond Pro by Jouve (UK), Milton Keynes

Printed and bound in Great Britain by Clays Ltd, Elcograf S.p.A.

HEADLINE PUBLISHING GROUP
An Hachette UK Company
Carmelite House
50 Victoria Embankment
London EC4Y 0DZ

www.headline.co.uk
www.hachette.co.uk

There are other places
Which also are the world's end, some at the sea jaws,
Or over a dark lake, in a desert or a city —
But this is the nearest, in place and time,
Now and in England.

T. S. Eliot

Historical Note

On Wednesday May 21st, 1952, at shortly after 4 a.m., a Post Office van carrying mail bags from Paddington station to the Eastern Central District office, was waylaid on Eastcastle Street, just off Oxford Street, by seven men in two cars. The robbers dragged the postmen from the van and drove it off, escaping with £287,000 in cash from high-value packets. At the time, it was the biggest heist in British history, and would remain so until the Great Train Robbery.

Nobody was ever charged with the crime.

The proceeds from the robbery were never recovered.

PART ONE
EASTCASTLE

I

TELL ME ABOUT THE CAMEL

May 20th, 1952

What came to mind when Adlyn Rowe thought of her mother was falling buildings and blown-off limbs and the end of the world. She was forever repeating the story of how she gave birth to Addie on one of the early nights of the Blitz, a look in her eye like the child brought into the world with her the bombs falling all about them from the sky. Blamed her for that, among other things. It was her favourite story to tell.

Through the wall, Addie could hear her mother talking to herself. Far as she knew, she never heard anyone talking back, but that was no doubt something to look forward to. Her little sister – Florence by birth, but Nees to everyone who knew her – fidgeted in the bed beside her, letting her know she was awake. Addie ignored her, pretending to sleep.

A small hand crawled across her face.

Warm breath in her ear.

'Addie? Addie. *Addieaddieaddieaddieaddie.*'

'Fine.'

A giggle, then Nees pounced on her.

'Nees!'

Another squawk of laughter.

'Get off me, Nees, it's too early.'

It wasn't, at all. All good intentions of getting Nees ready and off to the day nursery before going to school herself had gone by the wayside. Perhaps Mrs Harpenden would have something for her to do.

Nees pulled her nightshirt off over her head.

'I'm going to have eggs.'

'That's what you think?'

'And fried bread. Like Daddy does it.'

'Don't think there's any bread left, and I know we don't got eggs.'

'For breakfast?'

'For breakfast, lunch or dinner.'

Nees dropped her nightshirt and started to put on her dress from the previous day.

'Not that one.'

She popped her eyes like, *What, me?*

'You know you just picked it off the floor. Your other one's hanging right there where I put it last night and told you you'd be wearing it.'

Nees sighed and walked the three whole paces to the wardrobe to fetch the clean dress. Their narrow bed was pushed under the only window. Three chunky wardrobes, all with drawers at the bottom, formed an L shape around the corner of two walls, their mother's stuff filling two, their own and their father's squished into the other.

'What are you . . . Put a little something on underneath, thank you. Still got clean ones in the drawer there.'

'Got one pair.'

'You need more than that right now? And your socks.'

'Don't like them.'

'Long as we're listing things we don't like—'

A sharp rapping on the wall shut them up. Perfectly still, they waited, and there it was again, rat-a-tat-tat.

'Now you done it,' Addie said.

'Wasn't me.'

'Who else bouncing around waking the whole house up?'

Addie pointed for her sister to put on her socks. Swinging out of bed, she pulled on yesterday's corduroys and jumper, to loaded looks from Nees.

'I'll go see what she wants.'

The front door was open, as it usually was with all the comings and goings of tenants. The first in a long range of dowdy four-storey Victorian semis, the basement and ground floor were flats, the upper two floors rented as rooms.

Her parents' room at the front was dim, a dust-marbled shaft of light slicing in as the curtains hadn't been pulled tight. The left side was thicker where her mother had finished double-siding one curtain some years earlier but never got round to the other. A three-quarter bed, turned down with an ornate spread, didn't quite fit into the alcove and so was pushed up against a drop-leaf table slotted into the gap with disregard.

The bed was undisturbed other than having Stevie Rowe lying atop the sheets in her dressing gown, one arm draped dramatically over her face where the light from the window fell. Beside her was the brass curtain draw rod she'd knocked on the wall with.

The high-backed chair Addie's father always hung his work clothes on was noticeably bare, the low table in front of the green velvet sofa in the window bay was busy with empty bottles and stained glasses.

'Adlyn, would you be so kind as to do something about the sun?'

Standing on the sofa, Addie closed the curtains completely. She went to leave, but wavered by the bed. Stevie opened one eye, peering up at her from beneath her arm.

'Dad didn't come home?'

The eye snapped shut.

'Wonderful seeing you so early, Adlyn, but that's enough.'

Addie pulled the door closed behind her, the lock no longer catching because the frame was splintered around it. Nees was in the scullery, at the back of the house behind their room, looking for eggs in unlikely places.

'Told you there no eggs.'

'Dad would make me eggs.'

'Not unless he's a hen.'

'Where *is* Dad?'

'Working, I think.'

'What did Mum want?'

'For me to turn off the sun.'

Nees shrugged, it not being the most demanding request she'd ever made.

'Come on, sit down. See what I can find for breakfast.'

'And a story.'

The table was a place of chatter in the mornings, their father a great one for his yarns that always amused his daughters.

'Tell me about the camel.'

'Always the camel with you.'

It was Nees's favourite. The way their father would tell it, he'd lean back and take a deep breath, looking up to the ceiling as if searching for the right words, even though he told it the same every time.

'Now, let me see,' he'd say, hand on his chin as it all came back to him. 'As I recall, it was a warm-warm day. Kind of day you want to feel the sun on your skin, lie against the baked earth like a spotted lizard.'

'Spotted lizard!' Nees would say.

'A cold drink day. But of course, I had work to do. Back then I worked all sorts of jobs, but at that time I was loading at the marmalade place in Silvertown, down on the docks. My good friend from the fire service got me on there, the boss agreeing so long as there was no foolishness. He wouldn't stand for that, worked us like hounds.

'There we were, loading boxes of jars like it's kingly business, sneaking a little comfort in the sun as we worked, and then' – he'd bring his hands together in a loud clap, Nees jumping with delight – 'total uproar. Massive confusion. You know, they already dropped the bombs the night before, but we weren't ready for them along the sugar mile in broad daylight. Boom! Boom! Boom! And the ground rumbled beneath our feet, and the dark smoke come over our heads. Then it was more like an English bleaky day, away from the smell in the air, which had a dark sweetness to it.

'Men poured out of Silvertown, off the island, every one of them black as soot and kerchiefs over their mouths. The factories all closed under the bombardment, hearts of gold those bosses. But the sugar refinery took a direct hit. You never seen anything like it. The stores were ablaze, the sugar burning, and the streets was paved with bomb-cooked caramel. Great chunks of it just there for the taking. We chiselled up plates of the stuff, hands and clothes black and sticky with it. I don't know what damage I did to my teeth on the caramel road that day, but it was worth it.'

'Camel road.' Each time the tale had spilled out of her father, Nees basked in a soughing of fire, a scent of sugar so real she'd lick her lips, and it was all the sweeter for knowing what she had dreamed he had lived.

What could Addie offer in the face of that?

'Well, back then at the time of war, Daddy made marmalade, which, like eggs, we don't got none of right now.'

From her bed, Stevie listened to Addie mangle her father's war story. He'd told them it that many times that he probably now believed those fiery first days actually happened like he said. A wonderland where they danced between falling incendiaries, the roads ambered in tasty candy, and his courageous pregnant wife giving birth to their first child amid the destruction.

Stevie's recollection differed. They'd been apart from each other for long stretches, Reggie working at the factory and also volunteering with the Auxiliary Fire Service, on their toes during those early raids, and Stevie home along with the other young wives and mothers. Her neighbour Pat was a sweetheart and also married to a Jamaican, and had a young boy so knew exactly what was coming as unerringly as any German bomber. Like tourists they stood in the street to watch them overhead. A draughtboard alley near the docks, black and white families living side by side, black kids, white kids, some a bit of both. All of them with their arms spread wide, lips brrring like Spitfires as they ran.

Stevie didn't remember caramelised streets.

She remembered chalk lines scratched in the roads to direct bomb refugees to hastily arranged shelters.

She remembered being evacuated because of an unexploded bomb in Canning Town, not knowing where Reggie was as he hadn't been home in forty-eight hours.

She remembered lying awake on the floor of a school classroom, surrounded by other pregnant women and young mothers who must have had strange bedfellows coming out their ears, way they nodded off at the drop of a hat.

The school had been pandemonium. Six hundred people through there in a few short days. Brickwork bulging where it had already been hit on the first night. Buses were coming for everyone, to move them God knows where, but they never arrived. She hadn't been able to stand it, and talked Pat into returning home with her.

Pat, who'd helped her three sisters give birth, and who boiled water and fetched towels and made a sandwich for her boy to keep him busy. At exactly quarter to four in the morning, as the ground beneath them shook from nearby bombs, a baby girl emerged into the world, had a short wail, and settled comfortably on her mother's chest, swaddled with unreasonable love, for that was all there was in the world now.

Reggie never told the children about that.

Never told them that because he hadn't been home in days, he'd believed Stevie to still be in the school with the rest of the evacuees. The school that took a direct hit shortly before four in the morning and collapsed into its own basement with everyone inside.

The school whose rubble he was clawing at with bloodied hands, searching for what he knew would be nothing more than remains, when Stevie came walking down the street holding their daughter.

Never told them that.

Never told them how when he got to her, he threw up on the almost murderous shoes she'd squeezed her swollen feet into. How he sat on the kerb and cried. How the authorities stopped the newspapers reporting the dozens and dozens of bodies of women and children pulled from the ruins, or the hundred more they concreted over as they couldn't recover them. The single largest loss of life the Germans inflicted from the air, and nobody knew.

Perched on the kerb beside her weeping husband, holding the new-born Addie, it dawned on Stevie with a thrilling sinking sensation that they did not live in the land of the brave. All knotted together in the sooted sack of war, what choice was there but to bear it?

God forbid he told that story.

And now he was gone again, some tall tale about a special project he was on at the Post Office, where he'd worked the past nearly six years.

'Two, three nights, love, I won't be home. Overtime, you see. Bonuses. Easier to kip down with Jerry in Clerkenwell, near the depot. You know Jerry.'

Jerry, who'd never before been mentioned and who didn't exist. Only ever explained himself to assuage a guilty conscience, was probably off taking all night to do what they once did all night.

Not that she'd always been saintly herself.

She'd see what story he told when he returned home stinking of cheap tart.

When he came home—

A knocking at the front door aroused her from her reveries.

In the hall, someone called out, 'Hi hi hi.'

'Oh sweet merciful Christ,' Stevie mumbled, 'please just take me now.'

Hearing his voice, Addie rushed back into the hall in a panic.

Mr Grainger stood at the front door, a young man who looked middle aged, wearing a threadbare suit with the tie loose at the collar and blessed with the complexion of a slice of Spam. In one hand he held a tool bag, the other swiping at a persistent glaze on his forehead.

His late mother, from whom he'd inherited the house, had been favourably inclined toward theatrical types, it having been that sort of neighbourhood for many years, and that was what she had believed the Rowes to be when Stevie showed up a couple of years after the war, young Addie in her arms, looking for rooms and glowing with a residual glamour from her days as a nightclub hostess.

That her prospective tenant's husband was a postal worker was just fine, suggesting a stable income as it did. That he turned out to be Jamaican was less so, but Mrs Grainger overlooked what she considered to be a deception as even before the war she'd been accustomed to renting rooms to black entertainers on a short-term basis. And she was completely captivated by young Addie, feeling a child would enliven the house no end.

Her son was less captivated.

'Cup of tea, Mr Grainger?' Addie said, with the supreme confidence that she'd figure out what to do about not having either tea or milk somewhere between the front door and the scullery.

'Hello, uh . . .'

'Addie,' said Addie understandingly, the two of them only having met the three or four dozen times.

'Hello, young Addie. I'm afraid I have come on proprietorial business, and as such—'

Stevie threw open her door, wearing now her light summer robe with a tottery smile, and brushed her hair out of her face.

'Why, Mr Grainger, an unexpected but rare pleasure to receive you in our home.'

She always sounded like more than she was; maybe like something she once had been. Addie worried people thought she was taking an attitude.

'Mayhem yesterday, I hear, Mrs Rowe. Hollering and tomfoolery, destruction of property, confrontations with lethal weapons, things of that nature.'

There had been a spot of bedlam the day before when a man called Geronimo kicked Stevie's door in and stole the rent money he claimed Reggie owed him from dominoes, and the retired ventriloquist upstairs called to see if everything was all right and Addie stabbed Geronimo with a cheese knife and pursued him down the street at a benign distance instead of going to school, which was what she was supposed to do.

'Nothing more than a misunderstanding, Mr Grainger,' Stevie said. 'A poor soul, lost to the trials of tonic wines and turps, quite out of his mind, wandered into the wrong house and caused a minor stir. The front door, as you well know, is always left unlocked for the convenience of the more nocturnal theatrical characters upstairs.'

Grainger did not appear swayed by this, but wasn't in possession of nearly enough facts or intestinal fortitude to brave both Stevie's story and the precipice of her chiffon robe. Setting down his tool bag, he produced a chisel and hammer.

'How wonderful. We weren't expecting you to handle the work yourself.'

'If you want a job done right . . .'

And cheaply, Stevie thought. She sat on her sofa with her bare feet up on the low table, now mysteriously clear of bottles and glasses. Grainger focused as best he could on the busted door frame.

'There remains the issue of the outstanding rent, Mrs Rowe.'

Stevie stretched. 'I'm sure Mr Rowe will take care of that when he returns from work.'

There was a velocity to Grainger's eyes, roving here and there and everywhere but at Stevie's feet.

'Well, see that Mrs Harpenden gets it.'

The old widow in the basement flat was Grainger's creature, as she had been of his mother before him, organising cleaning and the collection of rent, saving him the hassle and herself a guinea off her rent.

Doubtless it was she who had informed Grainger of the whole Geronimo affair, there being nothing she looked down upon quite like those enabled to make scenes.

Throwing his tools back in his bag, he assessed his work, the frame now a mess of splintered wood and damp putty. 'That's as good as it's ever been.'

Stevie wiggled her toes by way of a goodbye and Grainger ran from the house, almost knocking over Chabon on the pavement outside. Charles Bonamy Chapple was Addie's best and only friend, and lived in a single room one street over with his father, Conrad. Chabon's mum had run off from Port of Spain when he was small with some fool idea of being a calypso singer in Miami, and they'd never heard from her again. Conrad brought him to London after the war.

'Mr Grainger in some sort of hurry.'

'Stevie can have that effect,' Addie said.

Chabon pointed to the scullery. 'Look like your sister did a massacre.'

Nees had clambered up onto the wooden table, by way of a chair that now lay on its back, and from a jar was scooping out handfuls of Mrs Harpenden's jam, made with wild raspberries from the bushes in the garden. It was runny and a little sour, but she was making do, red all over her hands and face and clothes and a lot of the table and floor.

'Wanted eggs,' she said.

'I told you, there no eggs.'

'I know.'

She tilted the jar to get another fistful, pressing the stuff into her mouth.

'Adlyn!' Stevie cried from her room.

Addie sighed.

'I'll get Nees,' Chabon said, removing the jam jar from the girl's reaching hands and lifting her over to the sink, trying to keep from getting red on himself.

Stevie was stretched out on her sofa. 'What, in the depths of her dissension, is your sister up to now?'

'She wanted eggs, you see—'

'I don't have time for prevarications, Adlyn. The whole story, as briefly as possible, please.'

'She made breakfast.'

'Made a mess, you mean.'

Addie shrugged. 'Chay got her.'

'And now we have to find the rent. That old witch downstairs will be loving every second of this, on top of yesterday's nonsense.'

'Mum, that man who stole our money, he coming back?'

'Why would I have the faintest idea? Never seen him before in my life.'

Addie knew that to be a lie. She had recognised the man from being round before, when her father had ushered him outside and they'd spoken in an angry huddle, the man departing with finger pointed and face creased.

'His name Geronimo.'

'His name *is* Geronimo, which cannot possibly be true.'

'His name is Geronimo and he lives in a ruined castle near tin town and you let him steal all the rent money and I chased him with a knife.'

Her mother had frequently intimated that her children were a conspiracy to ruin her, and Addie could feel that sort of notion taking hold again as Stevie pinched the bridge of her nose.

'Geronimo?'

'Uh huh.'

'There is no such person, Adlyn.'

'You saw him. That's what he calls himself.'

'Nonsense. And this ruined castle?'

'The Swiss castle,' Addie said, meaning the derelict Hero of Switzerland pub near a cluster of prefab huts put up on bombed lots by the Americans down near Loughborough Junction to temporarily house families those past eight years.

'You're making all of this up.'

Addie looked at the door with its clumsily fixed lock as if her mother was denying its existence. She could never doubt enough the happenings of other people, happenings that occurred outside her small world, and even some that happened within it.

'Mum, why'd he come here?'

'How on earth would I know? You seem better acquainted with him than I.'

'I've seen Daddy speaking with him.'

'Your father would know him. He can deal with it, then.'

'If he comes home.'

'When he comes home.'

Doubt embroidered Addie's face.

'Of course he's coming home, Adlyn. Where else could he go?'

'Geronimo said Dad owed him more. Said he'd be back.'

'I don't involve myself in your father's financial affairs. But we are going to have a talk about your conduct.'

Conversations about Addie's conduct were always threatening to break out.

'This is not the conduct of a polite young lady. Gallivanting off down the road after ruffians, inappropriately brandishing cutlery. Not something a young lady of class should do.'

A lack of class was another regular topic with her mother. Flicking through her magazines, there'd be much to say about what the women were wearing or doing to their hair, and class was her primary gauge. But Stevie had already grown tired of hearing herself lament her elder daughter's lack of finesse, and sat up straight on the sofa as if she might fully address the day at last.

'Be a love and roll me a fag.'

Addie cast about for her tobacco.

'Behind the sofa.'

She frowned. On the floor beneath the window, she found not only the tin of makings, but all the bottles and glasses that had been cleared from the table. She looked at her mother. In return, Stevie wore all the expression of a pudding.

Rolling was about the only thing Stevie had taught her to do, and then only so she'd not have to do it herself. Fingers larded with the previous day's yellow, she thumbed the pages as Addie nimbly went to work.

'Heavens, look at this one. That's certainly the dress for her, but I'd have made different choices with the hair. She used to wait tables with me, you know. Very intelligent, knew exactly what she wanted, but has all the taste of boiled cabbage. I'm terribly sorry she's had all this success.'

In Stevie's world, that she should run the rule over such matters wasn't in question. Addie had never thought of her mother as anything other than beautiful and sad, but there must have been a time when she had been at large in the world, a world bigger than two and a half rooms in a Brixton theatrical.

Addie lit her mother's first cigarette of the day, and as Stevie leaned back and inhaled, she gazed for a moment over the back of the sofa at the forest of bottles on the floor, but must have decided it too laborious a task to arrange a fresh drink from them and lay back again to smoke. Addie waited for her eyelids to droop, easing the cigarette from between her slender fingers and laying it on the edge of the saucer serving as ashtray.

Chabon had Nees looking as good as presentable in the previous day's dress.

'I had this on before anyway,' Nees shrugged.

Addie rushed her round to the nursery at the corner of their road, the matron commenting on the tardiness before asking after her mother in that patronising way, as if everyone was aware of her business (which they mostly were, Stevie Rowe being a topic of some interest among other mothers and the staff).

Addie remained scrupulously polite in the face of such provocations.

2

THEY DISMEMBERED BODIES TOGETHER

May 21st, 1952

Nobody had said it, not in those words exactly, but the men in the car with him would need killing, and he'd have to do it. Fred Martin knew that and couldn't get death off his mind.

There was the war. Six he knew of for sure, close enough to count them, and a grenade incident he didn't hang around for. A lot of men he knew had, and so had their fathers, and some of their sons too, the carrying-on in Malaya and Korea. His boy Ray might end up over there in a few years, National Service. Would there ever be another generation of men who didn't know killing?

The one beside him, who'd never given his name, sucked at his broken tooth again. Been doing it all day. The four of them in a Soho flat since the previous afternoon, kept there until Strong Arms Phil turned up with a motor and told them it was a go.

Now here they were, just gone four in the morning, sitting in a green Vanguard in the mouth of an arched passageway, and this tooth-sucker was still at it. Plucked from his tongue something he had dislodged and held it up on the tip of a finger for inspection before popping it back in his mouth.

Fred leaned forward and squinted down the dark road.

'That them?' Tibbs said, from the back seat, where he sat with a man Fred knew as Gwillim.

'It's them,' Fred said.

'It's someone,' said the tooth-sucker.

The van down the road waited at a cross-street. No traffic passed. Fred pulled his scarf up over his face, and the others did too. The only other car on the street was a black Riley parked up on the opposite kerb.

'Taking his own fucking time,' Tibbs said.

'Shh,' Fred and the tooth-sucker said together.

The van rolled forward, and the moment Fred saw for certain it was a Post Office van, he released the handbrake, holding the Vanguard at biting point, feet stiff on the pedals.

The GPO van slowed as it approached them.

'Turning red,' the tooth-sucker said, meaning the temporary lights just past where they were parked, where half the road was cordoned off.

The van eased gently by in front of them and everything happened at once. The black Riley roared away from the opposite kerb and blocked off the van at an angle, forcing it to veer, one wheel bumping up onto the pavement.

Fred released the clutch, jumping out behind the van to box it in. He kept it in gear as the tooth-sucker and the other two got out, joined by a pair from the Riley, and fell upon the van. Inside, the driver pawed uselessly at the alarm, silent because it had been disconnected by someone who knew how to do such things. The same someone who had flagged the van to the robbers in the first place. Door forced open, the van's three-man crew were dragged out and given treatment by pipe and bat, enough to dissuade resistance, and heaped untidily at the roadside.

Less than sixty seconds and the Riley was pulling away, just the driver in it now as the other two were in the cab of the mail van, which also took off. The tooth-sucker, Tibbs and Gwillim all jumped back in the Vanguard and Fred gunned it up behind the van until it headed west, that part of the plan unfamiliar to Fred, who tailed the Riley back the other way, through Seven Dials into a snarl of thin warehoused streets behind Covent Garden.

The Riley pulled up in the wake of a departing truck, the driver exiting and walking away briskly. Fred found a spot in the elbow of a crooked alley. Removing masks and caps, peeling off their overalls, they stuffed the lot in a travel bag and took it with them when they left the car. Streets and alleys already lousy with people, nobody noticed them.

They found Gyp leaning against an Oxford cab outside a bomb site down the road, dark hair in a scarf, blue eyes wild in the early sun. She clicked her fingers for the bag, Gwillim opening it so she could rifle through, satisfying herself it contained everyone's gear before stowing it on the cab's luggage platform beside the driver's seat. Fred opened the back of the taxi, letting the other three in before taking a rear-facing fold-down seat next to Gwillim. At a sedate pace, Gyp took the Strand and Fleet Street eastwards.

'Where we going, Gyp?' Tibbs said.

This was the part Fred knew that the others didn't, what the rest of their day looked like.

'Safe house,' she said. 'Somewhere to lie low, make sure we done this right.'

They drove to Cripplegate, where the morning was brighter from a lack of buildings to block the early sun. A gutted region that had never healed since the war because it was stone, and stone could not heal. Foundations were exposed and trains rushed through uncovered tunnels, loomed over precariously by what crumbling ruins remained. Bushes and wild flowers had the run of the place now, but nobody could call it bucolic.

Near the meat market they parked in a skinny war-smashed street and Gyp let them into what had once been a butcher's shop, the inside finished with white tiles and a glass-covered counter with chopping blocks behind. Out back, stairs led up to storage rooms on three floors, the top one motley furnished by a chesterfield and a couple of wingbacks and a small round table with three odd chairs and a stool. Two

boxes against a wall sported booze and basic foodstuffs such as bread
and cheese and cans of luncheon meat.

Gyp gathered them round. 'You don't leave here. Lav's on the
ground floor, behind the stairs. Other than that, you stay in this room.
You don't go out for any reason. There's a fire and the whole place goes
up, I expect to find your crispy remains right fucking here.'

Murmured assent.

'Single malt,' she said, pointing at one of the boxes. 'Should be cups
in there. Relax. Raise a toast. Way this works, someone will be back
here once we know we got away free and clear. For the first few months,
your cuts will be paid in instalments. So's nobody goes out buying
Rolls-Royces and fur coats. Everything settles down and the heat's off,
you get the rest. First payments will be later today, in a few hours.'

'Do we know how much?' the tooth-sucker said.

Gyp shrugged. 'I know what you know. The van got away from the
scene. You got away from the scene.' She looked round the room. 'You
shouldn't go tugging each other off too soon, but it looks like a job
well done, gents. Have yourselves a hard-earned one.'

Gwillim made everyone sandwiches and poured generously. The
other three played cards at the table while Fred sat in a wingback and
stared out the window. Voices in the street below. Smithfield winding
down. Buyers, sellers, butchers and bummerees clearing up and beginning to make their way home or hit the early houses for a jar or two.

'Deal you in?' Tibbs said. 'We're all flush. Or will be.'

'Maybe later,' Fred said. He topped up his cup.

'Breakfast of champions?'

He forced a grin. 'Post-job comedown, I think. Might have a kip.'

Closed his eyes and pretended to sleep, listening to them play for
money they didn't yet have, and never would. Not that he didn't have
the same urge. He was already wondering how he might put his cut to
use without it being noticed. It had been a long while since he'd been
able to make plans. Not since his butchering days before the war,

apprenticing under an older man, learning his trade with the idea he'd eventually take on the shop as the man had no kin.

But Fred couldn't wait.

Got involved in foolishness, thought he was a hoodlum, and did almost a year inside. Daughter still in nappies, Claire left to cope alone. He promised her never again and he'd kept his word, returning from war to work with his hands in the factories and mills of the Dale, living in a shabby rental with strangers on the top floor and running water in one room and a washhouse that in the middle of the night had to be found outside in the cold dark.

Since losing the job at the paint factory, he was more persuadable on the foolishness front.

The light had changed and the bells of St Bart's were ringing the hour and he must have dropped off for real. Was it six or seven? Peered at his wrist and realised he'd removed his watch before the blag. Waiting was interminable when you couldn't decorate it with time. He cleared his throat, sat up straight.

'Oh, look who it is.'

'We wake you, sweetheart?'

They laughed from the table, card game still on.

'Anyone been?' he asked.

The tooth-sucker took a sharp intake, clearing a morsel of sandwich from the hole.

'You think you'd have napped through that? Soon as the cash gets here, these two can pay me my winnings. Both owe me a tenner. Easier money than pulling the blag.'

Fred pushed himself to his feet, stretched and clicked his back.

'Going for a piss.'

Groped his way down the stairs, stiff from the chair, and found the loo. Went, then put the lid down and sat a while. Splashed water on his face. Drank some from cupped hands. When he heard a vehicle outside the shop, he unlocked the toilet door and stood holding the handle. Shop door went, and as soon as he heard feet on the stairs above him, he stepped out.

'Fred,' Mother said, pausing a few steps above him. 'Hiding in the carsey?'

Fred wiped wet hands on his thighs. 'How'd it go?'

'Fucking clockwork. So far.'

'Money out of the city all right?'

Mother laughed. 'You think after a blag like this we want anyone pottering about the shires with a truckful of stolen cash?'

Fred frowned.

'Did what you always do with valuables you want looking after. Gave it to a lawyer to keep in their safe. Last place the cozos can get into. Now, how are the lads?'

'Playing cards.'

'Drinking?'

Fred wasn't sure how much more they'd had whilst he dozed. 'A bit.'

'Not that it makes a difference. Be over in a flash.'

'Yes.'

Mother hopped down the steps, wrapped a reassuring arm round Fred's shoulders. In his other hand was a knife. Fred recognised it as a bayonet, the same kind he'd had for his Enfield during the war, but with the blade cut down substantially and ground to a new point.

Unimaginably sharp.

'Figured you'd be more comfortable with something you'd used before.'

'I was a butcher.'

'And as such you did a lovely cut. Boning and slicing with no little dexterity, I grant you. But butchers don't stab. Their knives aren't suitable for the dirty work. The hand can slip past the heel of the blade when met with resistance. Slice it open. This here is the right tool for the job. A tool with only one purpose.'

Fred took the knife, thumbed its quillons.

'Look, I don't—'

'You know what has to happen. Why it has to happen.'

Sleeves neatly rolled up to his elbows, Mother flexed his forearms, deep burn scars running up both.

Summer of 1948, the Battle of London Airport.

What should have been the biggest robbery in history.

Mother and eight men armed with bars and bats ready to lift half a million in cash, bullion and valuables, and a man inside the airport who was supposed to drug the other guards but lost his bottle and told the police, two dozen of them waiting in the shadows. Bedlam ensued. All said and done, sixteen cops and robbers were hospitalised, and seven villains went down for a total of seven decades' hard labour between them. Mother only escaped by spending the night face-down in a ditch and then clinging to the bottom of a police van, arms melting from the scorching metal.

Nobody would be allowed to lose their bottle this time.

'Think of what you could do with your share,' Mother said. 'For your family. For your boy. How he'll look at you.' His hand squeezed the back of Fred's neck. 'You need not believe in Him in order to be His instrument, Alfred. The wages of sin and virtue alike is death, and every man is the unsalvable son of the Christ.'

Fred didn't know about any of that, but he carefully slipped the blade into the belt loops at his back.

'When the time arrives, you only have to worry about one of them. Mother'll take care of the rest.'

He strode the three flights up to the top floor and crashed into the room like a music hall star, Fred breathlessly hurrying along behind.

'The fearsome wielder of the cosh,' he said, pumping the tooth-sucker's hand.

'He yelled.'

'But not for long, you saw to that. Fine work. Fine work.'

Clapping arms and squeezing shoulders, he had cups in everyone's hands and filled them to the brim with such zeal that nobody could refuse.

'Now, lads, before we get down to brass tacks – and you'll be glad to hear the score went very well, even better than expected – there are a few precautionary measures to take care of. You have the bag with the overalls and what not?'

Gwillim held it aloft.

'Good. Good. Right, follow me.'

Downstairs, he led them into the room behind the shop, which was tiled out floor-to-ceiling, with regular drainage holes in the ground. Hooked chains, from which meat had once hung, dangled down along one wall. A suitcase lay on the floor.

'Chaps, I require your togs.'

They stared at him.

'Any and all garments worn during the committal of this morning's good works should be disposed of, gentlemen.'

'Everything?' Tibbs said.

'Starko.' Mother patted his pocket. 'There's a century waiting for each of you, and new threads in the suitcase. Can't vouch for them, in fairness, but they'll get you home without scaring the neighbours. And then who among us won't be able to deck ourselves out with Jermyn Street and Savile Row clobber in the future?'

They looked at each other, reluctant.

'What am I saying? Still in work duds myself, which will also need dealing with.'

Shrugging off his jacket, he unbuttoned his shirt, and by the time his unbuckled trousers pooled around his ankles, the others were stripping down too.

'No trinkets in the pockets,' he said, hands on hips and naked as the day he was born.

None of them had brought anything, but they went through the pantomime of checking all the same. When Fred stood up, Mother looked pointedly at him.

'Sure you haven't forgotten anything there, Fred?'

'No . . . Oh.'

Kneeling, Fred drew the bayonet from the belt loops of his discarded trousers, sliding his fingers into the grip. Pleadingly, he looked up, but Mother's face was fast as stone.

He gave the nod.

Four sacks set against the wall.

In pieces, the men seemed more than the sum of themselves.

Mother and Fred hosed down the room and each other and Fred stowed the butchering blades back in the suitcase.

'That's it, then.'

'Not quite.'

Fred glanced up from where he knelt by the case. In his shock, he couldn't have formed words even if any had come to mind. Could barely draw air.

Axe in one hand and cleaver in the other, Mother bore down on him.

Fred couldn't believe he was being betrayed like that. They had a plan and it was working. Mother surely had the wrong end of the stick, it must be a mistake.

Hadn't they dismembered bodies together?

3

ROBBERY IS A GIFT YOU GIVE YOURSELF

Five hours earlier

Dave Lander never slept.

Windows open, a warm, airless night. No moon to talk of. At the knock on the door, he flicked on the table lamp beside the sofa. Two a.m.

Stood to the side of the door. Could hear two of them out there.

'Yes?'

'It's me, you soft cunt.'

Mother.

'It's late.'

'Don't be a pessimist. Maybe it's early. Maybe we're getting a head start on the day.'

Lander opened the door and let them in, Mother and Strong Arms Phil, who shoved a set of coveralls into his chest as he slid by.

'Tonight?' Lander said. 'Now?'

'Tonight,' Mother said. 'Now.'

'Not much notice.'

'That's the general idea, so no one gets breezy. Starts having thoughts of the second variety. Shake a leg.'

Lander went to the bedroom, leaving the door ajar. Emptied his pockets and put on a pair of dark trousers and a thin knitted pullover, both picked off a stall on the Portobello for this purpose. He pulled on the coveralls on top, leaving them open at the front.

'Make sure you're clean,' Mother said.

Lander made a show of going through his empty pockets again as he emerged from the bedroom.

'I need a watch?'

'No.'

Strong Arms was at the door of the second bedroom, hand on the knob.

'Not in there,' Lander said.

Strong Arms didn't press it. Lander grabbed a pair of gloves from a drawer in the sideboard in the hallway. Mother pointed at them.

Lander turned the cuffs inside out. 'Cut the labels out. Got them specially.'

Mother nodded and opened the front door, his Morris van waiting outside.

On a narrow street behind Bayswater station, two cars were parked in the broken shell of a bombed and derelict house, rest of the street the same, boarded up and empty the past ten years.

'Keys are in them,' Phil said.

Mother nodded. 'Dave, the Riley. Phil, the Vanguard. Peter Street, I'll see you there.'

East down the Bayswater Road toward the West End. In Soho, Mother peeled off to leave the Morris somewhere it was regularly seen. Peter Street was thin, barely room for two vehicles to pass without bumping the kerb. Strong Arms parked the Vanguard outside a rug merchant at the Wardour Street end, Lander pulling up behind.

Strong Arms remained in his car, so Lander did too. When Mother appeared on foot, he pointed for Strong Arms to go up to the flats above the rug shop, and then got in the Riley beside Lander.

'You got the new plan straight?'

'Falling off a log,' Lander said.

Mother side-eyed him. 'Take this seriously, like your life depends on it. Because it might well just.'

'I got it.'

'Then let's go to work.'

Essex countryside, the previous winter.

Mother and Strong Arms drilled everyone on the plan for the job, the big one. Out on a deserted lane, tyres marked out the streets and hazards. They ran variations on the scenario over and over, accounting for different potential mishaps. Caught in the snow once, the crews huddled in their cars trying to keep warm, and a copper came by on a bicycle, Christ knows where he was going or where he'd come from. Mother told him they worked for Ealing and were blocking out a sequence for a movie. Man asked if they'd bear him in mind if they needed a police officer, before riding off into the flurry.

They all laughed with relief.

'We haven't talked ackers,' Lander said, the risk fresh in his thoughts.

'You in a strong position to negotiate, Dave?'

He shrugged, opened the door as if he was going to walk off in the snow.

'Don't be a child. And shut the fucking door, colder than Christ's fanny out there. What do you think? It's a job. You get paid. That's how capitalism works, isn't it?'

'How capitalism works is bosses exploit labour. You haven't even said what the job is, past it being a hijacking. What are we knocking off? Payroll?'

'Mail van.'

'Bags off the trains not enough?'

For months, Lander had been up and down the country, slipping onto trains with a key for the GPO compartments and taking a razor to sacks, removing high-value packets. Back off the train at the same station when it all went well. Almost seventy grand since they began. Easy money, security was a joke.

'What's enough? There is no enough. It's just work. You stop when you're old, if you're lucky, and that's it.'

'Fee or a slice?'

'Slice.'

'What if we get nothing? What if the take's small? Slice can be peasant's work.'

'We're looking at a take of forty, forty-five grand.'

'What?'

'It's a big haul. The boss covers his costs, about five grand we reckon. Then he takes half. Remaining fifty per cent is divided equally between everyone else. If the take is what we hope, then you're looking at two, two and a half grand. Maybe less if the currency is traceable and we have to do a little smashing.'

Five years' honest wages for a single blag.

'Still sound like peasant's work? Still want to get out the car?'

Silence.

Mother shook his head. 'I should throw you out the car, make sure it's moving at the time. Fucking peasant work.'

Lander's teeth chattered. He thought everything through as a distraction from the cold.

'You trust the kink?'

'He's sitting behind you.'

Strong Arms winked.

'There must be an inside man. At the GPO?'

'There's always an inside man at the GPO.'

'He could talk, I'm saying. This ain't pulling sacks off a train. Blag this big, if he's not firm, he'll—'

'I can make cast-iron guarantees as to the tightness of his lips.'

'But—'

'Jesus. Do you think I haven't worked this all out? Sitting here in the fucking snow with seven men and the tyres out in the road, do you not think I've planned everything, Dave? Planned it out so everyone only needs to know what they need to know. It's been a real drag, let me tell you. People will read about it in the papers over their breakfast and think, what larks! Robbery and hold-ups. But it's a drag, Dave. It's a means to an end. It's fucking work. And, speaking frankly, it gets on my tit-ends when people question my ability to do it.'

'Just getting it clear in my mind.'

'It's clear in my mind, and that's all that matters.'

They'd run the plan till it was second nature. They were going to hit the van on Oxford Street, but it'd be four in the morning, when even that busiest of streets would be empty. Hard and fast, they'd be out of there in a minute.

Then, two nights ago, Mother had gathered them together. Slight change of plan – part of Oxford Street had been closed for roadworks, and the mail vans were running a diversion. He was tracking the routes. The plan was to select a new location and run the same operation as best they could, but they might have to change the timetable.

Eastcastle Street, behind Bourne & Hollingsworth, parallel to Oxford Street, was chosen.

'Roadworks there too,' Mother had told Lander. 'Temporary traffic lights, one side of the road shut.'

'So we only need to block the other half.'

'Fucking good job you're around, Dave, to offer essential strategising and advice on tactical manoeuvres.'

'And after?'

'Covent Garden. Place will be bustling with market traders and porters arranging the day's trade. Leave the car anywhere you can and walk away. Nobody will notice it for a few hours, God willing. Dump the overalls and get into Soho, make yourself seen somewhere you might usually be seen, and then Phil will come get you.'

That was the plan.

Strong Arms re-emerged from the rug merchant's building, four men in tow. They had scarves over their faces already, caps pulled down over their eyes. Lander knew them only from the practice runs, they weren't villains. Men with training from the war, men who needed the cash.

Men who were expendable.

They got into the Vanguard and drove off. Strong Arms squeezed into the back of the Riley, the car rocking as he sat.

'They're going to set up at the scene,' Mother said.

'Where we going?' Lander said.

'Noel Street.'

Behind Oxford Street, Soho-side, all trade premises, quiet that time of the morning. Parked there because of the phone box. A quiet half-hour before Mother got out, and less than a minute later the phone rang. He answered quickly, listening and saying nothing before replacing the receiver.

He got back in. 'Gents, robbery is a gift you give yourself.'

Lander rolled down his balaclava.

Afterwards, Lander left the car on Floral Street, handed off his overalls and gear to Gyp and walked into Soho. Next door to a butcher's shop in a paper cut of a court between two tatty streets, he took a seat in a café where he knew the staff. Somehow, despite the state of the nation, they had all the steak and eggs they could cook. He ate with the taxi drivers and sailors and his grub was cooked on a stove in the corner of the green-and-cream tiled room and was as fine as anything he'd ever had.

Two mugs of tea and extra toast and he realised he'd emptied his pockets before he came out, explaining to the owner he was caught short. The man waved him away, knowing what he did in Soho and who he did those things for.

He read an ice delivery man's discarded paper until Strong Arms showed up driving a pre-war Austin Cambridge, a Jamaican postman already in back. The inside man who had provided details of the mail van route, who several hours earlier had strolled unnoticed into the yard of the General Post Office at St Martin's Le Grand and popped the bonnet of said van, disconnecting the wires that powered the manual alarm system.

Nobody spoke.

In the cauterised wasteland of Cripplegate, they parked outside the old butcher's.

Mother's Morris was already there, as he said it would be. The door to the shop was unlocked, as he said it would be. Strong Arms steered the postman ahead of him and through to the cutting room at the back, where Mother kneeled nakedly over Fred's body.

'Jesus Christ!'

The postman wholeheartedly believed in betrayal.

He turned to run, but Strong Arms blocked his way, neck as thick as his head.

'Please, not with the axe.'

Behind him, Lander drew his blade.

'What do you think we are?' Mother said. 'Animals?'

Lander waited upstairs while another sack was filled.

Lit a cigarette and nosed about the boxes, fixing himself a sandwich and a couple of fingers of decent whisky. Strong Arms called and they loaded the sacks into the Morris.

'Everything went like clockwork,' Mother said. 'Team has been disassembled. The loot is safely stowed. The peelers' – he checked his watch – 'will probably be finding the mail van about now, and the fun and games will begin. Meanwhile, we're all done and can grab forty winks. Once we've dropped this little lot off.'

Mother drove the Morris, the other pair following in the car, to the thick end of St John Street, the other side of the meat market, packed with butchers, tripe dressers, sausage-skin makers, bacon curers, and cutters of every kind. Through a stone archway, they entered a covered yard where a walnut-faced crone sluiced blood from the cobbles with a bucket. The air tasted of tin.

This was the Kingdom Cold Storage Company. From a narrow street facade, the building stretched backwards and outwards in several directions, connecting to a separate structure backing onto the buildings of the street behind. A ramp gave access to a basement labyrinth of cork-lined cold storage where pallets of carcasses were delivered fresh from slaughter. An elevator brought them up to a vast chilled hall where curtains of meat hung, ready to be brought to market round the corner, or cut into chops and steaks for sale in the shopfront. Above that sat a floor of skylit offices where orders were taken, and a tearoom for the staff. As with anything Mother was involved in, his name didn't appear anywhere on the paperwork, but everyone knew who ruled the roost.

They unloaded the sacks onto the cobbles under the watchful eye of the old woman, who was known as Mrs Cruik to everyone except Mother, who was allowed to call her Avis.

Mother drew Lander aside. 'You're going to have people showing an interest. Close family friends, so forth.'

'Don't worry. I know how to handle them.'

'Good lad. Tonight, then. Dean Street.'

'All right.'

'We'll know where we stand by then. Himself will be at Peter Mario for his dinner.'

'I'll drop by if I hear anything.'

'Drop by anyway.'

'Sure.'

Putting down her bucket, Mrs Cruik dragged the sacks into a tilting shed in the corner beneath the covering, closing the door behind her.

Mother winked. 'Avis there prepares the finest ground meats imaginable. Perfectly seasoned and spiced, and piped into skins to make the king of sausages.'

'I'll stick to porridge for a spell,' said Lander.

4

DAUGHTER OF THE SWORD

The high-backed chair by the bed was bare again.

Addie noticed that when she brought Stevie her tea, earlier than she'd gone in the day before but not so early that she felt compelled to go to school after dropping Nees off at nursery. Stevie, as though born fresh every morning, passed no comment on her daughter's habits or her husband's absence.

Chabon had also not made it to school and was running hot water in the sink. Addie collected dirty clothes from her room and flashed a finger under the tap to see if she could take it. There was a rattling at the door beneath the stairs that led to Mrs Harpenden's basement flat, and the clearing of a throat. Feet conspicuous on the steps below.

'Better go see,' Chabon said, nudging her aside and pouring Rinso into the steaming sink. 'You know how she is.'

The staircase down to the basement had been enclosed, and every night the old woman crept up the steps and locked the door as quietly as possible. Every morning it was unlocked again, but only Addie ever crossed the threshold.

Knocking cheerily, she clattered down the stairs to make sure she'd be heard. Mrs Harpenden was in her kitchen, which was directly beneath their scullery and led out to a lean-to that had been built to shelter the space to the outside washhouse.

'Hello? Mrs Harpenden?'

The widow emerged from the kitchen carrying a tray.

'I've made tea.'

Addie nodded.

'Everything is fine upstairs, I trust?'

'Tickety-boo,' Addie said, which was something she'd heard Mrs Harpenden say.

'I thought I heard Mr Grainger yesterday.'

'Oh yes, bit of a palaver the other day. He came round to do some repairs. Thoughtful of him.'

'That sort of thing wouldn't have happened in Mr Harpenden's day, of course. Even the staff knew when to come and go discreetly then.'

This was her favourite pastime, unfavourably comparing the modern world to the classical times when her late husband had apparently owned the house.

'What did Mr Grainger have to repair?'

Addie was amazed at the old hige's slinkiness. There was no telephone in the house, so she'd slipped out sometime after Geronimo's incursion to either telephone or call on Mr Grainger. When did she manage that unseen? What was more mind-bending, though, was that Grainger had actually turned up to do anything about it. Usually the place would have to be falling down for repairs to even be considered.

In the large front room, sun starved in the mornings, Addie scooted the pouffe nearer the armchair and sat down. On the wall above the fireplace a sword was displayed on a wooden mount. She had seen it many times before, but after her work with the cheese knife she considered it now for the first time in practical terms.

'Belonged to Mr Harpenden's uncle, who was Mr Harpenden's grandfather's least disappointing son. Mostly on account that before he could really get the old coot worked up about anything, he got himself killed at Tel-El-Kebir, which as I understand it is in Egypt. They shipped back the sword, but somehow never managed to locate his body.'

She mentioned her late husband all the time, but rarely shared this kind of detail. All Addie really knew was that they used to own the house, until he died sometime before the war and Mrs Harpenden sold it, arranging to stay on as a tenant. They had originally bought it at the turn of the century. That was how Mrs Harpenden had put it – the turn of the century. It was impossibly long ago, but seemed to fit with the talk of Egypt. Pyramids, and so forth.

'Does it still work?' she asked.

'Most of a sword's work is done by its wielder, I'd say. I have no idea what condition the blade is in. I'm not certain I've ever had it out of the scabbard.'

Addie's wishes were written plainly across her face.

'Go on, then. But be careful.'

Standing on the pouffe, Addie lifted the sword from its mount and drew it from its sheath with surprising smoothness. It weighed about the same as a bag of sugar, but differently. The blade had a slight curve and looked as if it would effortlessly slice a person to slivers, if only she knew how to use it.

'Now then,' Mrs Harpenden said, pouring extra milk into Addie's tea and sitting in the armchair.

Addie slid the sword back into its scabbard and stood it against the fireplace.

'Since you appear to be at a loose end today, there might be some cleaning to be done.'

Addie nodded casually, like she could take it or leave it.

Fishing around in her purse, Mrs Harpenden produced some coins and piled them on the table. 'All the upstairs folk need doing. What you do with your own rooms is your business.'

Addie felt the risk of guilt rising to ruin her tea. 'There might be complications with the rent, but we can discuss that more fully at another time.'

'You know best.'

'And I don't think Dad came home the last few nights.'

Addie wasn't completely sure why she blurted that out, but it had something to do with guilt and money and the kind of esteem she believed Mrs Harpenden held her parents in.

'He always says letters don't deliver themselves,' she added.

Children feel what is going on, even if they don't comprehend, Mrs Harpenden thought. For her part, she had been waiting for something like this from Reginald Rowe ever since the family moved in almost five years earlier, although mostly as an enjoyable background concern. As Mr Hobart, the clarinettist upstairs, had said more than once, if she didn't have anything to worry about with the other tenants, she'd find more serious affairs to be anxious about. The leasehold, for one, which had only about ten years left on it and which Mr Grainger told her the Church Commissioners had shown no inclination to extend. Mrs Harpenden was nothing if not an optimist, however, and believed that particular problem would outlive her.

'I left a note for your father the other day,' she said.

Addie had found it on the hallway floor, where Mrs Harpenden had slipped it from beneath the door to the basement stairs.

'I haven't seen him since then.'

She slid the coins back to Mrs Harpenden's side of the table.

'No, child. That's your money, not for your parents. I can come to an arrangement with your father.'

'I'll tell him. If I see him.'

'Perhaps it might be better if you tell your mother that I'd like a word?'

Addie considered that. 'I'll try to speak to my father.'

Mrs Harpenden shook her head. 'I don't know whatever possessed your mother. Although I suppose we do know, really.'

'Yes, I suppose we do.'

Addie had cultivated the habit of acting knowingly whenever grown-ups hinted at secret things. She finished her tea quickly and, at Mrs Harpenden's insistence, took the shillings for the cleaning. Upstairs, Chabon was furious with the scrubbing of laundry, a sinkful of dirty water testament to his endeavours.

'Chabon, those are my socks.'

'Black,' he said, as if that explained something. A finger wiggled out the end of one.

'You should go to school,' Addie said. 'Your dad will go mad.'

Whilst it was true Conrad Chapple's wife had left him to be a bar singer in America, he too had fled Trinidad under a cloud. It began when an Indian obeahman got wind that Conrad could crack one of his toes so loudly it sounded like someone knocking on wood. They used this to run a scam about communicating with the dead, working the Indo-Trinidadian villages scattered among the sugar fields south of Port of Spain.

During the war, they played a few tricks on American personnel from the naval and air bases. A woman Conrad knew worked at Carlsen Air Force Base and fed him personal information about some of the men, which they used in harmless ways to entertain them. But one bomber pilot, whose trauma over his mother's death when he was a child they catastrophically underestimated, rumbled them after they'd taken him for hundreds of dollars.

Conrad fled, taking Chabon and hiding out with friends. The old obeahman was arrested but was deemed unfit to stand trial. Nobody ever knew if he had conned the head doctors, but he was taken to the lunatic asylum at St Ann's in the hills above the city, where he was the victim of a savage attack that cost him a foot. On hearing about that, Conrad got himself and Chabon on the first boat off the island and then on to London, where he believed there would be more opportunities for them both. That was a work in progress.

'Dad don't do darning,' Chabon said, studying his finger through the sock.

'Chay.'

'You cleaning for the upstairs folk?'

Addie shrugged. When it came down to it, they both had patchy school attendance, and a couple of days each week Addie spent either cleaning the house or taking in clothes from tenants and fixing them like Mrs Harpenden had taught her to. She enjoyed the clatter of the electric Singer.

She never wore herself out cleaning. There were cookers on the landings, but being theatrical types, the upstairs people weren't much for preparing their own meals, so they were rarely used. Old Mr Gattuso, the retired ventriloquist, had been known to warm the odd tin of soup, but long ago he'd set up a paraffin stove in his room so that he wouldn't have to risk bumping into anyone on the landing.

She held her nose whizzing through the toilet on the half-landing with Bar Keepers Friend. That was the only plumbing in the upstairs. Mrs Harpenden paid her to clean the shared parts of the house, but some tenants dropped her a few pennies to go over their rooms. Keys were tucked beneath stair runners, or left in never-used cookers. With no more than her usual diligence, she sped round the house spraying her can of Min.

Typically, Mr Gattuso was the only one home during the day. A neat and tidy gent, he let her do some dusting and wiping, mostly so he could ask her questions about the general doings of other tenants. She batted away his questions about the previous day's intrusion, buttressing her mother's story about the man having the wrong address.

Back downstairs, Chabon was paying particular attention to a minute splash of jam that had somehow found its way onto the door of her mother's room, which was open a crack. Without a mother of his own, he was protective of Stevie, who barely knew he existed.

He put his finger to his lips to shush Addie as she came down the stairs.

'She's sleeping,' he whispered.

'Well, it is afternoon.'

Addie slid into the room and retrieved the rent book from the bureau, string-tied in a bundle with the ration book and some stamps. She and Chabon went to the overgrown garden, filled with matted tufts of knee-length grass knotted with raspberry bushes. Trees ran along the sides and rear, offering shade from the day's rising heat.

'Due yesterday,' Addie said, studying the rent book. 'Nothing here for last week neither. Why Mrs Harpenden put that note under the door.'

'Your pa take care of it.'

'Wish I knew where he was. He's been out drinking before, but never two whole nights like this.'

'He'll be back. And I bet your ma got the money anyway. You'll see.'

Addie snorted. 'Got the money Dad gives her for food, and for her tonics and baccy.'

She emptied the pockets of her corduroys, gathering up the coins Mrs Harpenden had given her, and a few others she'd saved up. Stevie only rose from her pit when she needed booze or tobacco, if Reginald wasn't around to fetch it for her, and she usually sent Addie to the market for food, presenting opportunities to rescue a few shillings here and there.

Chabon counted. 'Don't nearly have enough.'

'It's a start.'

As if she didn't quite trust their existence, she counted the coins again.

'Going to be all right, Addie.'

'Yeah.'

'What happened to your ma's door?'

Addie grinned, the mortal fear she'd felt at the time having been supplanted by bravado now. She recounted to Chabon the events, and as happens with these things, the tale became embroidered somewhat, Geronimo growing a few inches and the cheese knife becoming a Household Cavalry sabre.

'I used to be a lion,' her father had told her about his youth. 'When my blood was young and I was a hot body about town. You're either a lion, or you're what a lion eats. You're a big cat, or you're prey.'

Looking back with a deep sense of satisfaction, Addie understood what he meant. Surely there were lions, who grabbed fate by the short hairs and flaunted swords and would soar in the world. And then there were wretched creatures, such as Geronimo, who lived existences of misadventure and iniquity and were certain to be punished (even if they did snaffle the rent money). There was a cosmic niftiness to it all.

'We were righting wrongs,' she said. 'We were lions.'

Chabon plucked a small pebble from the earth and threw it over the back fence. The first two terraced houses on the street behind had been bombed in the war and pulled down. The local kids called the debris site left behind Fairyland. It had been used by workmen when they built the nursery at the end of the road, and now stood vacant, a place for adventures.

'Don't know about lions, but there's frogs in the pond,' he said.

'Are not.'

'Is too. Seen them yesterday. Bet you won't hold one.'

'I'm not going to hold a frog.'

'Told you.'

'You hold one.'

'I held one yesterday.'

Addie laughed. 'I'd have heard you scream if you did.'

'I'll hold one if you hold one.'

'Deal.'

The back fence was about as well maintained as the rest of the house. They stepped right through one of the smaller gaps in it. Debris from the destroyed houses had been removed years ago, but the earth lay in big shovelled heaps, and the shallow foundations, along with half a dozen rows of bricks from the basements, were still there. Someone had boarded them off, but they'd worked a section of rotted wood away long ago to get inside. Rainwater had collected into an almost permanent pool in the hole left by the houses, which was known as the pond. The rest of the afternoon was spent chasing frogs, which Chabon wasn't wrong about, but neither of them managed to catch one.

Later, Addie said they better fetch Nees, as Stevie certainly wasn't going to, and they brushed themselves off and walked down the carriage path along the side of the house. As they stepped out onto Somerleyton Road, Chabon grabbed Addie, pulling her back out of sight.

'Ow, Chay, what—'

'Ah, he seen us.'

'Who?'

'Kindness over there.'

Chabon's slightly older cousin, long and rangy, stood on a bomb site a few houses down on the opposite side. Unlike the demolished houses on the other street, remnants remained of these bombed semis, half-walls and empty windows, basements heaped with rubble. They provided fun and hazard in equal measure.

Kindness had arrived six months earlier from Port of Spain, sent for by his father, who worked at the big laundry by the hospital. Older than the other kids on the street, but not yet running with men, he was a bully and a thief, and bullied others into thieving for him. Anything they could snatch around their homes – cigarettes, booze, occasionally jewellery or a watch.

'You know he'll take your money,' Chabon said, Kindness crossing over to them.

'What you two up to?' Kindness asked.

'Hey,' said Chabon. 'Nothing.'

'You been in school?'

'Have you?'

Kindness slapped him sharply round the back of his head.

'You don't worry about where I been. What you got on you?'

'Nothing.'

'Let me see.'

'We were just going inside to—'

Kindness feinted another slap, laughing when Chabon ducked.

'I said show me.'

He reached for Addie, and Chabon pushed him, not hard but he wasn't expecting it and stumbled over his own feet.

'I didn't mean—' Chabon started, but Kindness punched him, catching him on the ear where he tried getting out the way. He followed in with some more shots, clattering off Chabon's arms mostly as he protected his head.

'Leave him alone!' said Addie.

Kindness turned and started back, but suddenly fell on his face as Chabon kicked his legs away from behind. He cried out, grazing his hands and knees in the tumble. Leaping up, he tore after Chabon, who looped round the only car parked up that end of the street before full-out sprinting the other way.

'Go get Nees,' he yelled, a huge grin on his face as he flew by Addie, fear and exhilaration all mixed up together.

Addie laughed and willed him on, knowing even as she did that there was no way he was going to escape the older boy. To the sound of their feet slapping against the pavement as they disappeared down the road, she ducked inside her house and hid the coins behind loose skirting in her room, then hurried round to the main road to fetch her sister from nursery.

Nees was bored and hungry and a pest. Addie sniffed a bowl of rice and stewed peas from a batch her father had cooked up a few days earlier, and threw it all into a pan to heat. Nees sat at the table, feet kicking in the air, munching away happily, Addie sitting across from her awaiting whatever favours Kindness had done Chabon.

When eventually he returned, he wore a bright smile to go with his fat lip and skinned knee. One eye was already swollen, coloured like a split plum.

Addie was horrified. 'Chay, your eye. And your trousers are torn.'

'Didn't catch me till the end of the road.'

'Your lip's bleeding.'

He shrugged. 'Told him I didn't have no money and why's he chasing me anyway. Swear he chase anything that runs. Told him he must want to be police when he grows up.'

'That when he gave you many punches to the face?'

'Yeah.'

Grabbing the TCP from the cupboard, she mothered him some and took his trousers to darn the knee, as it wasn't much of a hole, and he sat in his underwear, happy as Larry and tonguing his split lip.

'We was lions,' he said.

5

THE RATS OF NOTTING DALE

Mother, who Claire believed would have unruly red curls down to his shoulders had he not been incredibly bald, was filling the room with one of his tales from the Great War, stumbling across some travelling circus in the Walloon Woods that had turned a farmhouse into a brothel, acrobats and lion tamers seeing out the war on their backs, big cats and pachyderms in the barn.

At first, she pretended not to be listening to him. What he would call feminine wiles, a trick that impressed and enraged him in equal measure. Then she actually wasn't listening to him. After the war, Fred worked in a timber mill on the canal, occasionally drinking with the men and going to the afters at closing time, crawling home before dawn. On those nights, she'd lie in bed on her wrong side, facing away from him and feigning sleep when he came in, no tea or powdered eggs waiting for him when he appeared the next morning. Fred liked a quiet life and believed they had a well-regulated marriage. Had the bite marks on his tongue to prove it. Years now since he came home sloppy drunk like that, and he'd never been out all night before.

Holding smoke down in her lungs like she was made of tin, she exhaled it slowly, coming back round to him talking about a bear.

'Can you imagine it, fighting a bear? Like I'd pay for the experience. Chained to a pole fixed in a bucket of concrete, I grant you, but how he expects this to work, I do not know. What am I going to do? Jab jab hook?'

'That's a lovely story, Teddy. Fred would really like that one.'

Crossing his legs, he laughed wheezily. 'Clips his bollocks and then offers him a look, rolling around in the palm of her hand.'

He stood abruptly, wiping sweat from his forehead. The living room was narrow, ungenerous. The open fire filled it. He removed his jacket, slinging it on the armchair beside the sideboard under the single front window. Still light out, the curtains undrawn, glass weeping from the crackling heat.

Fag in her mouth, squinting against the smoke, Claire knelt before the grate and poked at the glowing heart of the coals, raking a few into the centre and adding new ones round the edge.

'Roasting in here,' he said.

She sat back down, top lip glistening. 'I was chilly.'

Mother stood sweating in the window, visible for all to see. A terraced row, all of them three storeys and a basement, many split into flats or rooms. The kind of street disowned by its neighbourhood.

It's Kensington, but *North* Kensington.

It's North Kensington, but it's Notting Hill.

It's Notting Hill, but it's Ladbroke Grove.

It's Ladbroke Grove, but it's Notting Dale.

Peeling paint, crumbling plaster, tatty nets. Broken windows fixed with board. Tyres stacked in basement light wells. Irish, gypsies, blacks. Large families, broken families, single men, wanderers with violence in their eyes. Men grafting long hours beneath the smoke stacks of factories and works, women in bare feet hanging laundry and fighting in the streets. Gangs, whoring, illegal clubs, ageing gaslights, and the promise of the suburbs long passed by. Waiting for someone to come along and sweep the whole place up, start over.

He tried a different tack with her.

'You've looked better.'

'Fuck off,' she said equably.

'Tired, I meant to say. Nothing a good night's sleep wouldn't solve.'

'Well, my husband didn't come home last night, so I may have been a little short in the sleep department.'

'No. Pain in the arse all round. Needing to speak to him, like I said. You don't suppose he's . . .'

Claire laughed tonelessly. 'Christ. Who'd have him? No. Frankly, I thought he was with you.'

'Me? No. No. I was hoping he'd drop in one of the gaffs, quick drink or a spot of faro. I could have had that word.'

Every night, death crept a day closer, but sometimes it waited till eyes shut before leaping and prancing nearer, unnoticed until some sign arrived. The instant she'd opened the door to this man, this liar, it was the sign she'd been waiting for. Fred had been up to something since he lost his job at the paint factory. Disappearing during the day, returning with money saying he was working cash-in-hand. 'Fruits of my labour, hen.'

Now, the day after he's gone all night, Mother shows up, years since she last saw him, making a song and dance about looking for him. This man. This liar.

'You know, back in the clubs, you were never anything less than immaculate.'

'That was the clubs, Teddy. This is ten o'clock of a Wednesday evening, fifteen years, two kids and a whole entire life later. We've all gotten a little older.'

'I know this widow, lives down Chelsea way. Husband was some sort of minor baron, lost him in the trenches over there. Left her nicely positioned, as they say.'

'Teddy.'

'Yeah, half a mo. Tall old bird, she is, but completely lacking a chin. Like a chicken. Older than you, mind, but she's never let herself go. Asked her secret, I did, and she told me it was a regimen of pills. Little something to help her get a good night's kip. Little something to kick-start her day when she wakes. Maybe a wee mid-afternoon perker. Has a button-down pocket sewn in her gowns for her little box. Cock your ear, you can hear it rattle as she walks. Something very arresting about her.'

'Hard enough paying the rent, let alone thinking about treatments. Fred was working on something, though, said we'd get on an even keel.'

'He said that? What else did he say?'

'Nothing. Just that he was going to make some cash.'

'Money makes everything easier, I suppose.'

'Was talking about moving. Building something up to leave the kids.'

'Yeah, well I wish I knew where he was. Let me down tremendously, he has.' He glanced suddenly at the ceiling, as if he heard something. 'Where are the kiddies?'

'The kiddies are almost grown. Peg's upstairs in her room. Ray works with his uncle. Probably running the streets by now, with Joe in his cups.'

'Never fully came back, that one.'

She grunted.

'Not like your Fred. Wish I knew where he was. Most unlike him. You can rely on Fred Martin, I've always said that.'

A key scraped into the lock and Claire stood as the door opened.

'Fred?'

'It's me,' said a voice in the hall.

'Oh. Hi, Joe.'

Fred's brother was a big man. With oily mechanic's coveralls and a scraggy beard, he gave a general impression of being un-upholstered.

'What, he's still not back?'

He came to an abrupt halt when he saw Mother.

'Fuck does he want?'

'He was calling for Fred,' Claire said.

'Calling? You wanting to walk out with him, are you?'

'I was telling Teddy about Fred's plans,' Claire said.

'Like he isn't privy.'

Mother forced a smile.

'Good to see you, Joe. Been a while.'

'Not a while enough. Claire, why don't you fix a brew.'

'Oh, I'm all fixed,' Mother said.

'Claire.'

She nodded, half out the door already.

'Take myself for a fag.'

The corner's rats were large and voracious.

Living off the rich pickings of the empty plot at the heart of the Dale, the rubbish and rot, food chuckings left among the old mattresses dumped by the rag-and-bone men. A dead cat had been the attraction for a few days, nibbled at by plump rodents at first, now bloated and crawling with maggots.

Ray headed to the corner, as he did every evening, from uncle's garage where he worked after school, finding the neighbourhood kids there. The garage was a few doors from home, but he took the long way round so mum wouldn't spot him.

A crowd of about a dozen, mostly boys, were gathered. Clive, small and grubby, had pinched a box of matches, and they'd torn handfuls of weeds from the edge of the overgrown site, trying unsuccessfully to set them alight.

A house had stood in the space until a few years earlier, when it was pulled down. Nobody knew why. The other end of the block had been hit in the war, but it hadn't damaged that house, which had always been a state, so everyone figured the owner got fed up and demolished it. The rubble had been cleared, but nothing had happened since and now nobody was even sure who owned it. There was always talk of getting it cleared again, as it had been little more than a dumping ground for years, but the grown-ups would throw their hands up and nothing got done.

'You're wasting matches,' Ray told the kids.

They were a shade younger than him, and he was tall for his age, so they looked to him. Useless without him.

'Don't move.'

He returned to the garage, tucked away outside the bend on their street. Quietly he opened the hutch in the big double doors, but uncle wasn't there. Either at the pub, or an uncharacteristic early night. There was a cot in the small office out back, as sometimes he couldn't make it down the road to his basement flat beneath theirs. It wasn't the distance that was the problem; there were psychic spaces he was unable to traverse. On those nights, he drank rotgut and smashed the bottles against the wall, swearing up and down he was done with that place and they'd never see him again. He farted elaborately in his sleep. The air smelled like the inside of dead lungs.

Skidding out of the war, where he'd learned engines and mechanics, he crashed into Ray's parents' basement, spreading down there like damp until it was his domain, a place of tools and grease and inexplicable wood shavings. Bald tyres were stacked in the light well as if fortifying against bombardment, piled up past the windows. There was just enough room to slip through the downstairs street door.

They rarely saw him at the dining table. It was never considered that he would marry, shapeless and crude as he was, though he owned his own business and the garage he ran it from, and paid half the rent despite only inhabiting the basement. He gave the impression of places he'd left behind in the war. He was ageless, the product of a world saved but no longer functional. His capillaries bloomed. He was not long for this life but would outlive them all.

Ray took a can with a little petrol left, hurrying back in case the kids used up all the matches or lost interest. They were pulling up shrubbery. Ignoring them, he sloshed the dented can about, soaking the soiled mattresses. The others gravitated toward this new activity, an escalation. He took the matches from Clive.

'Stand back.'

Lighting three together in a series of small flares, he tossed them onto the rude pyre, the petrol catching quickly and burning a bright orange, smoking darkly. They all shuffled away from the heat as it got lively, fanned by the night breeze. Rats scurried out from beneath the mattresses and fled the scene.

Eyes black and fascinated, fire playing on their faces. None turned to look toward the clopping hooves as a cart drew up behind them, driver considering the blaze briefly before moving on. Billowing bigger and bigger, whipping against the blank wall of the end house, Ray pictured it leaping to the roof and taking the place with it. The screams of panic as the whole street went up.

As quickly as it had ignited, it was smouldering, the mattresses consumed and small flames licking the ashen mass left behind. Down the street were cries and laughter as the Ladbroke Hotel emptied at last bell, local dads tripping out the door. Kids ran faster than the rats to beat them back, save themselves a slippering. Ray checked if dad was among them. He hadn't come home the previous night, which was strange, but mum had dismissed it like it happened all the time. Dad was always home, though. Even before he'd been laid off at the paint factory, he wasn't one for being out past closing.

He ducked into the house next to his as a gang of men belched their way along. Derelict for years, the door was long gone and some of the lath-and-plaster walls inside had been knocked through, offering a view straight back to the garden. In the shadows, he waited for the men to pass, clapping backs and yelling farewells.

A few familiar faces, but no dad.

Maybe he'd come home earlier.

He ran back to the garage, dropping the can off before returning home. The front door was unlocked. Holding the latch, he closed it silently behind him. Lights were on throughout. The door to the front room was closed but he could hear male voices. He snuck down the hall, passed the crook around the stairs. Hopefully mum was in bed and had left something out for him, could eat a horse now he thought about it. At the end of the hall, three doors led off to the dining room, the scullery and the garden. Mum's legs stretched out from the small settee in the dining room.

He craned his neck round the door frame. Head back, blowing smoke at the ceiling, she idly flicked ash into the dregs of a teacup. He sized her up warily. Usually she smoked on the stool that held the back door open.

She beckoned him with a finger.

'Who's here? Dad?'

She shook her head. 'Your uncle's talking to someone.'

'You're smoking inside.'

'Don't you mind about that.'

'Thought you'd be in bed.'

'I bet. What time do you call this?'

'I was at the garage.'

'Oh aye? After your uncle?'

His feet became of sudden interest to him.

'And this fire I can smell is nothing to do with you, then?'

'Wasn't my idea.'

Like most of what he told mum, by the rules of the game not a lie exactly, but not the truth either.

'The corner?'

He nodded. Then, 'Dad still not back?'

Slight shake of the head, her eyes cast toward the thin scullery.

'Sandwich under a tea towel on the side. Ham from dinner.'

Eyebrows popped up, his favourite.

'Better you take it up,' she said. 'Eat it and get ready for bed. Quietly. There's milk on the slab.'

Fetching the plate, he poured himself a glass. It didn't get cool with the milk, like when you got it off the doorstep, but he was happy enough. He turned to go, both hands full.

'Excuse me,' she said, tapping the corner of her mouth.

He leaned down, kissed her.

'Thanks, mum.'

'Go on.'

He stole away down the hall to the stairs and up the first four steps, pausing at the fifth, which creaked awfully. Carefully he backed down and hovered edgily outside the front room, listening.

'No fool, that sister-in-law of yours.'

'Claire's not daft and never pretends to be. Nothing worse than someone playing the mug.'

'So, how are you, Joe?'

'I got tightness in my chest, which seeing your face is doing no favours. My feet are giving up the ghost. Taking a piss in the morning is a military exercise in patience and determination. What are you doing here, Nunn?'

'Dropping round on old friends.'

'You don't have friends. I'd give odds there isn't a single person on this earth who actually *likes* you.'

'You're hurting my feelings.'

'Where's my brother?'

'Well, as Claire said, I came round here in search of him—'

'Don't give me that cock and bull. He was mixed up with some bollocks you had going on. This robbery they're talking about on the radio, was it?'

'Now, Joseph, you don't want to make the mistake of—'

'Of what? Tell me what mistake I don't want to make? Think I'm afraid of you, or your white-feather boss? Tell him to come round with that chiv of his, see if I don't take it off him and cut his arsehole out, so he'll never again shit himself at the thought of soldiering.'

A weighty silence was broken by a crash, some item of furniture gone for a Burton. Ray heard mum sigh as she raised herself off the settee in the back room, and he scampered onto the stairs, keeping his feet to the outside and skipping the creaky fifth. He got to the landing as she reached the front room.

'Joe,' she said cheerily, as if calling him for his tea, opening the door. Uncle brushed past, didn't look at her. Stalked out the house, door slamming behind him.

Mother stepped away from the tall corner cabinet he'd been shoved into, its shelved knick-knacks left in disarray. He smiled.

'He's at that point in life, you ask him how he feels and he tells you.'

Claire left the room. She hoped he'd decide he'd been there long enough and see himself out, but he trailed after her into the dining room at the rear. She sat on the spindle-backed settee, with its cushions worn down to wafers, and crossed her legs, one foot going like the clappers and speaking more to her mood than anything she could say.

Mother held up his palms.

'What me and Fred had discussed, he was going to be back here.'

This man.

This liar.

'Teddy, I swear—'

'We've known each other too long to start kidding ourselves now. Or start asking questions don't neither of us want to hear the answers to aloud. If something's gone awry, I'll do my level best to rectify. My sense of the matter, though, is that he'll waltz through that door any moment and act like nothing unusual has occurred. Now . . .'

He disappeared into the kitchen, ran the tap and filled a glass.

'Here. Take this.'

Gave her a pill.

'What is it?'

'It's pharmaceutical. Quacks prescribe them, help you relax. Get a bit of shut-eye.'

If nothing else, a sudden loss of consciousness would get rid of him. She popped it in her mouth and washed it down. He sat beside her.

'I don't hold it against Joe. He's always been protective of his brother. And me and him, well . . .'

'He always thought you were a prick.'

'Now, that's not . . . I don't care for that language passing a lady's lips.'

'Heaven forfend.'

'You were always a class act, Claire.'

'Look good, Claire. Take a pill, Claire. Watch your mouth, Claire.'

'I can see you're in an uncooperative type mood.'

Feeling suddenly undiminished, recouping that merciless strength children possess that seldom survives into adulthood, she bared her teeth and snarled. He leaned away involuntarily. Content, she closed her eyes and sat back, melting a little into the seat.

She felt him stand, and peered up through one cracked eye. He was making a study of the room while he took a lap of the small table at its heart. Two Beswick ducks flew across the wall, their mate missing and presumed. The mirror above the tiled fireplace unsilvered in disgust. Two small photographs in a silver hinged double frame stood on the sideboard where the crockery hid, Claire and the two kids when they were young, and Fred in his battledress.

Post lay on the sideboard; he flicked through it. They were behind on rent and the landlord was talking about taking action. He had a quick nose in the scullery. Wouldn't find bursting cupboards, their feeding becoming opportunistic rather than comfortable. He returned to the letter from the landlord, and she snapped her eye shut as he tried to show it to her.

'What are you going to do about this? Claire?'

She turned her face into the settee. He shook her shoulder and she batted his hand away, muttering into the cushion.

'Claire, what are your plans? What if it's a while before Fred shows his face?'

A bit of voltage with that, her eyes cutting into him.

'Show his face? How's he going to do that?'

Mother straightened up.

'You're a liar,' she said slushily. 'So was he.'

'Don't know what you mean.'

Her mouth cascaded quicker than her mind.

'You're all liars. Vicious psychopaths and liars. I'm not afraid of any of you.'

'Terrific. Be homeless and unafraid.'

She made a face.

'I'll sort the rent. Not a handout – just a temporary arrangement.'

She laughed, a little too wildly.

'Life's a temporary arrangement,' she said.

Ray scoffed the sandwich, mum's piccalilli in it just as he liked. Nestling plate and glass on his chest of drawers, he undressed and put his clothes away neatly.

On the landing above, he heard creaking boards and flicked off his light. Opening the door a crack, he waited out of sight. His parents rented the basement, ground and first floors. Above that, two men rented rooms on the top floor. Mr Bowling was in insurance, on his feet all day, and kept himself to himself. It was the other one, the loser in the back room, who was the problem.

Vic Barlow.

Only a few years older than Ray, but might as well have come from a different time. Ray swore he listened to them from the top landing, maybe even watched sometimes. Probably he was into petty crime. Said he worked at the public baths, but that didn't mean anything.

Ray crept out of his room, keeping an eye out for any faces spying through the upstairs balustrade. Sister's door was open. True, it was unseasonably warm even for May, but she never used to leave it open. A recent development he thought not unconnected to Vic's sneaky interest. The hallway light was off, only the palest shadow of him cast on her wall as he stood by the door. She was asleep, that much was obvious, no way she'd arrange herself with a face like that if she were awake. Sheets pushed off, nightie twisted up over one knee. He refuted the shape of her, looking around it.

There must be other ways. He was an innovator, after all.

He pulled her door to and chanced a look downstairs round the banister.

Voices. Mum in neon hysteria. Then that man again, striding along the hall. At the door, he paused, feeling Ray's eyes, and turned. They peered at one another as if underwater, divers from different ships.

The man smiled.

Winked.

Just a flash, light off a blade. Alive in some way Ray didn't comprehend, like fire, but also containing the dimness of aeons.

He sat on the top step in his pyjamas long after the man went, feeling like a young boy. Of mum he heard nothing for a good spell, then she emerged from the dining room, pausing in the hall, leaning against the wall with one hand. Ray took himself back to his room, killed the lamp and concerned himself with pretending to be asleep.

He lay vibrantly.

Footsteps climbed the stairs and he turned away from the closed door, dragging the blanket up over his shoulder. The door opened, no knock. She picked her way through the darkness and sat on the chair beside his bed.

This was unusual behaviour.

This had all the signs of going badly for Ray, he could tell.

'Ray.'

Barely made out her voice, thought it might be in his head.

'Ray.'

He didn't do anything, even when he heard her move, felt her lean over him, her fingers running through his hair, stroking his brow. Slow, like she was swimming through something. Kissed his ear and sat back down.

'Your father's gone away.'

Her voice was funny. Sloppy, like uncle when he tied one on, but he didn't know her to drink like that.

'He's done something foolish and he's gone away. I'm not sure where we stand.'

Ray thought about rolling over, feigning waking up, holding mum's hand maybe. But doing something was seldom his choice when doing nothing was on the table.

'I don't know what I'm going to do.'

She was quiet after that, her breathing steady with a slight throaty rattle, and he wondered if she'd fallen asleep in the chair. He opened his eyes and waited for them to adjust to the dark. He dared not move. Just each other's breath for company, he matched his to hers, but quieter.

Shallow, shallow.

Keep it unheard.

Ray couldn't imagine ever sleeping again.

6

SHOW ME THE COPPER WHO DOESN'T NEED KILLING

Lander hid all day behind curtains.

Kensal Town, but felt like the Dale.

Working-class families packed in single rooms above sweet shops and laundries, or basements with the slenderest of light wells. His life would fit in a bedsit; kept the flat out of paralysis more than anything.

Early evening, off to Mum's for his tea. Sitting on the hallway bench, he tied his shoes before pulling on his jacket. On the way out, his fingertips brushed the door of the second bedroom that in the end had never been used. Hadn't found the stuff within himself to dismantle it.

Across the iron bridge, fetched the '51 Interceptor from a lock-up down near the Portobello. Two doors. Four litres. Straight six with a lion's purr.

Purposefully conspicuous.

Past the Scrubs, past White City dogs, to a townhouse backing onto Loftus Road, garden squeezed up against the terrace, turnstiles a couple of doors down. Bedlam on match days, street packed with supporters, every song and cheer echoing off the back of the house.

Lander's old man, a well-liked copper, died on the job (heart attack in a Bayswater brothel, but his brothers in arms lugged his corpse into a Wolseley and staged a more discreet discovery), and his uncle, another copper in a family thick with them, looked out for his mum. Bought her a flat on the new White City estate built on the old brickworks.

Doodlebug took that down in a heap of rubble in '44, his mum fortunately late home from her shift as a clippie on the buses. A prefab on Wormwood Scrubs with her new husband after that, until inheriting the townhouse from Lander's uncle upon his premature death two years later.

Eight steps up to the wide-open front door, inviting in the whole of the neighbourhood. His mother downstairs cooking, how she spent her days, preparing food for any straggling coppers who stopped by.

'How are you there, Mum?'

Housecoat and headscarf notwithstanding, Ivy Merriman was still a handsome woman. Lander pecked her on the cheek and sat at the table.

'You getting any sleep?' she said.

'I never sleep.'

'You look like it too. Sausages?'

'No, you're all right. Cuppa will do.'

'You weren't here for your breakfast either. Have you eaten at all today?'

'Was in the butcher's caff in Soho, had steak and eggs.'

'What were you doing over there?'

'Having steak and eggs.'

She gave him a look, plonked a tea down on the table for him.

'Your father's in the garden seeing to the birds.'

Henry Merriman wasn't his father. Nineteen and out of the house when his mother remarried, Lander never let a paternal relationship settle in. Another cop, he'd worked the same district as his father, waited a respectful period before discussing his intentions with Ivy.

'Still got the hump?'

The townhouse had been a dream come true for Henry, being a lifelong QPR fan. They won, he got six sheets to it at the Coningham

Arms and crawled home; they lost, he tripped right back for home-cooked hock and a hug. Two weeks earlier, they'd been relegated back to the Third Division, and he'd had a mood on ever since.

'Don't you go stirring him up. All I've been hearing about is this Mangnall chap and how he needs the boot.'

'Should make Henry manager. He'd show them a thing or two.'

Heavy boots kicked against the back step.

'You shush now.'

'There's a grey squirrel out there,' Henry said as he came in. 'If that isn't a metaphor for our present predicament with the colonies, I don't know what is.'

'Evening, Henry.'

'Ah, Dave, just up, are we? All night in your gambling dens, all day in bed.'

Lander wasn't exactly coy about who he worked for, but let the family believe the extent of it was running round the West End spielers.

'Should've stayed in bed, this welcome.'

'Good that you're here. We had Pete Vibart round for his lunch earlier.'

'Never knowingly turned down a free plate, that one.'

Vibart was Flying Squad, notorious for a twenty-stitch rip down his face courtesy of Billy Boy Blyth's razor. Wore it like a medal, like he had no fear. Lander believed men like that were dangerous.

'He was telling us about this fuss this morning.'

'What fuss?'

'Not on the wireless yet? Late editions will have it, I imagine.'

'Henry, what fuss?'

'The robbery. GPO van was held up.'

'One of them gets knocked over every other week.'

'Pete was at pains to suggest this one was different. When it's all said and done, he thinks it'll be the biggest heist in history.'

Funny that Mother hadn't mentioned that.

'How much could they have got? Forty, fifty grand?'

'Substantially more, from what Pete was saying. But I imagine you'll be able to tell us more in a few days.'

'How's that now?'

'Well, looks like it's your boss might be involved, what Flying Squad are saying.'

'My boss?'

'Billy Hill.'

'Christ, I've never even met the man.'

'Uh huh.'

'Meet the Commissioner many times when you were an odd, did you?'

'It's not the same thing.'

Lander slurped his tea. 'How about old Mangnall at the Rangers, then? Reckon they'll give him the heave-ho? After all, all he did was get them in the Second Division for the first time ever.'

His mother glared at him, and Henry adjusted himself on his chair, searching for an angle fit for conversation.

Pulled up at Shepherd's Bush, telephone box near the lavs opposite the Empire.

It rang sixteen times before they picked up.

'It's Lander.'

'Where have you been? Calling you for hours.'

'Turned into an interesting day.'

'We need to meet.'

'Where?'

'Rathbone Place car park. You know it?'

Did he know it? Less than a hundred yards from where the mail van had been taken off that morning, which already felt like weeks ago.

'Yeah.'

'There are ruins at the back. Half an hour.'

'Half an—'

They rang off.

Round the common, straight up Holland Park Road and the Bayswater, toms already on the prowl, leaning up against the Hyde Park fence. West End traffic loused up with the roadworks and closures, he dipped and dived through the red-brick canyons of Marylebone, leaving the car on a debris site on Great Russell Street, where the new Trade Union Congress headquarters was soon to break ground. Short walk to Rathbone Place, maybe three dozen cars parked up, and at the back thirty caravans in two tight rows, some housing whole families.

The way we lived now.

A city full of such sites. Small patches of erasure where buildings fell and nobody had the money or heart to replace them. What flat ground could be made was surrounded by exposed cellars and foundations. The car park had once been a decorative plaster workshop.

Though nobody thought of the war much, its scars were everywhere.

He was on time, but no one was there. Feeling exposed, he secreted himself in the corner of a ruin, smoking as he waited. When he arrived, he wasn't alone. Lander recognised the other three, knew them by sight but didn't *know* them know them.

Moving into the centre of the empty plot, the ruins hiding them from the car park's comings and goings, they looked about the place, wondering where he was. Suspicion that he'd been stitched up in some way, or was about to be horse traded, rose in Lander. He kept a lid on it and walked out.

'Dave, there you are.'

The General.

His guv'nor.

His vicar.

Superintendent Bob Lee, Flying Squad hatchet man and the only one who heard Lander's confession. A faint smell of pipe tobacco always accompanied him. The one in uniform stepped forward. The big man himself, Assistant Commissioner Ronald Howe, head of CID at the Yard.

'Good evening, Sergeant.'

Not a copper, but a lawyer. Appointed out of the office of the Director of Public Prosecutions straight into top brass as Chief Constable of CID. An AC now, and on his way to a knighthood via deputy commissioner at the very least. Would serve his twenty-five to the day and pension out on a pretty penny without having spent a single day on the street.

Lander took his hand anyway. 'Sir.'

Howe gestured to the other two, plain clothes like Lee.

'You know Commander Young?'

'By reputation.'

'And Chief Superintendent Tom Barratt.'

A serious-looking copper, he removed his hat to reveal a great bald dome. Lander had heard stories round the family dinner table about Barratt, a man who'd been eating out for years on collaring a New York hood, Jimmy Hynes, who'd blagged twenty grand's worth of jewellery off a very rich and very well-connected Park Lane widow before the war.

'Have you worked together before?'

Howe knew they hadn't. Knew Lander hadn't worked with anyone at the Yard apart from the General.

'Afraid not, sir.'

Handshakes all round. Trowelling it on with the sirs, not letting them get any read on him other than as a loyal little worker bee.

'Bob here has told us your story, Sergeant. We think you might be of some use to us.'

Everybody knew it as the Ghost Squad.

Officially, the Special Duty Squad. Teams of detectives put together in 1945 to work undercover among the villains of the capital in the face of the huge crime wave that surged through London in the aftermath of the war. With dire shortages and rationing came an inevitable uptick in black marketeering, and the Met chose to fight fire with fire. Cops who lived as gangsters, taking down firms from within. Some remained ensconced in the underworld for years, gathering intelligence and arranging raids and arrests in a manner that kept their legends intact.

At the close of 1948, despite posting their best results in terms of convictions and property recovered, the squad was wound down. There had been concerns from the outset. Relatively young detectives being given carte blanche to run about town without having to explain themselves to senior officers. Answerable only to Flying Squad bosses and Howe himself, they sailed close to the wind in terms of operating procedures. There were rumours of extracurricular activities, all done in service of the greater good. Whatever that was.

Quietly, without fuss or favour, the squad was put to bed. The city was beginning to regain its feet after the cataclysm of war, and more traditional methods of policing were appropriate once more.

That was the official word, anyway.

The Ghost Squad, the dirty little secret of the Metropolitan force, had always harboured its own dirty little secret. On paper, its members had been recruited from the ablest ranks of the city's CID teams. All detectives who had done time on the streets, had policed the city through the Blitz and six years of war. Who had earned their way through the ranks.

Off the books, there was a ghost squad within the Ghost Squad. A few select men recruited from outside the force, men who had returned from the war with certain skills. Men whom Bob Lee convinced Howe could be trusted to operate with minimal supervision for long spells in criminal circles. Even their families wouldn't know they were coppers. Brought in as detective constables, they remained sequestered from other coppers.

They wouldn't go to the Yard. They wouldn't file reports or make arrests. They fed raw intelligence directly to their handler. He never forgot a face, never forgot a detail. A walking filing cabinet of pedigrees on the town's villains, major and minor. Tea leaves, robbers, racketeers, fences, petermen, kidsmen, screwsmen, fitters, beasts and chickenmen, toms and nancy boys, chivvers and cutters, snouts and vermin, and every copper who collared them.

All stored away in the mind of one man.

The Memory Man.

Superintendent Robert Lee.

General fucking Lee.

Lander had sorta kinda known his face when he spotted him at his uncle's funeral. He'd only been demobbed a couple of months earlier and the city had a terrible brightness and an impossible dullness to it. His mum's fourth-storey flat had collapsed out of the sky, taking all his earthly possessions with it, and the prefab she lived in with Henry was cramped. The Gladwells, parents of his pre-war sweetheart Susan, offered him a room at the Paddington boarding house they ran, and work doing odd jobs around the place.

He assured them that nobody could be held to idle promises from almost seven years earlier, that they didn't live in the same world any longer, that he wasn't the same man. But they wouldn't hear of it. Within a week, he was accompanying Susan to the Coronet in Notting Hill Gate, their courting done almost exclusively at the cinema, so conversation didn't have to carry the weight. Running around looking like a gangster already in his slightly-too-big pinstripe demob suit.

Didn't get round to seeing his uncle before he was killed. After his father's death, Ivy encouraged Tommy Lander to take more of an avuncular interest in his nephew, which he did, but the two of them never clicked. His uncle talked constantly about toughening up, being a man now his father was gone. A kinetic storyteller, pacing back and forth, hands waving wildly, he recounted tales from his work as a copper. Clearing the slag, as he put it. Leaking light as he talked of gangsters and pimps, bookies and abortionists. Of politicians and bankers and lord's bastards. Lander used to think he drank, or was touched in some way.

'London is wide open for you, love. Too wide to be controlled by any one villain. Too deep to be policed by any one force. It is its own beast. A behemoth. People fleeing it in fear of being swallowed don't realise they are already in its guts. The man who knows that, who makes himself intimately familiar with its entrails, can find his way to the heart of the beast.'

Now he knew his uncle had been right.

Just everything else about him had been wrong.

When he was gone, everyone proclaimed him a hero. Hard to argue with the heroism of the departed. Any police brass worth their salt made an appearance at the funeral, Lander's mother accepting apologies from an endless line of blue trundling past. Lee didn't say much that day.

'I knew your uncle. A committed man.'

That stuck with Lander, as it could be taken any number of ways. No surprise when Lee approached him a couple of weeks later, sounding him out on a new project he was involved with. Lander didn't beat round the bushes. He'd thought about policing many times before, but returning from war it felt like dress-up to polish his buttons and hit the streets.

'I have something more to your taste,' Lee said.

He told nobody about his work, that was the important bit. Even kept on working for Mr Gladwell, maintaining the boarding house. Took his time with the other stuff, hanging around some of the West End clubs and spielers until his face was familiar.

They recognised his name.

They eyed him with suspicion.

He persevered. He bought drinks and favour for old-timers. He played the tables, lost some money, won some money. He was picked up in a raid, bound over for a score not to frequent gaming houses for a year. Back the next night, he was pinched in another raid a few months later, forfeiting his twenty quid recognisance.

Now he was bona fide.

Now he got nods and handshakes.

Susan was hinting toward marriage and he spoke to his vicar. Bob Lee told him to make a life, just don't share his secrets. Only the General could hear his confession.

'I knew your uncle.' First words Mother ever said to him. 'Could tell you a few things.'

'There's anyone I can't be told something new about, it's Tommy Lander.'

Mother had sidled up to him at the bar of an upstairs spieler over an ad agency on Gerrard Street. The ad guys were the biggest losers in there, they loved it. Throwing money at the tables, might as well have torched it. But they brought clients, gave them a night rubbing shoulders with villains and actors and the odd cousin of royalty. Greatest nights of their lives.

Lander knew why he'd be attractive to Billy Hill's firm, if they thought he could be trusted. Family full of police connections, that was a well of information they could draw from.

Started him slow, running messages and money between Soho dives. They had a motorised trike, but Lander bought a bicycle as it was quicker through Soho's alleys, bumping up the pavements of narrow streets. Told Susan and her parents he was managing a bar. Not the kind of place he could take them to, but eventually he wanted his own place. Her father liked his ambition, applauded his gumption. He gave his blessing and they were married, all the good that did him.

Soon enough, he was managing the places, flitting between premises that often lasted no more than a few months. He was trusted because he told Mother frankly how much he was skimming. Took what he thought was fair.

All the while, he fed what he knew back to the General. Sometimes it was acted upon, raids coming down, and sometimes it wasn't. Bob Lee liked to have the whole picture. He understood the black market was a wellspring, that all money flowed toward the legitimate sectors eventually. As long as citizens weren't getting carved up in the streets, then who was he to hinder the nation's economic recovery?

When the Ghost Squad was shuttered, Lander was bumped to detective sergeant. He was told he was more important than ever now because they had arrived at his true purpose.

He hadn't been put in place to supplement the Ghost Squad.

He had been put in place to outlast the Ghost Squad, an operation Howe knew wouldn't be allowed to go on indefinitely. He didn't know how many others there were like him, or if there were even any at all.

All he knew was his vicar.

The General.

Until now.

That morning, only three men knew about Lander, including himself. Now at least five did, and how many more would they tell?

Howe read his concern. 'Nobody else knows, Sergeant. Just the men standing here. Extraordinary circumstances.'

After what Henry told him Pete Vibart had said about the biggest robbery ever, Lander wondered what it was he didn't know.

'The mail van, sir?'

'You've heard something?'

'Only that it happened.'

Howe looked at Lee. 'Bob, do the honours?'

The General laid out the particulars; they had the basics more or less right.

'Well organised. Men who've seen service, probably. A tight-knit group, backed financially so they could prepare. Alarm tampered with, so an inside man.'

'Trucks have been knocked off before,' Lander said. 'What are these extraordinary circumstances?'

Lee glanced at Howe before he went on.

'The truck would normally carry somewhere between thirty and forty thousand. Occasionally a little more. Today was an unusual consignment. Bundles of soiled notes from banks in the south-west. Being taken for sorting, either to be redistributed or sent for pulping. We think there was almost half a million pounds in total. There was so much, they couldn't take all of it. We found the van abandoned in a yard behind Euston station, along the filled-in canal basin. They got away with eighteen sacks, containing just shy of three hundred thousand.'

'Jesus Christ.'

Mother definitely had not mentioned that.

'They had to leave the rest. Working theory is whatever vehicle they had brought to transfer the money into could only take so much.'

Lander thought it through. 'Strange.'

'Sergeant?'

'If they hit it today because they knew it was a bonanza load, then why didn't they have a vehicle big enough? Maybe they were just lucky.'

'Maybe. Or maybe they underestimated the volume of that much money. Almost all of it was one-pound notes. Old and crumpled, they soon stack up.'

Lander tried to picture Mother not planning for that. Figured the miscalculation came in underestimating the total score, not the physical volume.

Howe cleared his throat. 'Sergeant, why we asked Bob if we could meet you, we feel sure we know who was behind this.'

'Billy Hill, you're thinking.'

'Aren't you?'

Lander shrugged. 'Only so many people could have put it together. And there's definitely been something going on.'

'What do you mean?'

He looked at Lee.

'Other GPO-related robberies,' Lee said. 'London to Brighton train last week, ten grand lifted out of the secure compartment. Not the first time they'd knocked that route off. Local counters up and down the country, Harry Bryan's crew.'

'You got Bryan,' Barratt said. 'Sent him down on a ten.'

'Said at the time it was barely the tip. Duplicate Post Office safe keys were used. Intel on high-value packets. Nobody from the GPO was ever arrested, though. Then you had Bruce Grove, couple of months back. What, six grand out of the van there? George King's on remand, but it all feels like part of something bigger. Something organised.'

'Which brings us back to Billy Hill,' Howe said. 'Dave, this is your area. Tell us about him.'

'Three convictions. Knows he can be tugged for wiping his nose on his sleeve now. Did a five the last time and he doesn't want any more. Honestly, what I see, he's a background operator. You won't catch him red handed. He lets his boys do what he knows best.'

'Rackets?'

Lander nodded. 'The bread and butter, along with gambling. He knows the value of reputation, though. Doesn't do the dirty work himself any more, but goes out of his way to play the big man around town. Prince of Soho. Everyone pays fealty. Everyone kisses the ring.'

'Wife?'

'She runs a club, but they're strictly business now. He has another bird, regular like. They live together. Settled down, really. Turned forty, got different ideas about life. Cutting people up, running blags, that's all young-man business to Billy. If he was one of you lot, he'd have his years in, he'd be thinking about the door. What lies the other side. Take a more strategic view of things.'

'CEO of the underworld.'

'If you like. He's a schemer.'

'Could he scheme this?'

'Sure.'

'Did he?'

'I hadn't heard a dicky bird about it until my stepdad told me over his tea.'

'For my money, it looks like London Airport,' Barratt said.

The audacious attempted heist at the BOAC bonded warehouse four years earlier that ended in a riot when an inside man blew the job. The men who planned it were never found, though.

'We figured Comer for that blag,' Howe said.

Young tutted. 'Jack bloody Spot.'

'This isn't Jack Comer,' Lee said. 'But maybe someone has learned from his mistakes.'

'We should look for the inside man,' Barratt said. 'Shake up the GPO.'

Lander shook his head.

'You disagree, Sergeant?'

'Due respect, sir, saying they had inside help in the Post Office is another way of saying they need oxygen to breathe. Put a man on that job, give him maybe a month with nothing else to distract him, and enough pencils and paper to fill a suitcase, he draws up a list of names of people in the GPO willing to sell information, and we spend probably the rest of our lives going through it and getting nowhere.'

'What would you suggest?'

'Turn Soho upside down,' Lee said. 'If this is Hill – and let's be very clear, it *is* Billy Hill – then some of his trusted men will be in on it. Most likely Teddy Nunn, aka Mother. And Philip Carter, aka Strong Arms.'

'We'll bring them in,' Howe said.

'Of course, but you won't get anything. They're outlaws. They don't care about prison. They'd run any nick they were in. We need to identify a weak link.'

'Where?'

Lee shrugged. 'That's why we upend Soho. Find out what's shaking.'

'What do you want from me?' Lander said.

Howe adopted a fatherly tone. 'Dave, your brief might have to change a little bit. It's always been a long-term operation.'

'The plan was always thought of in terms of years,' Lee said. 'Dave has provided high-value intelligence, but we only picked low-hanging fruit.'

Howe nodded. 'Priorities change. The size of this robbery, the brazenness of it. Postmaster General is going to be dragged before Parliament tomorrow. The Prime Minister is personally keeping abreast of matters. It's perceived as a national embarrassment. You'll continue as usual. We understand the importance of your situation, and the precarious nature of it, but you'll have an additional objective now.'

'Identify who was on the job.'

'At the very least. The whereabouts of the cash is the real prize. It's one thing to have a solid notion of who pulled the blag. After all, as you said, there are only so many people who would even think about it, let alone have the ability. The press are going to have a field day. It is important that this sort of project robbery does not become *de rigueur*. They cannot be allowed to think they can walk away from a heist like this with the spoils.'

'Recovering the cash is a long shot,' Lander said. 'This was meticulously planned. They'll have thought through what they're going to do with the money.'

'We're hoping you can work miracles, Sergeant.'

'Those things have been light on the ground since about the twelfth century.'

Howe laughed. Handshakes and backslaps followed, like they'd solved the case in advance. The three bosses trotted off, leaving Lander with his vicar.

'Work with them so they don't muscle our operation,' Lee said. 'Otherwise it could be us the wolves feast on. The old worries about the Ghost Squad will resurface if they decide to out you.'

Lander nodded. It wasn't like the worries were unfounded. After all, here he was being tasked with finding himself and retrieving his own payday.

Some chance.

Driving to Soho, Lander parked on Lisle Street outside the café where the toms took a load off. Many of them knew him, knew the car. They'd keep an eye out. Nipped round the block to Gerrard Street, past the bombed theatre, and joined the late dinner crowd in Peter Mario. Rizzi, the owner, was showing people to their table, glad-handing as he did the rounds. Noticing Lander, he drifted over.

'He here?'

'Out the back,' Rizzi said, dropping the Italian accent he affected for punters.

'Company?'

'The hack, and another gentleman who I couldn't say. Looks the sort who wears a suit but holds his hand out for a living.'

'Is it a party?'

'Couple of somethings with long hair and short skirts for the guests, ordered in from over the road.'

'No Gyp?'

Rizzi shook his head. 'Phil is here.'

'All right. Cheers, Peter.'

'It's Wednesday, you know.'

'You got the osso buco?'

'Nice cuts. Do it just as you like it.'

'I better see himself first. His generosity might not extend far enough that I grab a bite.'

'You shout whenever you need something, Dave.'

Lander shook the older man's hand and slid between tables to a door at the back, knocking twice quickly and then once again. The door cracked open, Strong Arms peeking out. Looked him up and down, then around the restaurant, like he hadn't seen him a thousand times before, the most recent of which being the blag that very morning.

'He got a moment, Phil?'

'He's entertaining.'

'I've always thought so.'

The door shut momentarily before he appeared again, nodding Lander through. The small private room had a single table, but hatches opening onto the kitchen kept it noisy like the restaurant floor. Even at a round table, Billy Hill sat at the head. Back to the far wall, always facing the door.

Duncan Webb, who went by Tommy to his friends, was already red and shiny of face. Always wore the look of someone who lived a little too well, but if you watched him, as Lander did, he actually drank very little. Arm stretched along the back of the chair of the young woman beside him, his head lolled back in the uproar of a man laughing at his own jokes.

A Fleet Street character, the crime correspondent for the *People*, writing long-form pieces, investigative stuff. Made his name dragging the Messinas out from under their rock. He was also the de facto publicity department for Billy Hill, placing stories at his behest. In exchange, he got to be part of the inner circle, laugh it up with heavy gangsters and city captains, eat in the back room with the big boys and the thin girls.

The third man had a nervous smile plastered on his face, perhaps uncomfortable with Webb's humour, or simply unused to being so familiar with the kind of company he found himself in. His tie was pulled into a small knot, his wedding ring too tight to ever be removed. Lander recognised him as a London county councillor, but had never seen him with Billy before. If he was in the back room at Peter Mario, he had been earmarked, though, useful in some way. Gangster, politician, journalist. All they were missing was a copper or two. This was it right here, the great behemoth his uncle told him about. They were out of the digestive tract and into its beating heart.

Strong Arms dragged a chair over, setting it down away from the table, just off to Billy's side. That was how it was sometimes. Lander sat down, saying nothing, and if Billy had noticed his presence, he made no attempt to acknowledge it.

'You mustn't mind Tommy, Councillor Boys. He's spent so long in the gutter, bringing pimps and panderers to light, he sometimes forgets how to comport himself among civilised folk.'

Councillor Boys. Lander knew the name from the papers. Lambeth. An accountant by trade maybe.

Webb raised his glass. 'Our snouts are all in the same trough.'

'Remember whose trough it is, Tommy.'

Webb touched his chest in playful obedience, shooting a wink at the girl.

'Councillor, if I jest about a thing, that's how you know it won't end up in print. I'm very serious about the stories that run beneath my byline. I strive to make sure I not only get the facts first, but I get them right. And whilst Billy is correct, that I often consort with less-than-savoury characters – snouts, tip-off men, nosy parkers, outright villains on occasion – I also pride myself on my discretion. Trust is central to my work. Do you believe Billy would have me at his table if it were not?'

Rizzi appeared, wiping away crumbs, scooping up plates. He always saw to the back room himself.

'A drink, Dave?'

Lander shook his head. He wouldn't be so presumptuous at Billy's table. He considered Boys again. The soft, clammy hand of power. Wondered if he'd still be around a decade from now to feed on the scraps the behemoth dropped.

Boys caught Lander watching him.

'Which are you, Mr . . .?'

'He's not a mister,' said Billy Hill. 'He's a Dave.'

'But is Dave a tip-off man, or a nosy parker? Or an outright villain, perhaps.'

'Dave comes from a wholly different kind of situation. Tell the councillor, Dave, what does just about every other Lander ever born do for a living?'

'Thieve horses.'

Billy Hill ignored him. 'They're cozzers. Dave here was supposed to follow in the footsteps of his old man, and of his uncle, the great Inspector Tommy Lander. Do you remember that contretemps before the war, Councillor? The stranglings, women knocked off in their own flats?'

'The whores,' Boys said.

'Now, none of this made the papers, mind, whole thing brushed away neat and tidy, but the police got their man, and Dave's uncle was one of them who took him down. One way or another. The Soho Strangler, ain't that the legend, Dave?'

'Ballads written about it.'

'In-*spector* Lander. His heroism wasn't done there, either. Died bravely in the line of duty just after the war, saving a woman's life in a shootout with a Messina bravo. Tommy here will know more about that, being the man who took down the Messina brothers.'

'Made for a lovely front page,' Webb said.

'Made for a lovely career. But Inspector Lander got his due too. Medals up the jacksie, that one. Commissioners tripping over each other to praise him. But then, all dead coppers are saints, aren't they.'

Tommy Lander.

Hero cop.

Dead cop.

How do you live up to that whilst your own heart is still beating?

'And yet here you are, Dave,' Boys said.

'We all end up taking Billy's coin one way or another.'

Rizzi arrived with a bottle to refresh drinks, and Lander took the opportunity to lean in with Billy Hill, whispering.

'Had a bit of a blather over the family dinner table. Pete Vibart had been round.'

Billy shook his head, a gesture so small he could have been turning down a cigarette. He covered his glass when Rizzi tilted the bottle.

'Councillor, uncouth as he is, Tommy was right about one thing. We do all feed from the same trough, even the Daves of this world. And sometimes the trough needs tending to. I'll have to excuse myself, but you gentlemen enjoy the wine and the company. Everything's taken care of.'

He clapped Webb lightly round the ear.

'Don't you be leading the good councillor astray now, Tommy boy.'

'If I'm as astute a judge of character as I like to think I am, it's the councillor who'll be snapping the reins.'

Boys was grappling with the notion of forgetting about his wife for a few hours by telling his date all about the woman and the names of their four children, none of which was especially important in that moment other than to illustrate the frailty of his otherwise perfect life. For her part, the young woman listened very attentively, her hand resting helpfully on his knee.

The sun was long gone behind Wardour Street, but arc lamps and neon signs still cast sickly light over the village. The clock face of St Anne's, all that remained undamaged of the bombed church, read just gone ten. Things would be starting to jump off in the spielers, and Billy would want to show his face.

'Bit of a stiff, this councillor.'

'He'll ease into things just fine. These types, they lead lives of abnormal density. Layered on top of the usual home and familial duties, and whatever regular daily occupation they have, usually of the nebulous self-employed nature, you have to weigh the politics – real and otherwise – and the business – legal and otherwise – associated with his position. This crammed existence lends them the sensation of impenetrability. And the truth is, most of the time, if you merely act as such, let alone believe you are such, you'll get away with whatever opaque schemes you have riding.'

Paranoia was something of a rule with Lander, and he felt as if Billy was looking right through him.

'This suit, then, he's on some specially arranged panel or committee . . .'

'Licensing. And planning. Spot of rent assessment and tribunals too.'

'Finger in every pot.'

'It's not the pots themselves, you understand. It's the finger. It's the intersectionality. Therein lies his worth. The LCC has big plans. Half the city has already been levelled by war, and the other half is begging to be. Wide new boulevards reaching into the heart of the place, fit for the age of the motor car.'

'Thought they'd scrapped all that.'

'Sure, for now. Country can't afford it just yet. But these things move about as quickly as mountains at the best of times. Plans drawn up now won't come to fruition for another decade. Someone with the foresight and the capital could, if they were so inclined, position themselves very favourably in that time. And a councillor who deals with planning and with rent issues? Enterprising landlords who happened to acquire property that would need to be cleared for exciting new plans of the future might find such a person to be of use.'

Like blood in his ears, Lander could make out the distant dog-tail thump of the behemoth's heart.

Doing the rounds. Ticking off obligations.

Billy Hill, prince of the city.

They dropped into local boozers for some glad-handing and a gentle reminder of who kept the windows from being put in on a nightly basis. He palmed ten bob to an old derelict who'd pissed himself and was offering life advice to passers-by, and twice that to the street singer outside the Golden Lion.

He nodded at the ladies on the street, all platform shoes and fur coats. Soho's reputation for vice and iniquity was overblown. Reading Duncan Webb's pages in the Sunday paper might give the impression the place was a warren of freaks indulging in opium and unspeakable sex, but it was no worse than other quarters of the city, and downright sanitary compared to some.

The French pub was too bohemian for Billy, a place where tarts kicked off their heels and chatted with artistic types and, even worse, those who could lend money without losing friends. The floor above was the kind of restaurant where you took your life in your hands, but the rooms above that hosted private card games, and Billy made an appearance, shook some hands, extended some credit.

Further up Dean Street was Billy's main spieler, a rough-and-tumble basement joint beneath an Italian trattoria. Technically owned by two Cypriot brothers, the reason it was packed out with enthusiastic gamblers by midnight all week long was everyone knew it was really Billy Hill's place.

Outside, a Daimler Sportsman coupé was parked in the street. 5.5-litre straight-eight, powder blue with lizard leather interior. Only one person could have rolled up in that.

Billy smirked.

Downstairs was heaving, you had to shout to make yourself heard. Wall to wall with petermen and robbers, climbers and thieves, mobsters and murderers. But as well as the salt of the earth, the dregs washed up there too – blue bloods and lords' bastards, bankers and politicians, diplomats and film stars. Billy entered in style, everyone stepping away from faro or chemmy to greet him.

General Lee would have been quite beside himself, the roll call of faces in there. Villains major and minor from all across the city. Ganto the Dipper sat at faro next to his eighty-six-year-old mother, who smoked cigars an inch thick. Badger's Breath, Kipper Moon, Come-a-Purler Moe (also known as Morris, or Morris the Cat, or Opportunity Moe), Fat Dan the Fatman, and a crowd of other carnival acts. Putting birth names to them would be a proper night out for the General.

Someone tried to catch Lander's eye, but he walked right by.

Getting sidetracked by local fauna could be deadly. Seen him around, well-dressed older gent, kind of louche, talking to Mother here and there. Walked high shouldered like a cat and carried a small suitcase everywhere he went. His face shook a tambourine somewhere in the recesses of Lander's mind, but despite willing some ESP connection to the General's interior pedigree filing system, he drew a blank. A dealer or procurer, he guessed. Someone trying to jump themselves up a level. He'd talk to him only when he had to.

By the bar stood all the makings of a scene.

In a fur shawl not quite hiding her bare shoulders, Lady Norah Docker was letting the veneer of her well-earned respectability slip. Common born, in the thirties she had worked her way up through the clubs from dancer to hostess, and then worked harder from young wife of a wealthy old merchant to young wealthy widow. A year after her first husband died, she snagged his even older and even wealthier friend, a knighted salt producer who owned a stake in Fortnum & Mason but whose mind was already receding into dementia. In a coma for more of their short union than he wasn't, he left Norah with millions and the title of lady for life. Her third husband was managing director of the group that owned Daimler, and knew exactly what he'd married.

She was expressing her thoughts on some matter to Strong Arms, who often worked the bar on nights when Billy was in, with Gyp leaning against the counter beside her, watching with amusement.

'Aye aye,' Billy said.

They didn't get to the bar in time before Lady Docker slapped Strong Arms and threw a drink in his face. While he was deciding if it was appropriate to punch a lady, Gyp slapped him twice as hard, cackling with abandon at his confused expression, and let him have her drink too. The rest of the club barely noticed.

'This is all very ladylike,' Billy said.

'William Charles, your barman is demanding cash.'

'Terrible. Phil, what have I told you about trying to make money out of these people?'

'And he withheld the champagne for . . . whatever this is.'

She waved at the drink Phil wore.

'You know how he likes to wind your sort up.'

'My sort? I was born above a butcher's in Derby.'

'And nobody would ever know.'

She flashed him a look that could be taken any one of a dozen ways.

'Probably he just wants to know how much you carry underneath that fur.'

'Enough to be interested in a private game.' She brandished her chequebook in a threatening manner.

'And what's your excuse?' he asked Gyp.

She shrugged. 'What's good for the goose.'

Strong Arms towelled himself off. Billy kissed Gyp and told her to behave.

'Never.'

'Buy Gyp a drink,' he told Lander, snatching a bottle of champagne from the cooler on the bar and leading Lady Docker away to some-where he might more salubriously redistribute her wealth.

Lander sat on a stool. Gyp cocked an elbow on the bar and watched him.

'Two vodkas,' he told Phil. 'Old-fashioned glasses. Up. And keep a kind hand.'

'Take you on his rounds?' Gyp said.

'Yeah.'

'What did you do to deserve that?'

'Interrupted dinner.'

'With important developments?'

'I thought so.'

'Still haven't told him?'

Lander picked up his glass, clinked it against hers on the bar and drank.

She sipped at hers. 'Who was with him?'

'The hack. A suit.'

'Kind of suit a face wears?'

'Kind of suit County Hall wears.'

Mother arrived, holding aloft an unmarked swing-top bottle to hoots and cheers. In the corner, he led the boys in Morning Prayer – his dispensing of the panther's piss he brewed up from fermented plums picked off a tree growing amid the ruins of Cripplegate, in a copper still fashioned from a vat formerly purposed to boiling horse carcasses, the condenser coil ripped out of a cold storage facility. An underworld rite of passage, its foul taste was legendary, its twelve-hour incubation period of plutonium headaches the stuff of songs, and that everyone drank it regardless was, in Lander's view, down solely to the way Mother poured it with princely authority.

'Tarts?' Gyp said.

'No, I'm good for now, thanks.'

'At the restaurant, Davey. Were there tarts?'

'A little something for the guests.'

She smiled coldly. 'Davey Lander. Loyal to the last. How do you manage it?'

'Loyal to those who pay. It's good business acumen.'

Billy was back, talking with Mother. They looked over, and Mother nodded for him to join them. Lander got up. Putting cash on the bar, he pointed at Gyp's glass and Phil poured again.

She raised her glass. 'Amalgamation and capital.'

Not long after he married Susan, Lander had started doing a few extra things here and there for Mother, things he didn't report to Lee. The money was good, and it was easy. They had told him to fit in, to act appropriately. He had plans, after all. A life. All seemed like low-level white noise now, like a ribbon flowing from the grille of a fan.

Gradually, things escalated, got out of hand. Steal a few things here, hurt a few people there. Before you know it, you're more gangster than cop. You're lifting tens of thousands of pounds out of secure train compartments. You're holding up mail vans in the centre of the city.

You're killing men.

He'd never seen much sanctity in human life, and the war had disabused him of any lingering doubts on the matter. Brian Lassiter, first man he killed that wasn't in battle, was a piece-of-shit dipso who drove his car up on the pavement in the middle of the day and ran over a woman. It all happened so quick and those who saw it were so horrified that their statements were of little use to the police. The car was blue, maybe brown. Black, at a push. It was a man driving, though it certainly could have been a woman. About the only thing they agreed on was it barely slowed down at all. Weeks went by and the police said they couldn't identify the car or the driver.

Mother could, though.

Noblesse oblige.

You run the streets, you protect the streets, or at least make it look that way.

Turns out this Brian Lassiter took his car to a friend of his had a garage in Brentford, down on the river. Only this person he thought was his friend was really Mother's friend, word having gone out to keep an eye open for a car looked like it'd ploughed right through someone.

Lander found Lassiter in a grotty flat off Hammersmith Bridge Road and left him at the bottom of the Thames stitched up in a canvas bag with a load of bricks. Drunk for a week after.

One thing leading to another, now sacks of dead men were just some Wednesday-morning business. Six years perched on the razor's edge between cops and gangsters, Lander saw little difference between the two. It didn't matter at all to him which side he was seen as being on, except for the fact it would matter very much to either of them if they believed he was on the other.

Dave Lander never slept.

Lander followed the other two back up to street level, dustbins chaotically lining the hallway. The stairs up to the rooms above the restaurant were grubby and littered with fag butts and blood. At the front on the first floor was a single-room members' club where an iconoclastic Jewish duchess held sway over the great artistic minds of the age amid threadbare colonial decor. You might see anything there. Lucian Freud pumping another bastard into a passing acquaintance against the rickety upright piano. Francis Bacon in bare feet chasing peach-fuzz rent. Lander with his own eyes had witnessed a ninety-three-year-old Bernard Shaw goosestepping joyously while reciting the Sermon on the Mount and scattering pound notes in the air.

'Evening, cunty,' the duchess greeted Billy as they passed. 'Tonight the night you find the boiled eggs to come have a drink with me?'

'Muriel, I grow bollocks enough for that, tell me why I would waste them on drinking with the most magnificent dyke in the city when I could put them to use stealing the crown jewels or taking the government for the nation's gold bullion.'

She wagged a finger. 'One evening, when I'm steaming drunk, I'll tussle with that tart of yours and spend the better part of the night finding out what you're all about. Look at you, skin like undercooked pork chops. I doubt you'd last five minutes.'

Billy laughed, not doubting her for a second.

Lander had seen her put away pharmaceutical volumes of alcohol without effect but, ferocious as she was, his deep suspicion was Gyp would have cut her neck-to-knickers before she even got her dukes up.

Above Muriel's wonderland, on the second floor, was a club run by the Cypriots who fronted the spieler downstairs for Billy. Another hangout for villains, the occasional stabbing victim would descend clutching their uncoiling guts, and teenage Dexedrine overdoses poured down the stairs into puddles on the landing to be stepped over.

The room behind it, Billy had for private games, and the good Lady Docker had been set up with an entertainer and an aristocrat or two. This was slumming it for her. Billy had regular games in suites at hotels like the Dorchester for her, with all kinds of exotic players. In that small Dean Street room, a sympathiser was throwing sufficient hands to keep her interested long enough for a decent fleecing and a go round the block in the Daimler later.

In a low-ceilinged room on the top floor, a couple of old chester-fields, leather worn to knuckle skin, faced off before the fireplace. A drinks cabinet watched sullenly from the corner. Billy stood by the window overlooking Dean Street, spying the queue gathering across the road at the corner of Meard Street, waiting for the private lift up to the Gargoyle. The lights of the club's ballroom flickered through the warehouse windows of the upper floors, and Billy imagined his shattered reflection in the Matisse mirrors lining the walls, and hold-ing court at a table beneath the gold-leaf ceiling. He'd never be bohemian enough to be allowed in, even with the state of the current crowd that partied there.

Mother mixed him a little taste and blessed it before handing it over.

The pedigree on Mother went that as a young man Teddy Nunn had been a bright seminarian with a sharp eye for the politics of high papal altitudes, but ecclesiastical intolerance to his vast appetites in the narco-liquor realm quickly turned his collar back round, and he took to doing the Lord's work off-book, joining up and becoming a wildcat padre in the trenches of northern France, where God's delin-quency fomented a need for his representatives in any shape they might come.

Such frockless commitment had taken its toll, and upon his return to England he had nurtured a habit for vice that saw him become an integral part of the West End scene, moving from knifeman and rack-eteer for Jack Comer to Billy Hill's most trusted vicar. Men had sworn up and down to Lander that they'd witnessed him have a fistfight with a bear in a cold storage beneath Smithfield. Nobody could say what happened to the bear, but Mother had for several years now run a suc-cessful meat wholesale operation in the market.

Myth clung to the man.

He stood there now, counting out a fan of fivers before presenting them to Lander. Hundred quid. He stared at it in his hand.

'Exploitation of labour has already begun, then.'

Billy looked to Mother for explanation.

'Fucking Robespierre here,' Mother said. 'Concerned with the lot of the working classes.'

Billy pointed at the cash.

'What do you think, this is the pay-off? It isn't. We have to make the blag money safe. Most of it is marked, one way or another. That's why it was there, being taken back for evaluation. The banks, they keep notes on these things, descriptions of how the currency is soiled. Little Phil is organising a few hops for us across the Channel, change the money, bring back the francs and change them again. Figuring that to take a while, I went into my own pocket specially so you don't complain like an abortion at not receiving. And yet, what happens?'

Lander pocketed the money, sat down and kept quiet.

The tambourine shook in the back of his mind again. Little Phil, so called because he was smaller than Strong Arms Phil and because his name was Philip Little. That was the louche he'd seen down in the spieler. A money smasher for Billy, he worked under the cover of being a wine merchant, travelling to the Continent and bringing with him Billy's cash to sell at bureaux de change, getting rid of any hot currency. He'd be busy over the coming days.

'We'll build up the clean capital,' Billy went on. 'Two, three weeks, see where we are. Bit of luck, there'll be a bonus in it, seeing how well it went. That said, more of the currency was badly marked than we had hoped. Might not be possible to salvage. That'll be burned, so nobody can jam us up with it.'

He turned from the window, sat across from Lander.

'So. Family dinner. Pete Vibart, so forth.'

Mother sat beside Billy.

'Who's on it?' he said. 'Flying Squad, obviously. But the bosses.'

'Howe was at the scene.'

Mother guffawed. 'Fucking hell, the big man himself.'

'Way I hear it, Young and Barratt will be running it.'

'Until they're not.'

'Until.'

'Theories, ideas, latest thoughts?'

'They're working on the assumption there was an inside man.'

'In the GPO?' Billy said in horror.

Mother crossed his legs. 'They might further narrow it down by suspecting only bipedal mammals.'

'Nothing specific, then?' Billy said. 'No names?'

'Aye, you came up. But you come up any time anyone lifts anything off. Specifically, they noticed the resemblance to the airport job, which makes them think Jack the Spot.'

'Comer?' Mother spat. 'Fat pillock couldn't pull off a wank, let alone a heist like this.'

Billy patted his knee. 'Don't go letting pride in your endeavours discourage the odd from rounding up other suspects, Teddy.'

'Vibart intimated to Henry there would be raids,' Lander said. It was always a balancing act, selling what he knew through fabricated conversations with third-hand sources.

'To be expected,' Billy said. 'The spielers will get the once-over, and we'll all be pulled in, no doubt.'

'All known associates,' Lander said.

'Fine. Most of the chaps were down the Vienna. I'd laid on a bit of a spread, put a few quid behind the bar. Spitzel Goodman's got a piece of Billy Thompson, trying to relaunch him as a welter after Tommy McGovern napped him in the blink of an eye. He beat some South African kid, so we did it by way of a celebration. Most of them didn't get out of there until it was light. Couple of chief inspectors present will alibi them out, so none of that will fly. Teddy tells me you did good, though.'

The backslapping attaboy part of the evening had arrived, as it always did when funds were conspicuous by their absence.

'He held up,' Mother said. 'I've seen tears and mortal fucking panic on blags from men not half the cunt this one is. But he held up.'

Billy raised his glass and they joined him in the toast.

'In the blood, eh, Dave?' Billy said with a wink. 'Hero uncle of yours was pure blue steel under pressure. Must flow through Lander veins.'

'Let's hope I last longer than he did.'

'Yeah, well. Show me the copper who doesn't need killing.'

A concern that was always on Lander's mind.

PART TWO
UNREAL CITY

7

CLOSE YOUR EYES AND DANCE

Summer 1952

She knew by the quiet that it was early.

The thick old curtains leaked no light, but the upstairs people always made their day known, and traffic from Coldharbour Lane could be heard. Nees snuffled in her sleep. Addie carefully untangled herself from the blanket and got out of bed. She pushed the door shut tighter at first before turning the knob, so it didn't make a sound when she opened it. White moonlight painted the wooden boards of the hall.

Stevie's door was closed but unlocked, carelessly patched up with offcuts and filler that hadn't been sanded down. She had gone out earlier in the evening and hadn't returned before Addie fell asleep.

Her bed was undisturbed.

Looked roomier in there now, the alcove by the window empty where the bureau had been sold off cheaply. A heap of the gowns she seldom wore too, barely covering a few weeks' rent and food.

It was unlike Stevie to go out. Even before her dad had left, the pair of them rarely stayed out late. The worry in her stomach fed conspiracies. Maybe her mother hadn't sold her clothes, but instead had moved them out so she too could disappear. Joining her father somewhere and leaving Addie and Nees to fend for themselves. There was no other family that she knew of to look after them. Her father had arrived on his own from Jamaica, and her mother never mentioned any parents or siblings.

Addie didn't know that Stevie's mother had died when she was young, and at seventeen she had fled her broken and abusive home to look for someone with whom she could set up a similar arrangement of her own, finding Reginald Rowe to be just the ticket.

In the kitchen, Addie battled her worries by making porridge. After she had innocently told Mrs Harpenden that she didn't eat breakfast any longer as things were tight, the old lady had dropped off a huge box of the cheap stuff that didn't cook very quickly, claiming she had mistakenly bought two. That was a lie everyone accepted. Only old people and babies ate porridge, but there was precious little else in the cupboard so it would have to do.

'Hot pap for the just born and the nearly dead,' Reggie would tell her. 'But you make sure it nice and clammy, and add lots of sugar. Always find jam or marmalade stacked away somewhere in England.'

Nees woke in good time for nursery, albeit dressed up in one of Stevie's outfits, which looked like a large sack on her.

'Come on, Nees. Help me out here. You know not to mess with Mum's things.'

Leading her sister back to their room, she dressed her properly and sat at her at the kitchen table. When presented with a bowl of piping-hot porridge, Nees made a face and reared back from the smell.

'How about a dollop of Mrs H's jam?'

Nees nodded, and spent a good minute thoroughly stirring the jam into the porridge, still closing her eyes with every spoonful she heaped into her mouth.

'Mum up?'

Addie shook her head. 'She's tired. Gonna sleep in. Don't you go disturbing her.'

Nees played with her food. Big spoonfuls, small spoonfuls, arranging it into shapes in the bowl that slowly slid back into shapelessness.

'You get lunch at nursery,' Addie said.

'Beans and bread,' said Nees, as if that counted for something quite other than lunch.

They wandered round to the nursery just as it was opening, and Addie left Nees to go in the door on her own, scooting out of there before any of the matrons could buttonhole her for what they called a quick word.

The school day passed like the Dark Ages. When she got out, Chabon was waiting at the corner in the long grass behind a roofless bombed-out house with despairing windows. At the nursery, Addie went in to fetch Nees. The place was still more than half full, working parents using every hour they could get.

Nees was sitting on a matron's lap, pointing at something in a picture book. There were a few little black faces dotted around now, but when Stevie had presented Nees on that first morning, she had been the only one.

The matron lifted Nees onto the seat beside her and stood.

'Your mother, she's detained somewhere today?'

'I always pick Nees up on the way home from school.'

The woman was older than Addie's mother, short dark hair kept in no particular fashion, a floral shirt over her clothes flecked with paint and food and whatever else the day threw at her. She eased Addie toward a cupboard in a corner where they could talk quietly, seldom an augur of good news. The doors of the cupboard, decorated with children's paintings, were ajar and revealed an orderly collection of art materials.

'Nees is doing very well here. She's sociable, and good with new children. She never gets upset.'

Addie nodded, uncertain what was required of her. She awaited the dropping of the other shoe.

'There is an issue with the fees, however. All the parents that send their children here pay a daily fee of a shilling. We haven't received anything for Florence – that is, for Nees – in a couple of weeks. We do our best to accommodate different circumstances, and everyone knows of your mother's troubles.'

They do? thought Addie.

'The amount due would need to be settled before Nees could return. Do you think you could let your mother know?'

'Uh huh.'

'I really do think Nees does well here. It would be a shame for her not to be able to attend.'

'I'll tell her.'

Nees took Addie's hand, and they found Chabon outside kicking the low brick wall with his heels.

'How were your beans?' Addie asked her.

'Oliver Davenant fell asleep in his. I see him going.' Nees closed her eyes in instalments and drooped her head. 'Then he plonked right in them. He got beans in his hair.'

This was hilarious to her, still cackling about it when they reached the house. On the steps, two men who could only be police were exiting the front door.

'Hello,' said Nees.

Addie nudged her.

One of the men, the older of the two, took a step down and removed his hat, revealing his baldness.

'Do you live here?'

Addie nudged her sister again and none of the kids spoke.

'I'm Chief Superintendent Barratt. You can call me Tom. Would you be Adlyn?'

Her father always told her never to speak to the police. 'Nobody in Babylon-land going help you with the business of being black. And police going actively be unhelpful in that regard. Dog-drivers. Crazy white baldheads, all of them. String you up as soon as they figure what you all about.'

Addie considered this Tom's shiny bald head.

'Adlyn Rowe?' Barratt pressed.

'Don't tell nothing, Addie,' said Chabon.

'We're looking for your father, Reginald. Think he might be in a spot of bother, and we'd like to help him out if we can. Have you seen him today?'

'He's gone, and we're eating porridge,' Nees explained.

'Well I'm very sorry to hear that.' Barratt looked to Addie. 'Have any strange men been around recently?'

Addie thought of Geronimo, but looked from one copper to the other.

Barratt smiled. 'Apart from us.'

Barefoot in last night's dress, hair in a squall and hands on her hips, Stevie appeared on the porch looking like someone halfway through a fall from a plane.

'This is what you have time for? Molesting children in the street?'

'Now, Mrs Rowe—'

'Don't you Mrs Rowe me. I know what you think of me, and that's just fine because it's nothing next to what I think of you. Now, I've already told you all you're going to hear today from this family. Men out there murdering and robbing as we speak, but you want to accost a child on her own? You don't ever talk to my daughters. You have any questions, you direct them at me, and I'll direct you as to what you can do with them.'

The police retreated to their car, and the children followed Stevie inside, where she collapsed dramatically, face down on her bed. Hair and make-up a fright, but in that gown Stevie Rowe was still quite something. Addie caught a taste of what her mother must have been like when she was at large. Just a glimpse out of the corner of her eye.

'How exhausting everything is,' Stevie mumbled into her elbow.

Chabon stared at her, mesmerised. He'd never seen the like, and never would again.

Clack-clack-clack.

'Oh God,' said Stevie.

Clack-clack-clack.

Nees at the dominoes on the kitchen table.

'Why must she incessantly tap those bloody things?'

Addie nodded for Chabon to see to Nees. When the noise stopped, Stevie sighed. A small cough rose from the staircase down to the basement flat, Mrs Harpenden being conspicuous.

'I'll see to that,' Addie said, knowing it was going to be about their earlier visitors.

Downstairs, Mrs Harpenden sat primly in her armchair, embroidery hoop in her lap.

'Your mother must have been out very early this morning. I only saw her returning.'

'She out looking for Dad.'

'Hmm. And those gentlemen callers?'

'Police. They looking for Dad too, because nobody has seen him.'

'He's been reported missing, then?'

Addie shrugged. Mrs Harpenden squinted at her needlework.

'The first time the police ever called at this house – that is to say, the first time they called here during my tenure as homeowner – was shortly after we moved in, the late Mr Harpenden and I. Distasteful business about an employee and a theft from the factory. They needed to speak to everyone, and Mr Harpenden was home that day. Of course, things were very different back then. We had servants on the top floor, and kept horses and a carriage round the back. Mr Harpenden could recall Acre Lane when there were fields on either side, leading down to the Common.'

She paused for what must have been a particularly challenging bit of embroidery.

'When the police came, two detectives as I recall, a maid answered. Showed them to the room that your mother and father sleep in now. Goodness only knows what the neighbours thought.'

'Did they arrest anyone?'

'I simply cannot remember, it was that long ago. I suppose they must have done. It was the feeling of unease that accompanied their arrival that I recall most vividly. I must have spent a week trying to subtly work it into conversation with the women of the street, how Mr

Harpenden was too high up in the firm to have any dealings with such affairs, and was merely helping the police out as best he could.'

Addie nodded. 'Nees enjoyed her bowl of porridge this morning. I added a spoon of your jam.'

'A fine start to the day, getting out with some porridge in you.'

Addie left her to her embroidery. Upstairs, Stevie hadn't moved.

'It wouldn't be good if the police came round again,' Addie said.

'Oh, how she must have loved that. Wouldn't surprise me if she called them herself.'

'Someone called them?'

'I don't know. Probably not.'

'Why they looking for Dad?'

'Why do the police look for anyone?'

'Because they did something bad.'

'Or because they're missing. They wanted to know when was the last time we saw him, and was he here on some particular night.'

'Was he?'

'Good grief, Adlyn, I don't know. Do you think I maintain a journal, some reflections on the various household comings and goings? I asked them. No, I do not.'

'What night was it?'

'Sometime the week before the bank holiday. The second one.'

'That was the week he left.'

'I know. But I wasn't going to tell them that. Don't I have enough to do without taking on the responsibilities of the local constabulary?'

Addie didn't want to get into all of that. Stevie's shoes – what she called her dancing shoes, but Addie couldn't imagine anything more difficult than dancing in them – lay by the bed where she'd kicked them off. Addie straightened them.

'He ain't coming back, is he?'

'He is not coming back. And don't be daft, of course he is. He's always wandering off.'

'Not like this.'

Stevie had more faith in her husband than did Addie. Believed he would return and set things right, because he owed her at least that.

'You weren't here this morning when we woke up.'

'I was out with a friend. I need time for myself occasionally, Adlyn. My whole life can't be the pair of you twenty-four hours a day.'

'I didn't know where you were.'

'Where would I go?'

'To be with Dad.'

Stevie snorted. 'Don't think I wouldn't.'

'Nursery said Nees can't go back till we paid what we owe.'

Slowly Stevie sat up. 'They told you that? Was it the short-haired one? It was, wasn't it. She's been preparing her whole life for inevitable spinsterhood.'

'It's two weeks. A shilling a day. And then there's the rent.'

'Oh yes. We wouldn't want to forget that.'

'We already have. This week is due tomorrow, so that'll make three weeks.'

'Thank you for the comprehensive totting-up, Adlyn, I'm sure I wouldn't know what—'

A rat-a-tat knock on the open front door was followed by a brash 'Hi hi hi!'

'Oh God,' Stevie said. 'Quick, fetch that knife of yours.'

Their landlord's face appeared round the frame of the door.

'Mr Grainger, how wonderful,' Stevie beamed.

'Mrs Rowe.' He nodded, looking round the room and across the ceiling, as if expecting to find something dripping.

Sliding her feet into her dancing shoes, Stevie stood up her full height and primped her hair fruitlessly. 'Twice in such propinquity. We can barely rid ourselves of the treat.'

He stared at her evening gown. 'You off out?'

She tittered and touched his arm. 'Goodness, no. We were just playing dress-up. A little fun.'

'Mr Rowe about?'

'I'm afraid not.'

'Seems to not be about quite frequently these days.'

Resolutely Stevie maintained her smile.

'And what about today's visitors?'

Addie glanced at the door to the basement stairs. How had she let him know so quickly?

'Visitors, Mr Grainger?'

'The Old Bill.'

'Oh, that. Merely a few friendly questions.'

'Some criminal misconduct that they're looking into?'

'More of a pastoral matter.'

'Not to be repeated, I hope?'

'Well, I don't have any say on the whims and caprices of Scotland Yard, Mr Grainger.'

'Reputation to be thinking off. Rental values, tenant attractability, things of that nature. Police knocking the place up at all hours does nothing to help me there.'

Punctuating his point, he drew a tape measure from his pocket, the wind-up kind in a red leather casing.

Stevie fetched a beaded macramé clutch from where she'd stowed it on the floor.

'On the matter of the rent.'

'Mrs Harpenden tells me there's been some challenges.'

Rooting about inside the bag, she came up with a small sheaf of notes and started counting them out.

'Two guineas a week, I think you'll find that brings us up to date, including what is due tomorrow.'

Grainger stared at the money in his hand.

'A promising development for now,' he said.

With uncharacteristic efficiency, Stevie produced the rent book and a pen. 'If you could just sign here, Mr Grainger.'

Running a grubby finger along each short line, he scribbled his initials next to the dates and amounts.

Stevie smiled sweetly. 'Apologies for any misunderstandings regarding the dates due. Won't happen again.'

Grainger grunted. Teasing the end of the tape out of its casing, he gave it to Addie.

'Hold it against the wall there. Flat to it, come on now.'

Addie did as she was told and Grainger reeled out the tape and walked into the bay, pulling it until it was satisfactorily taut and making his measurement.

'I seem to recall you had dimensions for the rooms when we moved in, Mr Grainger,' Stevie said. 'Are you expecting them to have shrunk?'

'Pays to know exactly what you're dealing with. I believe the three of you could comfortably exist in this room. Might have to give up some furniture, but falling behind on the rent, complications of that sort, then selling a few items might well be a help rather than a hindrance.'

'You've just been paid your rent.'

He wound the tape back into the casing as he strolled through to the back room. In the hall, he looked in on the scullery, finding Chabon sitting at the table with Nees.

'How many children do you have exactly?'

'I've never seen that boy before in my life,' Stevie said, tottering after him into the girls' bedroom.

'Oh my, yes, those wardrobes would never fit with two beds. But a solid inventory of one's belongings, what is necessary and what is not, boiling things down to their essentials, which of us could say we wouldn't be all the better for that?'

'Mr Grainger . . .'

He had Addie hold the tape again as he paced out the room.

'Be careful how the white man makes you work' was one of Reggie's gems. 'He'll think nothing of showing you how to measure and cut rope, only to tie it round your neck.'

She let go of the tape, and it fell to the floor, where everyone stared at it.

'Oops,' she said, not picking it up.

Grainger began reeling it back into its case. 'The smaller of the two, but I think half the rent would be fair. Full use of the scullery, shared between you and the other tenants. Half the rent is a bonus for you, in acknowledgement of the time you've been here. I really don't think you can say fairer than that.'

'We've paid you the rent in full, Mr Grainger.'

'Things to keep in mind. Never hurts to be considering improvements.' He drew Stevie aside. 'In the future, Mrs Rowe, if you find yourself in a challenging situation with regards the rent, don't be afraid to reach out to me. I'm only down the road, and I'm always prepared to come to some accommodation with my favourite tenants.'

Stevie went for an appreciative purr, which came out more like a gag.

She saw him out to the hallway, where he paused to look around, as if considering the good work he'd done, and then left. The basement door had been left ajar, and Stevie heeled it shut and returned to her room, plonking down on her bed. She kicked off her shoes.

Addie sat on the high-backed chair that her father's clothes still didn't hang on.

'So?'

'So what?'

'Where'd all that money come from?'

'It isn't that much.'

Stevie tipped out her clutch bag on the bed, pulling the lining inside-out. Among the detritus were a few more pound notes and a handful of coins.

'I'll go to the market,' she said.

'Best if I go,' said Addie, picturing it turning into cigarettes and gin.

'Suit yourself.'

'Where'd you get it, Mum?'

'Friend loaned it me.'

'We'll have to pay it back?'

'More of a gift. They called it a loan so it was easier to take.'

'Huh. Good friend.'

Stevie swept aside the contents of her bag and lay back on the bed.

'Old friend. That's who I went out for a drink with. See? Wasn't all about me having a good time.'

'Must have been drinking all night.'

'We went up West for a dance. We were dancing all night.'

Addie glanced again at the shoes.

Stevie draped an arm across her face, voice slow. 'You just close your eyes and dance.'

This was typical Stevie – she accepted the prospect of dire straits as if unavoidable, stirring herself into action only when absolutely necessary, when eviction beckoned. From the kitchen, the clacking of dominoes started up again.

Stevie sighed. 'I shall never again have a moment's peace. She doesn't even know how to play the game.'

'It's the sound of the cards,' Addie said from the door. 'Reminds her of Dad.'

8

MAKE THEM EAT BRASS

Lander rose from the sofa when he heard the postman downstairs. Another letter, his name and address in familiar hand, postmark near the small coastal town where his in-laws had retired to. He put it unopened in the drawer of the hallway sideboard with the others.

He passed the day as he did most others, eating disappointing biscuits, despairing quietly, inflicting death upon flies. Went out for cigarettes and later went out for more.

Early evening, still brightness low in the sky, and the phone rang. It was Mother.

'Come get me.'

'Home?'

'No. Harrow Road nick.'

'You got touched again?'

'Hurry up.' He added, as if an afterthought, 'And bring a heavy hand.'

By Lander's count, this was the third time Mother had been brought in. The spielers and clubs were being raided twice a week, more than Billy had anticipated, and business was suffering. He was removing himself from the operations for the time being, setting new ones up without showing his face so the Flying Squad didn't poke their noses in. Lander had been picked up a couple of times himself, questioned by cops who didn't know he was a cop. None of the bosses showed their hand or interfered in any way. He took his lumps and was released.

Brass knuckles in his pocket, he fetched the Interceptor and hopped back over the canal, following the thick railway down the Harrow Road to where the police station sat next to the town hall. Mother was standing out front, a clutch of coppers watching him. He doffed imaginary chapeau as he got in the car.

'Anon, gentlemen.'

'Where to?'

'Breakfast. I'm starving.'

'Tad late for a spot of brekkie.'

'Serf mentality, putting a clock on breakfast. I've been having a kip in the cell. You break the fast when you awaken, when your daily endeavours begin. Don't allow pinstriped cunts in bowlers to put limits on when exactly that might be.'

Parking in an alley off the Edgware Road, they popped into a snack bar for a fried egg sarnie and a passable brew.

'Where'd they grab you?'

'Home. Pulled the place apart, again. Focus on floorboards and the lath-and-plaster this time. I said to them, I had a quarter of a marigold in tea-leafed cash, you think I'd keep it under my floor, you soft cunts?'

'They're taking liberties. It's not right.'

'It's perfectly fucking right, Davey boy. You get your villains who whine about this and that, ooh, the coppers turned up and ruined the Sunday roast. The babs in tears, the women wailing. Bang out of order, the peelers. Why's this happening to me? I'll tell you why. Because we're fucking gangsters. We rob and kill people. You want to moan about them turning the place over after we did the biggest blag in history? Pull the other one. This is part of the life.'

There was nothing to the night's work.

Mother ran his errands, kept his hand in on the streets. They kicked off with the wharf roads around Paddington Basin, a couple of Teds working late shifts at a timber yard who'd taken unreasonable chances with borrowed money at the faro table. Lander emptied their pockets and gave them the knucks.

Followed the canal to Harlesden, dropping in on a night security man at the paint works who was keeping notes on the weekly payroll for Mother. Over Thermos tea, he regaled them with his theory, well supported by bar-top fantasy and street supposition, that the Eastcastle Street job was the work of Scotland Yard, harvesting both a quarter-million to feed police annuity funds and justification to have armed coppers at every high-value postal haul.

'Think of how many more cozos there'll be. Historical recruitment drive. And they'll need to up pensions to attract new blood.'

All that was on anyone's lips was the robbery, and Mother was eager to hear all the tales, soak up what songs the streets sang. Looking to enliven a few tardy payers, they shook up a spieler in a mission hall basement and heard Americans had pulled the robbery. The mind of the landlord of the White Horse, on the corner of the vast and derelict Caledonian Market, was focused with a few benevolent slaps courtesy of a missed protection payment, but he had nothing more to offer than rumours of a commando crew, who'd hunted down fleeing Nazis in occupied Germany at the end of the war, re-forming for the heist.

For laughs, Mother outright accused two brothers who ran a banana warehouse in Covent Garden of being in on the blag, and initially they played coy, enjoying being connected to such a job by someone like Mother, until they saw the shine of Lander's knuckles.

Nothing they heard was reliable.

On Long Acre, they stopped off at the Enterprise, a boozer Mother owned in all but name, popular with newspaper types who enjoyed the company of villains and coppers who drank there.

Dorcas 'Darkey' Hutch had her name on the licence, and Mother let her run the bar as she saw fit. Hard as a horseshoe and just as bent. The first floor housed the Cabinet Offices, a private bar where police brass and select gangsters drank in peace, and the rooms above that were home to the late-night walk-up operations Darkey also matronised.

Behind the bar, Tabitha, Darkey's monstrous Alsatian, which answered to 'Tabs', had the run of the place. Nobody stepped behind there without an inquisitive, teeth-baring growl. Even Mother acquiesced to the dog's wishes as he did the rounds, shaking hands and sharing winks.

They took drinks upstairs and sat undisturbed in a private snug in the Cabinet Offices. Only others up there were the head of North-West London CID having G&Ts at the bar with an upstairs girl.

On their way through, Mother snatched a paper off the bar.

'Yesterday's. You see this?'

Copy of the *Mirror*, he opened to the second page, where the headline read, *Where do YOU think it is hidden?*

'Twenty-three days and not a trace of the £250,000 has been found,' Mother said. 'Opening it up to the readers, see if they can't come up with a theory or two. This could be big, Dave. Spot the Ball big. Have people pay a fee, send in their ideas. Get a chunk of the reward money if something pans out. Solve the Crime. The way us rascals run round doing places over, this'll be bigger than the pools in no time.'

'What's the reward?'

'Fourteen grand, it says. And all harmless fun. It's the banks' cash, and the insurance stumps up the bill. Christ, I'd do over insurance companies every single day of the week and twice on Sundays because it's the Lord's work. Look at them panic. There are no bigger criminals than banks, but nobody ever ends up in court for their rape and pillage. You turn a bank over, though, then you're an outlaw. Then the status quo has been shaken up and they'll come down hard. Well, *bonne chance, mis amigos.*'

He tugged on his ragged ear lobe, which had been gnawed off in a street fight in the twenties, though Lander had heard him tell it that a bullet claimed it at the Somme, whistling lead inches from planting itself in his brain pan.

'What have you been hearing over the family dinner table, Davey?'

'They're nowhere with the robbery, far as I can tell. They're pretty sure it's you, obviously. You and Billy.'

'The arrests and constant visits for interior decorating led me there already.'

'Most everyone they like for the crew was seen in the early hours at the Vienna by several chief inspectors, which don't help their case. They can't prove anything.'

'How could they, unless someone squeals?'

A reminder, warming up to a threat.

'How many times they had you in?' Mother asked pointedly.

'Twice.'

'And?'

'And nothing. Said I knew nothing. They reckon I'm little more than a bar worker at the spielers anyway.'

'So there's no way they find anything out, then. Only the four of us left that know.'

Billy's philosophy on killing was there was no angle to it as the risk was too high. Even chivving someone, he was careful to cut them downwards, as slicing up presented the opportunity for the blade to slip and open an artery, and then you had a real mess to clean up. Violence was business, and in business you only took the risks that were necessary to make a profit. Murder made no sense, unless of course nobody ever found out there was a murder.

'You start dropping bodies, the cozzers will be all over you,' Mother had told Lander once. 'You only kill someone if they absolutely need killing. And even then, you don't kill them.'

'How's that?'

'I'm saying, accidents happen. Even better, if there's no body, there's no crime. What can they prove? Can't even prove something's happened, other than some cunt's upped and vanished. I like to think of it as returning whence they came.'

Coppers didn't investigate bodies on the bottom of the Thames.

Or men who ended up in sausage links.

Lander thought of the million ways things could go wrong.

'Gyp knows,' he said. 'And who knows what farm animals Strong Arms worries. There's always something gets overlooked.'

Mother studied him.

'Anyway, what Henry tells me, they're not even that fussed about the arrests.'

'No? Funny way of showing it.'

'It's the cash. They need it back.'

'I had heard the country is broke. Perhaps they can't rebuild it without a truckful of stolen loot.'

'The robberies out of the trains were already an embarrassment. This one's tipped them over. Makes it look like they can't keep anything safe. The GPO is a laughing stock.'

'GPO is basically a Marxist operation at this point, redistributing the nation's wealth.'

Through the slightly warped glass in the window of the snug door, Lander spotted the louche, Little Phil, with his cat's prowl and suitcase in one hand. Discreet, he kept himself to himself and sat at the bar.

'I swear I know him from somewhere else. It's been bothering me.'

'Dorchester,' Mother said. 'Used to be the ballroom manager. Supplied what you might call executive services to wealthy clientele. Pills, powder, grumble and grunt. Pharmaceuticals were big for him back then.'

Lander stored that away.

Mother drank and wiped his mouth with the back of his wrist. 'Sorted the suites out for Billy's big-stakes card games too.'

'Lady Docker,' Lander said.

'Aye. Fell backwards into the wine business through the hotel, which afforded Continental opportunities. Went freelance.'

'And how's that going? Changing the money?'

'That's in hand. Speaking of which.'

Mother pulled out a wad of cash and tucked it thickly into the breast pocket of Lander's jacket. Lander didn't touch it. Fivers, looked to be about two hundred quid's worth.

'Fuck's that?'

'Tide you over.'

'Again, with this?'

'Complicated process, money smashing.'

'If I was a more suspicious man, I might think I was being led about by the nose here.'

'Dave . . .'

'Let me get this straight in my mind. Let's say we had a quarter-mil after Billy's expenses are taken out. It was more than that, but let's say. Minus his half, leaves a hundred and twenty-five large, to be split evenly seven ways. Let's say eighteen thousand each. Except for the minor point that there isn't seven of us because we chopped the other four up. So there's just me, you and Phil, leaving us with, let's say, just north of forty grand each.'

'There's a lot of let's saying going on here.'

'Let's say that's a fair distribution of the blag, and everyone has a great day. Best fucking day of their lives, in fact.'

Lander plucked the two hundred quid from his pocket.

'So run *this* by me again, just so I understand.'

'You know the money has to be smashed . . .'

'It's been months, so let's not pretend your man Phil over there hasn't been zigzagging back and forth across the Channel for most of that time.'

'One thing or another, it's turned out to be a lot less than we initially thought.'

'This is the part where you tell me the paper was too badly damaged?'

'The paper *was* badly damaged. That's why it was on the train in the first place, Dave. We've had to destroy a significant amount. Well over half, and I don't mind telling you that it twisted my tits having to torch that much cash. Look, the money is coming, and it'll be far more than what you were expecting going into the blag. But the size of the haul, it attracted more attention than we were anticipating. Your patience will be appreciated in the matter, Dave, if you don't mind. Please and fucking thank you.'

Lander shook his head, stuffed the cash back in his pocket.

'Most men, two hundred nicker in their pocket, that's a good few months' honest work.'

'Something neither of us know anything about.'

'Thank the merciful Lord. You ever meet anyone does an honest day's work for an honest day's pay who didn't, when asked to explain what they do, end up sounding like a cunt? I never did. That alone justifies the life of crime.'

'The money justifies the life of crime.'

'Davey.'

Lander dropped it.

Mother adopted a more solicitous tone. 'Talking of unwanted attention, how's the new spieler doing?'

In a Greek Street basement opposite the London Casino, which wasn't a casino, was Samson's Café, which was. Miss Samson, a spinster with prodigious appetites for double-pack rummy and much younger Mediterranean gentlemen, had taken over the operation from two Cypriot cousins, and still largely served a Cypriot clientele until ten on the dot, at which point everyone was unceremoniously tossed out no matter what they had on their plate. The tables were turned over and the gaming began at eleven.

A boarded-up bomb site on the corner gave access to a rudely con-structed side entrance, shadows of lost staircases climbing the exposed wall above it, supported now by great timber buttresses where the neighbouring building had fallen.

Mother sauntered into the place, a maharajah among his masses. They reached out to touch him, to talk to him, yearning just to be seen by him. Not as many as there had been at Dean Street, but rebuilding after constant Flying Squad raids would take time.

He and Lander stood at the back scanning the goings-on. Half-empty chemmy tables, and a barman with time to run his gums with the ladies between orders. Billy Howard joined them, a legendary street brawler loved by Billy Hill since he threw a straightener with Tony Mella to decide who controlled the bird food concessions at Trafalgar Square. Consequently, Billy Hill's brother Archie got to help tourists feed the pigeons, Howard was rewarded with a backroom spieler behind a trade union canteen for meat porters at Smithfield, and Tony the Greek was endowed with an outsized bare-knuckle reputation that saw more than his fair share of drunk punters trying it on at his new Soho clip joint.

Howard's Smithfield spieler proved popular not only with porters and bummerees, but local Post Office and rail workers too, so Lander had put him to work running this new gaff.

'Quiet night,' Mother said.

Howard shrugged. 'Nobody knows it's Billy's place.'

'Fucking conundrum. Billy's name brings in punters, but, current climate, Billy's name gets us shut down by the Sweeney.'

'We're doing all right. Nobody's losing out.' He glanced across the tables. 'Other than them who's supposed to, anyway. Here, what's the cagmag on that postal robbery?'

'Fuck should I know?'

'Reason I ask, we've got a dawdler, back at the canteen place. Regular, in there couple of times a week usually, so we run him a line. He's always down, but has straight work, so we let it slide a bit and he always pays up. Only, I haven't seen him going on a month. Reginald Rowe.'

Lander felt Mother's eyes flick to him momentarily.

Please, not with the axe.

'Remind me.'

'Spade postman.'

'What's he into us for?'

'Nothing too out of hand. Hundred and fifty or so. But it's the precedent it sets.'

'He's not going to have knocked over this mail van, is he?'

'No. Probably not. Might have known when it was running, though.'

'Then he really should have paid up his debts with his good fortune.'

'Fucked off back to the islands, what I'm thinking.'

'Fucked off whence he came, more like,' Lander said when Howard had drifted away.

A sharp look from Mother persuaded him to hold any further counsel on the matter.

'I've got a few things to see to around the neighbourhood.'

'Fine. Where to next?'

'No, you're all right. Might see how the next hour pans out here, then take a stroll around. I'll see myself home.'

'Yeah?'

'Been washing my own socks for a while now, Dave. See you tomorrow.'

'Sure.'

Letting his free taxi go was unusual for Mother. Many had been the night he'd have Lander hang around at the bar while he took care of something, having him drive him home at dawn, so this felt off. Not for the first time, Lander wondered how safe he was, working between two worlds as he was, and whether either of those worlds would help him should the time come when someone looked to return *him* whence he came.

Lander embraced paranoia, had learned to listen to those first tingles of dread, even if he had the suspicion that seizing upon them in such a fashion was inviting them to be realised.

He whipped the Interceptor down Old Compton Street to Brewer, where the art deco garage loomed over the junction with Lexington, chauffeurs for rich theatregoers rolling up in Bentleys and Daimlers. Spinning round the block, he approached the rear entrance and found an attendant he knew, Rusk.

'Jump in,' Lander told him.

'You need a spare ride, Mr Lander?'

'You got it.'

'Take her up to three.'

Lander climbed the ramps, before letting Rusk park the car using the turntable to navigate the tight columns of cars wagon-wheeling out from the centre. He returned in a tiny two-door Austin, looking pleased with himself.

'Something inconspicuous.'

Lander examined it as if he might not fit inside.

'Almost brand new, Mr Lander. Dorsets are fine cars. Straight-four pushrod, but more than enough for its size. More than enough. Nobody'll be looking for it until tomorrow afto.'

'It'll do lovely, Rusk. Here.'

He palmed him five bob and eased the Austin down the ramps and out the way he'd come. Parking up on Moor Street, he kept an eye on the back entrance to the Greek Street spieler, hoping he wasn't too late. Twenty minutes until Mother appeared, trotting along the bombed Bourchier Street, picking his way between open foundations of ruins now collecting rainwater, and getting into a car Lander didn't recognise.

Following anyone on quiet streets without being noticed was a challenge, let alone keeping pace with a maniac. Mother raced across Soho to Regent Street and up through Marylebone to Paddington. A sudden sense of terror escalated within Lander that they were headed to his own gaff in Kensal Town. Had something happened that night that had done for him? Had he given himself away in some fashion? He regretted now making that crack about the postman Reginald

Rowe returning whence he came. Mother was mad for the compart-mentalising of jobs, and perhaps Lander knew too much about compartments other than his own.

Before his fears could fully crystallise, they drifted toward Lad-broke Grove. There was little traffic and Lander kept his distance, often letting the other car disappear from sight. He thought he'd lost him completely at one point, having to cruise the back roads of Not-ting Dale until he found the car on a shabby street near the railway. He passed without slowing and circled round the block to park out of sight.

Only four other cars were parked on the road with Mother's, all down near a bend where there was a garage. Chancing that Mother had parked outside the house he was visiting, Lander slipped into the building next door, which was derelict, possibly bombed out. There was no door, the windows all boarded, and smashed walls inside offered a view right through from the street to the moonlit garden. A tiny courtyard sat next to the kitchen/scullery and what had once been a washhouse. He bunked over next door, which had an identical layout, remaining in a crouch when he landed, waiting for any sign he'd been heard or spotted.

The back door was open and led into a hallway, along which he could hear voices, Mother and a woman. They were in the rear room, its window overlooking the yard, lights on so they wouldn't see any-thing through the window. He crept as close as he dared, recognising there would be nowhere to run if someone came out.

'It's two a.m.,' the woman said. 'I haven't slept and I'm here talking with you. How do you reckon things are going?'

'Here,' Mother said. 'For the sleeping situation. Take the bottle. No, I can get more, as many as you like.'

'I don't want—'

'They work, don't they?'

'Yes.'

'And the other thing, that's fine. I need someone trustworthy, and you need a job. How is this not a good plan? You just need a few good nights' kip, and a regular routine with a pay packet.'

Abruptly Lander heard footsteps on the wooden boards of the hallway. Sliding in behind the open back door, he pressed himself flat against the rear wall of the house and held his breath. Mother breezed right past him and went to the WC at the end of the washhouse.

Pissed in short, feeble spurts.

Groaned and returned to the house without troubling the basin.

Lander was certain his shoes poked out beneath the door, but Mother hadn't spotted him. Inside, there was no more chat. Someone moved about in the house and lights turned off, then the front door banged shut.

He gave it a minute.

Couldn't hear anything.

Slipping through the door into the hallway, he was immediately met with a door on one side to the scullery, and another the other side into a dining room where the voices had come from. Edging along, a foot came into view, someone on a settee beneath the window. The leg it was attached to stretched out suddenly, foot pointed, and quivered like a cat's before relaxing.

Lander remained perfectly still.

Stared at the foot for a couple of lifetimes before chancing a look round the door frame. A woman in a dressing gown, slouched over and resting against a cushion. Asleep, he thought, until he saw the silhouette of the pill bottle on the windowsill. She'd had a little help.

Unopened post lay on a sideboard. He leaned over to get a better look in the dark. Mr Alfred Martin. The name meant nothing to him. There was nothing addressed to her, the wife he assumed. She moaned and shifted on the settee, heavy eyes opening just a slit.

He stayed very still.

If she saw him, she gave no sign, and turned her head a little, finding a new place to settle. Maybe she thought he was Mother. Maybe she didn't think at all. The robe had ridden up, revealing a full run of thigh. She had dancer's legs and he felt shame as he stiffened. What was Mother's interest in this woman? He couldn't ever remember seeing him with ladies. Or men, for that matter. He was a sexless, episcopal presence. Hard to figure him getting involved with a married housewife.

Beside the post, a small double photograph frame stood on the sideboard. The woman with two young children on one side, taken a few years ago probably, and on the other, to Lander's shock, a face he recognised. One of the men from the other car in the robbery, a man Mother had killed at the old butcher's shop, whose body Lander had seen on the floor before it ended up in a sack.

What on earth was Mother up to, entangling himself with the wife of a man on the blag? On the other hand, it was exactly the kind of thing he'd do. He loved playing the dangerous friend, someone who would grant favours whilst at the same time implying that he was in no way to be crossed.

Control was oxygen to him.

In the early light, the vast gasworks on the canal stood smog blurred like a giant henge. Deciding to return the Austin to Rusk later, Lander headed for his flat. A ridiculous plan was starting to take shape, that maybe if he could find the remaining money, or the exchanged currency, he could use it to barter his way out of the life in which he'd buried himself. It was pinning a lot on the hope that recovering the blag cash was worth enough to the brass that they'd let him slide on his part in the robbery, and every other thing, but if the worst came to the worst, with that much money he could always just run.

What he was going to tell the General about all this, he didn't have the foggiest. He always knew when he should contact Lee, or when he was about to receive a call or a note through from his guv. It wasn't a sixth sense or anything magical, he just thought back to when he last spoke with him, and if it felt like he was taking the piss, then one of them was about ready to reach out.

Started reconsidering that sixth sense part when he saw Lee waiting outside his flat, leaning against a 6/80. Looked like he was out for a stroll, hat tilted back on his head, folded paper sticking out of the pocket of his suit jacket.

Lander parked behind him and got out.

'Could have called.'

The look he received implied attempts had been made, and not just a few.

'Get in, Sergeant.'

Lander glanced up the road. Wasn't a person in the neighbourhood wouldn't know the 6/80 to be a police car. They took a scenic route out of Kensal Town, passing every works and warehouse, factory and bus depot, Lander on display for everyone to see.

Lee took his time looping down to the Bayswater Road and into the West End. It was good and light by the time he pulled over on Shaftesbury Avenue, outside the old Gaumont theatre, its art deco facade boarded up since the war. Directly opposite was the site of the Shaftesbury Theatre, obliterated in the war, the air it had inhabited now empty. Along the thin street beside it, they could see all the way to the front door of Peter Mario on Gerrard Street.

Lander blew his lips.

'Some point or deeper meaning I'm to infer from this.'

'Do I have to worry about you, Dave?'

'Be nice if you did. I was running ghost operatives, I'd like to think I'd worry about them all the time.'

'Weeks go by, we have nothing provable on this case, and from you I don't hear a dicky bird.'

'What do you want me to tell you?'

'Tell me something you know.'

'Know, or can prove?'

'At this point, I'm open to guesswork, deduction, wild speculation.'

Lander felt a spot more let's saying coming on.

'Let's say Billy Hill is behind it.'

'Crazy shot in the dark, but let's . . .'

'Which means Teddy Nunn did it.'

'Correct.'

'With six other men, according to eyewitnesses. Now, I can think of maybe two or three men, at most, who Nunn would trust. Really trust. So anybody else in on it he would have kept on a very tight rein, to the point they wouldn't have known anything other than their specific role. But even then, most of his crew alibi out, right?'

'Almost everyone involved with the firm. Except Nunn himself. And you.'

'Well, let's say I did it, and move on from there to picturing exactly how properly fucked that would make you.'

The early traffic was picking up, busy-looking men stepping off buses.

Lander pressed himself back in his seat. 'There's talk of a specialist crew.'

'Talk? Talk by whom?'

'Nobody who can be believed. Out-of-towners brought in so nobody from the Yard would know them. On the road back home right after the blag. Explaining why the usual faces all have airtight whereabouts.'

'You believe it?'

'No.'

'Has Nunn spoken to you about it at all?'

Lander snorted. 'He trusts me as far as running the money goes. The spielers, the nightclubs, the rackets, day-to-day stuff like that. But major heists? No. He did it, he's playing it close to his chest. There's no sign of new money, but I wouldn't expect there to be. Something this big, this precisely executed? They're not going to be running around with brand-new diamond tiepins and gold-heeled shoes. You got anything that could help?'

'Such as?'

'Some way of identifying the cash? A quarter of a million in small notes is a lot of readies, but if they were being returned maybe to be destroyed, then . . .'

'A lot are identifiable, but not in any organised fashion. We have bank clerk notes on some damage and markings, scribbles or what have you.'

'Probably too late anyway. Hill is careful. He'll burn anything incriminating. Clearing half the take is something he'd consider a good day. Destroying tens of thousands wouldn't bother him.'

'Crims don't burn cash.'

'You're thinking about him all wrong. His days of jumping Chelsea wives in the street for their jewellery are long behind him. He's not street slag. He's a baron. A capitalist. He puts in the long hours. Figures out the margins. He'll never allow himself to be put away, not again. There'll come a time when he's so legit he'll be stitched into the fabric of this city, and you'll never be able to touch him. You need to start thinking about him in different terms.'

'You're not giving me much here, Sergeant.'

Working between the lines as he did, Lander was adept at lying with the truth.

'Far as the crew goes, when you don't know exactly who you're looking for, maybe not seeing people you're not looking for can help.'

'People conspicuous by their absence.' Lee considered it. 'Perhaps lying low after a job.'

'If they're lucky.'

'You think Hill would kill his own crew?'

'He doesn't do killing. Doesn't see the angle in it.'

'Two hundred and fifty thousand angles is a different situation, though.'

'Usually, I'd say offing your own crew would be a reputation-killer. Nobody would ever work for you again. But nobody knew about this job before, and nobody knows anything now. No leaks. Everyone's talking about it, but there's nothing but nonsense rumours. Nobody knows the crew.'

'They must have people in their lives, though, the people who did it. People who would miss them if they're gone.'

'Exactly. Worth a look-see.'

'Got any names?'

'Some, I don't have their real names. There was a peterman went by Spider, had a lot of cash on the tables in the Dean Street spieler. Haven't seen him about.'

'Mark Cully,' Lee said. 'He's in Durham doing a four.'

'Fair dos. Then there's Moonie.'

'That's his name, Mooney?'

'Short for Moonraker.'

'He a simpleton?'

Lander shrugged. 'He's from Swindon. Sells French brandy on the black.'

'Sergeant . . .'

'And a fella called the Kink.'

'A man of lesser character than I might suggest you're making this up.'

'Paddy the Kink, something like that?'

'Patsy? Patsy the Kink?'

'Could be.'

'Patrick Dibdin. Decent car heister. Natural auxiliary to any big blag. That might pan out.'

Lander wished him good luck, as he knew for a fact Dibdin had nothing to do with the job and had gone to Canada a month earlier on false papers after two rather rambunctious twins from Bethnal Green told him they were going to saw off his feet, Patsy having dobbed them in for being AWOL from their National Service because they relieved him of a Ford Zephyr he had nicked for a Bond Street smash-and-grab.

'There's one other fella, but he might be nothing.'

'Go on.'

'Martin. Alfred Martin. Mother spoke to him a few times, but I haven't seen him since the job. Got the impression they went back a way.'

'Don't know him.'

'Lives in the Dale, off Ladbroke Grove.'

'You've been there?'

'Nah. Heard him talking about going for a sherbet at his local, the Ladbroke.'

'Talbot Grove?'

'Yeah.'

'I'll look into him.'

'Can I go now?'

'No, you can't go now. With Hill, is there any West Indian involvement?'

'In the firm? Blacks? No. That's not . . . I mean, I've never heard him opine on it one way or the other, but it's not the done thing. Although I have heard him speak about North Africa. Tangiers, maybe going there. Opening a nightclub. And there is Bar, of course. Big one-eared West Indian chap. You'd have something on him. Did a seven for shooting a bollock off a club owner during the war. He's not in the circle, though, just drinks at the Vienna. Has a huge grey-hound and can look after himself, so probably everyone is shy about telling him otherwise.'

'I don't mean someone who works directly for him. Maybe some-one who might have information for him, useful for a job.'

Please, not with the axe.

'Inside man, you mean? Like at the GPO?'

Lee said nothing.

What do you think we are? Animals?

'Thought you didn't have any obvious candidates. Nobody who jumped onto a ship for Spain the next day.'

'There are over three thousand postmen at Eastern Central. Another thousand in the foreign section in the same building. Hundreds of admin staff, not to mention the high turnover and seasonal nature of recruitment, or those that once worked there but have moved else-where. We haven't come close to tracking everyone down yet.'

'But . . .'

'It's just a theory at this point.'

That Lee knew about Reginald Rowe's involvement, or had his sus-picions, was clear. But Rowe had sizzled in someone's pan by now.

'I've never seen any West Indians around the West End gaffs. I'll keep an eye out.'

'You see this Alfred Martin chap again, you let me know.'

'Sure.'

'Good. I'll drop you back to your flat. Maybe on the way you'll search your mind and find something else you want to tell me.'

'Must be joking. I'll make me own way, ta.'

Lander got out and scarpered up Greek Street, keeping an eye on shop and car windows for any sign of unwanted company. The inner dimensions of his life were shrinking; he lived every moment in expectation of a gunman round the next corner. Any car he got into could be the one he never got out of. He really didn't know how he stood with anybody at the end of the day.

9

GANGSTERS, NOT COWBOYS

Mum toasted bread that was on the curl, laid out the butter and marmalade. It wasn't Golden Shred, but it was fourpence a jar cheaper from Leon's on Fulham Palace Road, which was a good hike from the Dale. Ray was in his pyjamas still, not having decided whether he was going to school or the garage with uncle, or rather having decided but not wanting to let on to mum just yet.

Sister simmered silently across the table, always something with her now. Mum sat down with only a tea, and now he thought about it, she was looking pretty fancy, hair and make-up not just the usual.

'What?' she said.

Shook his head like, nothing, but said, 'Where you off to?'

'I'm working, you know that.'

He nodded.

Uncle lurched in the front door, combover flying wild, laying the scent of tobacco behind him. His corduroys were grubby and paint marled, his pullover worn to an indistinguishable colour, and in battered old sandals he aired freely the ivory rhizomes of his toes.

'Toast on the table,' mum said.

He grunted and sat, holding a slice as he scraped butter across it and took a big bite, not troubling the plate in front of him. Stopped his chewing for a moment as he considered her.

'Working the afternoon shift dressed for the evening?'

Ray nodded vigorously. 'What I said. Didn't I say?'

'You're going to comment on my dress, looking as you do like something come out of a swamp?'

Uncle dignifiedly brushed crumbs from his front.

'Work more suited to someone younger, what I would have thought.'

'If thinking was something you had down to a fine art.'

It was early for uncle and he cut his losses. Sister slurped the last of her tea as she stood, taking her cup and plate to the kitchen.

'When are you in, Peg?' mum said.

'Nine,' sister called from the other room. 'Got Lady Bainbridge.'

'Never mind. At least she tips well.'

'Who's Lady Bainbridge?' Ray said.

'I wouldn't mind if she didn't go on so. It's a relief to get her under the dryer.'

'Who's Lady Bainbridge?'

'A nice old widow who gets a blow dry from your sister and tips her extravagantly.'

'After she's told me at length about her whippets.'

'Remember you told me you'd do the colours.'

'I know. I'm only in half-day, so I'll take them round the baths this afternoon.'

'Thanks. I'm going to be in till late, I think.' Mum turned to Ray. 'You're going to be late for school.'

'Yeah, yeah.'

He made no sign of hurrying until she stared at him, and he picked up his plate to follow his sister. The door was to, and through the crack he saw Vic Barlow come down the stairs with a towel around his neck, so he hovered by the door, pretending to examine post on the sideboard. He didn't like the upstairs tenant, working full time as he did and going out with money and girls.

In the scullery, sister's voice changed. 'Hello.'

'Morning.'

'You not working, then?'

'Getting ready.'

'Thought you'd grab a bath there.'

'Got to have my hair looking right before I get there.'

'For all the ladies in the first-class slipper tubs?'

'You should drop by. I'll let you in first class for free. Have a nice long soak. Pamper yourself.'

'Got to bring the colours in for a scrub at the laundry, so maybe when they're drying, I'll come.'

'When you do come, think of me.'

She laughed some other way, not like as if it were funny. Ray waited a little longer, making sure Vic was gone, but sister opened the door into him.

'What you doing?'

'Nothing.'

'Don't lurk behind doors.'

'I wasn't. I was bringing these through.'

She glanced back at the door leading out to the washhouse, seeing him suddenly for what he was. Her abrupt laugh set him on edge.

'Shut up.'

'Ray, don't talk to your sister like that,' mum said.

This was the way it would go, them ganging up on him. His blood up, he sought to change the subject, act as peacemaker. 'What time are you going to be back tonight, then?'

Mum shrugged. 'I don't know. I'm on the late, but the other girl is alone early, so I'm going in to give her a hand and clear the place up for the evening session.'

'Coming home alone?'

'You worried? That's sweet.'

Ray blushed, nothing quite going as he wanted that morning.

'The seven'll take me all the way from Oxford Street to Ladbroke Grove, drops me off outside the KPH.'

'Crazy,' uncle said. 'Trekking all that way. Why go to Covent Garden for bar work when you could pull jars at the Ladbroke?'

'Because the pay is better. More than enough to make up for the time and cost of the journey. Teddy's done me a solid.'

'Aye, I'll bet. What's his game, I wonder.'

'He's just helping out. Knew I needed something.'

'Why is he, my point.'

'I've known him a long time.'

'And he's always been a—'

'I don't mind working there. Quite like it, actually. Gets me out to the West End, and it means we don't have any problem making the rent. So unless you want to start covering all of it . . .?'

Uncle took a sudden interest in his toast crust.

'No, I thought not.'

Ray nipped upstairs to dress as mum cleared the table. He pulled on old trousers and his oily overalls and was tying his boots as uncle called upstairs to him.

Mum shook her head when she saw him coming down. 'I don't think so. You've got school.'

'School ain't going to help with the rent.'

'We've talked about this. My job covers the rent now. You should be in school. I don't need to be getting more visits about you.'

'Probably have to have him in with the infants, he's missed so much at this point,' sister offered, and nobody told her not to speak like that to him. Uncle even laughed, though probably just to counteract the meanness.

'Whaddusay?'

Ray lunged at her, more in the way of a warning than anything else, as he'd be the first to admit that deep down he lacked the capacity to actually hurt anyone. Even though it was unnecessary, uncle moved to stop him, but whilst bracing his meaty arm across Ray's chest he suffered a toe-stubbing that made him howl.

Sister stuck her tongue out, which was uncalled for.

Hopping about, uncle steered Ray out the front door, dancing clumsily into the street.

Between his initial amusement and arriving on the pavement, the toe situation had darkened uncle's mood, and though it was Ray who mostly owned this confected anger, he grabbed a second-hand piece of it.

'I don't know what your mother's doing working for that man.'

'And don't get me started on my sister, what she gets up to and the intentions others may be having in that regard.'

'What sort of man calls himself Mother, anyway?'

Ray nodded furiously, happy to find common ground on the apostate women of the family.

'What dad would have said, her trying to leave the house with the amount of make-up and other embroidery going on.'

'You keep your distance from this man, Raymond. This Teddy Nunn. There's a time and a place for violence, how could I be anything other than the last person to deny that, but for thieving? No. You keep a careful accounting of yourself, and if you find larceny in your heart, it's time to make changes. There's nothing lower than a crook.'

Walking on the heel of his wounded foot, uncle lumbered toward the garage, pausing every couple of steps to readjust his weight, though Ray knew he was observing a couple rounding the bend on the other side of the street, a young West Indian man with a white girl. He watched them too.

'They live on this street?'

'Never seen them,' uncle said. 'Going to church, maybe.'

Ray looked at his watch. 'At this hour of a weekday? And which church? St Mark's is the other way. St John's.'

'And those Peniel folk,' uncle added.

Ray wrestled with that one.

'St Peter's is a good walk in the opposite direction,' uncle went on.

'Methodists are the way they're going.'

'You think they're Methodists?'

Ray shrugged. 'Don't look like any Methodists. No, that can't be right.'

Uncle battled on with his hurt foot. Ray watched the couple to see if they went into a house on their street, but they didn't.

'You need liniment for that toe or something?'

Uncle considered his toe, which bore no sign of grievous injury.

'A little Sloan's couldn't hurt.'

That afternoon, Ray smoked stolen cigarettes outside the ABC on Lancaster Road. Uncle was always leaving packets here and there with a few snouts in them, so Ray collected them together and had almost a whole pack, even if they were these cork-tipped ones that barely tasted of anything. Made it easy to smoke more of them, mind.

Uncle had knocked off early, answering the call of a medicinal for his toe in his local, the Golden Cross, down on Portobello Road. That left Ray with a few free hours. The ABC had been part of his child-hood, right behind uncle's garage and a quick run round the block for Saturday-morning Minors Matinee and a dose of Zorro. Any kids with their birthday that week were called up on stage by the manager, and everyone clapped and they got a free ticket for the next week. Ray dreaded his birthday for this reason. Only one other kid had a birth-day the same week as him, Maureen Bennett, and when the two of them were called up on stage by the manager, he just wanted to die.

These days, Ray preferred Sundays, when they brought back a gangster picture or crime melodrama for one day. They were his favourites. Recently he'd seen *The Blue Dahlia*, *The End of the Road*, *Nick Carter* with Walter Pidgeon, *Pitfall*, *Murder Inc.* with Bogart, and his favourite, *On Dangerous Ground*. He liked the snow and he liked Ida Lupino.

That week was all right for the weekday shows, though, as Bogart was back with *Headline*. Looked like it might be more about newspa-pers than gangsters, but at least it wasn't a western. The B picture, *Quiet Woman*, he'd already seen earlier that week. Smugglers on the Romney, he'd liked it well enough but didn't want to sit through it a second time so was waiting for it to end, hanging around with uncle's smokes outside.

The other side of the street was almost entirely townhouse terraces, with a smattering of shops and pubs on corners, and along the pavement Ray spotted sister, coming from the direction of the public baths pushing the old pram they used for the laundry. Out of some perverse mixture of wanting to see and not wanting to be seen, he hid in the public telephone box between the cinema and the Jewish school, peering through the scratched glass with the receiver in the crook of his neck.

She was smoking, he noted, stubbing his own fag out on the shelf beneath the phone. He'd have her for this, mum not allowing either of them to smoke at home. She was walking with her friend Barbara, who Ray always found it difficult talking in front of, and they weren't setting any records for speed. Coming from the laundry, they should have taken the previous turning to get home, but they must have been headed for the shops.

He decided to follow them. In doing so he had no purpose in mind, but then he didn't know why he did most of the things he did, and was deeply suspicious of anyone who claimed to have anything clearer than mixed motivations for their goings-on. The idea appealed to him because he'd keep out of sight and they wouldn't know he was there. He felt that low inside himself, offering the same promise as the time he searched his parents' room when everyone was out (even though it turned up nothing of note), or the New Year's party when he snuck downstairs and outside saw Mr Redmond, who had drilled him at school on times tables and who he knew to be married, kissing the lady from the pharmacy who was also a palmist. Secrets, or things done in secrecy, no matter how mundane, were like a gift.

Before the surveillance portion of the evening could begin, however, sister threw a spanner in the works by stopping to chat to someone sitting on the porch steps of one of the townhouses. A black boy, about her age he guessed, but Ray couldn't believe it. From inside the phone box he couldn't hear them, but they conducted what was evidently a negotiation, as she eventually handed over a cigarette and lit it for him.

On Lancaster and Tavistock, he knew uncle had noticed more of them taking rooms in houses that were being cut up into smaller and smaller pieces. Ray personally had seen at least half a dozen. This one was making sister laugh, and Ray started running scenarios. If she wasn't careful, this type of behaviour got you in trouble. The newspapers had stories where they couldn't say everything that happened, but it certainly involved something like getting clonked over the head and dragged off by wild-eyed spades. Barbara he could tell was less interested, looking about how he imagined she would if asked about her tax situation.

Things petered out before they got to the head-clonking stage, though, and sister walked on with Barbara. Ray had lost the will to follow them, and ducked into the cinema to catch the main feature. The whole incident left a sour taste and ruined the film for him as he couldn't concentrate for thinking about sister and black boys. Furthermore, it ruined his plan to dob her in for smoking, as he couldn't think of a way to do that without bringing up the black boy, and knowing uncle's thought on matters such as jazz musicians and Indian hemp, he could only imagine what he'd make of this.

It all came to a head some days later, completely out of Ray's hands.

There was an order to these things, he felt, as uncle accompanied him home on the promise of roast chicken, normally forgoing the family table for the long bar of the Golden Cross, and they walked in on the squabble, mum really going into one, her wild gestures filling the narrow hallway.

'Here we go,' uncle said, as if he'd known all along something like that was going to happen.

'You went to the baths *once*, and just with the colours – which, by the by, did you scrub them at all? I don't think so. Went there because that boy is there. I'm working all day and still manage to boil your underwear for you and pick up your other clothes, dropped across the floor like breadcrumbs in a fairy tale.'

'It's my private stuff—'

'Oh, so they're private, but not the knickers I took to laundry, they're not private on account of you needing them washed and not being bothered to do it yourself. But these other items – how I'm supposed to tell the difference between one lot and the other I don't know – but these other items, they're private?'

'You were snooping.'

'I was picking up bras.'

'What's going on?' uncle said.

Hands on her hips, mum took a breath.

'This,' she said, holding up a packet of cigarettes. 'This is what is going on.'

'I knew it,' Ray said. 'I saw her smoking.'

'No you didn't,' sister said.

'Doesn't seem like the end of the world,' uncle said.

'They're hemp,' said mum.

Ray thought uncle preserved his dignity very well in the face of this revelation, knowing how he felt about such things.

'Where did you get them?' mum asked.

Sister rolled her eyes.

'Bet I know,' Ray said.

Mum held up a hand. 'Ray, stay out of this, please.'

'You don't know anything, Ray,' sister said.

'Oh, I know.'

'This wouldn't be happening if your father was here,' mum said.

Sister laughed, a single trump. 'The man who left his family is going to teach me anything?'

'He didn't—'

'Claire,' uncle said.

'I don't know what the big deal is,' sister said.

'We could start with having a little more respect for your mother,' uncle said. 'And for yourself.'

'This is nothing to do with you,' said sister.

'Don't talk to him like that,' Ray said. 'He's only worried. We all know what you've been up to.'

'What's that mean?'

Mum frowned. 'Ray, I don't think—'

'Tarting about with the black boys,' Ray said. 'Probably who she got those from. Ask her what she had to do to get them.'

Sister laughed at him. '*What* are you talking about?'

'I've seen you. I've seen her. Out on the steps on Lancaster Road with the West Indian lads. Giving them cigarettes.'

'When was this supposed to be?'

'With Barbara. When you was coming back from the laundry.'

Sister stared at him. 'Were you following me?'

'Was outside the cinema.'

'I didn't see you.'

'Too busy with the black boy. They're all up the street now. And Tavistock Road.' He looked to uncle. 'Aren't they?'

Uncle shrugged. 'I don't know. Peg, I don't think your mum's out of line if she found them cleaning up your room, especially if you're happy for her to do your washing.'

Sister crossed her arms.

'I don't want this in the house,' mum said, holding the packet up.

'What about who she got it from?' Ray demanded.

'Ray, go out and wash for your dinner,' she told him.

'Maybe she has them in the house,' Ray said, thinking she'd all but been clonked on the head by black boys at this point. 'Maybe—'

They were halted by a conspicuous creak on the landing above, and Vic Barlow bounded nonchalantly down the stairs. Ray had long been of the position that it was haphazard conduct at best, bordering on uncivilised behaviour, that the upstairs tenants could simply tramp through their home at will. But this was what things had come to.

Bunched in the hallway, they stared at him in white-knuckled patience, waiting for him to leave so they could once more take up arms. Instead, he cleared his throat.

'I believe this might be my fault.'

'Vic—' sister started.

'What do you mean?' said mum. 'This came from you?'

'I'm afraid so.'

'So it's always in the house. Great.'

Vic raised his hands. 'It isn't, I promise. I just . . . Look, with everything that was going on, Mr Martin and that, I thought Peg could . . . It was a mistake. I'm entirely to blame. I'd understand completely if you wanted to tell the landlord.'

'Tell the landlord?' Ray said. That was the very minimum that was called for, paving the way surely for the inevitable well-deserved beating that would be dished out.

Vic smiled understandingly at Ray. 'It certainly weren't no black boys.'

'Nobody's telling the landlord,' mum said.

'What?' Ray was beside himself. Fury thrummed in his ears as the outrage continued. This doper, this peddler, with his hollow apologies and he was still going now, charming mum right round his little finger, claiming it was a lapse in judgement and it'd never happen again, uncle nodding away as if it was all perfectly reasonable.

He was less than three steps away. Nobody would even realise what was happening before Ray struck him. Couple of good blows to fell him, fear spilling from his eyes as he looked up from the floor. As unpalatable a truth as it was, sometimes that was the only way to deal with—

'Ray?'

'Huh?'

The others were staring at him and he had no idea quite where they were with proceedings, except that he had not, in fact, managed to punch Vic in the face. For Vic's part, he was climbing the stairs, little finger wave to sister, and for all the world appeared to have smuggled himself back into everyone's good graces.

'This won't stand,' Ray declared.

'Go out and wash for your dinner, please,' mum said.

He looked from her to Vic's feet disappearing round the top step and heard him onto the upstairs staircase. Alone then in the hallway with sister, who rolled her eyes.

'What are you doing to do, Ray? You going to have a word with him? Go up and sort him out? Or just hide behind a door?'

He went out to the washhouse before he told them all what he really thought. It always came out the same. There's sister, flirting and smoking with black boys, tempting a good head clonking, and now sucking on reefers with older boys, but everyone takes her side and connives against him.

Dinner was on the table by the time he washed and dressed, and proceedings were navigated by manners and the best china. But even full of mum's faggots and mash and thick onion gravy, Ray wasn't going to be fooled.

He knew the score.

10

THE BRIDE WORE VISCERA

Like most other mornings, Addie got Nees up and dressed, sorted out her breakfast and made sure she washed her teeth and face. She fixed her hair and buckled her shoes and all was going swimmingly until Nees upped and vanished.

Addie checked their bedroom and the kitchen and the small wash-room out back. She called for her sister.

'Nees, we got to go. Come on now.'

She peeked in on Stevie, who managed to sigh her disapproval in her sleep. She checked the landings upstairs and looked out in the street and the carriageway round to the garden. Back in the flat, on her hands and knees, she looked beneath their bed. She pulled back the curtain to make sure Nees wasn't sat in the deep stool of the window, where Addie herself had once hidden for hours from their father when he was angry. Unable to find her in his rage, he believed she had escaped the house somehow and run off. Nees wasn't there either. Addie was beginning to get angry herself. Nees could be annoying at the best of times, either following her around or refusing to come along, but Addie didn't have time for foolishness that morning.

'Come on, Nees,' she snapped.

From one of the wardrobes came a snuffling. Addie approached quietly and opened the door a crack, peering in with one eye closed.

'Nees?'

Sat among the old shoes at the bottom, knees up beneath her chin and her little face crumpled, her sister wept quietly. Addie knelt beside her and held her tight.

'Everything fine,' she whispered. 'You playing hide?'

Nees nodded, wetness on her face. Addie rubbed a thumb across her cheeks and kissed her.

'Who you hiding from? Me?'

She shook her head. 'Daddy.'

'Daddy?'

'He always comes to find me when I hide.'

'Well, you were quiet like a little mouse. Maybe he didn't hear you this time.'

Scooping Nees up out of the wardrobe, she carried her to the wash-room and wiped her face. She couldn't believe this was what her father had intended. Leaving them fighting to make the rent, his youngest daughter hiding in wardrobes willing his return. And yet he was gone. Addie fully intended to find out why.

She walked Nees round to the nursery, all debts settled for now, but instead of going on to school herself, she hurried down Coldharbour Lane to Brixton Road, where Chabon was waiting at the gates to the library gardens, and the pair of them jumped on a 95 bus headed for Cannon Street station.

She had a plan.

The previous summer, whilst supposedly taking her for a day out to see the tribal art exhibition as part of the Festival of Britain, Reginald had mysteriously ended up several miles off course in a pub near the all-night meat markets, just to pop his head in, of course, say hello to the chaps.

This had been half nine in the morning.

He'd explained to her that the pub was an early house, allowed to open at first light because of all the market workers keeping unsociable hours, and so postal workers on nights often took advantage.

'You don't look the tenky horse in the mouth. They going to let you take a short drink at early doors, then you make sure that's just what you do.'

Given how often he had returned home carrying a bouquet of booze on his breath – Stevie sharing her opinions on this in no uncertain terms – Addie believed if she was going to track her father down, her best bet was asking some of his fellow morning drinkers.

She and Chabon sat upstairs on the bus, each clutching their sevenpence ticket tightly, equally thrilled and terrified by the prospect of being challenged by an inspector (though neither had ever seen one of these mythical creatures). From up there, they watched the city go by at unusual angles. Passing Kennington, Chabon pointed out where the cricket ground was, though even from the top deck you couldn't see it for the housing blocks. His father had taken him to watch Tae Worrell slap England's bowlers all over the place, the West Indies winning by an innings.

They giggled at Newington Butts and Elephant and Castle.

Ruins and debris sites became more frequent the closer they got to the river. The Thames was always exciting as they so rarely saw it. Bombed and fire blackened, Cannon Street station stood alone among the ruins of the north bank wharfs, something gigantic crawled out from the grey waters to die, iron ribs of its roof open to the skies.

When Reginald Rowe first arrived in Britain before the war, one of the first things he did was pick up a guidebook to London. For years now it had been stacked flat on a shelf, spine wallwards, between a photo album and tatty copies of *Home Chat*. It contained a fold-out map, but Addie used a single-page map of the western part of the City to plot their course out of the station and along Cheapside, up Giltspur Street to Smithfield.

A thin four-storey art nouveau in cast stone, the Fox & Anchor was from a different age. Inside, it was ill lit and even smaller than it looked from without, the bar along one side and small tables arranged amid the remnants of wooden partitions on the other, leaving only a narrow space to walk between. Old working men huddled over their ales, eyeing them with bemusement, the temerity of two children.

The place reached back a mile, and opened up some beyond the bar, where a group of men in GPO livery sat. Addie didn't recognise them, but couldn't really remember anyone from that day with her father. She produced a sheet of paper, upon which she had written in her neatest cursive the pertinent details as she saw them.

Approaching the group, she cleared her throat as if making a presentation to her class.

'You can't be in here.'

Behind them, the landlord had both hands flat on the bar, arms straight like he might vault over the thing. 'This is no place for children.'

'I'm looking for my dad,' Addie said.

'I don't think he's here, so go on with you.'

'Reginald Rowe,' Addie said, as if clarifying he was landed gentry.

A postal worker at the table turned for the first time to look at her. A sweep of blond hair fell across his face and he kept brushing it back with his hand.

'Reggie's your old man?'

She nodded.

He squinted at her. 'Christ, your mother must be a looker, then.'

The table erupted with laughter. The landlord stood back from the bar, happy now to let the punters handle the situation. His name was Eddie Monk, and twelve years later he'd have a heart attack getting undressed in a rented cottage in Mablethorpe on the first night of the only holiday he ever took, and wouldn't be found until a week later, face down with his pants round his ankles.

Addie held her sheet before her and read from it. 'My name is Adlyn Rowe, and my father is Reginald Rowe. Perhaps you know him, as he used to work at Eastern Central on the vans.'

'Not having the black in her, I meant,' the blond one said, as if Addie hadn't spoken.

'She's had the black in her all right,' someone else said to more laughter.

Addie persisted. 'Sometimes he still visits this area, stopping off in local public houses for supper or a quick drink on his way home.'

'Aye, Reggie and his quick drinks.'

'She mean the spade on the vans?'

'Uppity fella with the small moustache.'

'Thought he left?'

In the dimness, their voices were indistinct, inseparable. Only the blond stood out, and he spun his chair round so he faced her, his feet spread wide apart.

'Reggie ain't been around for a while. More'n a month, I'd say. He ain't home either, then?'

She shook her head.

'Learie, you know Reg?'

They looked to a corner nook where an older black man sat alone, smoking his pipe and drinking something dark. He looked at Addie rather than the men and shook his head. She wondered what he meant.

'Thought you all knew each other back there?'

Learie busied himself with his pipe.

'Very grown up of you,' the blond one went on, 'coming to a place like this, looking for your dad.'

'I'm old enough to take care of things.'

'Light with it.' He turned to his chums. 'You'd barely know with this one.'

His arm shot out and he clamped her wrist, pulling her in between his legs.

'Whyn't you sit up here on my knee and we'll see how old you are.'

'Let her go,' Chabon said.

'Piss off, boy.'

Chabon tried to prise the man's hand from Addie's arm but couldn't, so kicked him in the shin instead, earning himself a backhand.

'Chay!'

From the floor everything looked ungraspable and his mouth thickened. He spat blood.

'Your daddy's probably with his other woman,' the blond said. 'Way they are, his sort. Can't help themselves. Your mum was probably his tart when he was with someone else before.'

'Gents, drinks on the house.'

Eddie Monk brought a tray of brimming glasses to the table, concerned less with the children's welfare than his own early licence. All of a sudden it was as if nothing at all had occurred, the blond one releasing Addie and turning his chair back to the table. Addie fell to her knees beside Chabon, who was tonguing his lip.

'You all right?'

'Thame playth.'

'We should go. Maybe we should talk to that crazy white baldhead policeman.'

The blond's ears perked up at this.

'You talking to the police?'

'Come on, Addie,' Chabon said, getting up and tugging her sleeve to go with him.

'He came round to talk to us,' Addie said.

'Police think Reggie's missing?'

'Teddy Nunn did say something about him,' one of the others said.

The blond one nodded. Standing, he grabbed Addie's collar and steered her through to the back of the pub. Chabon stepped in and got knocked down again for his troubles, one of the blond's mates dragging him along the stone floor behind him. Chabon looked for Learie, but the old man had left. In a subdivided area a long way back, he and Addie were thrown into a snug about the size of a train compartment. Its double doors were secured from the outside.

'Chay, you got a cut on your head.'

He looked at her funny. 'Eye got an echo.'

Touching his mouth, his fingers came away red. He bent over and spat out a coil of blood.

'I'm sorry, Chay.'

'You didn't hit me.'

'I made you come here. Stupid.'

'Made me come nowhere. I decide where I come.'

Addie tried the doors, which didn't budge. A rush of heat bloomed in her cheeks and sent tears to her eyes. She wondered where that lion with the sword had gone.

'I'm scared.'

Chabon scooched along the banquette and put an arm round her.

'Be fine,' he said, rubbing her shoulder.

'I really thought they could tell me where Dad is.'

'They do know him,' Chabon shrugged.

She licked her thumb and gently wiped the blood from the graze on his brow.

'You know it's nasty when you put lick on my face.'

'Yeah.'

She dabbed away a little more.

They could hear voices outside the nook, but even pressing their ears to the frosted glass couldn't make out what was being said. When the door finally opened, the burly blond one stood over them and they slid to the back of the snug.

'We want to go home,' Addie said.

'Later. Someone you should talk to. About Reggie.'

'I have to fetch my sister from nursery.'

'This won't take long.'

Addie shook her head and the man roughly hauled Chabon out, handing him over to two of his pals, who held him like a plank under their arms. The blond wagged a finger.

'He'll be unharmed, unless the pair of you become more trouble than you're worth. Then things could get a mite hairy. You with me?'

Addie nodded, reluctantly going with him. She followed the two carrying Chabon, the blond one behind her, out through a tight door into a tiny courtyard behind the pub. A gate gave access to a bigger, covered yard, and they were led through a smokehouse out onto St John Street, and almost immediately turned back on themselves through an arched passageway into another covered yard, which had a shed in one corner.

Inside the building, men were busy dragging racks of chilled meat to and fro, hanging the white carcasses of pigs on hooks, or taking them off to be transported or cut. A large lift took them down into a subterranean space, where a snarl of cold, dark corridors opened up into a large room with vaulted ceilings. Frost-furred pipes zigzagged above them and their breath smoked from their mouths. Addie shivered uncontrollably. The men dropped Chabon carelessly to the ground, and the first thing he did was remove his jacket and put it round her.

A group of men jostled a younger one who looked nervous. Mother watched over them, smiling. He noticed the children and their escort and walked over.

'This her?'

The blond one nodded.

Mother leaned down over Chabon, tilted his chin up to get a good look at his wounds.

'What happened here?'

'He kicked me.'

Mother looked the man down to his boots.

'You couldn't handle two kids?'

'They're handled.'

'My apologies. I must have meant to say, anyone who can't handle kids without resorting to brute force is as much fucking use as an old nun's slit.'

The blond started to say something, but thought better of it.

'Get off out of here. Tell Billy Howard to stake you a fiver on the faro.'

'Sure, Teddy. Cheers.'

'Letter twat.'

Addie couldn't imagine who this man was, or what connection her father could have had with such a place. The nervous young man still looked nervous, whatever his predicament was. Chabon wasn't helping matters much, closing one eye and peering around with the other, then switching them over.

Mother studied him closely.

'Do you require help?'

'No thank you,' Chabon said. 'I am a lion.'

Mother addressed Addie in confidence. 'Sometimes a blow to the cranium taken in anger can uncotter all manner of workings, lead to unexpected or delayed consequences.'

'He's fine.'

'Usual type behaviour, what you're saying. Well, you know him best. I understand the pair of you have been asking around for Reginald Rowe.'

'He's my pa.'

'Is that a fact?'

'He works for the Post Office.'

'Yes, he does. Good honest work, too. And I've occasion in the past to have a drink with him, and a bit of a chinwag. Even a spot of breakfast in one of the canteens. Reason I asked you down here for a chat, I haven't seen your pa for a spell, and it seems as if you were wondering the same.'

'He hasn't been home in weeks.'

'Is that right?'

'Mum's worried sick about him.'

'I can only imagine. Worried as she is, would the involvement of the police be something she has looked into?'

'No. But they was asking for him.'

'Poking their noses in of their own volition? Typical cozo behaviour. Did they speak to you?'

Addie thought about the crazy white baldhead. She shrugged.

'And these coppers, dolled up in uniform were they, or wearing their own duds?'

'No uniform. He had a hat and was bald.'

'Ah, was he. And what did you tell him, this copper with a hat?'

'Nothing,' Addie declared. 'Pa always say never talk to no crazy white baldhead.'

Mother guffawed. 'Quite right too, young lady. No good comes of talking to coppers.'

At the far end of the room, two men entered pushing meat trolleys, one empty and one heaped with foul-smelling waste. The head of a pig sat on top.

'As it turns out,' Mother went on, 'your visit here coincides with an auspicious day. We're having ourselves a wedding. This is Albert, our young groom.'

He beckoned forward the nervous young man.

'Bert,' said Albert.

Mother didn't look at him. 'Formal occasion, Albert. Some decorum, please.'

The empty meat trolley was stood up on its end, making it as tall as Addie. Men clanned around Albert, whose eyes were wild like prey watching the dripping jaws of their own devouring. To his vociferous complaint, they began to forcibly strip him, two of them holding him fast as the others tore every stitch from him. Addie moved closer to Chabon, panicky fear rising like cold waters around them.

She squeezed her eyes tightly shut. 'When white people making white people fuss, you got no business with that.' Why did she only listen to her father when she already knew he was right?

Mother swept an arm toward the sides of pork hung on hooks along one wall, crates of smaller cuts stacked against another. 'Do you know what we do in this place? In this vault we cold store the meat so it's fresh for market. We deliver sides or entire carcasses to butchers, but we are butchers ourselves too, have a street-front shop. I once had working for me a struck-off surgeon, a soak who let it go to his hands. Less precision needed for cutting dead swine. What he told me, the anatomical similarities between human and porcine thoracic and abdominal organs are such that learning dissection on one is instructive for the other. Pig or long pig, if you know how to gut one, you can gut the other. If you know how to kill one . . .'

Her father's temper.

The man Geronimo.

The feeling of being locked in the snug.

Addie thought she knew anger. Knew violence. But they were pale shadows of the terror she faced now with this man in his underground domain, a sunless world that bore no consideration of the one above in which she had lived her entire life. Through cold or pure-spun horror her hand shook and she tried to stay it with the other, but then they were both at it. Chabon laid his hand across hers and she thought she might weep.

Albert was roped tightly to the upright cart, arms by his sides and shoulders fixed between its handles. She had only ever seen her father's body and this was nothing like that. The men laughed and Albert did too, but it was a hollow, fake thing.

Mother led matters.

'Blimey, lad. I know it's chilly down here, but you've got husbandly duties to perform.'

Against a roaming black-gloved hand, Albert squirmed and protested, but Mother hushed him.

'Where's the blushing bride?'

The other cart was pushed up in front of the boy and Mother lifted the pig's head. Addie saw the dead face had been made up in grotesque, and daisies hung about its ears. Mother planted it on the end of the cart before Albert's crotch and stuffed his shy prick into its mouth.

'Nice and fresh. Brought it in special, hasn't been hanging in the cold, so no fear of frostbite.'

Tubs were upended over Albert's head, shrouding him in ox blood. Men threw offal and rotten eggs at him, fruit and vegetables on the turn.

'Come,' said Mother, leading the kids to the cart.

He had them take handfuls of wet pluck and rotting greens, and draw back their throwing arms. Addie clenched her jaw in the hope her face didn't collapse, tears fattening in her eyes. On the brink of shrieking, she saw Chabon launch his sloppy stuff, slapping against Albert's reddened skin, and felt him at her side, hand on her arm to help her feeble toss.

Mother selected a dripping organ of his own, and as he threw it, he chanted, 'Tell a copper, come a cropper.'

Under encouragement from the others, Addie and Chabon returned to the cart for more and pelted vile muck at Albert in some heathen ritual of blood and guts, and they cried and yelled as they did so and Mother egged them on and spoke of binding them to the family, and how you never spoke or acted against the family, especially not to the police.

'*Tell a copper come a cropper tell a copper come a cropper tell a copper come a cropper tell a copper come a cropper tell a copper come a cropper* . . .'

They sang the incantation until they were screaming it like it possessed magical powers, and the cart was emptied of its organs and compost and Albert stood entangled with swine and waste and forcing a brave face. Garlanded with intestines, a crown of hooves was placed upon his head. Fistfuls of flour were thrown, caking his skin white over the gore.

Addie could no longer recall her purpose when she set out that morning, such was the fear and madness that engulfed her in the icy cellar. It seemed to her as if this was the only end she was ever going to have met by leaving her home, and in Chabon's face she saw he knew it too, an understanding between them that they needn't ever talk of what had happened there, just so long as they survived it.

'We're a family down here, see?' said Mother. 'You marry into it. The price we pay for love.'

Taking hold of Chabon's chin, he tilted it from side to side, examining his bruises. Chabon fought the instinct to pull away, his breathing quick and ragged with fear. The worst his life had offered him was the odd beating from his cousin Kindness, or occasionally his father's shoe when he gave some lip. He'd never known anything like this man, who seemed capable of bringing nightmares into being on a whim.

Mother winked at him.

'He knows what I'm saying. I haven't got you wrong, lad, have I? You're not one for the prick, so she's got you throwing yourself into bother. If it's not a bird, it'll be your mother. There's not been a wall erected, a poem written, a war waged that wasn't to impress someone. You fell into this world out of one cunt and will spend the rest of your days trying to climb into another. That's what life is, son. One long fallopian pursuit.'

He was interrupted by a fuss in the door to the storage vault, two porters in heated dispute with three black men. Addie didn't recognise any of them, but one, taller than the others, looked at her as if he knew her, and there was something strikingly familiar about him.

'Did you bring gatecrashers, young Adlyn?' said Mother.

The tall one apologised to him.

'We don't mean no disrespect, Mr Nunn, but I'm responsible for the girl.'

'And how's that?'

'Reggie Rowe, he's my brother. This girl, she don't know nothing, don't mean nothing by coming here, other than to find her father. She don't really know about him, what he's like.'

Mother looked intently at him. 'Is that so? And what is Reggie Rowe like really?'

'He fly-by-night. Sort of man who up and abandon his family one day, right out the blue. Up sticks and probably find his way back to the island. Probably find his way to a new woman. New life.'

Mother nodded, pulling the man aside. 'That does sound like old Reginald, if we're being completely honest. And what do they call you?'

'Everso. I'm Everso.'

'I have no doubt. Problem with our Reggie, fly-by-night operator that he is, one never knows when he's going to reappear, flitting back and forth from parts unknown.'

'If I know anything, I know Reggie won't be heard of again in London town. Never be no botheration again. And never be anybody looking for him again, neither.'

'I like the cut of your jib, Everso. And it's not as if your brother is an irredeemable cunt. I happen to hold winnings of his, fruit of his endeavours at the faro table, which I know he'd wish for his family to have.'

'I would expect him to send the odd dollar back to see to his family.'

Mother smiled. 'On account of his young daughter.'

'And there being another daughter, younger still. Before we even consider his wife.'

'Now abandoned and fending for two children. Indeed.'

Mother pulled something from his pocket.

'There's a two-er there, speaking to Reggie's remarkable success beating the house, and handing it to you I'm acknowledging some accommodation to be reached regarding any commission the carrier might be due. Terms down to your discretion and conscience, what you can live with, so forth.'

Everso stuffed the wad in his pocket.

'I'll see to the family. No more surprise visits.'

'I surely would appreciate that. You know, you should come see me, Everso. Dean Street. Anyone will tell you the way. Basement below an Italian place. I'm sure we can be useful to one another.'

They shook hands, and Everso ushered the kids out, back through the grim corridors and into the lift. Addie was confused. Her father had never before talked of having family in London, and yet here was a man who bore a resemblance and seemed to know her.

He caught her staring at him and winked.

'I don't got an uncle,' she said.

'Don't go much expecting to, neither.'

In the street, Everso was exhilarated. He and his boys strode alongside the vast market buildings at such a lick the kids had to break into a run to keep up.

'How much he give you?' one of them asked.

Everso glanced at Addie. 'Sort that later.'

'Teddy fucking Nunn,' the other one said.

Walking backwards, Everso addressed Addie.

'How'd you two make it here?'

'Bus,' Chabon said.

Everso tutted.

'Where they live?' the first one said.

'Brixton,' Everso said.

'We got that thing over that way, get the stuff for the Bucket.'

'Yeah, they just down the road from there.'

'Need a car for that, though.'

'All right, we'll do this. You come with us to the Grove and we'll drive you back to your mami as we going that way. Only conjure how excited she going to be, I turn up at the door.'

'You know Mum?'

'Long time back. Come on, we'll get the Tube.'

At Aldersgate they jumped on the Hammersmith & City and rode it to Ladbroke Grove. It was loud, but Everso and his boys rabbited away the whole time.

'Playing the fool for that backra, and he talks of winnings. Talking about accommodation, like where I'm staying meaningful in any way.

Get him out of his pig cave, get him up the Grove or round the Court, see where he is then. See what he makes of my jib then.'

He went on like this, making no mention of the wider situation, his relation to Addie or her mother or where he might have kept himself her whole entire life. Chabon had uttered not a word since they got out of the cold storage, shaking his head once to refuse the return of his jacket. Addie took his hand, but it hung limply in hers, as if unaware of being held.

When they got off at the Grove, they walked round the block and Everso's boys said it was about time for breakfast, which felt late for Addie, and ducked into the Rainbow Café on the corner of Everso's street. A short, damp dead-end road, the houses were in disrepair, walls stained and crumbling, window frames rotting. It ended abruptly in the brick wall of a factory or workshop.

Prams stood outside a couple of doors, wailing from one, but no grown-ups showed themselves. Last on the left was number 10, the door locked. Everso knocked to no response.

He stood back and looked up. 'Her window open.'

One of the second-floor sashes was raised right up, the light breeze sucking out grubby floral curtains. He cupped his mouth.

'Bess! Where you at?'

Addie glanced down the road, fully expecting someone to come out demanding explanations. A face eventually appeared in the window, a woman peering down.

'What you want?'

'What'd'you mean?'

'You only just done running off fast as your legs can carry you.'

'I had to rescue my niece,' he said, presenting Addie as if she were evidence.

'Your what?'

'Reggie daughter.'

'When did you speak—' She stopped herself, looking down the road. 'Wait there.'

She vanished, and shortly they heard the door unlock.

'Come in and we sort this out upstairs.'

The kids looked at one another.

'I ain't gone bite,' she said. 'Ever the one with fangs.'

The house was dark, the downstairs doors all shut and no light getting in the hall. Upstairs, curtains were drawn across the window on the half-landing between the first and second floors. There were two doors on the top floor, no scullery like the floors below, and she led them into the front room. It was big and bare, and the flapping curtains killed most of the sun. A bed against the far wall, a sofa beneath one of the windows, dresser in front of the other. A small table had two unmatching chairs, and there was a narrow bookcase. The wallpaper had been ripped off in places, damp showing through where it clung on still.

She cleared a plate and some papers off the sofa.

'Have a seat.'

She had an accent, but not quite like Everso or Addie's dad. The children sat and Everso guided her over near the bed, where they spoke low but the kids could still hear.

'When you see Reggie?'

'I didn't. Haven't seen him in for ever. Neither has Stevie, way I hear it. That's what the fuss was earlier when I left. Old Learie, work at the Post Office, he sees Addie here in the Fox & Anchor up near the meat market, making a scene, asking after Reggie. Learie call Moses, and he come get me before it all get out of hand.'

'So where Reggie?'

'I don't know. Listen, I need that car.'

'What car?'

'Come on, now. That Sunbeam the fella let you use.'

'What fella?'

'You got bags of fellas now? White fella manages the bakery down near the Canterbury Arms. You know what fella.'

'What'd'you need it for?'

'Run these children home, for one thing.'

'And for another thing?'

'Woman, you are a hard day's work.'

'That don't seem like the attitude to take when you need something from me.'

Everso clasped his hands, fingers interlaced as if in prayer. 'Bess, I would like to go see the man, one who makes the rum with the bones and pepper, so we can collect a few boxes and bring it back for the blue tonight at the Bucket. If you would find that pleasant and acceptable.'

'You fooling to set this up in Clovis's basement?'

'Yes, I am. Moses got a Plessey, play twelve records. Once I get the rum from the man in Brixton, we're all set.'

'Yeah, real sound system.'

'We can go to four, five pubs instead, maybe get a dram down us before someone put us in our place? Tell us where we can and can't drink? That sounds like fun. Let's do that instead.'

Bess gave him a key.

'He walks to work, leaves it outside his house on Silchester.'

'Yeah, I seen him. Right across from the baths?'

'Do not damage it in any way.'

'I damage it, less chance me getting the rum back here, so you know I'm not looking to do that. You watch these two while I fetch it? I'll be sweet as honey later.'

'Uh huh. Hurry up.'

Everso all but ran from the flat, leaving them with Bess. Dragging across a dining chair, she sat facing them.

'Ever say your name Addie?'

'Adlyn Rowe. And this is Charles Bonamy Chapple, my best friend.'

'What's happening, Charles?'

Chabon nodded as if in agreement.

'You two not kin, then? She looked at Addie. 'Reggie only your father?'

'Chay's dad is Conrad.'

Chabon concentrated hard on some spot above Bess's head.

'That so? My name is Bess.' She stood suddenly. 'Get you something? You come a long way? Drink, something like that?'

'I live on Somerleyton Road,' Addie said.

'That so? Was on Geneva for a spell myself. I think I got some milk. There's water.'

A low rumble built into something more, and the children looked about as if the place was on the brink of toppling in on them, and Bess laughed.

'Just the trains pulling away. Some of them louder than others. Railway behind the houses across the street there, imagine what it's like for them.'

She nodded as if that had settled the drinks matter and walked through to the back room. Addie searched the place with her eyes, craning her neck but too afraid to leave the sofa and root about the place for real. She didn't know what she was looking for, but felt certain she would know if her father had been there recently.

Bess returned with two small glasses of milk. She sniffed one before handing them over. It wasn't cold, but the children drank, Chabon suddenly terribly thirsty and downing it in one, leaving a trace of blood on the rim that he wiped away with a thumb. Bess studied this specimen some, waited for his floating eyes to settle on hers.

'You got a good one to that lip.'

'Yes, ma'am.'

Addie gave him a look, as if his talking to this woman now was a betrayal after his prolonged silence.

'Come up nice and fat.'

'Postman wallop me.'

'You ask him about Reggie?'

Chabon looked at Addie.

'Uh huh,' Bess said. 'Likely to happen, go about poking your noses in.'

'You know my dad?'

Bess shook her head. 'Never met the man. Heard about him from that other one.'

'Dad never told us he had a brother.'

'They grow up with different mamas, different homes. Everso come over here since he was young, before your daddy. Thought he was going to play in a band, but that went about as well as anything else the man do.' She scratched her nose. 'Reggie not at home, then?'

'He's missing.'

'How long?'

'More'n a month.'

'He do this often?'

'Not more than a night or two. The police are looking for him.'

'What sorta police? Them hard hats?'

'Not bobbies. They wore their own clothes. Chief something.'

'Big police. What they ask?'

Addie stiffened. 'Never speak to the crazy white baldheads.'

Bess laughed. 'Reggie tell you that?'

Addie nodded. 'He got some bald too, though. He doesn't like it said, but right up on top there, just off to the side so it looks like a mistake.'

Bess laughed again. It was a good laugh, a high sort of cackle that was infectious, and the children laughed along.

'Mum chased the police off. She said they asked about some night, where he was, and how long since we'd seen him.'

'Questions sound like they got something else in mind. What night?'

Addie shrugged. 'Around the bank holiday.'

'Reggie, Reggie. What did you do?'

'What did he do?' Addie said, face creased.

'What I'm wondering.'

Chabon stood abruptly, bolt upright. Addie leaned back, wondering at him.

'Charles?' Bess said.

'Ma'am, could I use your bathroom?'

'You can stop with the ma'ams for one. I'm Bess. And for two, there's no bathroom here. Loo outside, downstairs out the back. Mean going along the hall through the downstairs flat, out to the garden. And they lock it sometimes. There's no key, but they use a knife to turn it. He don't like us down there. Crazy old baldhead.'

Addie laughed, but Chabon was sensing an emergency.

Bess leaned in conspiratorially. 'Sometimes I go in the sink next door in the other room. But you can't go telling anyone that. Can you go in the sink? Otherwise, it's round the corner to the baths.'

'I can go in the sink,' Chabon said, suddenly excited by this prospect. He hurried off and they heard him move something to stand on and then heard him pissing in the sink.

'Boy had a powerful urge.'

Addie nodded. 'He got punched in the face, and there was blood and the head of a pig at the wedding.'

That skidded their conversation to a halt, but Addie always had questions about something and just then what was on her mind was something Everso had mentioned a couple of times.

'What's the bucket?'

'Oh Lord. The Bucket is some of your uncle's foolishness. He always has something on the go. Back in Kingston . . . you know where Kingston is?'

'Back where Dad comes from.'

'There's a club there, a nightclub, called the Glass Bucket Club. Now Everso, what he thinks is that he can have a few dozen folk popping out of a basement room like the stuffing coming out a teddy bear, with a crate of booze and a gramophone, and call it the Glass Bucket and some of the original will rub off on it. Stupid, because back in Kingston, that club is only for white Jamaicans and tourists, making a joke of Everso's whole plan. But once he got something between his teeth . . .'

Chabon returned, drying his hands on his shorts.

'You got a bed in the kitchen.'

'It's as much a bedroom as anything. Fella name of John rent that, two pound a week. We don't have a real kitchen up here, so that room got cold water and a heater. Little stove. He leaves it open so I can use it. You want to know a secret?'

Both children nodded furiously.

'People who lived in here before? They had both rooms. Married couple, and the fella killed his wife.'

'He killed her?' Addie said. 'Killed her how?'

Bess made a strangling motion, tongue in the corner of her mouth. Chabon glanced round the room like he might see a foot poking out from beneath the bed.

'Baby daughter too. Hid the bodies in the washhouse downstairs.'

'Good job for that sink,' Chabon said.

'Good job for the stranglings,' Bess said. 'Didn't rent to no black people before that man did murders. Owner got shot of the place right quick, and Mr Brown bought it up. Now it's two pound a week for a room, but the previous fella never would have rented to me.'

Whistling got them looking out the window to the street, where Everso poked his head out of a cream-and-burgundy saloon, a pre-war model with headlights mounted on the wing, the spare wheel attached to the body just behind. He told the kids to come on, and Bess showed them down. Though still light, the sun had dipped and Addie suddenly thought of Nees as she climbed in the back of the car.

'Moses not in the café,' Everso said. 'We'll go by his place, just up the road.'

'Don't get these children mixed up in any of your foolishness,' Bess warned him.

He waved her off and spun the car round in the quiet road, the kids thinking this was great sport. Addie couldn't remember ever being in a car. Her parents had never owned one, and most of her life was spent hurrying between home and the nursery and school.

They went back up the road they'd come along from the station, parking up across the road from a cinema. The terraced townhouses on their side weren't so different from the ones on Somerleyton Road, a little narrower, with more steps up to the front door. Young men clustered on the steps smoking, catching the last of the day's sun. Her father often did the same, and Addie enjoyed watching the chatter and raucous laughter. Three older men were playing dominoes, the clack of the cards carrying over the music wafting from an open window. They spotted Moses in a bay window, dancing and clapping to the music, and the children got out and danced on the pavement until he came skipping down the steps.

There was happiness.

There was joy.

Addie didn't know that to some people there was nothing more terrifying.

There were no other cars on Somerleyton Road when Everso swung the Sunbeam off Coldharbour Lane. Rolling to a stop outside number 1, he told Moses to remain in the car and escorted the children up the steps. Addie saw the basement curtains flutter.

Stevie was in absolute horror.

From her usual repose on the sofa in the window, when she saw Everso she shot to her feet and grabbed a thin vase, brandishing it upside down like a throwing axe. Its dead flowers slid out and, brittle as they were, broke into flakes on the floor.

'What are you doing here?'

'Calm yourself.'

Her eyes flicked to Addie and back to him.

'We agreed.'

'I'm not here to . . . Listen, you know where your kid was? Running around looking for Reggie. Going in pubs, asking questions, irritating gangsters and about looking to get herself cut. What am I doing? I'm bringing her back safe.'

Slightly less certain about the vase in her hand, Stevie glanced at Addie, who was amazed by all this as her father had a brother she never knew about and she couldn't imagine how this was a bad thing.

'Dad's gone to Jamaica,' she offered.

Stevie laughed out loud and put down the vase.

'The last place on earth Reginald Rowe would go is back to . . .'

She read Everso's face.

'Oh.'

Stepping backwards, her legs hit the sofa and she stumbled into a sitting position. Everso went to her, but she held up a hand and he stopped.

'He's gone?'

'He gone.'

'And he's not coming back.'

Everso shrugged, as if that was merely a detail. He pulled four notes from his pocket.

'Score there.' He looked back at Addie. 'Said he'd drop a few quid your way when he could.'

Stevie laughed again, but it had an edge now, a delirious cut to it.

'Yes! From time to time.'

Everso backed away like she was contagious.

'It's not much.'

Addie's eyes clamped on the money. She knew from her parents' robust discussions on the matter, which could be heard through walls, that this was almost three weeks' wages, and probably didn't involve the tax and overtime parts of the discussions that seemed to make Stevie laugh so often.

'I suppose he'll send this money to you, who he'll know where you are despite you never staying in the same place more than a few months, rather than sending it to me. That's the plan, I suppose.'

'What do you want from me, Stevie?'

'I want someone to say it.'

'I only know what I know. Just take the money.'

'Yes. Thank you so very much.'

She turned on the sofa, arm draped over the back, gazing out the window. Everso left her to it, pulling the door to her room closed. At noises from the kitchen, he went to investigate, finding Nees at the table, amusing herself with the dominoes.

'This your sister?'

Addie nodded.

'Nees, this Everso. He's your uncle.'

Nees held up a double three. 'Hi.'

'Hi there.' He glanced at Addie. 'Knees, her name? I thought . . .'

'Florence. But Daddy said he had a new berry coming, and Mum said she was eight and a half pounds, so Dad said she must have been a naseberry, and the way he say it he called her Nees.'

Everso grinned.

'She sure favours him. Got that darkness Reggie got. Now you, you're light like me. You practically red. Must have lots of your mother in you.'

'Why would you say such a thing?' Addie said.

Her hair had fallen across her face and Everso hooked it back with a long finger.

'Listen, Red, I'll try to drop round some—'

'Now who the bloody hell are you?'

They both turned to Geronimo, standing hands on hips in the hallway.

'You her new one?'

Everso guided Addie and Chabon behind him. 'New one? What am I a new one of?'

Stevie's door opened and she sighed dramatically.

'You.'

'Yes, me. Told you I'd be back, and you'd better have my money.' Geronimo jerked his head to Everso. 'Maybe your new man can pony up.'

'Sort it out between yourselves,' Stevie said, shutting the door and locking it.

'She's crazy,' Geronimo said.

'He says Dad owed him money,' Addie whispered.

'That right?' Everso said. 'Reggie owe you?'

'That's only your business if you're going to settle for him.'

'Maybe I make it my business regardless.'

Geronimo drew a screwdriver from his pocket.

'I'll get the sword!' cried Addie, but she found the door down to the basement locked.

Everso didn't so much as blink at the screwdriver. He strode forward, grabbing Geronimo's wrist, twisting it viciously and tearing the tool from his hand. Before Geronimo had the time to reassess his position, Everso plunged the tip of the screwdriver deep into his shoulder, through thick muscle and scraping terribly against bone.

He cried out, but Everso, gripping the handle still, walked him backwards out the front door until he fell down the steps. Geronimo, for whom events had escalated far too quickly, sat on the pavement staring at the screwdriver sticking out of him. Moses got out of the car, but Everso motioned for him to stay back. He knelt beside Geronimo, whispering close to his ear, Geronimo nodding uncontrollably, an innocent fear on his face.

Everybody understood their place in the order of things.

With that accord reached, Everso helped Geronimo to his feet and watched him hurry off down the street. A smatter of light rain fell, though from where Addie couldn't tell, as the sky was clear, the sun bright. Devil rain, Reggie would have called it.

'Rain and sun one time. Mean the devil and his woman tussling for that last bit of hambone.'

She couldn't imagine how that explained the rain, but it had seemed reasonable at the time. From the door, she saw Kindness across the street laughing, and Everso go over to him. They looked back toward Addie and Chabon, then shook hands.

'No good going to come of that,' Chabon said.

Everso returned to the car, looking up at the kids.

'That man won't be back,' he told them. 'Don't worry on that debt.'

They waved him and Moses off, going to collect their rum from the man near the railway arches on Canterbury Crescent. Stevie looked out of her room.

'Why do you bring these strangers round here, Adlyn?'

'He said he was my uncle. You knew him. And that other one I didn't bring around.'

Stevie scowled at Chabon.

'I meant this odd child.'

She disappeared back into her room and pulled the curtains.

'We got a loaf,' Addie said, nodding back toward the kitchen.

Chabon shook his head. 'Think I want to see my dad.'

'All right.'

He stood there as if still unsure on the matter, and she grabbed him in a hug, his arms hanging lifelessly at his sides. When she let him go, his eyes were damp.

'Chay?'

'Bye then.'

Addie felt there was something she should do, but had no idea what. She watched him drift off down the road, before returning to the front room, where Stevie had lit a rollie and lay back on the sofa.

'How come I never knew I had an uncle?'

'His complete absence from your life until today should be explanation enough. He and your father weren't . . . aren't . . . close.'

'He said to this other man that Dad's gone to Jamaica.'

'That would be typical of your father in a moment of crisis. Up sticks and run for the islands.'

'He said . . . he said he went to a lady?'

'Men will sometimes start new families. You can't really blame them, it's in their nature. Like cats. They're anybody's for the flash of a leg and will abandon their young to the mother's care without a second thought.'

Addie sat on the high-backed chair near the bed, drawing her feet up onto the seat and hugging her legs. Stevie sat up.

'How on earth did you find Everso?'

'Didn't. He found us.'

'What was he saying about gangsters?'

'I don't know. Dad took me to this pub before, ages ago, so me and Chay went there to see if anyone knew where he was.'

'Why did he take you to . . . Actually, I don't want to know. Where was this?'

'Near that meat market. It's a pub that's open in the mornings.'

'Sounds like Reggie.'

'These men took us to a place where they had meat hanging on the walls and it was cold, like we could see our breath and there was frost everywhere, but it was inside. And there was a man . . .'

She stumbled over how to explain the young groom Albert and what happened to him, or the exact nature of Mother. Words seemed a paltry way of conveying whatever he was.

'Adlyn?'

She knew perfectly well she was sitting in her mother's room, but some part of her lingered back in that freezing cellar. Felt now like a bad dream, or perhaps this room was the dream, and it was that cellar she was still in and would never leave. What walls can be raised, or doors bolted, against such nightmares?

Stevie touched her hand. 'Adlyn, what of this man? What happened? Did he—'

'He asked us about the police. Then Everso and Moses came and they took us out of there and we met Bess.'

'Adlyn, what on earth are you . . . and who's Bess?'

'Everso's friend. She lives in a house where a man killed a woman and buried her in the washhouse.'

Stevie pressed the heels of her palms into her eyes.

'Give me strength. How did he know you were even there?'

'I think Learie told him.'

'For heaven's sake, who is . . . You know what? I believe I'm going to call an end to the subject, except to say this – I don't want you talking to or visiting or having anything at all to do with Everso.'

'Why?'

'Nothing at all. Am I understood, Adlyn?'

'But why? He's my uncle.'

'He's never been an uncle to you.'

'Why's he called Everso?'

'His name. He has his mother's name. Michael Manly. He's ever so manly.'

Addie laid her head on her knees. She thought she might cry and battled against it, Stevie not liking fusses that weren't of her own making.

'Why'd he go, though?' she whispered, hiding her eyes from her mother.

'Your father? Probably he thought he was doing the best thing for all of us.'

'How is him leaving the best thing?'

'Plans have a funny way of not ending up where you thought they would.'

Addie couldn't make sense of it all, but was sure it had something to do with her new uncle. He was something she needed to get straight in her head.

'Everso has a club.'

'That what he told you?'

'He was getting rum for it.'

'Adlyn, if a person owns a legitimate club, they don't buy unlabelled bottles of moonshine from rascals under the railway arches.'

'Well, Bess says it's named after—'

'I don't want to hear any more about Everso or this Bess or any of it. I've had it up to here with the situation.'

'But he's Daddy's brother.'

'I don't care.'

'Why?'

'If you're going to insist on me requiring reasons for my antipathies, we're simply not going to get anywhere, Adlyn.'

II

THE WAR ROOMS OF VIENNA

In a mistaken attempt at improving his day, Lander went round his mother's for brekkie. He had been lying on the sofa listening to the weather report about thunderstorms overnight in the west, leaving a trail of July showers across the country. Who needed that? He smoked a fag on the drive round, and stood outside a few minutes smoking another, but dallied too long and was accosted by Pete Vibart.

'Morning, Detective Sergeant,' Lander said.

Vibart always looked at him as though he brought shame upon his family's name, which was good as it meant word hadn't leaked down from the bosses that Lander was law.

'Dave. Heard you've been collared a few times over this robbery business.'

'Hasn't everyone?'

'Someone will give it up.'

'You reckon?'

Vibart ran a finger down the scar that seamed his face.

'Your mother in?'

'Hope so. Looking for my breakfast.'

'You take advantage.'

'She's my mother,' Lander said, snuffing out his fag under a heel. 'What's your excuse?'

Ivy had the kitchen going like a caff, sausages and bacon on the sizzle, eggs lined up. Lander kissed her on the cheek.

'Morning, Mum.' He nodded at Vibart. 'Someone left this on the doorstep.'

Henry practically pulled Vibart's chair out for him. Ivy rustled up plates for the three of them and they set to it, big pot of tea and loads of toast.

'Enjoying that, Detective Sergeant?' Lander said. 'Doesn't trouble your conscience, butter and meat all procured on the black market?'

Vibart ignored him.

'What's the news from the Yard, Pete?' Henry asked.

Vibart grinned, crunching into his toast. 'Had an absolute whopper last week, though to be frank, it's not really for a lady's ears.'

'Hasn't been a lady in these walls for years,' Ivy said.

Vibart proceeded with his tale about a well-to-do foreign bird, a stateless Magyar who fled the White Terror and who had been nicked over fifty times for lifting trinkets and doodads from West End and Knightsbridge department stores but hadn't once been convicted.

'I've stumbled into this as I was in Harvey Nichols on an unrelated stolen goods matter, and she's stuffed a silk scarf up her skirts and tried to make off with it. The guard stops her and attempts to lead her to the office without fuss, but she's moaning and whining and acting like she can barely put one foot in front of the other and he has to carry her there with a small crowd gathering to gawp.

'They call me in for ease as I'm already there, and I'm going to arrest her when the manager says they've had her before, several times, and the courts don't do nothing, so they don't even want charges brought. Only he won't explain why, tells me to speak to the woman.'

Egg on his chin, Henry said, 'So what she say?'

'Accent that could cut solid oak, and classily dressed, this woman. Clothes a few years old maybe, but of good quality. At some point down the line there has been money of the real variety, which makes me wonder about stealing a silk scarf that was overpriced at two quid.

She pulls out a letter from some eminent Harley Street loony doctor that goes a long way to explain all the carry-on. This quack, he's certain that being detained by police or security and the like brings this woman to orgasm – I apologise for this, Ivy – and her sole motivation for pilfering these small objects is to fetch herself on the thrill of being arrested.'

This made Henry giddy, slapping his knee with his napkin and laughing so hard he might unpeel. 'So what did you do? Let her go?'

'Had to. Harvey Nichols weren't interested in pursuing it, and I called B Division at Lucan Place and the desk sarge knows her straight off, gens me up on the fifty-odd arrests and every other thing. She's a local character now.'

'Gets off because she gets off,' Lander said. 'I try that, a different set of results, I imagine.'

'You try that, expect to be struck in an educational beating.'

'Of course, if whilst keeping a lid on my own urges and invigorations I made off with not a silk scarf but a mail van containing almost half a million quid, my chances of a clean getaway would be greatly increased.'

Vibart pointed threateningly. 'I could have you brought in again on that matter.'

'For one of these educational beatings we've been hearing about?'

'David, do stop provoking Peter,' Ivy said.

'Thank you, Ivy.'

'I'm sure he's doing his best to catch the robbers.'

Lander snickered. 'As damning an assessment as any.'

'What we hear, a good amount of the cash is unusable. Will have to be burned. And we've got some of the rest back already. Identified from clerks' notes.'

'Oh aye? Day out at the races chasing smashed notes?'

Vibart smiled like he knew something he wasn't going to spill for a change.

Ivy walked behind her son, hand on his shoulder. She ran her knuckles lightly against his jaw. 'You need a shave,' she said, before drifting out of the room.

Vibart tilted his head. 'You do have your mother's face, you know.'

He took after her, so everyone always told him, and still had a lingering boyish charm.

'Only someone born looking as unfortunate as you would consider that an insult, you grape.'

Lander idly traded barbs over another mug of tea before getting on his way. In Covent Garden, there was plenty of parking near the ruins on Shelton Street, behind Long Acre. Walking back round the block, he entered a yard off Seven Dials where, above an apothecary that never seemed open, lived two Belgian sisters who had a somewhat officious attitude but were among the more reliable pushers Lander knew.

'What do you want?' said the one who answered the door, talking through a thin gap.

Lander could never tell one from the other. 'Bit of a wake-up. Strong but not too strong.'

'Amphetamines, sure. Dex.'

'By the bottle?'

She disappeared for a moment. The door didn't open more than a foot. Solid blocks were screwed into the floor inside, just beyond the swing of the door, and they laid heavy planks against them during business hours that prevented it being forced in from the outside.

Her face returned in the gap. 'Got a whole bottle and a half.'

Lander paid her and took both, and bang on eleven, he was entering the Enterprise on Long Acre, Darkey adding a little something to his tea to warm up his soul. He perused his paper, and this being England it was mostly supercilious reporting on foreign politics, and coverage of a child killer strangling little girls in Bath. He was thinking about the money, though. Picturing Billy Hill throwing fistfuls of soiled notes into a fire, tens of thousands turning to ash.

The money offered hope. If he found it, it represented his best shot of getting out scot-free. Handing over a big haul would get him right with

Scotland Yard. He could leave the force, get away from the city so Billy Hill wouldn't find him. Of course, if Billy and Mother had changed what they could abroad, and then changed the francs back into sterling, chances were the cash had been legitimised somehow. And if it was still liquid, it'd be in a solicitor's safe somewhere, untouchable.

Deciding to stay for his lunch, he went up to the bar, finding a bunch of chaps making a lunch order of their own. From the ink on their hands, they worked in one of the printing works that lined Long Acre. Of more interest was the barmaid – he recognised her as the woman Mother had visited in Notting Dale, widow to this Alfred Martin who got himself chopped up for sausage meat.

The print workers were having themselves a good time, one of them a little too good. He held the barmaid's hand when he passed the money over, making a real show of it, the others leering over her.

'Oi,' Lander said softly. 'Knock it off.'

The one who'd done the grabbing looked for all the world like he might have some point to make, but Lander met him with a level gaze. Perhaps recalling what sort of place the Enterprise was, who it was owned by and the sort of characters who frequented it, he decided on discretion and a scowl, skulking off with his mates.

She said nothing, but offered an appreciative look.

'Pint of bitter,' he said. 'And is there some sort of lunch on?'

'There's a pie they called home made.'

'What's that mean? They put the rats in it?'

'I can hear you,' Darkey called from out back somewhere.

He made a face and the barmaid smiled.

'Thanks,' he said, as she put down his drink. 'You're new.'

'Claire.'

He nodded. 'Lander.'

'That a first or last name?'

'Just Lander. Like Rembrandt.'

She laughed and it was a good laugh, the kind you want to hear again.

'I'll bring the rats over when they're done.'

As it turned out, things got busy and Darkey brought his pie, slapping it down on the table like a winning hand. Lander ate merrily enough and had a few more pints, missing Claire each time at the bar, and read a couple of other abandoned newspapers. Afternoon started to edge toward evening, and he figured he should show his face at the Greek Street joint, see if anything needed looking to.

Lacking zeal for his task, he shook out half a dozen Dexedrines and swallowed them with the dregs of a pint. That was when Mother appeared, talking to Strong Arms and Come-a-Purler Moe, and Lander felt his night take a turn.

Mother didn't immediately come over, so Lander got himself a fresh pint. The walk to the bar had apparently got longer and it occurred to him that he had overestimated his ability to remain credible under the dose he'd taken.

Darkey served him.

'One last sherbet, if you please.'

'What's wrong with you?' she said, not fooled for a second. 'It wasn't that pie, and I won't hear anything from you along those lines.'

'I am as fit as a fiddle could be.'

He lifted his pint and took a long drink, then found Mother at his side.

'Chop, chop. We got places to be.'

'You didn't even know I'd be here tonight.'

'But you're here now, so let's get to it.'

'I have an unfinished pint.'

But Mother was already off. Lander chased after him, drinking the pint on the move, most of which escaped his mouth. In the Interceptor, back through the West End to the Edgware Road, yodelling distance from Paddington nick, and an upstairs chophouse-cum-spieler called the Vienna Rooms, run by a Louis Schneider, who insisted his name was Taylor. A Jewish refugee, like most of the faces in the Vienna, he took an idle cut of the dice games that were the only action the baize of the billiards table saw.

Mother's flat had been turned over again, the small garden ploughed up this time, which was the cause of his current rant on coppers.

'The properly constituted human mind rejects all authoritarianism, including the police and all their works. Why they're currently pushing to have all children in school uniforms until they're sixteen, so they'll muster enough lily-brained idiots to continue wearing someone else's uniform later in life.'

Lander charged up the stairs to the Vienna, banging the doors open loudly. Mother gave him the once-over and he strove to contain himself. The place was about half full. The regulars in there for a nosh and a natter about the homeland, Billy sitting with Gyp and a pair of generous gin and tonics at one end, and Jack Comer drinking alone down the other, each pretending not to watch the other.

Jack Spot, erstwhile prince of the city, his firm now in tatters, his crown taken up by Billy. Still, he took his morning shave on the Edgware and strolled the streets kissing babies like a parliamentarian, settling in for the day in the Cumberland Hotel to dispense favours to his constituents before getting a taste of the action at the Vienna after dark.

Lander could see his future at the end of a blade.

At the bar stood Bar, a six-and-a-half-foot Bajan who was always accompanied by his equally long greyhound, Bar's Choice. The dog scrutinised Lander through narrowed eyes.

'You're alone,' Lander said when they sat with Billy and Gyp. 'No protection. Is that the new protocol?'

Billy looked at Mother.

'He's in a funny mood.'

'I am chatty,' Lander allowed.

'Does that chattiness extend to our friends on the force?' Billy said.

'They've got some of the cash,' Lander said, relaying what he'd heard from Pete Vibart. 'Said they'd identified them from bank clerks' notes about markings on the currency.'

'You heard that?'

Lander sensed the greyhound taking a perverse interest in him, and considered how he might get across his points in such a way the animal couldn't understand, in case it was listening in.

'Dave? Did you hear that?'

'I did hear that.'

'They say where they got them from?'

Lander shook his head. 'I tried to press him without sounding interested, but he didn't spill. Racecourses?'

'Wouldn't be the courses,' Mother said. 'Post Office counters up north?'

'Maybe,' Billy said.

'The West Indians, too,' Lander said.

'What fucking West Indians?' said Mother.

'I heard talk of West Indians. Vague and nondescript talk. Talk of general West Indian involvement, which I took to mean they were looking at someone from the GPO. That's my sense of the West Indian involvement, being as you don't ordinarily see blacks pulling blags like this, or working with the big firms.'

'Well they're not going to find the West Indian they're looking for, are they?'

'Return from his deathbed of the Nazarene aside, such occurrences are certainly uncommon.'

Like he was speaking directly into the greyhound's gaping jaws, the hound standing over him, its breath hot on his skin, and then it snapped back to the bar, where it had been the whole time. Lander wiped his slick brow.

Gyp pushed her gin and tonic across the table toward him and he accepted gratefully, taking the whole thing down in big gulps. The three of them stared at him. He burped.

'You speak to our wine merchant?' Billy said.

Mother shook his head. 'Not home. Wife says he's nipped across the Channel.'

'Not for us?'

'That's all done. Legitimate business, I assumed. I'll catch up with him.'

Lander made mental notes of what was being said, all the while sending psychic deterrents to the giant greyhound. He studied the faces that appeared in the club. Spitzel Goodman, who'd managed Primo Carnera, looked as sharp as ever. Alexander Medavoy and Leopold Rodan, stick-up artists who Billy had used to take unauthorised card rooms before, played double-pack rummy with two women at a small table. Jacob Schenkman, bookie and probable pederast, was watching over the baize. He was Taylor's partner in the gambling operation, but Lander knew from General Lee that he was a snout and would give anyone up at the drop of a hat.

'You attached to this place?' he blurted out, interrupting Gyp's thoughts on a coupon scam. 'Other than it being good sport, setting Comer's nerves on edge just you being here.'

'Is this chattiness going to be something of a habit, Dave?' Mother said.

'I like the ambience,' Billy said. 'And the police are turning the Soho joints inside out, so it's best I steer clear, see if we can get business back to normal on that front. Five-minute drive for me and Gyp, this place.'

'Only, my suspicion, on a deep instinctual gut level, this place is ripe for a raid.'

Mother watched him as if he were a thing in a jar. 'On a gut level, is that so?'

'Nothing concrete, but putting things together, evaluating the broader picture, there are opportunities present for an ambitious superintendent to rack up seemingly small-fry unlawful gaming charges, assisting in the conduct thereof and what have you, that would, taken in accumulation, present difficulties to anyone who had previous pedigree.'

'Did you take a bang on the head today?' Mother said.

But Billy was scanning the club.

'What do you see, Dave? Who do you know about that I don't?'

'Schenkman.'

'The bookie? He's been collared several times and took it straight.'

'For making book, took his lumps, no doubt. For getting off a lag on account of being a kid-stretcher, I'm saying.'

'Schenkman?'

They all looked at him.

'This is from family breakfast?' Billy said.

'Absolutely nothing concrete, but over convivial after-dinner brandies with the folks, yeah.'

'A shame, should some serious injury befall him,' Billy said. 'Trips over, sits on a chiv that unmans him.'

Mother had a better idea. 'Or, given he makes book out of this very gaff and watches the dice thrown, perhaps leave him in place and avoid it for a while, getting a warm tingling sensation inside when the cozos raid it and as gravy wrap up that prick Comer. Then see what deserts Schenkman is due, on the double count of being a snout and a fucking animal.'

Leaving Mother with Billy and Gyp, Lander decided to make a pass of the Enterprise before going home, hoping to catch sight of Claire. Sporadic rain fell. It was gone closing by the time he got there, but with the lights on he could see her clearing up. Parking outside a small tearoom across the road, he waited for her to leave, praying that the rain kept up.

When she came out, she said goodnight to another woman and hurried round to Endell Street, pulling her cardigan up over her head. Lander drove up and pulled alongside her.

'Hey,' he said, winding down the passenger window.

She ducked down to see who it was.

'We met earlier. In the Enterprise.'

'I remember. Rembrandt.'

'You don't look prepared for the rain. Can I give you a lift?'

'My bus is just up on Oxford Street.'

'You're getting soaked.'

She looked about, unsure.

'Look, I live in Kensal Town, if that's any use to you. Teddy wouldn't forgive me if he knew I left you on the roadside in this.'

Teddy's name sealed it. She got in and brushed a hand through her wet hair.

'Does Rembrandt have a first name?'

'Dave.'

'I'm Claire.'

'I remember. Nice to meet you properly.'

They shook hands awkwardly.

'You're out west then?' he said, putting the Interceptor into gear.

'Ladbroke Grove. Round the corner from the station.'

'Practically neighbours.'

'Don't know about that.'

'Only the two railways and a bridge separate us.'

She stayed quiet. He battled on.

'I hadn't seen you in the Enterprise before today. You been there long?'

'Not long, no.'

Pulling fucking teeth, and he was still feeling chatty after his liberal medicating.

'I'm not good at chit-chat, but can't do uncomfortable silences either, so forgive me if I prattle on or ask too many questions.'

'Teddy gave me the job.'

'Me too, I suppose. Bit of a hike for bar work, though.'

She smiled. 'You sound like my son.'

'Oh aye? What does your husband do then?'

'Uh, he's no longer around.'

'Oh shit. I mean, sorry. Like I said, prattle and inappropriate questions. My specialities.'

'It's all right. He . . . left. Was just gone one day. I've known Teddy a long time, and he wanted to help. I needed work, so . . .'

'How old's your boy?'

'Fifteen.'

'Get away.'

'His sister's three years older.'

'Blimey. I can't imagine how strange it must be to have made grown people. It's just you and them now, then?'

'My husband's brother has lived with us, or in the flat below, since the war. Don't ask, it's an odd set-up.'

'Better than being alone.'

He sped up on Notting Hill Gate to beat a milk float nosing out of a side street, and swung a little wildly into Pembridge Road and even wildlier into Kensington Park Road, narrowing avoiding the cabmen's shelter that divided the street. His heart was pumping the sound of the sea through his ears.

She looked across at him. 'Do you think anyone alive knows us?'

'Well, that's the eternal dilemma, isn't it? Can one ever really be known? I once thought there was someone who knew me, really knew me, but not now. Frankly, I'm not even sure I have friends any more. People I work with, acquaintances, sure. But friends? Somewhere along the way, I either discarded them or maybe I never really gathered any up. Never nurtured them. Something about confessing feelings to another person, allowing myself to be seen. There's a fear I'd later be ashamed.'

He became aware she was staring at him.

'I said, do you think you could drive slower.'

'Oh. Shit.'

She laughed, and it was just as good as the first time he'd heard it. A laugh that reassured him, as if nothing could go awry in its presence. Despite knowing this to be utterly untrue, he laughed along with her and felt good.

On the Grove, she directed him to her street, and he parked outside the house he'd previously sneaked into. It was still raining lightly and she remained in her seat.

'I'm Claire Martin.'

'Dave Lander.'

They shook hands again, but it was neither awkward nor formal. It was the most he had touched another person in as long as he could recall.

'Are you really a Dave?'

'It's what people call me.' He thought about it. 'I was David as a boy. And still am to my mum.'

'I think you're a David. There you are. Now you are known to someone else a little better.'

She got out and dashed through the rain to her door, glancing back slyly.

Christ, he thought. Had he been tricked into feeling something, and if so, who was to blame for that?

I2

FIELDS OF A THIN CRY

A series of fiascos was apace, as usual.

Stevie came home late. The front door was unlocked, and she stepped out of her shoes on the porch so they wouldn't clack across the hall floorboards. She was careful not to fumble her key, and lifted the bedroom door so it didn't scrape against the frame where it had been fixed. She left the light off. Placing her shoes down carefully, her bag slipped out from beneath her arm and thumped on the floor. She screwed her eyes closed tight and waited.

Nobody came.

Sitting on the edge of the bed, she felt something open up inside her that hadn't been there before, but she knew now would never leave. It was light, not in a good way but making everything it came into contact with insubstantial. She didn't have an exact word for it, but if pressed she would have said despair was close.

She found herself sobbing, and turned on her bed, pushing her face into the pillow so the children wouldn't hear. Salt from her tears ran into the grazed skin of her bruised eye, which was closing up nicely now, adding insult to injury. She had returned with no money, and realised now what she should have known before, that what she had fooled herself into believing would be a regular source of income was actually no source at all. Was worse than that – it had helped itself to what it wanted; had lessened her.

A board creaked in the hall and she held her breath suddenly, fought to get control of her trembling lips. She didn't move from where she'd buried her face, willing with everything she had for her daughter not to knock on the door.

She knew if Adlyn had heard her cry, she would be afraid. Crying wasn't something she'd ever seen from her mother. In truth, Stevie couldn't remember the last time. Her own mother had died when she was so young she didn't recall much about that time, and she learned quickly that tears didn't have the effect on her father that she'd seen them have on other fathers. If anything, he enjoyed them. He never touched her in what people would have called a wrong way, but she was intimately familiar with the back of his hand, and tears were no defence.

Adlyn only knew Stevie to be theatrically upset. Melodrama she could handle, she'd been dealing with the histrionics all her life. But not this. The board creaked again, and Stevie heard the door to her daughters' room shut. She opened her mouth and wept in near silence. In its thinness it sounded even more desperate. Stevie didn't enjoy the sensation, as if she was giving something up. Emptying herself.

Calming down, she sat up straight, waiting in the dark until she captured a stillness within herself. Pulling off her dress, she draped it over a chair and dressed for bed. She tried to keep her mind empty, but didn't sleep.

The girls were up and sorting themselves out in the morning. She heard Adlyn tell Nees to wash and get dressed, and shortly afterwards there was a knock at the door. Stevie didn't answer, but the door opened all the same and Adlyn placed a cup of tea on the seat of the chair beside the bed. She pulled the curtains some. The window was west-facing and the morning light dull, but she still kept it off the head of the bed.

She busied herself picking stuff up, pointlessly folding clothes. She kept this up until Stevie moved, propping herself against the wall, squinting through one eye.

'Knew you weren't asleep. Could tell from your breathing that—'

She stopped, catching sight of Stevie's face.

'Mum . . .'

'Is it grotesque?'

'What happened?'

'Things didn't pan out.'

Before Adlyn could ask anything else, Nees's feet came slapping down the hall and she rushed out to intercept, steering her toward her own room so she wouldn't see Stevie.

'Mum's still tired, and you need to get dressed because we're going to surprise everyone and have you in nursery early.'

Stevie got up and went to the mirror on her dresser. Had to go up close to the glass to get a good look as she could only see out the one eye. Ugly bruises browned beneath the bad one, blood crusted her nostrils. The good side, her cheek was still red and puffy from crying. Spitting into a handkerchief, she worked off the worst of the blood and firmly ran a thumb beneath her good eye.

In the hall, she heard Nees ask, 'I going to be there all day?'

'I'll come and get you when I get back from school,' Adlyn said.

'I'll get beans.'

'Yes, you will.'

Stevie scavenged in her purse for money, not finding much. Adlyn ducked her head in.

'Taking her round.'

'I have some coins here . . .'

'I got some. I'll see you in a minute.'

Stevie knew Adlyn hid money behind the skirting in her room. She had never let on she knew, and had never taken any of it. Often, it was all that put a meal on the table for the girls. Adlyn was only gone a few minutes, and when she returned, she fetched a damp cloth and the bottle of antiseptic from the scullery.

'I'm fine, Adlyn.'

'Got blood on you.'

'Where? I'll—'

'Sit still, I'll do it.'

Stevie perched on the edge of her bed and Adlyn wiped her face and dabbed at it with antiseptic, to much hissing and fussing.

'You all right, Mum?'

'I suppose I must look a fright.'

Her good eye opened a crack and Adlyn looked into it.

'S'all right.'

'I didn't mean to frighten you.'

'Didn't.'

'You're being very grown up. Helping with your sister and every-thing. I'm very appreciative.'

But she couldn't quite make her face like that of someone who was appreciative. Just a marzipan smile to go with her throaty voice. She took her daughter's hand.

'I think sometimes that I sneaked into my life. That I came into being without permission. Married in just the same way. That I was always waiting to be turfed out in one way or another.'

She could see Adlyn didn't understand, that she was worrying her.

'I want you to know you were wanted. Are wanted. You and your sister both.'

'We know, Mum.'

'I wanted to say it. And to say that when you're a child and doing your growing up, you don't realise that your parents are still growing up too. You don't see that. Don't see they've barely begun to realise they're not the person they thought they were going to be.'

'Mum, we need to talk to Everso,' Adlyn said, disarming her somewhat.

Stevie smiled. 'And sometimes the child grows up slightly quicker than the parent. But no. Absolutely not. I forbid it.'

'Mum—'

'I don't have a phone number for him anyway, and he hops from bed to bed like a flea.'

'I know where his friend lives. Bess. Me and Chay went there.'

'Bess,' Stevie said, as if talking about a lizard.

'He might have money from Dad.'

'He hasn't.'

'How you know?'

'How do I know? I know because it stands to reason that if Everso wanted to help us, he would have brought round any money your father might have sent him. And if your father wanted to help . . .'

'What?'

Stevie's voice shrank.

'If he wanted to help, he would have sent money straight to us.'

'What we go—'

'Adlyn.'

'What are we going to do then?'

'Something always comes up. We'll make do, won't we?'

She made an effort. Day's end on Electric Avenue, picked up cheap a lonely piece of fish, not stinking too bad yet. The fishmonger's mate tipped empty crates into the gutter, the ice making the sound of applause as it slid into a puddling heap. Couple of onions and the cider vinegar that the father of Adlyn's odd little friend made at home, and Stevie had what passed for Reggie's scobeech going, along with some rice and beans in a pan.

She made up her face, hiding the eye as best she could from Nees, and the three of them ate dinner at the table. She was loud Stevie, fun Stevie, telling the girls they'd play dress-up after dinner. That was the thing Nees loved the most, pigeon-stepping about in Stevie's heels, wearing gowns miles too big for her. The hats and fascinators and clutches and jewellery.

When they'd cleaned up, Nees ran to their room and she and Stevie pulled gowns out of the wardrobes. Dresses laid out for the dead, given a final twirl up the hallway and back, before being heaped on the bed like raked leaves.

Stevie lingered in a black calf-length sheath, because she liked herself in black, liked the way her hair touched it and it touched her pale blue eyes. The past, a fleet and awful thing, snuck up on her: wearing the dress when friends came round; Reggie making drinks; her chewing a slice of lemon from her glass; Adlyn little more than a toddler; music from the sold gramophone.

Blouses big enough on Nees to be gowns, sleeves hanging long and empty. Stevie helped her apply lipstick, and they all giggled at Nees's pout. Shade on her cheeks, a little round her eyes, she was all hips swaying along the hall.

It was a good evening, one of the best, and Nees went to sleep quick and happy. Stevie took the pile of clothes to her room. The kids never knew when or how she took them from the house, but that was the last time they saw them.

'Hi hi hi.'

Stevie stood up from the sofa. The make-up was a touch Soho-nights, but it disguised the fading bruises, and their landlord would think it was for him. She arranged for a smile.

'Mr Grainger.'

He stood in the hallway with two young men, the types that lived with their mums and had enemies in their spare time.

'Couple of strapping boys at the ready,' Grainger said, rocking on his feet like a bobby.

There first was a series of negotiations, furniture bartered for future rent, and before the heavy lifting could begin in earnest, Grainger's tape measure had to make an appearance.

Addie and Nees waited them out on the stairs, peering between banisters. A few old faces hovered over the landing above them to see what the fuss was about, before retreating to their rooms, daylight no time for the upstairs people.

Two wardrobes were hauled into the front room, one squeezed into the window-side alcove beside the fireplace, where their father's bureau had once stood, and the other against the wall opposite it. Stevie joined her children on the stairs, watching with uncharacteristic equanimity as her sanctuary was polluted by their belongings.

The third wardrobe, along with the girls' thin bed, remained in the back room, awaiting a new and potentially dangerous tenant. Stevie was already working on worries in that direction. The two young men, casually employed by Grainger at his builder's yard, fetched a settee from the back of a van and pivoted it inelegantly along the hall and into the front room, swapping it out for Stevie's beloved sofa. It was a bed settee, for the girls to sleep on, whilst during the day it would be folded back up for Stevie to maintain her usual repose in the window bay.

When the men left, Stevie had Addie roll a cigarette for her, and she sat on this settee and smoked it under duress.

'I am not quite myself.'

After a few weeks, Adlyn no longer complained about the smell of tobacco from the grubby walls as she slept. Reggie, who smoked like a steam engine but had frighteningly arbitrary rules about such things, often sat out on the front steps playing dominoes with his friends in the freezing cold to escape the odour.

'I'd lay cards in the snow with dead fingers rather than with your mami in there smoking that funk into the walls,' he told Adlyn.

Sometimes she woke with a start, or in tears, and Stevie even allowed her into her bed. She wouldn't say what it was that invaded her sleep, but Stevie suspected Everso to be at the centre of it, the events of that day when her daughter met him.

Her school attendance improved, as she got out of the room as early as possible each day, but they were behind in Nees's nursery fees again, and Adlyn's cleaning pennies from Mrs Harpenden wasn't going to do it.

Stevie did her drinking during the day, when the children couldn't watch her. She was often asleep when they returned home in the afternoon. She spoke less. They seldom saw her eat. She sure as hell made certain the room was tidied spick and span for the visit from the National Assistance Board, though, and help was approved, covering the rent and an additional thirty-four shillings a week, which Adlyn collected from the Post Office each week.

A woman not much younger than Stevie moved into the back room, unmarried and heavily pregnant. She'd left three young children with her mother in Saint Ann's Bay to come join her fiancé in London. She'd worked as a packer and shared a room with him on Geneva Road under the promise of marriage, right up until she fell with child and he scarpered and married another woman in Stepney. Her Jamaican landlord wouldn't tolerate a single mother and told her to leave.

Stevie galvanised herself with gin against the impending wails of a newborn. She went through brave faces like socks. If one could subsist on put-uponness alone, she had such fields the grain would have staved off famines.

'What does love lead to?' she asked nobody in particular. 'Hope, and children, and . . . this.'

13

BY A MAN'S PLACE SHALL YOU KNOW HIM

Mother liked to scare the newspaper writers in the Enterprise, and they liked to be scared, talking about it for weeks at their desks, what larks they had with faces in a villain's pub.

'This is a place for men who work with their hands,' Mother roared at them, and held up his fists to nervous laughter.

A rota was pinned on the wall in the room behind the bar that led to the cellar. Lander kept note of Claire's shifts and built his days in accordance. He'd bring sandwiches in a paper bag from the café down the road and they'd share them after three o'clock closing.

He collected glasses from tables, brought them to the bar and she washed them. Mother watched carefully from the door leading to the stairs.

'Just giving a hand,' Lander said when he noticed him, embarrassed somehow.

'You must be mistaking me for your father. Or hers.'

On a warm night, Claire had stayed longer than her shift helping Darkey get ready for the evening, and was looking to leave before it got busy.

'I've to get my car from Bayswater,' Lander said. 'Give you a lift if you keep me company there.'

'That's almost home.'

'Think of the thrilling conversation you'd starve yourself of, though.'

They walked to Tottenham Court Road to jump on the Central line. At the station, Claire pointed out a poster advertising the city's free art galleries.

'Do you like art, David?'

'I respect it.'

'What does that mean?'

Lander felt about art galleries and museums much the same way he did about churches. There was a sense of grace in the becalmed stone, but he'd never recognised the presence of any gods there.

Before he could begin to try to explain that, she said, 'We could see the Iveagh Bequest at Kenwood House. Go for a walk on the Heath. Says here we get the trolleybus out to Archway or Highgate Village, and the 210 along Hampstead Lane.'

A plan had formed without him having to do anything. All that was required of him was not to ruin it. 'Or I could drive.'

'Well, if you're going to be hoity-toity about it.'

He looked at his watch. 'A little late now, though.'

They stood in easy silence on the noisy Tube, and the sharp evening air was refreshing at Lancaster Gate. She walked with him without asking where they were going, which wasn't far. The Interceptor was parked behind a partially burnt wardrobe left at the kerb on Sussex Gardens, a broad avenue with thin service lanes sandwiching the main thoroughfare, strips of greenery between them. The ground-floor stucco of the brick terraces was grubby, their Georgian grandeur now succumbed to more prurient trappings. Many were private hotels of a certain sort, whose rates started by the hour.

He opened the passenger door for her, glancing up at a nearby house.

'Wait here for a sec. I just have to pop up and collect something.'

'Not likely,' she said, grinning. 'I'm coming too.'

'These aren't places for—'

'If you say a lady, I'll scream.'

He hesitated.

'We both work for Teddy,' she said.

Two houses in the row had collapsed from war damage, their fascia partly standing, the rest boarded up. Innards open to the skies. Across the street was a bigger gap where three houses had been cleared completely but not yet replaced. The shabbiness of the street and the scars of war were almost disguised by the trees in bloom.

The third floor, only the garrets above them, and he told her to wait on the staircase, in the shadows.

'Trust me, this will go a lot smoother if I don't turn up with a . . .'

She gave him a pointed look.

'. . . bar wench.'

'We'll talk about that when we're done here.'

Secreting herself away in the dark of the stairs leading up, she watched as he knocked. A man opened, his face freshly bruised. She looked quickly into his eyes and knew Lander was responsible, knew the man held an equally fresh fear of him. There was something terribly thrilling in that.

Increasingly Claire harboured a resentment that her life was not what it might have been. There had been a war, and amid the fear and death people had done exciting, exhilarating things, women included. She had brains and talent, but to what use had they been put? Keep on top of the darning, but be aware the roof could fall in on you at any moment. Then, when she fled the city with the children, a few years on a farm that came to nothing.

As a child, she had thought she might be an artist. She loved to sketch and paint, and her father had taken her to the national galleries. At some point, though, such dreams became absurd. She'd happily have settled for driving a truck in the war, though. Doing *something*. She worried her unused brains and talent had turned her into something sharp.

It hadn't been too bad when she was merely reconciled to a quiet life. But now age had laden her with something else – the resentment of having once been young and excited for a life that had passed her by. The blessed fortune of her husband returning safely from war, or she and both her children having come through unscathed, wasn't lost on her. Yet she was done with feeling guilty or indulgent for wanting more. She loved her children and her husband, but now they were almost grown and he was God knows where, and she had no memories beyond survival, which was the bare minimum one could expect, surely. After all, nobody believed in their own death, not really, and those of others were an outrageous inconvenience.

This night-time jaunt with Lander was a salve to her disappointments. An illicit thrill. But she wondered about him, wondered what he was to Teddy Nunn, what he might have been to her husband. She felt reckless, hiding in the shadows watching him going about his racketeering. Reckless and excited. She couldn't quite pick up the mumbled conversation between Lander and the bruised man, but an envelope was exchanged and the door closed. Lander smiled and nodded for her to join him going back down.

In the street she looked back up, but realised the room must have been at the back.

'Who was he?'

'Local entrepreneur.' He waved the envelope. 'Got a little behind on his rent.'

'A pander.'

He shrugged.

'That's what you do for Teddy?'

'It's one thing. This is more of a favour for someone else.'

They got in the car and he watched her closely.

'I'm not a fool.'

'You said you wanted to come up.'

'I mean, I know what happens at the Enterprise. The upstairs rooms.'

'I have to drop this off on the way.'

'That's fine.'

'It's just round the corner.'

They drove up by Paddington station, the nearest street a mixture of ruins and hourly hotels, and onto Bishop's Bridge Road, the south side of which had been almost completely demolished. In the place of the old houses was a newly constructed estate of tower blocks on concrete legs.

'We'll need another war soon,' he said.

He parked on Westbourne Grove, at the corner of Monmouth Road, and knocked on the basement entrance round the side of the end shop, beside which a sign read, *Express Agency Letting Services*. A portly little man, balding with glasses, answered. He squinted, not as if struggling to see, but that he might hear better.

'How you doing, Papa?' Lander asked him.

'Good. Very good indeed. Do come in.'

He shuffled aside, letting Lander and Claire in. Behind him, a bathroom door was ajar. Down a short staircase was a set of two windowless offices, the lights on in one.

'From our friend on Sussex Gardens,' Lander said, dropping the envelope on the desk.

'Ah yes. Excellent. Very appreciative, Dave, very appreciative indeed.'

His voice was oddly squeaky, like a teenager's on the verge of breaking, and he spoke with an accent. Claire thought he looked much older than he probably was. Fussing about his desk, he searched through notebooks and scraps of paper.

'I have it here somewhere.'

'Don't worry, Papa. I can drop by any time.'

Papa held up a finger. 'No, I had it only a short while ago.'

'You look worn out. Should take the odd night off.'

Papa sat behind the desk, opening drawers.

'I am buying my first house. The first one I shall own for myself.'

'That so?'

'Indeed it is. Only on the one floor is there vacant possession, but that will be for Gloria. The rest, it will pay for itself in no time. Come, look.'

He found a photograph of an end-of-terrace townhouse that had seen better days.

'St Stephen's Gardens,' he said proudly. 'The Colonel is letting me have it for a song.'

'You wily old devil.'

'Ah, here we have it!'

He presented a crumpled envelope to Lander as if bestowing him with honours.

'You know he doesn't expect this from you, Papa. The one thing has nothing to do with the other.'

Papa waved a hand. 'I respect Billy, and am appreciative of his counsel on all matters. I want everything between us to be extremely strong signals. Transmissions received loud and clear.'

'Roger that. I'll let him know.'

They left him sitting at his desk squinting at rent books.

'He's a funny bird,' Claire said in the car.

'Papa? Polish. Came here in the resettlement scheme after the war. Story goes he and his brother were involved in resistance against the Nazis. His brother was arrested and executed, but Peter escaped to Russia, only to end up in one of Stalin's camps. Never quite recovered from it. His voice. I dunno, something they did to him. Rest of his family perished in the Nazi camps.'

'Why do you call him Papa?'

Lander shrugged. 'Everyone does.'

'Another pander?'

'No, actually. He doesn't run birds. He was a bit of a spiv, always had something on the go. You could reach him at a phone box on the Bayswater Road. He'd be there for a couple of hours, early evening, taking and making calls. Started renting and subletting rooms, and opened this place. He does have his fair share of brass take rooms off him, mind.'

'Sounds like a pimp.'

'He marks up on the rooms, but the girls are happy to pay. They can't always get rooms, and he doesn't muck them about. Don't involve himself in their business or take a cut. Just a landlord. He has straight tenants mostly. He's canny, knows the law.'

'Oh?'

'One girl in a flat can do what she pleases, and charge what she likes for it. Two like-minded birds in rooms in the same house, then it's a brothel. Papa knows who to put where to keep the cozos off their backs.'

'Who's Gloria?'

'A tom he has a thing for. I don't really know how the pair of them work exactly. Billy reckons she gave him the cash to start the agency properly. Think he might be a customer. Not sure about this flat he's got her. Thought she was shacked up with some Jamaican tuba player.'

'I'm learning a lot about you here.'

'I'm an open book.'

'Hmm.'

'You in a rush?'

'No.'

'Might drop this off at Billy's then.'

He spun the car round and looped past Whiteley's department store and onto Moscow Road, where Billy lived in a plush nine-storey apartment block.

'I've never met Billy Hill before. He's been in the pub, but . . .'

'Never has to buy his own drinks.'

'Right. What's he like?'

'He's like a company director, only for a different sort of firm. I'm not taking you in for tea and bickies, though. This time you really can stay here.'

He got as far as the front door to the building, and Billy emerged with Gyp on his arm.

'Davey boy. Can it wait? We're off out for a nosh-up.'

'Bertorelli's,' Gyp said.

'Sure. Been to see Papa.'

Billy smiled. 'You sort out his difficulty?'

'Yeah. He was keen to show his gratitude.'

'You mind keeping hold? We'll count the ways in which he was grateful tomorrow.'

'Course.'

Billy glanced at the Interceptor. 'That the barmaid from Teddy's place?'

'Yeah. Giving her a lift. She's on my way.'

'Loose lips sink ships, Dave.'

'She doesn't know anything she doesn't pick up from the boozer.'

Gyp was amused. 'Not what I would expect for you.'

'I'm just—'

'Giving her a lift. Yeah, I know.'

Lander waved them off, watching them wander down toward Queensway before he got back in the car.

'Off for a late nosh,' he said. 'Italian. You like spaghetti?'

'Never had it.'

'Get away.'

'I'm a mum from the Dale, David. Who do you think takes me out for Italian?'

'You peckish?'

She shrugged.

'I know a place.'

'Not on the table next to the Hills.'

'Christ, no. I wouldn't do that to you. Or me.'

'Yeah, all right then.'

In the pokey basement of a yellow terracotta hotel on the Bayswater Road, a scowling waitress with a fag behind her ear worked until three in the morning serving the best spaghetti outside of Soho for three shillings a bowl. The clientele was an odd blend of Kensington stiffs and Bayswater brigands, brought together by judicious use of olive oil and the tobacco smoke that clung to the mustard walls. Claire sliced her Milanese with a knife and scooped it with a spoon, and Lander approved of such barbarism.

They ate happily, not saying much, and she didn't mind that he watched her eat, wasn't embarrassed. Something else. Something warm. She stole glances at him over the edge of her glass as she drank.

'Ask,' he said.

'Ask what?'

'Whatever it is you're not asking that you want to ask.'

'It's not really a question.'

'Began every interrogation ever.'

'You hear things, around the pub.'

'What things?'

'Things you do for Teddy.'

'Oh aye?'

'The man at the flat earlier. His face.'

'Oh. *Those* things.'

She took a heaped spoonful of chopped spaghetti.

'You're asking if I'm a thug.'

'I wasn't asking.'

'My family are all police.'

'Really?'

'For all the good it's done them. Dad had a heart attack doing surveillance, was found in his car the next morning. Mum married another copper later. And my uncle, Dad's brother, is something of a Met legend. He was shot dead saving the life of a jazz singer from a Messina brothers gunman. Got a medal to pin on his corpse for his troubles.'

'A hero.'

'He was a prick.'

'You weren't tempted by the family business?'

'I was all set to join and the war happened. When I got back, I didn't fancy more time in a uniform.'

The scowling waitress whipped the bowls from beneath their noses and asked if there'd be anything else in a manner that made clear there wouldn't be. The place was loud and busy and they let themselves be hustled along, laughing as they left.

The Interceptor was parked across the road, outside an eighteen-room pile on the park owned by a Labour MP who had inherited it from his tin merchant father who had been a Tory MP, and Lander gave it the two fingers it deserved as they scudded off down Notting Hill Gate.

'Home?'

She sighed. 'I can't face home.'

'What's waiting there?'

'Complaints.'

'I've been known to make a cuppa.'

Her face suggested accord without her saying so, and once again life took on the appearance of arranging itself. Gone midnight, and around the Tube station the Grove was alive, though the townhouses beyond that were dark save the occasional lit window. Not fancying the walk from the lock-up, he parked outside the flat in Kensal Town. He scooped post from the mat and put it on the sideboard. The place was neat and she liked it.

'Tea?'

'What are you having?'

'I thought coffee.'

She nodded. In the kitchen, he fetched a can of Lyons and sorted the electric percolator.

A wry smile. 'How much was that, then?'

He winced. 'Fiver?'

'The joys of bachelorhood. Can I use the washroom?'

'End of the hall.'

'Indoors? Luxury.'

Listening to the percolator, he made up a tray with two cups, milk and sugar. She'd been gone a while, and he popped his head into the hall and saw she'd been having a look around. The door to the other bedroom was open, the one he didn't go in. He approached quietly. She stood in the middle of the room staring at the cot. The bedding was in a neat pile, never properly laid out. He made no sound, but she turned suddenly, startled.

'Oh David. I'm so sorry. I was being nosy. I should never have come in here.'

'No, you're fine. I just . . . I haven't been in here in a long while.'

He didn't move. It was impossible his legs would ever move again; he'd be rooted to the spot until he collapsed. She stepped in close and held him. He was unsure what to do, but in her tightening embrace he found resolve again, at least enough to move. His fingers found the soft of her arms and remained there.

Into her hair he whispered, 'I made coffee. It's French.'

They sat on the sofa and drank by lamplight.

'Mmm.'

'Chicory,' he said, shrugging.

He was quiet and she knew it wasn't that he was upset with her, but just that he was upset.

'You don't have to get back?' he said eventually.

She wrinkled her nose, a small shake of the head.

'Or sleep?'

'I rarely get any without taking a little something.'

This surprised him.

'Teddy gave me some pills after . . . when my husband left. Can't sleep without them now, and then I wake up feeling like death. But if I don't take it . . .'

'You don't sleep and you're knackered in the morning anyway.'

'Yeah.'

He found the half-full bottle he'd got from the Belgian sisters in his jacket pocket and gave it to her.

'Take half of one when you get up, see if it gives you a spot of cheer in the morning. The other half later on if you're flagging.'

'What are they?'

'A helping hand. You can get them on prescription, but this way you don't have to sell your doctor a line. I use them all the time.'

She slipped the bottle into her bag. 'Apart from that, I don't want to leave you alone.'

'I don't sleep anyway. I mostly sit here at night, if I'm not working.'

'Then we'll sit here together.'

Hours later, he woke with her head on his shoulder, early morning's silver light gradually annexing the room as the sun crept round the curve of the earth. It was foolish, dangerous even. She could be a witness in any investigation, and getting involved could compromise that. She also had some strange connection with Mother, and Christ knows how he'd take such things. But until a gun was pressed to his head, danger would be diluted by other feelings. Humans might recognise the long term, but in truth they didn't handle it much better than four-legged creatures.

He stayed there until she stirred.

'Oh God. Won't hear the end of this off the kids.'

'Tell them you slept with one of Billy Hill's boys.'

She smiled at the thought. And then at another thought.

'I have to work.'

'Tragedy of the human condition.'

'Pays the rent, though.'

'I'll give you a lift.'

She checked her watch. 'No, I'd like to walk. It's a nice morning.'

'Kenwood House,' he said, thinking about walking with her on the Heath.

'Tomorrow? I'm not working until seven.'

'Me too. I'll pick you up. What, eleven?'

She nodded, then laughed.

'What?'

'Don't know. I feel daft.'

'Good way to be, daft.'

She kissed him on the cheek, lingering for a moment. He thought she was going to say something, back out perhaps. Then she was gone.

He ran a bath and had a cuppa while he soaked. Towel round his waist, he left damp footprints on the carpet as he fetched yesterday's post from the sideboard. Familiar handwriting on another letter. And a handwritten note on a folded sheet. He read it twice, turned it over and looked at the blank back. He read it twice more.

If a bent copper were to write him a note making vague suggestions about the Eastcastle job, about knowing what happened to the cash and implying a few quid might be thrown their way, then it would read just like this.

Why had they chosen him? Did someone know he was with Scotland Yard? Had Howe or Barratt been less than discreet? Or was it merely someone making the not outrageous leap that he might be involved, given his position with Mother and Billy.

He considered telling Mother. Then he considered telling the General. If this was a bent copper, it might be a chance to find something out. Either about the money, or about the copper. Something he could pacify Lee with.

The note said nine o'clock Saturday morning at the Mount Royal Hotel.

He'd chivvy things along, still make eleven for Claire.

Taking a pill to get up, he burned the note in the sink, watching the flame chase the paper into ash and washing it away.

14

NO CURE FOR WHAT HE'S GOT

Claire rose late. She'd left Lander's early the previous morning and gone straight to a twelve-hour day at the pub, still needing a pill to get down when she finally returned home. Now, the kids were already out and the house was empty. Even the upstairs tenants were gone. She made herself fried bread for breakfast and enjoyed sitting at the table in peace.

Eleven o'clock came, and he didn't show up, as she'd known he wouldn't.

He was a lure. A reckless attraction. After she'd walked home from his flat, she could smell his aftershave on her hands, like she'd been eating fruit. She'd touched her nose, her lips.

There was something childlike about him. Something unreliable, something dangerous and yet naïve, like all the males in her life. She had married Freddie in spite of those same concerns. David was harder edged than Freddie, leaning more toward dangerous than naïve. And his sadness. Yes, it was probably his sadness that she had got herself caught up in. She was jealous of it. An infinite reservoir of grief that connected him to countless, nameless others with whom he sipped from it. But not with her. Not that sort of grief.

She took half of one of the pills he had given her, to shake off any remaining sleep. The day passed pleasantly, ignoring the kids' laundry and shopping for a few bits instead. She had lunch and decided to go to the Enterprise a little early. She enjoyed working. Sometimes it felt like night was the only time one was allowed to legitimately anticipate pleasure, so walking West End streets before her day shifts always provided her with a furtive afternoon kick.

She thought about seeing him there later, and hoped she wouldn't. All the same, she planned what she would say, whether she should make a scene, or ignore him, or just carry on as if nothing had happened.

Taking the other half of the pill, she left to catch her bus.

She wasn't going to let anything ruin her day.

It was the third day of the Test and England were in a comfortable spot. Having declared on 326/6, they had the Indians five down for 49 overnight. They'd be asked to follow on, and were expected to set England a modest winning target at best. It could never be said that a miracle was required, of course, because this was England in August: it duly rained, and the whole third day had so far been a washout.

Ray had uncle's wireless on in the garage, tuned in to 1500 metres, listening for the hourly updates from the Oval on the Light Programme. Alf Glover had nothing to report, except the weather outlook wasn't promising for the next few days either, and coverage of the motor racing from Goodwood was expanded.

February, back home on some dustbowl pitch in Madras, India had won their first Test, only taking them the twenty years. The death of the King had been announced at lunch on day one, so what did anyone expect, making England play under those circumstances. This series was different. Only rain was going to prevent a whitewash.

What would India ever know of cricket?

Ray was mostly messing around. Uncle hadn't shown up, and there was only so much he could do on his own. He'd changed the oil in Mr Hardigan's van, as he knew he was coming to get it later on. That was a straightforward job he'd done dozens of times, though. Uncle didn't like him going under the bonnet unsupervised on more complicated work. The Morris that had been dropped off the previous evening, that had some problem with the cylinder-head gasket.

Ray could fix it, no sweat. Out back there was a gasket from what he was pretty sure was the same model car. He couldn't imagine it being too much of a trial. After all, there wasn't much uncle could do that Ray couldn't. But he didn't like getting uncle wound up, and there was nothing he'd get wound up more about than unauthorised repairs.

He couldn't face lunch at home. Mum would be there, and she was acting out. He hadn't seen her in a couple of days, but night before last she was out all hours and crept in the house when it was light. This on the back of being out late three or four times a week on account of that job of hers. He couldn't stand the sight of her just yet, so went round to the pie and mash shop on the Portobello for his dinner.

When he was done, he popped into the Cross to check on uncle, only to be told he'd turned up at opening already trousered and was refused entry.

'Where'd he go then?' Ray asked the landlord.

'I know anything about your uncle, he'll have settled down in the first pub silly enough to serve him, and he won't be moving until the three o'clock bell.'

Ray didn't have time to be searching every boozer in the Dale. Walking back to the garage, he thought about how there should be some kind of work uncle could do where he wouldn't do anyone any harm, but that would keep him out of the pubs, at least for the mornings. He'd have to reconsider his position on waiting on uncle to supervise the starting of work. Perhaps not that afternoon, but soon. Otherwise nothing would get done.

He tinkered with a few things, took a chamois to Mr Hardigan's van to give it a good shine. Maybe he'd notice that, the extra mile Ray always went, leave a tip or something. The wireless was on low, and he held out hope of some play at the Oval, but it didn't come. All they needed was one good day. Mop up the tail and send the Indians out again. Victory by an innings was inevitable.

Having moved the replacement gasket into prime position near the Morris, Ray gave the place a well-needed tidying and made a brew with the battered old Swan electric. By the time all that was done, there wasn't much point starting anything new. He drank his tea, waiting until Mr Hardigan came for his van. He not only left without giving Ray a tip, he told him he'd settle up with uncle during the week.

Ray locked up. Whilst having a few jars in the morning was hardly cause for alarm as far as uncle went, it was unusual for him to disappear for an entire day without a word. Ray did the rounds. He returned to the Cross, but they hadn't seen him and said he wouldn't be welcome, state he was in. Further down the Portobello he checked the Warwick Castle and the Blenheim Arms, but he didn't know anybody in those pubs, and they didn't know him or uncle.

The Ladbroke was next. Uncle rarely graced the place with his presence, as it was dad's local, and uncle's position on that was he'd seen enough of dad over the course of their lives that he didn't need to look at him over a pint jug every night at this stage. But it was also tripping distance from home, so if he was on a mission, he might pop in there for the luncheon session, especially as dad hadn't shown his face in months now.

The landlord – a potato-nosed old Jack Tar known as Forks, as many a drunk punter had suspected him of lifting their wallets when they were passed out – claimed he hadn't seen him, but made sure to ask absolutely every punter in there.

'Lads, Freddie's boy has lost his uncle. Anyone seen the soused shite?'

No one had.

'Ye lost your daddy too, young Ray. Misplacing one brother I could see being an accident, but both and should we be asking questions?'

Laughter from the toothless wrecks on their afternoon rums.

'All jesting aside, how's your mother doing? Claire's a fierce handsome woman for a man to be up and leaving.'

'Maybe we'll drop round,' offered one old mop at the bar.

'Provide comfort and moral support, like,' Forks said.

Red cheeked and laughter ringing in his ears, Ray left before he lost his temper. Mum could always cause consternation without even being there. He looped round the Little Sisters of the Assumption to the large Roundhouse on Lancaster Road and down to the Bee Hive, but no joy. Back on Ladbroke Grove, in the Elgin, an old-timer called Long Reach Larry said he'd seen uncle in the KPH up the road before lunch, and that was where Ray found him, ensconced in a dim corner, sweat pasting hair to his head, debagged and irrevocably drunk.

Ray was unsure if uncle recognised him, eyes like the bottoms of bottles. He said his lungs were ragged and shot and complained of nausea, and with the next breath demanded more whisky from the landlord and hurled imprecations when service was refused.

'How long's he been here?' Ray wanted to know.

The landlord shrugged. 'He was here before noon, legless by lunch bell. I let him sleep it off when I closed, and he went right back to it after.'

Ray was beside himself. 'Where are his trousers?'

'They made their exit about the same time as his senses.'

'Don't listen to that shithound,' uncle cried. 'He did time for his short-hand pour. And for farmyard offences too numerous to cite.'

'Get him out of here now,' the landlord warned Ray.

'I can remove myself from any premises that withholds liquor, thank you,' uncle said, standing up in his briefs and wrestling with his coat.

'Here,' Ray said, grabbing a sleeve.

'I can manage,' uncle said, pulling the coat on. He held up the skirts and studied the buttons. 'What snakefucker deemed this an appropriate method of fastening?'

'Christ.'

Ray dropped to his knees and brushed uncle's hands away, doing up the buttons. Once out on the Grove, he had to steer him away from chasing the chickens that roamed wild around the alley leading to the railway mews.

'Let's go home.'

'I will not.'

'We're not going to another pub.'

Uncle watched him askance, as if just noticing his presence.

'My cot,' he said, meaning the put-up bed in the back room at the garage.

'Fine.'

With Ray holding him up, they staggered down the road, making a wrong turn as uncle insisted he knew a shortcut. They ended up in the yard behind the ABC cinema, scaring off a group of lads playing back there. Ray knew a couple of them, had snuck into the cinema through the rear door with them before now.

'This isn't a shortcut,' he said.

Uncle pointed at the back of the garage, visible behind the school next to the cinema, separated from them by a garden or two on Ladbroke Crescent.

'Right, and how are we . . .'

With the aid of a dustbin and the crumbling buttress, uncle hauled himself astride the five-foot wall at the back of the nearest garden and rolled off it into a bed of sweet peas. He upturned a barrow full of live eels, the shifting knot unravelling on the now waterlogged lawn, but kept moving and piled over the fence into the yard behind his garage. As a shortcut, it wasn't remotely quicker than simply walking round the block, but he didn't care to hear about that or any concerns for other people's privacy.

He wouldn't get up off the damp, mossy ground and Ray called him a wet-souled old josser who wasn't worth a shit to anyone, and uncle punched him in the shin and crawled after him until he forgot why he was doing that and pulled himself to his feet on the downpipe.

Inside, he collapsed on his cot and started to weep in grief at the state of his existence. Ray handed him a handkerchief to dry his tears, though he felt nothing for them. He had done this too many times to be fooled. Uncle would go to sleep a drunk and hating himself, and wake up in the morning unable to do anything about either of those things.

Ray spread a blanket over him and uncle got short, told him to buzz off. Ray locked the doors only to prevent him escaping during the night in search of petrol to drink. He returned home and found the place empty.

No lights on, no dinner on the go.

Turning the wireless on to the Light Programme, he sat in the dark to listen to *A Book at Bedtime*, but found only Billy Ternent and the Ternenteers live from bloody Butlin's in Filey, and remembered it was Saturday and he'd somehow missed the final instalment of *Memoirs of Hecate County*, read pungently by Sid James. He flicked over to 464, where they were discussing some dead Frog whose work the Pope had just added to the Index of Forbidden Books because he possessed a taste for profanation carrying as far as blasphemy, and a sincere desire to roll over deeper in filth and to defile what was purest in the life of men. He defended not only homosexuality, but pederasty and also the Greeks. Had he ever given a saloon of Rotting Hill degenerates an eyeful of sagging brain through threadbare undies, though, was what Ray wanted to know.

Hearing a key in the door, he peaked through the nets. It was mum, and she was alone and apparently had arrived on foot. Previously, he had seen someone dropping her off in a car too flash for the Dale. That was something he'd bring up with uncle tomorrow – if it was some character from this Teddy Nunn's pub she worked at, he'd want to know about that.

'What you doing sitting in the dark?' she said, flicking the lights on.

'There was nobody here.'

'You couldn't figure out how the electric works yourself?'

'Where was everyone, what I meant.'

'I was working. Peg said she was sleeping at Theresa's tonight. They were going to the picture house.'

'There was no dinner.'

'Well, you're not a schoolboy any more, Raymond. Old enough to make that decision, you're old enough to get yourself a spot of dinner.'

'Had pie and mash for me lunch.'

'There you go. What are you complaining about?'

He frowned, unsure what he had wanted from this conversation, but certain it wasn't going as he had expected.

'Uncle didn't come to the garage all day.'

'Oh? Where was he?'

'Found him eventually in the KPH, paralytic. They tossed him out the Cross before it even opened this morning.'

'He's drunk, then?'

'Drunk? He could barely walk, he had no trousers on and he spilled eels everywhere.'

'Somehow none of that is a surprise.'

'And it's Saturday, so there was no bedtime book.'

She dropped down beside him on the sofa and brushed his hair with her fingers, which he didn't duck away from.

'I got sausages from a bloke. Fancy a sausage sarnie?'

Ray was scandalised. 'It's almost midnight.'

'Who's here to tell us we can't, though?'

Uncle didn't come over in the morning. When Ray went to the garage to check on him, he hadn't moved from the cot, where he complained about light-headedness and nausea.

'You were honkers.'

'Did you fix that gasket?'

'You told me never to do anything without you being here.'

'This would be an exception to that rule as the fella's picking it up first thing.'

Ray ran home and got tea and toast to bring uncle, who sat up in the cot and directed him in the replacing of the gasket. He refused all offers to join them at the dinner table, explaining it was quite impossible for him to move from the cot.

'At least put some trousers on,' said mum, who had come to see his display for herself.

Uncle compromised and pulled on oily coveralls.

'Should I call for Dr Turnbull?'

'You having a tin one?'

'He's just round the corner. He'll drop by.'

'That old goat can't possibly still be alive.'

'It's his son.'

'I will not be treated by my doctor's son. I have some dignity.'

'Christ.'

'He's a parsonical old coot. Always has opinions.'

'He's dead.'

'Bedside manner of a furniture dealer. Feel like I'm going to be given away with the chesterfield, being examined by him.'

She left him to it, noting her bottle of Red Hills had somehow found its way to the garage.

Early waking moments, Claire stretched out to her full length in the bed, which she enjoyed being all hers. Monday was her day off and bloomed with possibilities. Of course, she knew nothing would happen beyond the doing of chores, a run to the washhouse at the baths, picking up the groceries, cooking dinner for the kids.

She lay there in modest contentment a while longer, the day not really breaking until the curtains were pulled. Ray could manage his own breakfast. Her mind was empty, but a fatal longing crept up on her and took the form of David Lander, and she humoured it for a while before shooing it out of her head. That was what she would do with feelings from that point forth – tamp them down so they didn't encourage misbehaviour. She hadn't seen him since his flat. Saturday night had been busy in the Enterprise, with all of the usual faces except his. Didn't show on the Sunday-lunch session when she was there either. Nobody had mentioned him in terms of anything unto-ward having happened. Perhaps he was embarrassed, but despite his claims that he didn't sleep, he didn't strike her as a man kept awake at night by his conscience.

When she made an appearance downstairs, Peg was munching toast and Ray was standing at the stove frying eggs badly. He looked at her helplessly, and she guided him to the dining room and a few minutes later brought him a plate of scrambled eggs on fried bread.

'I used to paint, now I make eggs,' she told her bewildered children.

She'd quite taken to violating the accepted mores of their home, and so instead of joining them at the table, she poured herself a tea and went to sit in the front room for a spell. The longcase clock in the hall had wound down, but it could wait.

Ray washed up and left for the garage, mumbling a goodbye before the door clattered shut. There was no order in the household whatso-ever since dad left. He imagined similar carnage in homes across the land where fathers hadn't come back from France. What future did the country have?

And now there was some fuss outside the garage, the owner of the Morris banging on the doors.

'He's not opening up, and I need my car. I told him I'd be here early, and he assured me that was fine. Did he even fix it?'

'Your car's ready to go. Let me get the door.'

Ray unlocked the wicket in the large barn doors.

'Stay here a minute and I'll see what's gone on.'

Pissed up on the bottle of mum's Red Mills he'd had Ray sneak over, no doubt, lying puke-encrusted and pitiful in his cot. He opened the door to the back room, and though uncle was exactly where he had expected to find him, Ray immediately knew everything was not right. Uncle's eyes were drowsily open, but showed as much spark as marbles. He was a colour less than life. Ray edged nearer. He bent over and had a closer look, reluctant to touch him.

He wasn't sure what to do.

Who to tell.

It didn't seem to be an emergency, and yet he felt a pressing need to do something.

Hurrying back through the garage, he locked the door again and left the Morris owner standing there spouting about his car. With the heel of his hand, he thumped on his front door until mum opened it.

'Ray, what on earth—'

'You need to come.'

He tugged at her sleeve.

'All right, hey, careful, you'll rip it. What's going on?'

'Mum . . .'

Boyish, scared. She pulled the door closed behind her and went with him in the clogs she wore round the house. She ignored the regimental Morris owner insisting about his car and ducked through the wicket.

Her brother-in-law was most certainly dead, and an unpromising but mostly idle day off now threatened an unwieldy fullness.

'He said he felt sick, but he'd been in his cups since I don't know when, so I just thought . . .'

Claire touched her son's arm.

'Not your fault, Ray. I asked him if he wanted the doctor yesterday.'

'Who do we call now?'

'I'll get Dr Turnbull.'

Ray looked at the body. 'For what? He can't fix him.'

'No, Ray. He can't fix him.'

'No cure for what he's got.'

15

THE EXCOMMUNICATION OF DAVID LANDER

Lander had had every intention of meeting Claire on Saturday, of going to Kenwood House and walking with her on the Heath. He toyed with the idea of bringing food for a light picnic, but was unsure if they were going to be doing the art bit first, and whether walking around with a bag of food was allowed in such circumstances. But he'd have the car, of course, and could leave it in the boot, not even mention it to her until the occasion arose.

Yes, that was the thing. He'd stop in somewhere mildly upmarket before picking her up. Let them suggest picnic wares so he wouldn't make a hames of the whole thing.

This was what he was thinking about, whether there were specialised picnic foods of which he was unaware, as he stood outside the Mount Royal. It took up an entire block on Oxford Street, right up near Marble Arch, but the entrance was round the back on Bryanston. A modern brick building raised in streets of stone, with its wide curved windows wrapping its rounded corners, it bit its thumb at the monumentalism of other recent constructions.

Leaning against the wall of the Mostyn Hotel opposite, Lander smoked and watched the happenings. Taxis and limousines came and went, dropping off and picking up. Seemed posh for a covert meeting, but he supposed that was the point. Who were they likely to run into there, other than fading Hungarian aristocracy or travelling Hollywood stars?

When a large party arrived in two cabs, he waited for them to get into the lobby and followed, using all the fussing over them to make his way to the lifts unseen.

A book about art.

That was what he should get.

He could pick something up from Charing Cross Road, read up, something that might interest her. Though, to be frank, conversation was easy between them, and the silences even easier. He didn't want to introduce unanswerable questions into proceedings. How do you feel about Gainsborough? Or the grand manner of Reynolds? She was too sharp not to see through that.

His wife, Susan – another sharp one. They were pictures people, hitting the cinema every Friday. A couple near them up in the Rise, the Odeon and the Palace, and the Royalty down in the Grove, but Susan preferred the bustle of the Embassy or the Gaumont on Notting Hill Gate, or even the Empire on Leicester Square, where he occasionally wangled gala premiere tickets from a cunny-haunted treasurer at Loew's who'd got himself in a pickle with upstairs brass and downstairs cards.

Lander had mistakenly thought this was a stepping stone to bettering themselves, perhaps becoming show people. He talked about getting theatre tickets as if it were some other magical life they aspired to.

Susan, who knew they weren't show people, tilted her head.

'If we're going to be show people, I'll need new show people clothes. Perhaps a martini gown.'

'What's a martini gown?'

'A gown for spilling martinis on.'

'That doesn't sound like it would help us with the show situation.'

She pouted and shook her head. 'I couldn't possibly go to the theatre wearing martini.'

'That wouldn't do at all.'

'And I'd need help getting out of my martini gown so I didn't get damp.'

'Funnily enough, my fingers are dextrous with both button and zipper.'

'So you see what would come of all this show business.'

'No good whatsoever.'

And so they saw Rita Hayworth at the Embassy and hurried home for a spot of dexterity. A happy marriage, neither of them ever straying. Away at war, Lander had a couple of adventures – a Cairo whore in an Italian caravan that travelled the road between Tobruk and Matruh (who was killed when the SAS mistook them out in the desert for Axis forces and riddled them with a .30 Browning), and a peculiar encounter amid the debris of a haberdasher's with a German widow – but had been with no other woman since courting Susan upon his return. Though the thought of her with another man would have been heartbreaking, what he would have mourned most would have been his own infidelity.

This line of thinking got him to room 365 in two minds, both of which cleared up with the immediate realisation the door was open a crack. Instinctively, he pulled back to the opposite wall and looked up and down the corridor. There was nobody making their presence obvious, but why would there be. There were a thousand ways this could have been a set-up, and he'd run too many of them through his head. What it came down to was his faith that whoever was behind this wanted something from him, and so wouldn't just put the barrel of a gun behind his ear when he walked into the room. Anything else, worst came to worst he felt he could rely on Lee to sort things out.

He toed the door open. It brushed thickly over the carpet, slowly widening his view of the room. It was spacious. Aside from the bed, two sofas faced off before a fireplace, and there was a small kitchenette along one wall.

The room was turned down and there was no sign anyone was

staying there. There were two doors, presumably a bathroom and a closet. He was figuring on trying the first one when someone behind him spoke.

'Help you?'

Nice suit, but the wearer was rough round the edges. Hotel detective, probably ex-Met, someone to clean up, keep the secrets of wealthy clientele.

'I don't think so.'

The man smirked. 'What are you doing?'

'Nothing.'

'This is a private room.'

'Aren't all the rooms here private?'

Silence.

'There doesn't seem to be anyone staying here, anyway,' Lander said.

'You break in?'

'Door was open.'

'That so? I should probably ask you to come with me so we can sort this out.'

Lander nodded, as if that sounded reasonable, but moving like he was going to come with the man he shoved him hard in the chest, sending him tumbling backwards over the corner of the bed.

That was when the cozos turned up.

Piling into the room like there were free meals on the go, twisting his arms behind his back and driving him face-down into the surprisingly deep carpet.

'Fuck's going on?'

'You're under arrest.'

'For what?'

'Looked like assault to me.'

Bracelets snapped on, he was led out through the lobby to where a car was already waiting on Bryanston Road. An obvious set-up. But why? They had nothing on him. The note had been sent to him specifically, so he hadn't incriminated himself by coming. They did a couple of laps of Grosvenor Square on the way to West End Central on Savile Row, their opening line of questioning some baloney about a spate of robberies in the hotel. He kept shtum, ignoring their inquiries and their slaps round the head and kidney punches, and when they reached the station walked gingerly to a windowless room for what he assumed would be a more enthusiastic interrogation.

Detectives he didn't know, and more importantly who didn't seem to know him, braced him about his presence in the hotel room. If they knew anything about the note he received, or why half the uniformed constabulary of Savile Row had been lying in wait outside a hotel room that technically wasn't in their division, they didn't let on.

'I was there to see a woman,' Lander said.

'A tart?'

'How many toms do you roll up from the Mount Royal? Jesus, that'd be an eye-watering hourly rate.'

'Look like you could afford it, from your wallet.'

'I carry enough cash to get bail when you lot play silly twats like this. Bail and a brief, never leave home without the readies to cover me.'

'So, what? This imaginary bird gives you a number, and you got the wrong room?'

'From the welcome I received, I'd say it was exactly the right room, wouldn't you?'

Stony silence.

'Look, I thought she said room 365. Maybe I'm mistaken. Or maybe she lied.'

'Coming on a bit strong, were you? She wanted rid, so fobbed you off, give you the wrong room number.'

'I think she found me incredibly charming, actually. Most people do. I suspect she found me so charming that she felt compelled to send me to the wrong room in case she never escaped my spell.'

They left him alone for what felt like hours, no offer of a brew or a pastry of any kind, and it was Pete Vibart who came in when the door opened again.

'Chasing skirt, is it, Dave?'

Lander shrugged.

'Problem I have, this whole mystery woman scenario, is I hear from a snout that you're connected to the Eastcastle Street blag.'

'Christ, you've had me in twice over that already.'

'Someone points you firmly in the picture for it. And at the same time, as part of a discrete and independent line of inquiry, we hear about a sit-down of the Eastcastle crew, room 365, Mount Royal Hotel, this very morning, and lo and behold, who should turn up but Dave Lander.'

Lander laughed.

'All right, Pete. With your independent lines of inquiry.'

But he could see it in Vibart's eyes that he believed the whole line of shit he was selling. Maybe someone had fingered him, though he couldn't imagine who. The only people who knew for sure were Billy, Mother, Strong Arms and Gyp, and if any of them had turned rat there'd be more trouble afoot than a hotel room stitch-up. Somebody taking a punt, probably. Seeing him around with Mother and Billy, guessing if it was a Billy Hill production then Lander was likely in the crew. Coupled with the note he had received, it was starting to feel like the stitch-up was made to measure.

'I want my brief.'

'What does an innocent man need a brief for, Dave?'

'Nobody needs a lawyer more than an innocent man. And I want to call mine.'

'Maybe let me know who he is, and I'll give him a bell.'

'Sure. Patrick Aloysius Marrinan. Let me just think of the exchange. Yeah, you might reach him at Fuck You 2868.'

Vibart left.

Lander had no idea how long he'd been there, his watch having been taken along with his wallet and keys, but waiting was something he had down to a fine art. He would outlast them. Though if he was being honest, he had what he might characterise trifling concerns – but no more than that – about being locked in that box at length without recourse to his pills.

When Assistant Commissioner Howe walked in, alone and without his uniform jacket and hat, alarm bells did start to sound. Lander looked round the room with something approaching panic.

'Nobody is listening to us, Sergeant.'

'So this is me being dangled out to dry, then.'

'I don't know what you mean.'

'You set this up?'

'Set what up?'

'The hotel, the note telling me to go there, so forth.'

'I don't send notes. You received a note?'

Lander laughed. 'Right. Sure.'

'What did this note say?'

'It implied it was from a copper who wanted to talk about the robbery cash.'

'Where is it now, this note?'

'Where do you think? I burned it.'

'Convenient.'

'Not particularly.'

'Presumably you reported the receipt of this note to your handler?'

'You serious? You know it doesn't work that way.'

'Oh? You receive intelligence, potentially evidence, that is germane to both your long-standing objective of identifying corrupt police officers, and also more specifically to your new priority of the Eastcastle Street robbery, but you inform nobody?'

'I thought it might have been bollocks. I mean, it *was* bollocks. It was you lot.'

'*You* lot.'

Lander scoffed.

'The protocols of your role, Sergeant Lander, are very clear. When the Ghost Squad was shut down, it was out of concern for behaviour such as this. You are to maintain contact with—'

'Maintain regular prearranged contact with my superior officer or other authorised parties throughout active operations.'

'And did you?'

'Sir, if you could show me the operational brief for this investigation that sets out exactly what the prearranged contact I am supposed to be maintaining is, then I could confirm if I have done that. As for this particular instance, I received the note in the early hours of yesterday morning, so no contact had been prearranged or could be prearranged for a future time.'

Howe let a silence hang that Lander was too keyed up not to fill. Falling into the simplest of cop traps.

'I've been doing this for six years, and in practice the protocols aren't worth the paper they're not written on. I know that. You know that. Superintendent Lee knows that. If it's such a problem, why has nobody ever raised it before?'

'Perhaps because you weren't suspected of being involved in a quarter-of-a-million-pound armed robbery before now.'

Lander laughed.

'Perhaps because awkward questions about your lifestyle had been overlooked, but now the meagre results of your work no longer justify the leeway you've been afforded. The size of the flat you keep.'

'In Kensal fucking Town?'

'The car you drive. Running around like half a gangster, and consorting with the wife of a man suspected of being involved with the Eastcastle robbery.'

'Sounds like I've been doing my job.'

'You associate with Edward Victor Nunn. And William Charles Hill.'

'Suffering Christ O'Reilly. Associating with them *is* the bloody operation. My brief is to associate with them. How is this a development?'

'Your brief, Sergeant Lander, is to associate with known members of the Billy Hill firm and report back regularly to your superior officer with usable intelligence to shut down their enterprises. To identify corrupt police officers in Hill's pocket. If, on the other hand, that relationship has been turned round somewhere along the way . . .'

'You know the drill. The whole point is that they think I'm one of them. If I look like it to them, then obviously I'll look like it to you if you take this outsider's view.'

'Which makes it the perfect cover for a bent copper.'

Lander held out his hands.

'Then slap the bracelets back on. Charge me and bring me before a court. On what grounds and with what evidence, I do not fucking know, but I'm sure you'll manage to finagle something.'

'You forget yourself, Sergeant.'

'It isn't me who has forgotten, *sir*. I was sent to do a job, that's what everyone has forgotten. Why am I not being debriefed by my handler? Why am I being interrogated by the head of CID? Christ, you didn't even know who I was until the robbery, and then you wanted to put the whole operation in jeopardy out of professional embarrassment.'

This was what it meant to be a ghost, to be able to generate indignation. Lander was what he needed to be. To do one thing, he needed to be able to do the other, needed at the drop of a hat to be able to act like he believed he was righteous, no matter which side he was talking to. Because when the throat-cutting season was upon him, there was only one side that counted.

His.

Howe leaned back, took a different tack.

'This woman you're involved with. Claire Martin of 7 Camelford Road—'

'You're having a fucking laugh.'

'The wife of Alfred George Martin, now considered a person of interest in the Eastcastle Street robbery.'

'Only because I identified him as such. To my guv'nor. In an un-prearranged contact.'

'Relationships with witnesses or suspects are strictly verboten in—'

'Relationships with witnesses or suspects is literally my job description.'

'Not that sort of relationship, Sergeant.'

'Fuck off. I've never touched the woman.'

'Sergeant, you will address me in—'

'This here is an interrogation, not a briefing. I'll address you with the same contempt you do me, only I'll be honest about it. *Sir.*'

'I can take your warrant card in an instant, Lander. Stories in the papers about an undercover officer gone rogue, released from his job. See how you survive without our help then.'

'Fact you'd even consider that is what separates you from real police. About what I'd expect from a man who has never spent a single day on the street. Lawyer turned brass, no idea what policing is about, and you want to talk to me about working undercover?'

'I've had just about enough—'

'Good. Off you fuck, then. I'm done. Not saying another word to you. Either get me my guv'nor, or charge me and get me my brief.'

Here was what it meant to be split in two. Lander meant everything he said about Howe, with the caveat that, though he wasn't going to allow this to alter his feelings, the man was absolutely bang-on-the-head right.

Lander had gone native.

At the same time, he also genuinely believed that Lee was his guv'nor still. Despite everything, some latent aspect of cop remained inside him. He believed everyone had some cop inside them, because they internalised their oppressions. They took what their friends and family told them to do, and what their laws and leaders told them not to, and fed their inner cop to police themselves and to police others.

The cop inside needed to be destroyed if you were going to get anywhere.

'Hello, Dave.'

Superintendent Bob Lee.

The General.

His guv'nor.

His vicar.

'You been here the whole time?'

Lee sat down. He had a quiet grace that Lander imagined he shared with Oxford dons, or novelists who lived on unearned income and wrote great works of the suffering middle classes. He crossed one leg neatly over the other beneath the table.

'Leaving me to Howe, you think I'm dirty too.'

'Cigarette?'

He took a packet from his pocket and placed it on the table. Lander took one gratefully. He was aware of a patina of sweat he was wearing, and really wanted something to get up, but a fag was as good as it was going to get.

'The note, that was you?'

'Why didn't you tell me when you received it, Dave?'

'When was I supposed to have done that? And why? You've always left me to my own devices.'

Lee produced his pipe and pressed down a pinch of tobacco. He tested it with a few short draws, a lip-popping sound that always grated on Lander, and lit it.

'Why am I here?' Lander asked.

'You were arrested on suspicion of assault, I believe.'

'Come on.'

'And breaking into a hotel room.'

Lander shook his head. 'Are we really going to play silly bollocks?'

'Sergeant, before we go on, before things start getting entered onto the record, is there anything you'd like to tell me?'

Always with this. Confession and penance.

'Like what?'

'I could ask specific questions, but a full and frank accounting of your own activities would be better for both of us.'

'Guv . . .'

'Fine. Are you dealing narcotics?'

'What? No.'

'Possibly as a means by which to ingratiate yourself with the Billy Hill firm. It makes sense.'

'I'm not dealing narcotics.'

'Are you an addict?'

Lander hesitated. 'No.'

'You should be aware that your home has been thoroughly searched. Pharmaceutical amphetamines and barbiturates were found.'

'That's . . .'

'Yes?'

'A little pep in the morning. I'm not a junkie. It's nothing a doctor wouldn't prescribe.'

'Did a doctor prescribe them?'

'No, but—'

'A not insubstantial amount of cash was also found. You put the two together, and . . .'

'You know why there's cash. You know the things I do.'

'I wonder about the things I don't know, Dave. Would you like to tell me about them?'

Somewhere in the world was the one person who helped themselves by telling coppers what they wanted to know, but Lander had never met them. Nothing he could tell Lee would make things better for him. Better to stick to the bullshit and bravado. Better to prove to them he was dumb rather than guilty.

'You confiscated the cash?'

Lee stared at him.

'Only, if you're going to mount a case against me, I'd need it to pay for a decent silk. So if I could have it back, that'd be great.'

'If under cross-examination they try to paint you as a criminal mastermind, you repeat what you just said. The doubt will be more than reasonable.'

'I'm not distributing drugs.'

'This is you and me, Dave.' Lee jerked a thumb back behind him at the door. 'This isn't them.'

'You and me? You send me a note to lure me to this hotel, so forgive me for being sceptical on the whole you-and-me thing.'

'Tell me about this note.'

'You know about the note.'

'You told Assistant Commissioner Howe that you felt it had been written by a police officer.'

Lander took a drag. This was how it was going to be, being talked in circles until he washed down the drain.

'All right, Sergeant. Let me tell you what we know. We were told by a confidential source that you were involved in the Eastcastle Street caper. As in, you were in one of the two cars on the day, in active committal of the robbery. Independently, word reached us that individuals with knowledge of the robbery, and the fate of others who had committed it, would be in room 365 of the Mount Royal Hotel this morning.'

'What is this? You come here, it's me and you, Dave, tell me what's in your heart, Dave, and then feed me the same line of horseshit as the others.'

'I'm telling you what I know. I might not be able to prove all of it, but there are many things I know without being able to prove. I know Billy Hill financed and planned the robbery. I know it was Teddy Nunn who put the crew together and pulled the blag itself. And now I hear that the person who is closest to Nunn is you. That if he was going to do anything like this, the two people he'd definitely have with him would be Philip Carter, otherwise known as Strong Arms, and David Lander.'

'You really think that?'

'I've said you can tell me anything, Dave. There are very few things that aren't fixable with the right friends.'

Please, not with the axe.

'Where is Fred Martin, Dave?'

'I don't know Fred Martin.'

'Just his wife.'

'She works behind the bar at the Enterprise.'

'Did he go to ground after the robbery? Or was he dealt with?'

'Mum used to have a gramophone that would get stuck and keep looping the same bit of records.'

'You have to give me something, Dave. Given the spot you find yourself in, coupled with the last few years not exactly having been productive on your part.'

'Bullshit. You know what I gave you.'

'Penny-ante stuff. A couple of constables in Bayswater on the take? A vice sergeant in this nick?'

Lander laughed. 'I gave you stuff so big you were too afraid to act on it. I gave you Ted Greeno and that prick Bert Sparks, on a plate. And you did nothing. They're still running the streets, because taking them down would be too big a scandal for the Met to bear.'

'Hard proof was always lacking and—'

'All due respect, sir. Fuck off. Intelligence was my brief. Proof was always your end of the bargain. Tell you what the score is so you could drill down into it and nail them. Only, how much do you really fancy looking into bent coppers now that you've realised just how many of them are on the tit? Let's face it, Billy Hill is good for the police. West End gangs aren't carving each other up any more. Fewer citizens are getting beaten up because everyone's paying the same boss. Suited you down to the ground taking what I told you and filing it away in that big brain of yours, letting everything tick over because there was no violence. Then a mail van gets knocked over and there are questions in

Parliament and the big brass are embarrassed and it's suddenly Dave Lander's fault? This the best you got?'

'No violence? No moonlit visits to Paddington pimps? Beatings getting out of hand?'

'Must admit, I didn't see that one in the news. Who made the complaint?'

'It's funny that nobody can put names to the crew that pulled the heist. Like they vanished into thin air.'

Lander fought the urge to say anything. Everything the General had was vague. An approximation of the truth. Nobody who knew anything for certain would have talked to him, but there were people who could make educated guesses with a gun to their head.

'We're closing in, Dave. Not long before we put it all together.'

'Just biding your time for the odd month or three.'

'We have some of the cash. Identified from notes made by the bank clerks. We're working on tracing it backwards.'

'Oh aye? Where'd you find it? Been molesting touts at the racetracks?'

'No, Dave. Not the racetracks. The French found it and sent it back.'

Lander imagined Flying Squad officers stacking soiled notes sent to them by the Gendarmerie, adding insult to injury.

'I don't know anything about no French. Look, what am I doing here? Why all this palaver just for a sit-down? You could have just asked.'

Lee laughed. 'This conversation has an echo to it. I've heard it before.'

'Last time you came and got me in your car. What's the score here? You going to charge me with this hotel nonsense? Or the pills?'

'We'll see.'

Lee uncrossed his legs. Pipe hooked in the corner of his mouth, he left Lander the box of fags when he departed. Lander passed the time smoking. Eventually he was removed to a cell, without the cigarettes.

The thick-glassed windows offered no view and the bench was hard. For once, he wanted to sleep, but it was too cold and he ached. He needed something to dampen it down.

It was Lee who came for him when the sun was up, with tea and a sausage sarnie. He ate appreciatively and smoked two cigarettes. Lee left without asking a single question. Lander remained there the rest of the day, a parsimonious evening meal served with water, and another sleepless night. When Lee fetched him again, he was wired.

He rubbed his eyes. They were dry and weak.

'We're keeping you out there on the job.'

Lander's laugh sounded more like a bark.

'What was the extra day for? Just to make sure I was good and torched?'

Lee handed him his personal items. He fastened his watch on his wrist and pocketed wallet and keys.

'Fags seem to have mysteriously disappeared.'

Lee showed him across the road to where a bomb site had been bulldozed flat into a car park during the war. The Interceptor sat beneath a scaffold hung with tarpaulin. Its seats were out, their upholstery unpicked. Door panels had been removed, and all the chrome had been taken off and lay scattered around it.

'Were you astonished not to find a quarter-million stuffed in the boot?'

'We had to check everything.'

'All these years, all for nothing. They're not going to trust a word I say now.'

'You think they saw you get picked up?'

Lander laughed. 'Brings me to West End Central, where half the cozos are living on Billy Hill's charity, and wonders if the man knows I've been nicked. Wonders if he knows they've had the head of CID in talking to me. Had the Sweeney's tartar, Superintendent Lee, in running the rule. Wouldn't be a surprise if they were waiting at my gaff to chiv me.'

He tossed his car keys back to Lee.

'Have someone drop it by when you've got it back in one piece.'

'I'm always here, Dave, should you want to talk.'

'You need me, look in the local canals. I'll float up sooner or later.'

His front door was busted, the flat a tip.

In the hall, the sideboard was upended, its contents scattered. The letters he'd been ignoring lay opened and read. Kitchen cupboards had been turned out, cans opened and left to congeal on the side, packets of dry goods decanted onto the floor. The upholstery had been slit. His mattress unstuffed.

The other bedroom was trashed, the cot in pieces.

He imagined who might have been there. Pete Vibart was top of the list. Pictured his hands round his neck, flesh twisting in his grip, watching the shine in his eyes dull.

'I'll kill those pricks.'

He heard something, but before he could turn, a bag was pulled over his head and someone had him round the throat. Someone large and powerful, and fear didn't even reach his heart before everything was gone.

16

KISS THE BLOOD FROM MY KNUCKLES

What should he recognise?

The dregs of consciousness. Face against metal through the sack. Lying prostrate, hands bound behind him somehow. Rocking side to side. Face clammy, sucking cloth into his mouth fighting to get air. No voices.

The van lurched to a halt and the engine died.

Now, he told himself.

The doors opened, the fresh air not penetrating the sack. Hands under his arms lifted him out and onto uneven ground. Steered him along.

Now, he told himself, before they get you inside.

He could still hear the city, and a door unlocked, his feet stumbling on the sill.

And then he knew.

The smell of stale beer and fucking. The back stairs at the Enterprise, climbing them blindly, up past the Cabinet Offices to the second floor.

Now, he told himself, while people can still hear you.

Tripped on the next flight and was held up, lifted back to his feet. The floors where upstairs business was conducted, straight down the hall and up more stairs, all the way to the top, the garret rooms.

The sackcloth was thick.

The room was dim.

Quiet. A church silence.

Now, he told himself. Your last chance.

Someone was close to him, their breath all he could hear. All he could smell. Until they kneed him hard in the balls. He cried in pain and dropped to the floor, chin whacking off the bare boards where his hands were behind his back. Didn't know which hurt more. Tears in his eyes.

Dragged to his feet.

Thrown onto a hard chair.

Hands cuffed to the back.

Slapped round the head.

Punched in the gut.

Slammed in the nose.

Caned across the shins.

Belt round his neck.

Lifted until his arse was off the chair, until he couldn't breathe, until nose blood poured back down his throat.

Until he thought that was it.

Now, he told himself. Now you get what you were looking for all along.

Released, he dropped back into the chair, choking on his own blood as he fought for air like a drowning man. A mousy squeak escaped his lips to laughter all round.

Tears on his cheeks from his slammed nose and his stretched neck and his mortal fear and his too-quick acceptance – no, not acceptance; it wasn't that benign – his too-quick embrace of his own death.

Tears dirty with blood and shame.

He tried to remember his wife.

He tried to remember his father.

He tried to remember being a boy, remember his mother's hands, remember what it felt like to receive gifts from the world.

There was nothing there for him to hold onto.

The sack whipped off his head.

'Wotcha,' said Strong Arms, inches from his face.

Grabbed Lander's chin, turned his face this way, then the other.

'Looks all right to me.'

Mother stepped into view, watching him in some secret way only the two of them understood.

'Nary a scratch upon his visage, save what befell him at your own fair hand, Philip. What say you, Davey?'

Lander tried to blow blood and mucus from his nose, but it clotted around his nostrils and bubbled as he breathed.

'With kidnappings and the like, it's a rule you have to talk like previous centuries?'

'First inspection, nothing wrong with the mouth,' Mother said. 'Phil. If you please.'

Slammed in the mush.

Lander and the chair he was cuffed to would have toppled over backwards had Strong Arms not held him up with almost the same movement in which he threw the punch.

'Bloody hell,' Lander said miserably, blood on his chin.

Mother leaned in. 'Two days enjoying the hospitality of our friends in Savile Row and the first sign of a fat lip you get from Phil here.'

'They questioned me.'

'Two days in Savile Row without being struck must be some type record. Some unprecedented event, an eclipse of the sun and the moon and three planets in conjunction.'

Lander ducked away from another Strong Arms haymaker that never came.

'Why wasn't the first thing out of your mouth "I want a brief"? You know Billy would look to your interests and his own by providing a needle-nose at no expense.'

'It was. I told them Marrinan. They did nothing.'

'Denied your fundamental right to legal representation, yet forwent the traditional beating, when usually they'd leave a trail of bloodied crooks behind them as happily and thoughtlessly as a cow shits.'

'Someone dropped me in it.'

'Ah, the introduction of some mystery party at whose feet all blame can be laid.'

'They said someone fingered me for Eastcastle.'

'Who would possibly know?'

'There are people who could make a decent stab,' Lander said, like a desperate child found next to a smashed vase, scratching around for a plausible explanation. 'Could guess it was a Billy Hill production. Ask themselves who works with Billy's right-hand man, Teddy Nunn. Doesn't take a genius to look to me or Phil. Christ, the cozos already tugged me twice over it previous.'

'Didn't set you up VIP those times, though, did they?'

'How's that?'

'Visits from the Assistant Commissioner. Visits from the exalted Bob Lee.'

'Sign of their desperation . . .'

'So an unnamed snout, in possession of nothing more than a hunch, fingers you to the peelers, who take the word of this obvious man of honour and integrity so seriously that they dispatch the highest brass to question you on the matter. And with kid gloves, no less, rather than the many punches to the head with which such inquiries are usually delivered.'

Lander shrugged and Strong Arms punched him in the eye.

'Davey, if it hasn't dawned on you yet, you're in a jackpot here. Cooperation and forthright sharing of information being the only ways to forestall future clobberings.'

'Christ, I didn't tell them anything. Third time they touched me up, and did I say anything before? Why would I now? And what the fuck would I say? Yes, Mr Assistant Commissioner, now you bring it up so politely, I will allow that I did nick your quarter-million quid and do a bunch of murdering besides. What arrangement might we reach over that?'

Earned himself another cuff round the head.

'Why am I getting tuned up now?' he screamed.

Mother stayed Strong Arms's fist.

'Quite right, Davey, should have explained the circumstances more clearly. Lack of a beating and nice chat with high-ranking cunts aside, while you were having a weekend away, the Vienna Rooms were raided on the back of new information originating from the very police station you were holidaying at.'

'Shit. Was Billy there?'

'No, Davey, Billy was not there. Having decided to take your now incredibly prescient advice and avoid the joint.'

'Well, there you go. I told you there was a rat in there. You can't say I didn't say that. Pointed him out to you. Weren't nothing to do with me, the Vienna getting knocked over.'

'Timing of the raid, occurring with you in custody – write it off as coincidence, you're saying. Whims and caprice of chance. You buying that, Phil?'

'Narks will say anything in the face of a good doing.'

'What they say when they're spared a beating is what interests me.'

'Let me go or get my brief was the extent of my side of the conversation. They kept me there to search my flat, the state of which you've . . .'

He tripped over the thought that maybe the police hadn't torn his flat apart, but Mother and Strong Arms had instead, and which of their throats he'd cut first for trashing the other bedroom.

'Yeah, they left a mess all right,' Mother said. 'Haven't got to the floorboards and wall laths yet, though, so count yourself lucky.'

'They've got the Interceptor in bits too.'

'Find anything?'

'Pills, in the flat, which they hope to hold over me, but which I am being frank about to you here. They're making it look like—'

'This isn't my first harvest, Dave. I was bringing the crops in when you were crawling about in beshat nappies. I know peelers and all their ways, making the one thing look like the other to see what reaction it might provoke.'

'And knowing that, you still think if there was anything I was withholding that having Phil knock out my teeth is the best way to spill those beans?'

'No. No, I do not.'

Mother stroked Lander's head.

'But I would have lost your respect if I hadn't given you at least a taste of diabolical violence.'

Strong Arms uncuffed him and pulled him to a bed against the wall behind him, bare mattress on an iron stead. Handcuffs already hung from the posts of the headrail. Lander glanced at Mother.

'We have to be sure, Davey. Just now, our trust is not something you have in spades.'

Strong Arms pushed him down on the bed, securing one wrist to a set of cuffs.

'No,' Lander said, but Strong Arms held him and fastened the other wrist.

Mother dragged the chair across and sat beside him as if visiting the poorly.

He held Lander's hand.

'It's all going to be okay, Davey. I don't want you to fret.'

'Fret?'

'Don't you worry.'

Fear like a stone within his chest, and one of the upstairs girls, Martha, appeared with a hypodermic.

'Fuck off with that shit.'

'Easy, Davey boy. What did I say? You're safe here.'

Lander squirmed, pulling against the chains so hard the cuffs bit into his wrists.

'Philip.'

Strong Arms sat beside him and clamped his arm still as the girl tied it off and slid in the needle.

'See now? That's better.'

Warmth, like he'd pissed himself but inside his own veins.

'What you . . . what you done?'

'Doesn't it feel good? Doesn't it feel like laying down your burdens? Like the comfort of the womb?'

Lander smacked his lips. He couldn't feel his hands and feet, but his heart surged.

Mother's lips to his ear.

'This is the black bomb, Davey. This is Saul on the road to Damascus. Help you sift through your thoughts on the matter.'

It was crazy to Lander that he had never done this before. He grinned a sloppy grin. Why on earth would anybody not want to feel like this all the time? Mother's fingers ran up the inside of his arm, stroking him gently. He wasn't alarmed, though, because he could wait obscurely among the flossy webs in the high corners of the room. And as he sank back down, Mother was as fractured as images between passing seconds, what is seen on the cusp of sleep or other places where time is lost for ever, never to be regained.

There was a surprising delicacy to the man's fingers on his cheek.

His lips brushing his forehead and temple.

A soldier's whisper.

A deathbed comfort.

He sang to him like he might a troubled infant.

Stroked his hand like he might a dying lover.

'Tell me what you know, Dave. Tell me on what matters you and Assistant Commissioner Ronald Howe spoke.'

Lander compelled himself into the past.

'Questions before Parliament?'

Mother nodded, patting his hand in reassurance.

'Bringing the postman to heel,' Lander said. 'It's all go at the GPO! Marine David Thomas Lander, sir! C H stroke X one-nine-nine-seven-four-one, 41 Royal Marine Commando. That's all I have to say about that.'

Mother whispered in his ear. 'What did Mr Howe want from you, sweet marine?'

'I don't believe he knew who I was until we met, sir. Still doesn't understand. Silk heart, copper head. Not a day on the streets.'

'A most terrible cunt, goes without saying. Who else was there, lad?'

'Say two Hail Marys and an Our Father in penance and you will be forgiven, my son.'

Lander squeezed Mother's hand and looked into his eyes, tears in his own.

'He didn't believe me.'

'He?'

'The General.'

'Bob Lee?'

'Called me a liar and a brigand and left me for dead.'

'There, there. You're with family now.'

He gave himself over, sliding into a recreant euphoria that bridged the estranged halves of himself. The compartments he'd constructed within himself loosened and fell, and the divided David Landers cleaved to one another. He recalled his wife's face. Her sly smile and thin lips. The way the bottom one stuck out when she concentrated, tackling Ximenes in *The Observer*. She was soft and warm and so was his skin against hers until the crack of a good slap brought him back and Mother rubbed his cheek some and kissed it better.

His shirt was torn from him. His belt unbuckled and trousers dragged down until he was as he was at birth, the warm tickle of words he didn't know in his ear. Hands free now, but too heavy to raise. He imagined Claire there watching him and felt himself stiffen into the manly state.

Dog soldier, ear to the ground.

Widow running, horses for steaks.

Fair jacket, fair jacket.

Door may view, door may view.

Sunny lemontina, sunny lemontina.

Gendarme come, gendarme gone.

Bring the gold home.

Shame shrivelled him and silenced him, the only thing that ever does. All the blood of his life on his nicked and scarred knuckles.

Mother kissed them clean.

Claire watched carefully from the door.

Had she contributed to this? David was in a state, drunk at the very least but probably something more. Naked too, but for a chain round his neck. She looked away but her eyes were drawn back. She felt like she did when he looked at her across the dinner table over her first spaghetti.

She had been feeling bereft of something she probably never had, and David had seemed capable of giving her that thing. On the other hand, there was everything else he could give.

He sang now in the tune of 'Frère Jacques', but his words were gibberish.

He was delirious.

Mother tried to comfort him. Held his hand. Stroked his cheek. Something obscene in the gesture; this time she did look away.

'Ah, Claire love. Good.'

He waved her into the room. 'Wonder if you might give Davey boy here a helping hand, you two being friendly and that. He's got himself a bit the worse for wear.'

She wondered if this was all somehow for her benefit, Mother making some point. More of his games, his compulsion to control people.

'Where are his clothes?'

He looked about as if they might be lying around someplace. 'A mystery for sure. Gallivanting around the West End in his altogethers.

Good job we found him. Who knows what turn the night may have taken?'

Martha, who worked upstairs and was sixteen if everyone was turning a blind eye, came with a grubby blanket and a look for Claire that spoke to experience beyond her years. A look any woman would interpret as a warning not to ask questions and to get away as quickly as possible.

Claire took the blanket and wrapped it round David, covering him. He looked at her with unseeing eyes and his empty stomach welled and she ducked aside as he spewed foul acids and little else.

'Christ,' he said, and wiped himself on the blanket.

As if he were a rolled-up rug, Phil heaved him onto one shoulder and carted him out of the room, Claire hopping along behind. Down in the street, Mother waved down a hackney and pressed a fiver into Claire's hand as Strong Arms tossed Lander in the back.

'Won't need a key,' Mother said.

The cab driver was in two minds, but knew where he'd picked them up from and knew which side his bread was buttered, so said nowt. In Kensal Town, he helped her get Lander out, leaving them on the kerb and speeding off. Holding the blanket together to maintain some semblance of dignity, Claire struggled up the stairs with him and found the door to the flat ajar, the frame splintered around the lock.

Her grip on him loosened when she saw the mess inside, and he reeled sideways against the wall. Blanket sliding from his shoulders, they tangoed obscenely toward the bedroom, cool and dark where the curtains were pulled and the sash raised a crack. He collapsed onto the bed and muttered into the mattress springs. The fine chain on his neck pooled around a St Christopher. Something a mother would give, she decided.

He was out instantly in his stupor, feet twitching in riotous kitten dreams, so she closed the door and left him to it. Starting in the kitchen, she reordered the house as far as was possible, tossing out ruined foods and repackaging what she could. She found a carpet sweeper, again wondering at his domestic arrangements, and cleaned up spilled cigarette ash and general waste in the sitting room, battling stains new and old in the rug and on the sofa.

With something approaching a pallbearer's reverence, she reassembled the cot in the smaller bedroom, folding the blankets and laying them inside. A mobile was broken, but she fixed it with a hairpin and dedication, hanging it in its rightful place.

She struggled with the sideboard in the hall, but righted it and replaced its emptied drawers. Their contents she fitted back as ordered as she could manage, pausing when she found the flutter of letters. She'd seen him hide one away unopened before, and knew immediately some violation had occurred. Reading snatches of one or two as she gathered them up, she judged them not for her eyes and shuffled them into a neat pile on the side.

Everyone hid things.

Everyone lied.

She made tea and drank alone in the moonlit sitting room. Sleep wouldn't come. In the early light, she heard him rush from his room to the bathroom and vomit. She put on coffee and returned to the sofa.

Five days of growth couldn't disguise the muddy bruises on his face.

'Morning.'

'I cleared up a little.'

'The police were here.'

She nodded. He couldn't discern her mood.

'I made coffee. There's some in the percolator.'

'Forgive a foolish question, but what day is this?'

'Tuesday.'

He counted back days in his head. 'And the last time I saw you . . .?'

'Thursday night. Friday morning.'

'Yes. Sorry. I was arrested, Saturday morning. Otherwise—'

'I knew you weren't coming.'

'I was. The police held me until . . .' He couldn't quite straighten it out in his head. 'Yesterday? Yesterday morning. Then Mother came for me.'

'What does that mean?'

'Sack over my head. Choked unconscious. Bound up and thrown in the back of a van.'

'I didn't think it was as he said.'

'What did he say?'

'That they found you naked in the street.'

'They found me here. Took me to the Enterprise, I think.'

'I saw you there.'

He sat on the sofa, head in his hands.

'What do you remember of last night?' she said.

Helpless, fingers steepled beneath his chin like a shriven child.

'Claire . . .'

'You sang.'

He frowned.

'Some French song. You had the words all wrong. I brought you home. Teddy gave me money for a cab and said to see you back. You were in a bad way, and I felt somewhat responsible for that.'

'You? Why?'

She shook her head.

He hesitated, recalling something.

'My clothes.'

'You only had the blanket when you left. I had to keep it wrapped round you in the taxi.'

She looked away.

'He shot me up with a speedball. Something fast and something slow. Methamphetamine or maybe cocaine, mixed with an opiate. A bad bomb.'

'Why? Why would they do that to you?'

'Mess me up. Hoping I'd tell them something. Give myself away.'

'Away how?'

'They think I narked to the coppers.'

'You didn't?'

He shook his head. 'Flying Squad pinning me in a corner. Coaxing Mother into worrying about me. When they had me locked up, they raided a joint Billy sometimes frequents.'

'Make him worry you told them about it.'

He nodded.

'Make him worry you might have told them more. All the things you do for him. The robbery, for instance. And the men who did the robbery.'

His eyes gave away nothing.

'My husband.'

That fell between them like a guillotine.

'Is Freddie dead, David?'

Now her eyes were full of confusion. A betrayal he could never comprehend.

'Actually, I don't want to know. I couldn't stand it.'

She stood.

'I'll see myself out. Please don't follow me. Do that for me, at least.'

17

DECAYING TOWERS, LURID LANES

Fragments of a dream he never dreamed. A dream he lived.

Lander smoked two cigarettes, all he could find in the flat. He didn't go out for more. His wife was on his mind. The letters gave him the evil eye from the sideboard. He put them in the drawer and closed the sitting room door, but still they gave off a hum. They had a half-life of a million years.

His position was fraught.

The General suspected he was a gangster.

Mother suspected he was a rat.

All Lander knew was he needed a way out and the money was his best and only chance. Barter with it or run with it – he needed it first. And the only avenue he knew to anywhere near the money was Little Phil.

In the mirror, he barely recognised himself, but supposed that suited his purposes. He dressed, leaving on him the foul odour of his days and nights in the hands of others.

Little Phil only went into Soho when he needed to see Billy. Usually he drank in the Star in Belgravia, a regular haunt for faces of all kinds. The upstairs room was where the rarest sights were seen, where the Chelsea set of beggared aristocrats, penniless writers, jobbing thespians, pimps and prostitutes rubbed shoulders with bona fide film stars, royalty on the currant from their protection, and occasionally

the richest man in Britain, who made his fortune tinning pigs' arse-
holes for troops in Africa and adroitly misdirecting tax bills.

On various nights of culture, Lander had heard tell of Princess
Margaret, coke dusted and frock thrown over her head, joyously dancing the cancan on tables with Diana Dors. Sid James, fresh from
losing a packet on exclusive gambling boats sailing from creaking Bat-
tersea Reach wharfs, punching an erstwhile armed robber down the
staircase for besmirching the Jewish brothers who once ran Gainsborough Pictures. Or the landlord, an Irish poet who'd married into the
licence, telling Elizabeth Taylor, panda eyes courtesy of Nicky Hilton,
to shift her hotel-sized arse so the house hound Danny could reclaim
his favoured chair.

Tucked away on a narrow cobbled mews off Belgrave Square, it
wasn't somewhere Lander was well known, but anyone important
would at the very least know of him. He nodded at the landlord,
Paddy, who gave him the once-over, rightly sizing him up as a victim
of the age.

Past the bar was the staircase to the smaller private lounge, membership of which was a nebulous and tacit affair. The late-afternoon
crowd lacked blue blood, though Eddie Chapman leaned against the
bar. A professional safecracker and explosives man, he had been a
double agent during the war and MI5 had to talk him out of attempting to assassinate Hitler when the Führer wished to personally award
him the Iron Cross. He'd done nick for armed robbery, and for public
indecency when he was caught rooting a minister's daughter upon the
plinth of Achilles in Hyde Park. A man of impeccable standing in his
community.

At a window table near the fireplace, Little Phil sat in a wingback
chair guarding his suitcase.

'Phil?'

He looked up, startled. Immediately glanced at the door to the
stairs.

Lander took off his cap. 'Dave Lander.'

'I know. Teddy's . . .'

'Probably best not to try finding the word.' He pointed to the other chair at the small table. 'You mind?'

'No. Of course.'

Lander sat down heavily and sighed.

'Been on the sauce, Dave?'

'It's been an interesting time. Was about to head home, but thought I'd have a settler.'

Little smiled, relaxing. 'Heard you got your collar felt.'

'Fucking slops. Had me in two nights. No brief. No charges. No questions.'

Little pointed to his own face, meaning the bruises on Lander's.

'Aye, generous with that,' Lander said, stitching his story together.

Paddy brought over a brandy that barely touched the sides as Lander tipped it down his throat. He grinned, battling the nausea that eddied inside him.

'Not sure that's going to hit the mark.'

Phil opened his suitcase on his lap and toyed mysteriously with its contents, pressing a fold of paper into Lander's hand.

'What is it?'

He winked. 'The cure.'

In the bathroom, Lander shook out the powder into a tiny heap on the back of his hand, dubious about the volume even without knowing it was diluted with boracic. He inhaled deeply and listed against a wall. It wasn't coke. That same sensation he had upstairs at the Enterprise seeped through him. Dope drunk and daffy, he wandered back along the narrow corridor, pulling sleaves of wallpaper loose as he went, and rejoined Little, who had refreshed their glasses.

Lander drank. Matters were under discussion.

'I skim from the clubs and spielers,' he said. 'Trick is forthright honesty in your own crookedness. They expect you to garnish the salad to some extent.'

'I value too much my throat remaining uncut.'

'You had all the job cash. No doubt you slipped some aside.'

'Counted down to the very last note. Receipts retained for every exchange. My racket, I charge a healthy percentage of each transaction, so the theft is baked in.'

Lander tapped his head knowingly.

'A lot for Bill to stuff beneath his mattresses.'

'Run through the nightclubs by now, no doubt.'

He nodded, though he hadn't seen any extra cash on the takings, and he'd been scrutinising them. 'That what wasn't burned, anyway.'

'Yeah. Burned.'

'And you feather the nest with the powder.'

'Got into that when I was manager at the Dorchester. Cocaine and pethidine to the posh crowd. Girls and boys for them upstairs. Billy's high-stakes games in the suites.'

'Lady Docker.'

'*Lady* Docker! Christ. The stories I could tell you. Fucked up the arse by George Raft in a downstairs cloakroom. They had him over, shooting some hokum at Teddington about a gambler. There's this charity gala in the ballroom, which became a bit of a do because Princess Margaret agreed to attend. She likes the Dorchester. Discreet. We looked after her. They manage to rustle up George Raft and Colleen Gray off this picture, who usually wouldn't touch this sort of thing with a bargepole, but since there's a royal going. Bit of Hollywood spice for the princess.

'Now, Raft, he is really something. You should see him dance, absolute dynamite. The ladies love him. Make you reconsider which bus you take to work. On top of that, he's half a gangster. Bugsy Siegel, and then Mickey Cohen, he's tight with these guys. They want to be like him, see. Because he has class. There are no classy gangsters outside the movies. You could take Billy Hill home to your mum and not be embarrassed, but that shouldn't be mistaken for class.

'Halfway through this gala, one of the cloakroom girls, she finds me and tells me there's a bit of a rumpus going on. One of the cloakrooms is locked from the inside. Now, I got the master key, opens all the doors for fire and safety reasons, you understand. I open it real quiet, sneak in. These are fancy bathrooms, Dave, not some shat-out washhouse. The likes of you and I would happily make roost in one, spend our remaining days in luxury.

'Anyway, there they are, Lady Docker bent over the basin with her skirts flipped over her back, proffering cheek and taking it Greek-wise from Georgie boy. He's heard about her title, see, and decides he needs a bit of posh to tell the chaps about back in Hollywood. Nobody had the heart to tell him how she got that title.'

Lander was losing track of things. Feverishly warm, sweat mapped his shirt and he leaned his cheek against the window in search of coolness.

'The night has some burn in it,' Little said. 'I know a place.'

'I like places.'

Lander stood abruptly and made for the door, careening off several tables on the way. Little had him under one arm. Perched at the top of the stairs, a wretched helter-skelter, he readied for the end.

'Brace yourself with this.' Little offered him a small silver case. 'Keep it.'

Lander opened it and took a pinch of powder. The thing about coke, you did one snort and you were already thinking about the next. It was in that attitude he danced down the stairs and out into the street, where an antediluvian duke was being helped by his driver into an outrageously long Silver Wraith.

'Take us to the place he knows at once,' Lander told the driver without reply.

'Ignore him,' said Little.

'What you see before you is the product of past wars and future indiscretions,' Lander said to the perplexed chauffeur.

He followed Little, for he held the key. Through leafy squares and gardens and onto the Old Brompton Road, where Lander lifted his hat at the cemetery. On a curved crescent of once-grand houses, they entered a basement beneath a ratty London brick hotel, a den of ill-lit rooms with low ceilings and smoke-tarred walls.

'Appear plausible,' said the louche.

Walk upon the fucking moon, thought Lander.

Though he hadn't noticed it happen, a woman of lazy sensuality now hung from Little's arm. Lander sank into a deep armchair, the bottom of which was gone in some way, so he was low to the floor.

'You want to go first?' Phil asked.

Lander stared at him. 'I need to be somewhere.'

'You need fixing, is what you need.'

And he fixed him, its warmth spreading through his body.

I am invisible, Lander told himself, and was convinced of it. Light spilled from a lamp on a small table and he shrank back, it being important he wasn't illuminated in any way.

He wasn't privy to its terms, but some parley was beat, and that was fine, for where were they now? No longer in the chaste city, but the unreal city, some province of equivocacy where the upholding of decent standards was a matter to be taken under advisement, at best.

A hand was waved before his face, but he was long gone, deep beneath the blue Ypresian clay staking out new territories. One of them would stick, the law of averages would see to that.

The way his heart felt, bursting at the seams. Make peace with your ends, for they are with you at all times. He was fine with that. Death could not come soon enough.

Little was a malady of the soul, an organ of menace. He steered her over the sofa and she suffered him vocally. Pin a red rosette! There was shit on the air, and no mistake.

Neither of them paid him any mind because he was dead, dead and slumped in the corner where he may as well have been furniture. He had become both of his purposes, the killer and the killed. A spectral aggregate.

Could only be a matter of time before they discovered his ruse and realised he was no corpse, and then all hell would break loose. Everything could be taken two ways.

Little was disappointed in him frankly, but no more than he was in himself. He was stood up and expected to walk, but his legs were not his own. Come on, feet! Treacherous dogs, they let him down at every turn.

He fumbled for the silver case and had a little pinch, little livener. Ushered unhurriedly out the door, money left in the pool of light on the table, and up the stairs into the street. He floundered but was caught by the embrace of a cab.

Paradise.

Time was a mockery.

'I know a place,' Little said.

Lander laughed. He knew all the places.

'It's in Brighton. We can get the last train, come back with me. This place is an oasis. You can spend days there.'

Lander nodded. 'No, I can't.'

'Leave the city. It'll be good for you. They think you're a snout, you know.'

Lander shook his head. 'I know. That's what the cozos want.'

'They figure you for the Eastcastle crew?'

'Think I'd still be hanging around here if I had part of a quarter-mil, I asked them. Must be joking.'

The hackney swung quickly onto the King's Road, Lander hanging on so he didn't slide across the seat.

'Who'd you suppose they had on it, though?' Little said. 'Wild guess.'

Lander shrugged. It was the kind of idle gossip went on between criminals everywhere.

'Dunno. Most of the chaps were down the Vienna when it happened.'

'Exactly. That's where I was. But you weren't.'

Lander guffawed. He'd set out to find the location of the money, but had managed only to get stocious and then probed by Little. Didn't know why Little was so interested, mind. Perhaps he was simply a nosy parker. Dangerous thing to be.

The louche clicked his fingers. 'There was a fella someone mentioned a while back, at the place on Dean Street. I never saw him, but I think it was Phil brought him up. The other Phil, Strong Arms.'

'Yeah?'

The coke had worn off and the only solution he could think of was more coke.

'What was his name? One of those names that's two first names.'

'Like Philip Little and Little Philip.'

'Funny man. No, it was Alfred. Alfred Martin.'

Lander's veins froze up. 'What?'

On the strength of that lie, he grew bolder.

'Yeah, Alfred Martin. I heard he was on the Eastcastle crew. Don't know him, though. You?'

The man was sitting there point-blank asking him about a dead man. No possible way Strong Arms told this idiot about Fred Martin. Definitely no way Mother or Billy did. Who else knew? Gyp? Fuck would she talk to the louche about the crew for? Could Claire have mentioned her husband in the Enterprise? To Little Phil? Made no sense.

That left just one person.

The only person Lander had told about Fred Martin.

The General.

His vicar.

Bob fucking Lee.

The taxi pulled up outside Victoria.

'You sure you don't want to come down to the coast? Weekend at the Metropole?'

Lander shook his head. He was spinning.

'Nah. I'm good, Phil.'

'You want the cab?'

'I'll walk, I think. Could do with it.'

Little paid off the driver and they said their farewells. Lander could barely get away from the man fast enough. Claire had told him he sang a French song with the words all wrong. *Gendarme come, gendarme gone.* Lee told him they received cash back from France, but how would the French have known so soon to do that? Someone knew where to look. Who to ask.

Someone like the rat fuck who exchanged it in the first place.

Turning on his heel, he headed back for the station.

18

HE BECAME A KNIFE

Bright. Brighter. Brighton.

Third-class ticket in hand, Lander darted among the sparse crowds beneath the departure board, watching Little at the news kiosk. Two nuns, freshly alighted in the city, were helped with their luggage by a porter. Lander nodded to them gravely.

Stalking Little at a distance, he two-stepped quietly between the pillars on the platform holding up the great iron trellising beneath the glass roof, remaining unseen. When Little was aboard, Lander waited out of sight until the last moment and boarded the same carriage, cap tugged low. A collector glanced at his ticket.

'That's third.'

Lander nodded in mute agreement, it being the third-class section of a split carriage, after all. The man waved vaguely at an empty compartment and Lander took a seat. The train rocked into life and pulled from the station.

The great chimneys of the electricity works signalled they had crossed the Thames, and soon the suburbs rushed by in a smear of light from the back windows of houses, and eventually disappeared so completely that he couldn't see beyond his own reflection in the blackness of the window.

Little was two compartments down, the only other third-class rider on the carriage. A dining car attendant stood in his doorway talking to him.

'You are drunk again.'

Little allowed that he was.

'I'll fetch you some coffee.'

Lander waited in his own compartment for the man to return with the drink.

'Get some shut-eye before the missus sees you,' he said, closing Little's door.

Lander gave it another ten minutes. The attendant didn't return and nobody else showed their face in the corridor. It was a non-stop express, so there would be no new passengers. Tipping out a reckless heap of cocaine into his palm, he snorted it up like a cow eating grass. Studying his reflection in the glass, he wiped himself off and adjusted his tie.

Little was dozing in his compartment. The light flickered, some faulty connection.

'Phil.'

One eye snapped open, then squinted.

'Thought you were walking home?'

'Changed my mind. In for a penny.'

He sat down, removed his cap. Little rubbed his eyes and stretched.

'Phil, I'm in trouble.'

'I know it.'

'Billy and Mother, the police got them thinking I narked. The raid on the Vienna.'

'You're in a tight spot.'

'I need to get out. I need money.'

'You need a friend.'

'Sure, if that friend's got money.'

'What if this friend had something better?'

'Better than money? I've heard stories about such things, but never seen them.'

'This honour-among-thieves shit, Dave, it doesn't exist. You know Mother would cut your throat before he went down for something himself. But everyone else is expected to be loyal. Do their stint if nabbed. Where are the rest of the Eastcastle crew? What loyalty were they shown?'

'You're going to get us both killed where we sleep.'

'Meet my friend. He's what I like to think of as indemnity against contingent mishaps.'

Christ, he didn't know Lander was a cop. Didn't know he was trying to turn a cop into a rat.

'Fucking hell.'

'He knows it was Billy Hill's operation. Knows it was Mother pulled it. He knows about France and the money.'

'Then why aren't we all in cells?'

'Only got my word. He wants more.'

'They touched you after you'd smashed the cash.'

Little nodded. 'Customs. Fucking stupid.'

'You got nicked over *wine*?'

'Nah. Diamonds. I'd been in Antwerp. Something I do on the side.'

'And you asked for Flying Squad. Offering them what? Billy?'

'At first I offered grounds for mitigation: that previously my snow had found its way up an august pair of royal nostrils. That Margaret Rose certainly is a lively one. I told them, I'm prepared to tell the truth, the whole truth and nothing but the truth. That backed them off some. Then my friend got interested. The money, how it was done. How I might open a window for him into Billy's world. Future smashings. The upstairs card games.'

'But not the cash.'

Little shrugged.

Lander shook his head. 'No, because that's gone, isn't it? What wasn't burned was put through the clubs.'

'That what you're after, Dave? Steal the stolen cash and run?' Little laughed. 'That story in the paper, over a hundred thousand torched as it was useless? Billy got Duncan Webb to do that. We burned, at most, two thousand quid. It was nothing. The rest was exchanged, clear and free.'

'Bollocks.'

'You think you're on the same side, but there are no sides. Or everyone's on their own side, whether that allies them with friend or foe. Come and speak with my friend. He can be your friend too, at least for a while.'

'You're taking a risk, Phil.'

'No. I'm taking my chance. I'm getting out. If we can give them Billy Hill and the robbery, then I'm gone. My family are already in Switzerland. Wife and my girls. I mean to follow. I've put hay in the loft. We'll be comfortable.'

'I need to think about this.'

'I don't think you do. You need to take care of you and yours. You married, Dave?'

'No. Well, yeah, but not now.'

Little frowned.

Something about the man talking so freely opened a tap inside Lander.

'We didn't have a telephone, is what it was. A man I didn't know knocked on the door, said his wife sent him. I didn't know her either, but he said she knew Susan, that's my wife, knew her from the bagwash. Fair enough. Told me I should go down to the Portobello, where the public lavs are outside the Carnarvon Castle. Told me that's where I was needed.

'What I'm thinking is, she's pregnant, you see. Quite a way along. She went off out to get us some dinner, bit of meat and some veg to cook up. Usually I'd go with her. Carry the bags and that. I enjoyed it, walking the market with her. Couldn't cook much, but I'd peel and chop and everything, two of us in the kitchen. I'd been working on the car, though, and was covered in grease. She told me to wash up and she'd be back before I knew it.

'So I'm panicking something's happening, she's dropping sprog in the middle of the market. Leg it down there full whack, and I don't know exactly what's happened but he must have lost control, or lost track of where he was. Car bumped up the kerb and mounted the pavement. Struck her right there. They told me she would have died instantly. Don't know how they can tell that, but it's what they said. She died instantly. *They* died instantly. What I learned subsequent, that we was having a girl. I was going to have a daughter.'

'God, Dave, that's awful. I'm sorry. Terrible.'

Lander couldn't remember ever telling anyone that stuff, but now it was all he could do to hold his tongue with this louche he barely knew.

'Sorry, Phil. Don't know why I burdened you with all that. It's not something I talk about, usually.'

'Not at all. You can't hold onto a thing like that yourself. Better to get it off your chest. I don't know what I'd do if anything happened to my Maisie and the girls. What happened with the driver? The police got him?'

Lander shook his head. 'He drove off. People described the car in general terms, but it happened so quick. Coppers never got anywhere with it. No, it was Teddy who tells me who this man was. Brian Lassiter. Told me who he was and where he lived.'

He shrugged. Glanced at the door. 'We got a loo on this thing?'

'End of the carriage.'

He excused himself and locked himself in the lav. Only when he looked in the foggy mirror did he realise he was crying.

'Jesus Christ.'

He washed his face and took a couple of pinches of snow for luck.

Little smiled warmly when he sat down again.

'You mind if I smoke, Phil?'

'No, go ahead.'

Lander shook his carton out to offer one.

'No thanks.'

He opened the window, the burst of fresh air a balm against his warm skin. He didn't need the cigarette, but it occupied his hands and he liked the feel of it between his lips. In the corner of his eye, the lights outside stretched out into unbroken berserking streams of red and white brainfuck that distinguished the coke from the more requiescent high of heroin.

'This Lassiter,' Little said. 'The one who killed your wife.'

The bulb flickered. In querulous light, Lander realised why he'd told Little all of that stuff. Discarding his cigarette out the window, he opened the door and let it smack wide open against the carriage. He tossed the suitcase out first and gouged his thumb into Little's eye. As he howled, he grabbed him by the throat, yanking him from his seat and hurling him out into the night. His body thudded damply against the side of the tunnel mouth as the train whooshed into stone blackness.

Collar up, cap down.

Calmly out of the station and down the Queen's Road, a neon arabesque of pubs and hotels and cinemas, people spilling joyfully into the street. The sea at the end of the road, glistening so bluely by day, monstrous and unseen at night, booming against the shingle. Its salt on the lungs conducive to lapses in moral judgement, the coastal lands betwixt and between, all wild permissions granted.

He sheltered in a telephone box on the esplanade. Took three calls to find him, difficult to judge where he'd be that time of night. They came to an arrangement and Lander started walking. Quiet residential streets, heading north out of town, following the railway for a couple of hours until he saw the lights of a garage on the London Road. In the dark just off the road, he concealed himself behind the brick crown of an air shaft from the railway tunnel beneath.

Mother arrived shortly in a car Lander didn't know.

He got in the back and lay down across the seat, closing his eyes.

'There, there,' Mother said. 'We'll get you home.'

They drove back to London in dark silence, Mother leaving the car the other side of the canal. Lander dumped his coat and cap in the water and they walked into Kensal Town, Mother adopting the attitude of a drunk and singing loudly as they fumbled their way into Lander's flat.

He made coffee. They emptied liquor bottles down the sink and left empties in the living room. They lit cigarettes and let them burn down. They set the scene.

'You met Phil for a few jars. Left him at the station. Met me in Soho, and we ended up back here, drinking and smoking and telling some lies. The police ever come knocking, that's what you say. Now, we need to make a new man of you.'

Mother filled a bucket with water and sat Lander in front of the standing mirror in the bedroom. He brushed soft soap into a lather on his face and ran the razor over a strop.

'Tell me everything.'

Lander told him a story of truth and omission, how during the interrogation at Savile Row Lee had told him of recovering money from France, and how later Little had attempted to recruit him. How he put a stop to him.

Mother ran the blade in clean lines up Lander's throat and across his jaw. His eyes flitted in calculation.

'What *exactly* did Little tell you?'

'Everything.'

'You'll be feeling slightly put out, then. Slightly let down.'

'Slightly.'

Mother wiped the blade clean. 'Nothing's broken here that isn't fixable, Davey. Everyone will get what they're due.'

He slipped out into the night. Lander found a nightcap of dregs and collapsed on his bed, pillow cool against his face.

He was a stranger, a fugitive from himself.

In his dreams he became a knife.

19

IN ANOTHER WORLD, I AM YOUR ENEMY

She didn't break into tears.

Life was about keeping on, or so it had seemed since Freddie vanished. She hadn't cried over him, and she knew she wasn't going to now over his brother. Was it perverse? Fred was gone, but life had gone on much as before. The worst Claire had felt about it was those occasions when it occurred to her how infrequently she thought about him at all. It was unquestionable that Joe would be missed more, and he'd never met anyone he couldn't make himself repellent to inside five minutes.

Halfway through dressing – and the day was going to be unreasonably full so she didn't have time for this at all – but halfway through dressing she sat on the bed and thought she might force herself to have a cry. Get it over and done with.

Her black dress hung on the front of the wardrobe. Bought for her mother's funeral, it only ever saw the light for burials. A shapeless sack, she would keep her coat on over it, the day being helpfully overcast.

The smell of fields suddenly visited out of the blue, taking her back to days of farm milk and collecting breakfast eggs at first light. When war happened and Freddie signed up, she went to his father's cousin and his wife in Somerset. Bert and Nora, the only family he had left. Nora's funeral was the last time she'd had the dress out.

Bert hadn't woken up the morning of the Normandy landings, had never seen the news. Nora battled on with Claire's help and the hands she had, two men in their late fifties. Everyone understood that Claire and Fred would take the place on, Nora living there with them. When he returned from war and came to the country to his wife and children and the offer of the farm, Claire was so sure what the rest of their lives would look like, living in open space, living free, that it never once crossed her mind Fred would say anything other than yes to the offer. Until he did. Everyone married a stranger. There was no way to know. No way at all.

It was too big a what-if to imagine their lives if they had stayed in Somerset. Freddie had never seriously considered it – he was from the Dale and of the Dale – and so she had packaged the idea away somewhere in her mind and never unwrapped it in the years since. She hadn't fought him on it as she had enjoyed the life they'd had before the war, before the children. Bars and clubs and restaurants.

The life they never returned to.

Besides, the kids might have played in a barn and a hay bale could easily have fallen and crushed them. Anyone could play what-ifs.

There were smaller choices she thought of more often. What if she had insisted Freddie told her what he was involved in when he came home flush with cash? What if she'd known he was involved with Teddy Nunn again, what if she'd talked him out of it? Would she have rediscovered value in their life together without first having lost it?

But Freddie had known Teddy for years, they both had. Being involved with Teddy was what made him money before the war, and what led to him doing a short spell in prison. It was a complicated entailment that would have had to be unpicked in the open for her to keep him out of this latest scheme. This last scheme.

Really, the only choice she could have realistically changed was how she reacted to it. What if she had refused Teddy's offer of a job? What if she had told him to leave her alone, told him that she believed he had killed her husband, or at least led to him being killed? Or what if she had kept it to herself but invited him round for a meal? He'd have enjoyed that, the game of it. Rat poison would be too obvious, too easily discovered.

Crushing up the pills he gave her had a seductive irony. He'd have passed out on the sofa having a brandy afterwards. She'd have pressed a cushion over his face and held it there just long enough, then gone to bed, claiming to have left him there the night before. Or maybe Joe would have helped get rid of him.

What a funny thing the wandering mind was, conjuring another world in which you were a murderer as a positive alternative to the world at hand. She got up, dry eyed, and put the dress on, resolving to buy herself new blacks, smarter blacks.

The only impartial witness was the priest.

He spoke of a man he'd never met, effortlessly eulogising a stranger by baking his constituent parts down into tasteless unrecognisable comestibles that might easily be swallowed of anyone.

The others, gussied up in their Sunday best for death, had unequiv-ocal opinions. Ray, for instance, didn't like the shirt and tie he had been made to wear.

He wanted to be in his oily overalls.

He wanted them to see uncle off in a pub.

He wanted someone to go up and say he was a weird drunk old prick and I miss him.

But there was no truth in a church.

Hastily buried in Kensal Green cemetery, beneath the implacable gaze of the giant gas holders, uncle was toasted by an inconveniently large party of mourners back at the house.

Ray immediately sequestered himself upstairs, but knew he couldn't fully commit to not showing his face, so didn't change his shirt and tie. Sitting on the landing, he listened to the hum of grown-up chatter downstairs. Mum and sister had prepared food, but not nearly enough for this lot.

Slipping into sister's room, he had a nosy round her dresser. Curtain dark, he found nothing of interest, so drew them open. Dull northern light like his own room next door, with a deathly view of the school, closed for the summer now, so not even the veiled joy of a day off the other kids didn't get.

Tried the drawers, but knew the wood catches and scrapes, had heard it through the wall. Got one a couple of inches open and could see underwear and the hair of a cloth doll she'd kept through the years. Sniffed at the gap and some meaning bloomed coldly in his guts. He resolved to throw out his own childhood one of those days.

Mum and dad's room faced south and lay in lowering sun. He rifled through drawers but found nothing instructive. His mother's bedside cabinet yielded no evidence of obviously aberrant behaviour. In the wardrobe, right at one end, hung dad's battledress blouse that he stole when he was demobbed, forage cap folded flat and tucked under a shoulder strap. He could never imagine dad as a soldier, or what he might say to other soldiers or they to him. He existed in his own life barely more than he did in his vanishment, and he's in the field killing men? No. Taking the cap, he stuffed it in his pocket and wandered out into the hallway.

At a whistle from above, he looked up, Vic Barlow hanging over the banister and beckoning him on up. They'd never really talked before, and Ray wasn't sure why he disliked him beyond his obvious interest in sister. Perhaps because he wanted not to dislike him, wanted to have a friend who wasn't one of the younger street kids. Nothing was to be trusted less than getting what you wanted, of that Ray was certain. What you wanted had secret ways of undoing you.

Ray'd never been up to the top floor. Pretty much the same as the first floor, but the back room hadn't been split into two bedrooms, so Vic had a large space. An enormous sofa cut the room in half, a bed and wardrobe down the far end behind it, an armchair and some lounge furniture in the end nearer the door.

Vic had a reefer on the go. Ray didn't do it but knew the smell.

'You want?'

Ray hesitated, shook his head.

'It's all right. You don't have to. It don't prove anything. You smoke fags?'

'Yeah.'

Vic nodded to the low table between the sofa and the armchair.

'Pack of Flake there.'

Ray sat on the sofa beside Vic and took one, studying the box.

'Never had these. Honeydew?'

'Came off the back of a truck. They're fine. More so for being free.'

Vic laughed easily. He snapped his Zippo and lit it for Ray.

'Sorry about your uncle.'

'Yeah. Thanks.'

'Grumpy old codger, but I liked him.'

Ray smiled. 'Should have had you give the service.'

'He was in the war?'

'Africa. Where he learned engines.'

Vic held it in and spoke when he exhaled. 'Made it through that and got taken by the Dale.'

'Dunno if he did make it through that.'

'Peg says you've not heard anything from your old man.'

'Nah.'

'No idea where he is?'

Ray shook his head.

'He was always telling me how he was going to get his own shop, how I'd work there with him.'

'He was a butcher?'

'Long time ago. I don't remember it. Anyway, I like the garage. Like machines. What would I be like with a knife?'

'Probably he liked the idea, a family business. Martin and Son.'

'My uncle, he thought dad was involved in some way with that Nunn bloke.'

'Teddy Nunn?'

'Yeah.'

'Fucking hell. You know who he is, don't you?'

'Who?'

'Billy Hill's main man.'

Ray thought about mum's words.

Your father's gone away. He's done something foolish and he's gone away.

And uncle's.

You keep your distance from this man, Raymond. There's nothing lower than a crook.

'Fuck him,' Ray said.

They looked at each other and broke up laughing. The door swung open and sister came in, noted them sitting shoulder to shoulder on the sofa with a raised eyebrow, and laughed.

'What are you two doing?'

'Nothing,' both said.

'Cackling like old friends making up after a hundred years or two. There's just me and Mum, come downstairs.'

Ray wrinkled his nose. 'He didn't really like people. Why are they all here?'

Sister shrugged. 'Dunno, but they ain't going nowhere.'

Vic stood, swiped loose bits of baccy and makings off his shirt.

'You coming, Ray?' sister said.

'Yeah,' he said, not moving. 'I'll be right down.'

'Here,' Vic said, tossing him the pack of Gold Flake. 'Get you through the day.'

'Cheers, Vic.'

Sister eyed both of them with suspicion and led Vic downstairs. Ray gave them a moment, smoked his fag down before stubbing it out. He went down to the first floor and hung about on the landing.

'Ray!'

Mum downstairs.

'Ray, I need some bottles of milk stout.'

The man in the shop on the Portobello near the Golden Cross served Ray as he knew he was getting liquor for uncle. He'd probably help him out today, especially if he knew it was for the funeral. Who turned up at someone's house and expected milk stout, though?

'Fuck this.'

Quietly he went into mum's room and raised the sash. The roof of the washhouse was just to the left, easy to step across to. Carefully, as he wondered how sound the structure was, he scrambled over it and dropped down into the garden of the derelict ruin next door. Walking through, he checked the road was clear and made off the long way round the block, so he didn't pass the house.

Didn't realise where he was going until he came to the Golden Cross, that he'd fished uncle out of so many times. He went in seeking some of his uncle's spirit to rub off, but it felt like a land where the rules no longer held sway. The landlord was absent and he didn't recognise any locals who'd bent their arms with uncle. The pretty young barmaid looked at him as if he didn't belong, and he was scared to death of what she might say and how he might look after she said it, and so left as abruptly as he'd arrived.

Craving familiarity, just to be in the presence of anyone who knew who he was, he walked back to the Ladbroke Hotel, dad's old local. Behind the bar, Forks eyed up some likely victims among the career drinkers who'd set up stall for the day. He nodded at Ray.

'Shame about your uncle.'

'Yeah.'

'Monstrous old fart, but he kept my boxy little Minx running long after it should have been.'

Ray took a stool at the bar.

'Mum wants milk stout.'

'Can't serve you that.'

'Yeah, I know. Not for me. There's people over at the house, for . . .'

'Go you a pop or two if you sit quietly.'

Ray nodded brightly. Didn't even mind when it came with a straw like a kid would have it. Forks tossed a bag of crisps in front of him too. Ray sipped and felt content, the Ladbroke being somewhere he could imagine uncle and dad.

'You Freddie Martin's lad?'

Head cocked, one eye closed, an old-timer squinted at him from a booth. Ray recognised him from being at the service, but had never seen him before that.

'You know dad?'

'Knew your uncle. Don't know Freddie so well.'

'How'd you know him?'

'Was in Africa with him.'

He nodded to the bench opposite him, and Ray brought his pop and crisps over.

'You fixed engines too?'

'Aye. Not like your uncle. He'd get anything moving, no matter what was wrong with it. Sand and bugs that'd get into stuff over there, he brushed it all off. A wizard.'

'Was he always . . . you know, he could be . . .'

'A right royal prick?'

Ray shrugged.

'Yeah. The desert never did that to him. Point of fact, I reckon he could have turned the sands back, he was that much of a prick. But he was my friend over there. And that counts. I'm Barnabas Mawle. People call me Barnabas Mawle.'

'Ray,' said Ray. 'People call me Ray.'

There was something funny with his jacket, and when he saw Ray staring, he pulled it back to reveal a furious-faced little monkey with a crest of white hair flowing down its nape, who'd clearly had enough of being tented up.

'That's Mister. He's not going to put up with this much longer.'

'Where'd he come from?'

'Originally, Colombia. That's the only place tamarins like him live.

But I got him in Panama, where a man was using a hot stick to make him dance, until I took that stick off him.'

'Ain't much bigger than a squirrel.'

The monkey ran up Barnabas's arm and sat on his shoulder, content to receive favours in the form of peanuts and snarl at anyone who came too close. Forks came over to remonstrate with the seating of a monkey in his establishment, but Barnabas talked him round and soon Forks locked the place up and called the other locals over so they could drink to uncle's departure.

Mister was thrown nuts, which he occasionally threw back in spiteful reciprocity, and Barnabas told them everything he was minded to about his life, which was so much that in no time they felt they'd known him their whole lives. A merchant seaman, he'd travelled the world since the war, including the few places worth seeing and a whole rake that certainly weren't.

The life of a seaman sounded just fine to Ray. Barnabas told him who to make friends with on a ship, including the cooks and the stewards and the purser if possible, and that on deck the second mate always knew the best whores in any given port town.

'Also get you out of your National Service, being a seaman.'

'National Service is stupid,' Ray said.

They drank to that and drew up lists of pastimes for a new national service.

Painting poetry on the walls of prisons.

Stealing milk bottles from the rich.

Throwing eggs at priests.

Having the monkey kiss bar girls.

Setting fire to schools.

Resurrecting the men of Ray's life.

The age of enlightenment had passed.

People milled about the house, men mostly, drinking everything there was and sending out missions for more. The few women sat in quiet huddles and talked of the men and of the food and how there were too many of one and not enough of the other.

Claire wondered what would happen if she left. Who would notice? She couldn't put a name to half these people, and the others she hadn't seen for years.

All crawled out of the woodwork now.

Peg appeared with Vic from upstairs. That wouldn't last, he didn't have enough aspects for her to be interested in. Then again, she thought of Freddie.

'Where's Ray?'

'Up there.'

'Mr Maskell—'

'From the fish shop?'

'Yes, Mr Maskell from the fish shop would like milk stout. He's not fussy about which one, he graciously informed me, but milk stout would be the thing.'

'What's he even doing here?' Peg said.

Claire held out her arms, like what are any of them. From the bottom of the stairs, she called to Ray.

'Ray? Ray, I need some bottles of milk stout, please.'

'He said he was coming,' said Peg.

'Good.'

She fussed about, checked on a few of the women, resisted strangling them till their eyes popped out, the looks of pity they shot her as a woman who'd misplaced a husband and now buried his odd brother. Peg and Vic slipped out the front door and she knew she wouldn't see them again until late. Good on her.

'Shall I kick some people out?'

Mother, who to add to this comforting threat smiled.

'I'm hoping the paltry stock of food and drink will chase them off sooner rather than later.'

'I'm very sorry.'

'Why? He thought you were a common thief and you didn't think any better of him.'

'Certainly, but one must maintain manners in the face of death's awesome dominion.'

'Yes. Mustn't one.'

He looked around.

'Dave's not here?'

'Dave? David Lander?'

'Pally, you two, I understood.'

She laughed, which only knocked him off his stride for a second.

'Sorry business, him getting arrested and all.'

Now she couldn't stop, and he wasn't sure of himself any longer.

'You and he—'

'There is no he and I,' she said. 'Is that why you're here? To ask me about David Lander?'

She struck a wicked grin and saw it in him that he got the impression she found him funny, which she did, but the anger that caused crumbled quickly as he saw also that she wasn't afraid of him.

'No, I—'

'I should find my son,' she said, leaving him in the hallway and climbing the stairs.

She poked her head into Ray's room, but he wasn't there. In her own room, she found the sash raised, which she hadn't done. She looked out the window.

'Little fucker.'

Still, she admired it, really. Downstairs, she took her coat from the hook by the door. Her departure drew a few strange looks.

'Won't be a sec,' she said. 'Back in a mo.'

Why did people always abbreviate time?

She fled the scene like an arsonist. Rather than heading to the nearest shops on the Grove, she walked in the opposite direction, down through the Dale past the tight Norland streets to the shops of

Princedale Road. Even then, she had no intention of looking out stout for a rash-faced ball of a man who probably hadn't spoken to her brother-in-law for years. Boys ganged in the road, some holding thin sticks or smoking cigarettes, but parted for her when she was drawn to the confectioner's.

On a whim, she thought to buy some milk chocolate, but saw the small shop had a refrigerated case with bottles of pop.

'Chilled,' she said, delighted.

'The future,' the shopkeeper beamed.

She bought a cold Coca-Cola, and had the shopkeeper open it for her. In a less than demure manner, she drank it down in several long gulps and silently burped, enjoying the sensation of the gas easing its way back out. She picked up a packet of Cadbury's Milk Wafers, which she considered to be an altogether superior biscuit, even as she wondered whether technically it was a biscuit at all. It cost her 2/9 all in, and as she was waiting for change, she noticed the board of wanted ads and business cards on the wall. A small handwritten help-wanted note caught her eye. A local artist needed someone for secretarial and administrative duties, as well as 'general help', whatever that was.

'How long has this been up?' she asked.

'Just this morning, madam. The address is across the road, the first street off on the other side there.'

Why not? she thought. Can't do any harm to see if they're in.

First time she knocked, there was no response. There was a garage next door, and she ducked her head round the corner of the cobbled alley that led to its yard behind the street. An old mechanic was watching the legs of a young man who was otherwise beneath a car, directing him in what to do. She didn't want to believe in serendipity, but there it was.

She knocked again, more insistently, and a harried-looking man opened the door. He glanced back over his shoulder before speaking.

'Yes? Can I help you?'

'Mr Delaney?'

'Yes.'

'I saw your card in the shop window.'

She pointed back toward the main road.

'Oh. Yes. I only put that there this morning.'

He hesitated, taken aback by her all-black attire.

'I've come from a funeral,' she explained.

'I see.'

'Is the position still vacant?'

'Uh, yes.' He looked behind him again. 'I wonder if . . .'

A man appeared in the other doorway of the small lobby room inside the front door.

'Hello there,' he said.

'Good afternoon,' Claire said.

He looked at Delaney for an explanation.

'This is my assistant,' Delaney said, inexplicably.

'Yes,' said Claire.

'I sent her out to order some of that paint I was telling you about.'

The man nodded, no longer interested. The three of them walked through to a large workshop, a barn-sized space that reached up two storeys. Mezzanine levels were visible on one side at the far end of the building, with separate staircases leading up to them. Against the walls stood large boards with incredible landscape scenes painted on them. On close inspection, Claire realised they were parts of the same scene, designed to fit together into one huge image.

Another man was in there, apparently with the disinterested man but dressed rather shabbier than he. For a moment they all looked at Claire.

'Can I offer anybody a tea?' she said, because it seemed to be the thing to do.

Both men muttered that they could suffer some tea, and Claire turned to Delaney, who was watching her with imploring eyes that she understood to be some cocktail of desperation and contrition. He glanced toward the staircase at the far end of the workshop, and she trotted off as if she'd had the run of the place for years.

Upstairs was more studio space, desks and tables laid out with sketches and some cut fabrics. Another staircase led up to rooms in the attic, arranged around the exposed beams. There was a lounge, with a lot of art and photography on the walls, and a kitchen behind that. She set about making a pot of tea, finding matching cups and a tray. Ripping open her packet of biscuits, she fanned out a dozen or so on a plate.

She wondered if they'd want the tea in the lounge area upstairs, but decided to bring it down, negotiating the open stairs like she was carrying nitroglycerine. When she got down to the workshop, the disinterested man and his friend had already left.

'Oh! You actually made tea. My God.'

'Should I have just counted to a hundred up there?'

'They had another appointment and had to dash. I'm so sorry about all of this, I have no idea what possessed me to introduce you like that.'

'It was the easiest way to explain my intrusion.'

'They were here to see some of my work, to decide if they want to hire me.'

'And?'

'Oh yes. I think they will. I have to go to the theatre tomorrow.'

'Tea to celebrate?'

He beamed and then took the tray from her. 'Let me carry that. We can go upstairs, the sitting room by the kitchen.'

Back up in the rafters, she took a seat and Delaney was mother, pouring their teas.

'I don't know where to begin,' he said. 'I haven't even asked your name.'

'Claire, Mr Delaney. Claire Martin. And don't worry about what happened. I don't expect the job based on that.'

'My name's Edward.'

'Edward,' she said. 'Not Ted, or Teddy?'

'Lord above, no.'

'Good. I like Edward.'

He gave her a subtle once-over again.

'Did I understand you correctly that you've come from a funeral?'

'Ah, yes. Well, people came back to the house after the funeral, and I'm not really sure how so many of them turned up, I'm sure they weren't all at the service. I was supposed to pick up some milk stout, but honestly, they can take care of themselves. I was walking around and I saw your card and thought, why not.'

'Right . . .'

'And we buried him already, so don't worry about that. Should have seen some of the things he came home covered in. My son was right, we probably should have all worn overalls.' She smiled gratefully. 'All of this has just happened in the last few days and hours, otherwise I could never be talking about it.'

He slurped his tea and she picked up a biscuit and had a nibble.

'You found biscuits?'

'I had them with me.'

'You brought biscuits with you from a funeral to see about a job?'

'It worked out that way. Go on.'

He selected one.

'It's not orange, is it?'

She shook her head. 'Milk Wafers.'

'I bit into what I thought was a chocolate sandwich recently, received a rather unpleasant surprise.'

She took a big bite of hers and showed him the inside.

'See?'

Satisfied, he ate his own in neat little mouthfuls, other hand cupped beneath to catch crumbs.

'I'm not an expert,' he said, 'but this interview seems to be going rather well.'

'I'd say so.'

When they'd finished the tea and eaten most of the packet of biscuits, he showed her round the studio and explained the work. They fell into working on a woodland backdrop with textile foliage, Claire passing him fabrics to cut and keeping track of the finished pieces.

'I was going to ask if you could start Monday, but it seems you've begun today.'

'Monday would be fine. Tomorrow would be fine too, if that's what you need.'

Delaney nodded. 'Tomorrow it is then.'

He locked up and said he was meeting a friend at the Crown if she fancied a drink.

'At some point I should probably see what's going on with the horde of mourners at my home.'

'Oh, milk stout,' he said. 'They have a carry-out licence there.'

She picked up a few bottles of Mackeson and was happy as she walked home.

The Ladbroke was in the midst of a farce.

The pub was locked up and locals lay about the place in various states of havoc. Old Forks had hit the rum hard, and after exhausting his repertoire of shanties had gone to sleep atop two tables pushed together, his boots for a pillow. Barnabas Mawle sat with his eyes closed, mumbling half-verses of songs from his war days.

Only Ray was upright, having been on the pop, and had been tasked for the last hour with pouring drinks at the bar, which was beyond the ken of anyone else by that point.

Mister sat on the bar eating peanuts. He took an interest in the ale pumps, and hung from one, pouring beer into the dregs trough. Ray cupped his hands beneath it like he was receiving communion, like a hunter washing away the blood.

'Stop it, damn fool monkey.'

Mister splashed ale on him before dodging Ray's grasp and dancing down the bar top. Bored of yanking the pumps, he perched on the edge of the trough and drank the dregs. Ray thought about stopping the creature, but as small as Mister was, he figured the situation would regulate itself sooner rather than later. Lying in the beer, the monkey drank itself into a stupor, culminating with a squeaky bout of hiccups before it passed flat out on the bar.

Ray took this to be his signal to leave.

Taking three bottles of milk stout from the shelf, he left cash enough to cover and slipped out the back way, the main pub doors being bolted. Down the road he saw mum and waited for her. He held up the bottles and so did she.

She hooked her arm inside his and they looked at the house across the street.

'I hope they're all gone,' he said.

'Me too. I really do not have the patience.'

It was quiet, but the door was ajar. They found it empty except for Mother, sitting in the living room.

'Holding down the fort,' he said, 'as all Martins had scarpered.'

'Thank you, Teddy,' said Claire. 'We won't detain you any longer.'

He hesitated, not sure where he stood with her.

'No need to come in for a few days, if you don't want. Get all affairs settled, so forth.'

'I won't be coming in at all, Teddy. Thank you for the job. It's not for me, though.'

He grinned, like it was a put-on.

'What are you going to do? I don't think the lad is going to bring the bread home from the garage.'

'I'm joining the merchant navy,' Ray announced.

'You are?' Claire said.

'There was this alcoholic monkey from Panama.'

Mother laughed. 'Going to sea!'

'I'll be selling the garage, then,' said Claire. 'And I've got a new job.'

He was incredulous. 'Doing what?'

'It's nearer to home.' She looked at Ray. 'It's not in a pub.'

'Well, I'll drop by,' Mother said, finding himself at the front door, having been steered there without noticing.

'That's very sweet of you, but there's no need.'

'Keep an eye on the boy.'

'I'll be at sea,' Ray shrugged.

Mother laughed thinly. He looked at her.

'Why'd you involve him, Teddy? Could have used anyone. Why my Fred? Why did you come here that day he disappeared? Why are you here now?'

He smiled and suddenly felt too old to do so, as if at his age he needed new armour against such talk, and against unpicked truths and the coming of death.

'Why do you need to possess people?' she said.

'Long day. Hard day. You're not quite yourself. Possess? Think maybe you're possessed.'

'No. I'll never be possessed, Teddy. You hear me?'

'I am your friend, Claire.'

'You ever think about what would have happened if you'd made different choices? How your world would look? How any of those innumerable other worlds would look?'

'What?'

'In another world, I am your enemy.'

'Claire—'

'Stands to reason. Choices made differently, events played out some other way. You're my friend here, but there . . .'

'But I am your friend.'

He was out on the street now.

'Yes,' she said, gently closing the door.

That other world was so close she could touch it.

Smell the dinner she cooked him.

Feel the pills crumbling as she rolled the thick tunc of a glass over them.

The woven fabric of the cushion.

20

THE SOUND OF ACCOMMODATIONS

The last day at Somerleyton Road began with a death threat and went downhill from there.

'Speak again and ready yourself to be thrown to the bottom of those stairs.'

Stevie was in no mood to be trifled with, having finished off what remained of a bottle of gin before she'd even got dressed, reasoning it left less to be carried.

'Well I never,' Mrs Harpenden said. She backed out of the hallway, ducking through the door beneath the stairs.

'Yeah, get back down to your cellars.'

'Mum, she's got a sword,' Addie whispered.

'Only sharp thing that old harpy possesses is her hateful tongue.'

'Given the choices you've made in your life, it's of no surprise to decent folk that this is what it has come to.'

Stevie rolled her eyes dramatically. 'Hark the crawthumper. Imagine being so ashamed of the entire circumstances of one's own life that you tell anyone who'd listen you used to own the house, the basement of which you now blight, and your husband used to run a biscuit factory, or whatever fantasy it is you're selling them these days.'

'I will not hear a word against the late Mr Harpenden, and what is more—'

'Late! I bet you wish he was.' Stevie turned to Addie, though was delighted that a larger audience had already congregated on the landing above. 'Do you know who her husband was? A music hall singer who ran off with an organist thirty years ago. That's why she's living in an old theatrical, because that's exactly what she was.'

'This is slander and outrageous filth.'

'Filth is that it was an organist called Derek your old man ran off with because he knew his way round prick better than you did.'

'This coming from a woman whose husband fled the country to escape her, leaving her with two stained children so every time she looks at them she'll remember—'

'Oh, you'll get to know all about that when Grainger moves half a dozen Jamaicans into the room. Will you lock your door at night then, or lie in the dark in hope of being invaded?'

Mrs Harpenden slammed the door shut. In silence they listened to her departing footsteps on the stairs.

'You done with the scenes?' Addie said.

Stevie straightened her back.

'I shall dress and ready myself for the day.'

'Tremendous.'

She retreated to their room and closed the door. Beulah, their pregnant neighbour, watched in fascination from the kitchen, Nees perched on the table beside her.

'I'm going to miss your ma. She turns bother into an art.'

Three cardboard suitcases stood by the front door, holding almost everything Addie and Nees possessed. Two pillowcases were stuffed with toys and the few books they owned.

Their existence had become increasingly tenuous thanks to Stevie's drinking and flamboyant managing of their financial affairs. Grainger had been pressuring her over the room, which he could rent out for far more money to new tenants, and she had finally come to some accommodation with him whereby he was putting them up elsewhere for little or no rent. Addie wasn't exactly sure where that was going to be. Stevie was vague on the details, but kept claiming it was a fine deal,

with the relish of a defeated king selling his subjects on the magnani-
mous terms of their surrender.

Chabon skipped up the steps to the porch and knocked on the
open door.

'Hey.'

'Mum threatened to push Mrs Harpenden down the stairs.'

Chabon shrugged, as if that wasn't nearly the most unreasonable
suggestion he'd heard.

'Look what I found,' he said.

On the pavement outside stood a scruffy looking walnut drinks
trolley. In an art deco style, it had three-tier shelves with what had
been an enclosed glass section at the front, but the glass was missing.

Sensing Addie wasn't exactly bowled over, he said, 'Thought we
could move stuff to the new place with it.'

Grainger was supposed to have brought his van round to help them
move, but hadn't shown up. She rolled the trolley forwards and backwards, as if testing the soundness of its casters. It was probably the
most apt fashion in which they could move home.

'Where'd you get it?'

Chabon looked toward the bomb site across the road.

'Behind the ruins, down by the railway. Just lying there at the
bottom of the embankment. You think someone threw it from a
moving train?'

'No.'

His face fell.

'It says Loughborough Hotel on it, silly.'

She pointed to a dulled brass plate on the thick edge of one of the
shelves.

'Assembly Room,' he read, looking at her quizzically.

'Where we saw *Dick Whittington*. The ballroom upstairs.'

He nodded. A couple of years before, Mr Gattuso upstairs had got
them tickets for the show and they'd spent a couple of awkward hours
sticking out like sore thumbs.

'Some drunk musta wheeled it out,' he said.

Nees came out and clambered onto the trolley, squealing delight-edly as Chabon rolled her up and down the street. Inside, Addie coaxed Stevie along with her packing, which she had yet to start, like this entire plan of her own making had suddenly been foisted upon her. Not having thought about the need for more cases or bags, she carried armfuls of clothes outside and heaped them upon the trolley. Her jewellery and cosmetics cases followed, and her shoes in a neat line on the bottom shelf.

When everything she was bringing was piled on, there was only room for the smallest of the children's cases. Knotting the pillowcases closed with the ends of a length of string, Addie wore them round her neck like milk pails, a suitcase in either hand. Nees clung to the front of the trolley like the figurehead on a ship as Chabon set to pushing it along. Stevie directed him from behind, carrying nothing more than an air of authority.

'Does this coloured child work for Mr Grainger?' she asked Addie.

Grainger lived in a large house round the corner on Coldharbour Lane, opposite the nursery. Damaged in the bombing that destroyed the row of houses that stood where the nursery now was, he got it for a song. Its neighbour suffered worse in the blast, and had remained unoccupied ever since. The gardens of the pair of them, along with the next two houses along, had at some point during the war become one big yard, which Grainger also leased on a peppercorn rent.

As they passed along the pavement, the upstairs nets twitched, a dark shape behind the curtains watching them. Mrs Grainger was seldom seen, suffering from nerves and existing cloistered away in the front bedroom.

The rear yard was accessed from the side street. This was where Grainger operated his commercial concerns, including a cartage busi-ness, storage facilities and, allegedly, a builder's merchant, though of that there was scant evidence. Two horses roamed freely, skin and bones the pair of them, nibbling at shrub here and there, and a

Dobermann was chained to an iron post, a situation about which it was loudly expressing its feelings.

A row of sheds lined the edge of the property, and a large workshop sat at its heart. Around that were arranged half a dozen caravans, which Grainger had originally bought to do up and sell, but soon realised, with the housing situation being what it was after the war, that he could do better by renting them out. To these he had added several other makeshift homes, including a small caboose, a shack on wooden piles, and a bus, which Addie now learned was to be her home.

Long shorn of its wheels, and settled on piles of crumbling brick, it was single-decker and much shorter than the red buses Addie knew from the city's streets. A stovepipe poked through the roof at an angle and was belching smoke.

'Hi hi hi.'

Grainger stepped down from the rear entrance.

'Got her all warmed up for you.'

He showed Stevie onto the bus, leaving the children to bring in her belongings. All of the seating had been ripped out, including the driver's cab, which was now a storage cupboard. Sleeping areas had been arranged at either end, serviced by the front and rear doors, with a living space in between that could be roughly isolated by concertina doors hung with grubby fabrics. A small settee had been put in opposite the stove, specially for Stevie.

Addie couldn't believe what she was looking at. For her part, Stevie wasn't remotely perturbed. The shank-end of life, she accepted it almost gleefully without hope or fear, for where else could she tumble from there?

Grainger made a show of lighting the wood-burning stove, declaring that tea could be made, though Addie wasn't sure where the water was supposed to come from as there wasn't a tap or a sink of any kind on the bus. She and Chabon did another run with the trolley, collecting what meagre provisions remained in the pantry, and all the kitchenware and crockery. When they returned, Nees was already making friends with a horse, chuckling as it ate weeds from her palm.

'Watch your fingers, Nees,' Addie called.

'What was Stevie thinking?' Chabon said.

Addie shook her head. 'How are we going to live here?'

'You get used to it.'

They turned and found a woman sitting in the door of a caravan, sewing what looked like a mask of a wolf's face.

'Costume,' she said. 'Me and the husband make 'em for theatre productions. I'm Maggie Moxon.'

The children introduced themselves and accepted Maggie's offer of a drink. Her caravan was packed with rails of clothing, and boxes stuffed with more.

'Got a second-hand clothes business too,' she explained. 'Upstairs in Gerrard Street. Just ask for Linda's, everyone knows.'

'Who's Linda?' Chabon said.

'I've got Tizer,' said Maggie.

This quelled any questions about Linda. Addie only got Tizer on special occasions as Stevie couldn't stand looking at the red lips it made. Pouring into cracked china cups, Maggie showed them round the yard as they drank.

'Most importantly, there is a washhouse.'

Addie pushed a rotting wooden door and peered inside a crumbling brick annexe to the empty house next to Grainger's.

'It flushes, and there's running water. What there isn't is electricity, so there's no light. Get yourself a torch for evening visits.'

'I never knew there were horses here,' Chabon said.

'For Grainger's cartage, though now he has the van he uses them less and less. Just about keeps them fed, though if the winter is ruinous, I'd lay odds he'll eat them. He's had pigs and sheep here before now, and a recalcitrant cassowary who he was keeping for a fella runs a travelling menagerie. That bird was a pest.'

Walking back to her caravan, she lifted a canvas tarp and presented them with a pile of wood that looked like smashed-up furniture.

'The other important thing – wood. Get it in any form you can. Spring and summer seems fine living out here, but come winter you'll need that stove going to keep warm. All night, sometimes. Stuff gets dumped round here, so if you see any furniture, grab it. Keep it dry as best you can, and that's your fuel for winter. Grainger will offer to sell you some, but it'll be extortion.'

Finishing their drinks in the caravan they listened to Maggie's stories about being a variety artiste, part of a singer-and-accordion act with her husband, of whom there was no sign. Nees found them and complained of being hungry, and Maggie sent them on their way with a few broken chair legs to help with the stove.

Stevie was in her bed hugging a bottle of gin.

'Tizer lips!' she cried, and lay back asleep.

Happy to avoid any intense negotiations, Addie relieved her of a few shillings to go shopping with and told Nees to stay in the bus as it was getting dark. In Brixton market she picked up a dented can of salmon rissoles and some swedes with a small corner of fresh butter.

Chabon took the items to carry, and she knew from the worried creases on his face that he had something to say.

'Don't bottle it up.'

'I got something to say.'

'I know. I'm helping you get it out.'

'I'm moving.'

'Could be doing it a little quicker.'

'No. Pa and me. We're going.'

Addie felt her insides plummet. 'Back to Trinidad?'

He shook his head. 'Might as well be. Other side of the river. Notting Hill.'

'Where Everso live.'

'He's part of it.'

'How's that?'

'You know Kindness been speaking with him.'

'No.'

'Your uncle got some new job for some white man. Looking to places he rent out, collecting money and that. And Pa, he got laid off at the ticket factory. He was looking at a job at the hospital, but Kindness, he tells Everso and Everso come speak to Pa, offer him work and a place to live come with it. Two rooms. Addie, I get my own room.'

'In Notting Hill.'

'Yeah.'

'What's your pa doing for him?'

'Dealing with people, mostly. Your uncle, he's not really one to be handling people's complaints except with his fists. Why he and Kindness get on. Now he's got this crazy dog too. We get two rooms in this house, and Pa looks after it for him. Collect rent, fix things, stuff like that. There are a few other houses on the street, he looks to them too. Mostly folk from back home, Pa said. Not so different from round here nowadays.'

'I haven't seen Everso in ages. He don't bring no money from Pa.'

'He got his own money, I can tell you that.'

'You didn't tell me, though.'

Chabon looked at his feet as they walked along.

'No. I was scared you'd be upset.'

'We don't get to choose where we live. Look at this mess Stevie got us into.' She shoulder-barged him playfully. 'What am I going to do, though?'

'I'll still come round.'

She made a face. 'From Notting Hill?'

'The Tube.'

'To where? Clapham? Chay, that's miles.'

'Buses. Something.'

'Not the same, though, is it?'

He shook his head and was afraid suddenly he was going to cry, battling with his own eyes. Her hand slipped into his and he squeezed.

'When you go?'

'Day after tomorrow. Pa ain't paying no more rent on where we are.'

Addie fell quiet. A lot was happening altogether too quickly.

'I'll be round,' he said. 'You'll see.'

At the bus, they dug out her father's London guidebook and studied the Underground map, plotting routes from Clapham North, changing at Moorgate to head west. Nees danced around them, chanting about starving to death, and Chabon said he better go. Addie said she'd be round the next day to help him pack, and then she set to dinner, boiling the rissoles and creaming the swedes as best she could with the little knob of butter.

Stevie had drunk her fill and was passed out on her bed. Addie waited for her, fending off Nees and trying to keep the food warm for as long as she could.

By midnight she gave up.

The world was louder without walls.

Traffic and commerce, the nagging wind, and a nickering at the window. Addie pulled up the corner of the thin, light-bleached curtain and found the horses whispering to each other. Two old plugs with no food to speak of, brushing up against one another, necks entwined. Nothing wasn't an absence. When you had nothing then nothing was everywhere, the world teemed with it, a fullness of nothing.

She was not quite cold, the blankets having mysteriously wrapped themselves round Nees during the night, who murmured quietly in her sleep, silvered snot above her lip. Addie rose. A chair leg snapped in two and a few cheap offcuts that would burn in moments sat beside the stove. She decided against lighting it until she had to.

The washhouse was colder than the outside and she hurried. Already, she couldn't imagine it in winter. They had no bucket and she kicked around the junk piled up against the workshop in the middle of the yard looking for something to carry water to the bus in but came up with nothing. The Dobermann went garrity when it saw her, tugging against its chain, before giving up and lying down, a snarl never far from the corner of its mouth. In the bus, Addie dug out the kettle and the biggest pan they had and filled them with water from the washhouse tap, walking back slowly.

'No bucket?'

Maggie was in a thick robe and nightcap, a cigarette on the go. Addie shook her head.

'First thing you should get. Come winter, you won't want to be making multiple trips for water.'

'What do you do about washing yourself?'

'Got a basin in the caravan. Walk to Camberwell baths sometimes, or just down to the lido.'

She laughed at Addie's long face. 'It's not so bad.'

Reggie would have laughed. 'Even when you dead, the crows can still eat you.'

It was beginning to dawn on Addie with a mounting sense of horror that things could always be worse. She made tea for Stevie, who took it in bed.

'Chabon moving to Notting Hill tomorrow, so—'

'Chabon is moving to Notting Hill.'

'Chabon is moving to Notting Hill tomorrow, so I'm going to help him pack up.'

'What about school?'

'Still be there Monday.'

Stevie sighed. It was all too much, the burdens her family placed upon her.

'You'll have to collect Nees from nursery,' Addie said.

'Hmm.'

'Mum!'

'What?'

'You'll have to collect Nees before they close.'

'Do you think I'd forget my own child?'

That didn't deserve the answer it wasn't asking for. Grabbing her father's London guidebook, Addie dropped Nees off across the street and walked to Chabon's flat round the corner. In truth, he and Conrad didn't have much stuff to pack up, and they weren't bringing any furniture. A couple of hours and they were done, leaving the rest of the day to study the guide's fold-out Tube map and plot routes to and from Notting Hill.

'Pa, which station we near?'

'Up on the railway near the canal. Westbourne Park, or Royal Oak.'

'Not Queensway?'

'You want to make a walk for yourself, sure.'

Chabon followed the map with his finger. 'Go to Moorgate and then get the Northern line to Clapham North.'

'That'll take for ever. At least an hour. And you're still a half-hour walk away.'

'I can get off at the river and get a bus to Brixton.'

Addie looked miserable. 'It's not going to be the same.'

She told him about the water situation and Chabon came up with a plan. When Addie left, he followed a minute later, charging out of his building with an upturned tin bathtub over his head, yelling, 'RUN!'

She ducked under the tub with him and like a pantomime tortoise they galloped down Coldharbour Lane. Laughing hard as they veered into the yard, they stopped abruptly when they found Nees sitting in the doorless hulk of an old car, in tears.

'Nees?'

Addie knelt on the ground beside the car and her little sister almost fell out reaching to hug her.

'Everything fine now. Everything just fine.'

'Mum never came,' Nees stammered.

'You cross the road on your own?'

Nees nodded into Addie's shoulder.

'That's my fault. Shouldn't have believed she'd remember. Should have been back myself. She in the bus?'

Nees gripped Addie's sleeve tightly in her tiny fist.

'There sounds.'

'From the bus?'

Nees nodded and started crying harder again.

'All right now. Nothing to worry about. Chay?'

Chabon took Nees by the hand.

'You want to go in my boat?'

'That's not a boat.'

'Is too.'

'That's a tub.'

'Tub nothing but a small boat. Get in, you'll see.'

Nees sat herself in the tub and Chabon rocked it from side to side, mimicking the roll of the open sea, to laughter from the girl. Addie approached the bus quietly, fearing what Stevie might have done to herself. Crouching outside the rear door, where her mother slept, she too heard the strange sounds.

The sounds of accommodations being come to.

She ran back to the old car and sat inside. Nees got out of the boat and climbed up on her lap.

'Mum's fine,' Addie said. 'Just leave her be for a while.'

Chabon got in the driver's seat, and the three of them sat quietly staring out the cracked windscreen. Wasn't long till the bus door opened behind them and Grainger stepped out. Unseen in the car, Addie watched in the rear view mirror as he scurried off to his back door.

'I'll be back,' Chabon said. 'You see, I'll be back all the time.'

Addie rested her head on his shoulder. Nees nestled into her chest and closed her eyes, and Addie thought how profoundly unfair it was, the stony sadness her young heart had no right saddling her with.

21

RULE 36

leftright *slamslam*
leftright *slamslam*
leftright *slamslam*

a tooth came loose, couldn't spit it before swallowing. Chair tipped back too far and he crashed onto the floor, hands trapped beneath his back. Cried out but it was lost in the backpour of blood, nose somewhere in the roof of his mouth now.

Pete Vibart grabbed hold of the chair and hauled him upright, just in time to be slammed in the face again with his mate's loaded gloves. A cop he didn't know, but he was doing a number. Brow shredded, he could see the flesh hanging in his eye.

The cop leaned in close to his face. He had narrow eyes, smooth features with a flat nose. Looked like a fucking turtle. Lander laughed.

'You finding this funny?'

'Look like a fucking turtle.'

slam

'Tuesday night,' the turtle said. 'Where were you?'

'You fixed my car yet?'

slamslam

In the ribs, felt them crack where he was stretched out by his hands bound behind his back. Tried to take shallow breaths, anything else like glowing pokers stabbing his sides.

Vibart leaned against the wall, ankles crossed, checking his nails.

'Dave, why are you doing this to yourself? We know. We *know*, you know? We just need to hear you say it.'

'Say what?'

'Tuesday night.'

'Drinking in the Star. Then home. Told you a million times.'

'Teddy Nunn is not an alibi, Dave, when you are out doing killings *for* Teddy Nunn.'

'One of them what-do-you-call-'em. Paradoxes.'

'Just tell us, Dave.'

'Where I was?'

'Once we're all agreed, we can work things out together.'

Dribbled blood down his chin. Lip torn right through, it hurt just doing nothing.

'This turtle-faced prick knows. Don't you? Why'd you think your wife couldn't sit down right?'

'Oh Dave,' said Vibart.

slamslam

Blackness.

He awoke in the chair in agony. Face in tatters, his hands behind him wrong somehow. Beginning to wonder how far they would take this.

Paddington nick, down in the vaults where they took the spades and the queers and the wrong 'uns for a good seeing-to that'd never trouble the occurrence books. A traditional educational facility. Wasn't sure how long he'd been there, but he was sitting in his own urine, if that was any measure.

When the General came, he came alone.

Arranged himself neatly in the chair opposite.

'Have you anything to tell me, Dave?'

Lander laughed bubbles of blood.

'Forgive me, Father, for I have sinned.'

'I'm here to listen.'

'Think my gums are on the wall over there.'

'It was a nice job, Dave. Nicely laid out. The bottles and glasses. Fag butts. And the singing, a particularly nice touch.'

'The hell are you on about?'

'We're talking to everyone at Victoria and Brighton. Everyone who was on the train. If just one person can place you there, you're done.'

'Train?'

'Let's not play the fool at this point, Dave. I'm not even entertaining the notion you don't know what happened. If you were responsible for shopping him, that's one thing, and it's bad enough. If you did the thing itself, then you'll hang.'

Lander laughed.

'That "if" carried your turtle-faced bastard's fists a long way here, guv. Why go to all this bother? Wouldn't take me forty-five minutes to find someone who'd swear on their nan's eyes you were in the room when the King kicked the bucket, your hands round his neck. If you're going to fit me up, make sure it fits proper.'

'I don't have to fit you up for the things you do, Dave. When we take you to court, the case will be undeniable.'

Lander grinned, teeth ringed with red.

'I'll scrub up lovely for a beak.'

'You'll be arrested soon, an arrest that you will enthusiastically resist, requiring your subjugation.'

'Put a bow on me.'

'You know how it works, Dave. It's easier if you cooperate.'

Stripped naked.

How many days in the cell?

Light. Dark.

Hot. Cold.

In the grip of screaming fever – blood, sweat and shit everywhere.

A doctor's hand on his face. Stitched up and fingers splinted and wrapped. The General looming over him, no longer interested in his confession.

'Look at you. Junk-sick. Pitiful. To think I once believed you were my best man.'

Sounded like he was miles away, at the end of a tunnel. Lander snarled, bared his teeth. Clammy, slick with his own fluids.

Give it up, his own weak heart told him.

Give them Mother.

Give them the robbery.

But what did he have to offer, really?

No evidence of the robbery. No bodies left to give the game away. No sight of the cash. Nothing but his word, and what was that worth now? All he could give them was the train murder, which was all his own doing.

He kept it tight.

He said nothing.

Lights on full. No light at all. New coppers came with a hose and sprayed him down, blasted off his filth with icy water. He howled and they laughed. Taken to a new room where clothes were brought, smart court clobber. A stone of fear at the pit of his stomach.

'Where's Lee?'

He was cuffed, pushed down into a chair.

'The Superintendent has washed his hands of you, you miserable rat.'

'There's only us now.'

'And you'll do as we say.'

'Unlawful possession, to wit, heroin and cocaine.'

'Bollocks!' Lander said.

'The defendant will plead guilty.'

'The fuck he will. You've got me on the pills, and that's it.'

'The defendant will plead guilty, or the investigation will have to widen in scope. Include other parties not currently suspected of wrongdoing.'

'Namely, Mrs Claire Martin of Camelford Road.'

'Turn her life upside down and inside out.'

'Bring her down to the vaults.'

They held him when he went to get up.

'We'd rather the defendant didn't look any worse than he does when going before the court.'

'But we're not going to fret over it.'

He slackened.

'Husband missing, presumed. Brother-in-law recently deceased.'

'Oh, look, he didn't know that.'

'The defendant is out of the loop.'

'Mrs Martin gets banged up and those children of hers are suddenly all alone in the world, no roof over their heads.'

Back of a Maria, half a mile to Marylebone, in the dock lickety-split. Stood up like they told him to, pleaded guilty like a good boy.

Still didn't see it coming. Didn't get a whiff of it until his ears heard it.

Unlawful possession while on active operations for the purpose of gathering information for the Metropolitan Police.

Like that, they outed him to the world as a copper.

The General up in the gallery to watch, walking out as the beak sent down his sentence. Years buried so deep that nobody but he and Lee knew, now anyone with eyes on a newspaper would be privy. And him on his way to nick, nine months courtesy of the judge who was doubly disappointed given his position. There'd be a stiletto primed to be plunged in his back before the night was out.

Lee was waiting in the cell downstairs.

'You've killed me,' Lander said.

'Rule 36.'

'Oh aye. They'll be falling over themselves to help me out. And going on the rules only confines me to my cell, where I can't get out when they come for me.'

'Nobody's going to come for you, Dave. You'll have some time to reconsider your position. Make better choices for what's best for you.'

'You pious twat. Still the priest. Still trying to hear confession.'

'Not me, Dave. It's in God's hands now, and His son died for our sins.'

Lander laughed.

'Joke's on him, then.'

A thousand men jammed together and yet still resolutely hard and unable to help one another, like teeth in a rotting mouth.

First and only thing he said to the screws was he needed to be in segregation. He was locked in a cell on his own for eight hours while this request was taken to the governor. No food, no water, though maybe no bad thing. If meals were brought to his cell, he dreaded what they might contain. A copper in prison. Might as well have been a rat or a child raper.

He kept himself busy with bouts of exercise. Push-ups, sit-ups, sprinting on the spot. Full suit still on, sweat steaming off him like a horse. Long after dark, the door was unlocked and swung open, a head screw shining a torch.

'Your request to be made subject to the provisions of Rule 36 of the Prison Rules, for your own best interests, has duly been considered by the governor and granted. Being as night shift is operational now, first thing tomorrow morning you will be removed to a D Wing single-prisoner cell, where your time will be spent in segregation rather than in associated labour or common activities.'

'What did—'

The screw turned on his heel and left, the door pulling to behind him.

But it remained to.

It remained unlocked.

This was how it was going to happen.

He listened at the door. The wing was deathly quiet; the silence of birds before a hurricane lands. Then footsteps.

Lander knew what was coming, had been expecting it. He stripped off his clothes so there would be nothing for them to grab hold of. He was tired from his exercise, but his skin was slick with sweat. Twisting his trousers into a tight coil, he wrapped it round his left hand, grimacing as his splinted fingers were squeezed, and held it taut with the other.

He recognised the man who came.

Benno Kosoff. Benny the Jew.

Halfway stick-up man who chanced his arm in a bank heist gone wrong. His getting caught was nothing to do with Lander, who didn't even know the job had happened until Benny was nicked, but any face he'd breathed air in the same room as who was now banged up would be blaming their misfortunes on him.

Benny was big, but the slob didn't know how to fight. Thought his bulk would work for him. Lander had boxed a bit in the marines, waiting to be sent to the Med. Knew how to put that torque into his punches.

Knew how to hurt.

He knew he enjoyed it, too, but this was something else.

This was fighting for his life again.

The slob looked at his naked body and grinned. Piece of metal in his hand filed to a point, a cloth-wrapped handle. An amateur weapon in amateur hands.

Lander stepped toward him so he could move back away from the first slash, whipping his trousers round the slob's arm and grabbing hold. Benny couldn't get a grip on him, finding no purchase on his slippery skin. His hands clamped onto Lander's face, who bit down hard, so deeply his teeth hit bone.

The slob wasn't done screaming before Lander landed elbows to his nose, two, three, four, blood exploding across his face, followed by a cross hook to the jaw. He felt a knuckle go where he didn't catch him quite right, but he'd done more hurt to the jawbone.

On his hands and knees, Benny spat undecipherable threats, cut off by a choke when Lander jumped on his back. Squeezed with all his might, delivering short rabbit punches with his other hand.

The screws arrived, not finding what they'd expected.

Three trying to pull him off, but Lander held on with everything he had.

The slob was out cold, but he wasn't going to let go till his skull burst.

He thumbed his eye.

Bit a chunk from his shoulder.

Gnawed on an ear.

Benny wasn't moving when they finally beat Lander off him, dragged him roaring from the cell.

'You tell Lee I'll fucking kill anyone who comes for me! You tell him that!'

Voices from the cell:

Jesus, someone get help.

He's done him proper.

Someone get someone.

PART THREE

BEHEMOTH

22

THE DELUSIVE DISAPPEARANCE OF
LADY DOCKER'S GOLD

Six years later – summer 1958

Rachman remained unflustered, telling Paddy Kennedy that 'The room is engaged, I am afraid,' when the landlord of the Star Tavern opened the door to the staff bathroom and found him receiving an ardent blowjob from the young barmaid Brenda.

The door closed and Rachman patted the girl on the head.

'Nothing to worry about.'

She seemed even less perturbed than he did, and he decided probably she was a zealot. Their negotiation had been completed with startling haste. Rachman had launched into his usual spiel, lamenting that such an attractive young woman should be wearing such an ordinary watch, and producing from his coat one of the 22-carat gold Kutchinskys that he bought in bulk for such opportunities. It slid up and down her wrist now as her hand worked on the base of his piebald cock.

He was not one for charvering the girls, especially ones as spirited as young Brenda, as one never knew quite what one was going to walk away with in the way of unpleasant venereal surprises. But a spot of cannibalism was fine.

That Kennedy had obviously told everyone in the upstairs lounge what he'd seen did not embarrass Rachman at all upon his return.

Why should it? These days, none of the circumstances of his life did. His days of humiliation were behind him. Over years, it had turned into anger at being a victim, at not being taken seriously. Then the fury had soured into despondency. Now, he didn't think about it at all. Since settling in London after the war, he had turned his hand to anything so long as it didn't involve honest work. He was happy to play the obsequious easterner if it got him the things he wanted. Things like young Brenda.

What did these people know of being conscripted into Nazi road gangs, or of the shit-eating privations of Siberian labour camps? Even after their war, such things were abstractions to them. They hated him, he knew that from their eyes. Not in any overt or ill-mannered fashion (although there were plenty who certainly did feel free to express the full range of their opinions), but a subtler, under-the-skin kind of hate, something more instinctual than emotional.

And so, at the small window table, he sat tubbily in his white shark-skin suit and silk shirt, diamond cufflinks and tinted glasses even indoors, and went back to losing heavily at cards to Billy Hill, who had a second pack open brazenly on his lap that he picked freely from.

'Another brew, Papa?' said Billy.

Rachman nodded politely. He never had a proper drink unless Billy did, which was getting rarer and rarer now. Rachman suspected something he and Billy had in common was their bodies had aged in advance of their years, courtesy of maltreatment at their own hands and those of others. Billy poured from the pot on the table, swapped out three cards in his hand and declared gin.

'Very good,' Rachman said.

Billy's woman, this Gyp, fiddled with the monstrous rings on her fingers. She lived for a fuss. Her position on her husband's card habits was unimpeachable: cheating was a tactic for Billy, but should anyone try to have one over on him, then blood was called for. Rachman had heard a story about a private game in Cannes. When a local player was caught stacking – a self-styled duke, eldest son of a family ennobled in the seventeenth century, and half a Rothschild to boot – it was hardly Gyp's fault when his ear came adrift after a corrective haymaker from a beringed fist.

Rachman, however, was genuinely happy with proceedings. The fleecing was part of some grander understanding between him and Billy, one which, through various business affairs, kept money flowing for both of them.

Mad Fred, on the other hand, was less impressed. Ostensibly Rachman's bodyguard, Norbert Fred Rondel sat in the corner stewing at the idea his boss was being taken for a ride.

Rachman's major-domo, Serge Paplinski, had found Fred during a brief foray into wrestling promotion that was only useful insofar as it provided them with a source of muscle. An Austrian Jew, Fred Rondel had been abandoned at six years old when, following the death of his mother, his father moved to Palestine with his new family and left him behind. Even back then, Fred had been wrong. 'A handful' was how people would describe him. He was relocated to England before the Nazis arrived and claimed to have studied for a while at a Talmudical school to be a rabbi, a thought so laughable that Rachman assumed its concoction was part of Fred's malady of the mind. Blessed with preternatural strength, his wrestling career was hampered by the fact that he frequently struggled to appreciate its scripted nature.

In truth, as far as personal security went, Rachman suspected that in an actual pinch Fred would prove about as useful as a kitten. He had the mind of a child, and wouldn't recognise a threat until it walked up and biffed him on the nose. However, his size discouraged bad intentions by itself.

'Have you any other games coming up, Billy?' Rachman asked.

'You not losing enough to me, Papa?'

'You know how I like to make an evening of it in interesting company.'

'Next month, I'll be putting something together.'

'What of these games John Burke is putting on with John Aspinall?'

Burke was an Irishman from a well-positioned family in Tipperary who had never troubled himself with a career but was more than handy with a pack of cards. Aspinall's mother had married into money several times and he was comfortable with the fox-hunting set, and had been the great gambler at Oxford when he studied there. Now the pair of them ruthlessly used his connections in the upper classes to host high-stakes card games in Mayfair apartments or luxury hotel suites, taking five per cent of the winnings. Rachman had never been more desperate to lose money to anyone, and hoped Billy could grease the wheels of an invitation.

But Billy laughed.

'Papa, even I don't get to play in those games. The Earl of Derby and the Duke of Devonshire sit at their tables. They socialise with Her Majesty. They can't risk being photographed with the likes of you or me. But you're always welcome to my private games, Papa.'

'With your Lady Docker.'

'It's as close to royalty as you'll get, my old son. Speaking of which . . . Teddy.' He beckoned Mother with a curled finger. 'We need a little chat.'

Mother gave Paddy Kennedy a fleeting glance, something passing between them, and the landlord ushered the handful of other patrons out of the private bar and downstairs to the saloon. Rachman stood, as if to make his leave.

'Don't trouble yourself, Papa. This isn't so sensitive that you can't hear it.'

With a tiny nod, Rachman sat down again.

There was one other exception – a well-dressed Indian man sitting by the furthest window from the bar smoking a cigar. The former Maharajah of Baroda, once considered a deity by his people and still well liked in the pub, he was seeing out his days in shameful exile, having fled his homeland with a woman of monstrous reputation who had smuggled most of his kingdom's jewels into her luggage on their way out the door and later divorced him. Now she jetted around the

Mediterranean with her son on the proceeds of melted-down gold and recast diamonds, nimbly dodging tax authorities and bedding strapping young deckhands on private yachts.

Billy was unworried by his presence.

'Don't worry about Boss, he's a retired demigod and has more celestial matters on his mind. Don't you, sunshine?'

'Hear no evil, speak no evil, Billy.'

A stateless Jew slumlord, a disgraced Indian king and a racketeering robbery mastermind. Rachman loved London.

Mother joined them at the card table. Billy's other creature, Frankie, stood by the fireplace where the poodles warmed themselves, and Fred took up a wall opposite the windows.

'What's the rumpus?' Mother said.

Billy chose his words carefully. 'Been asked for a favour. By a friend.'

Gyp scoffed.

'We don't need this every time,' Billy said.

'*Friend.* Don't think I don't know. Don't think I ever don't know. There's nothing about you I'm unaware of.'

Billy leaned back and cast his eyes up to the ceiling.

'Jesus.'

'What friend?' said Mother.

'Summoned, we was,' said Gyp. 'An audience with Lady Muck and her cuckold knight.'

'Oh aye, Docker? What's she want?'

'Got done over by a passing sailor and felt our Billy, boss of the underworld, might make things right.'

Mother looked at Billy. 'You what?'

'Someone nicked twenty-five grand of jewellery from her pile out in Hampshire. She wants me to locate it.'

'What made her think you could do that?'

'Because of his immaculate standing in the community,' said Gyp. 'Reach out to pawn shops and Hatton fucking Garden, no doubt.'

'Right.'

'And that he stood her a good rooting in the cloakroom of Gennaro's at the launch of that arsewipe book of his probably played on her mind too.'

'That's an outrageous slur,' said Billy.

'Yeah,' Mother said. 'I didn't think the book was that bad.'

Gyp pointed at Frankie, attempting to slide along the wall and escape down the stairs.

'Don't know where you're going. You're the one who saw him giving it her and told me what he got up to.'

'Cheers, Frankie,' said Billy.

'I only told her 'cos she asked in a manner made it seem like she already knew.'

'I did already know. Just needed someone to tell me.'

Frankie threw up his hands. 'See? What do you expect me to do with that, Bill?'

'Anyways,' Billy said, 'about this bit of thievery. Told her I'd put my best man on it.'

'Oh?' said Mother. Then, realising, 'Oh.'

'She scribbled down descriptions of a few pieces that went walkies.' Billy slid the note across the table. 'Just ask about. You never know.'

Mother looked at the list.

'Mostly solid gold.'

'Yeah.'

'She won't be getting that back. It'll be gone, like it never existed.'

'Well, we can ask anyway.'

'Why?'

'What do you mean, why?'

'Why do I give a shit Lady Docker lost her gold?'

Gyp laughed. 'My question exactly, Teddy.'

'Because she's one of us.'

Mother straightened his back. 'Is she fuck. She thinks she's something else now. Penthouse apartments and palatial estates. Probably hangs crystal chandeliers from her ceiling.'

'Firstly, go fuck yourself,' said Billy, who'd just had chandeliers fitted in his new flat in Barnes. 'And secondly, she's been a good fleece over the years, and should continue to be.'

'Why don't she go the police like the rest of her lot do when their gold gets nicked? That's what the cunts are there for, to serve the rich. Report it and claim the insurance.'

Gyp cackled.

'She can't,' said Billy.

'Why not?'

'Because it was nicked by a sailor is why not,' Gyp said. 'A sailor who she brought back to her home and who took her over the kitchen table before he took her for twenty-five long.'

'Where was the good Sir Docker while all this was happening?'

'Watching, I shouldn't at all be surprised.'

Billy shrugged. 'So you see, it's sticky.'

'What she tell you about this sailor, so we might identify him?'

'Nothing. Just a sailor.'

'I see.'

'What do you reckon?'

'I reckon she told you fifteen grand of gold was twenty-five.'

'Probably.'

'And I reckon she didn't go to mentioning the sailor was black.'

'Black? Nah. She'd never—'

Gyp exploded laughing.

Billy stared. 'Teddy, what are you getting at?'

'That she ain't getting that gold back.'

Mother slapped an envelope of cash down on the table.

'Your cut.'

Frankie shook his head in awe. 'Mother, you're something else.'

'Jesus Christ,' Billy said. 'What do I tell her now?'

'He was a sailor, so she thinks. Tell her probably he got on a boat, that he's far away and the gold is with him, being pawned under different skies. She'll still have you back to the castle for dinner. Still class up your card games.'

Billy shook his head sadly. 'She don't have that Daimler money no more.'

The racking-up of colossal expenses on the company dime had not gone unnoticed by her husband's employers, who had considered them so gargantuanly egregious that he had been forced to step down from the board.

'Course she doesn't,' Mother said. 'That was only ever on loan. It's always only ever on loan to the likes of us.'

Billy frowned.

'Bill, you want that life, I know. You want to be rich, yet unencumbered by the consequences of your criminal enterprise. You crave a schism between what your life has become and what made it that way. But you can't have that. People like us, we got a choice. Live inside the law, or be outlaws. The people you want to be like, they don't need that choice. They were born above the law, and live their whole lives out of its reach.'

'Don't see you turning down money.'

'Course you don't, because it's all about money. It's fucking work.'

'Thieving ain't work.'

'Might not be a job, but it certainly is work. How lost you are, Bill. I don't dream of settling down in a manor house with staff and hunting dogs. I see those cunts, and yeah, I want to take everything they have. But I don't want to own it in the same way. I want to liquidate it. Make its worth my own, the way I want it. I don't want the life they have. I don't even believe in their right to lead those lives. If I could, I'd burn the lot of it to the ground. But that's out of my purview.'

'Steady on, Wat Tyler. Bloody hell.'

'Look what happened to him. Slaughtered at Smithfield along with the cattle. It's not realistic to end the system, or even fix it. It's been around for centuries, unchanging, unrelenting. So we take what we can and last as long as we can. They'll take it all back eventually. Nothing we do lasts.'

'Don't know why you even bother, then.'

'What else am I going to do? Be a muggins and work a job like some cunt? I'd put a rope round my neck first. Even if you fight the system, you're part of it in ways you cannot comprehend. You want to help Lady Docker out, tell her to take precautions when bringing home wild prick. She's one of them for as long as she can hold onto it, and for however long as that is, we'll take her for all she's got.'

When Rachman decided he'd lost a suitably deferential sum, he stood and shook hands with Billy. Mad Fred pushed himself away from the wall he filled and glowered at everyone. Frankie looked like he wouldn't mind half a chance, but Rachman knew he was not a man who led with his fists and ushered Fred out the door. He would dream up something for him to do so he felt of use.

Mother met him out in the hall at the top of the stairs.

'Where you going to be later, Papa?'

'My office, as usual.'

'See if you can't get Everso to come along, and I'll drop by.'

'I will make sure Michael attends.'

Mother glanced back at Billy Hill counting his winnings.

'You know you could just put a little extra in the usual package.'

Rachman shook his head. 'You English like to pretend that your rituals are of no importance. But they are the way everyone prefers to do things. I will see you later.'

Down on the street, holding open the door of the Rolls for Rachman, Fred looked back up at the upstairs window of the Star like he wanted to do something.

'Norbert, it is all theatre. In the same way we allow Michael to behave as if he is a gangster, because Ladbroke Grove is his territory. But in which direction does the money flow?'

They drove round the park and South Kensington became Notting Hill Gate became the Grove and back to the office. Rachman telephoned what was known as the estate office, a small room on the ground floor of one of the Powis Terrace slums. The one they called Kindness answered. He adopted the attitude that Everso would come round the office in his own good time, until Rachman suggested that Teddy Nunn was not a man to be kept waiting.

Everso was there within the hour.

He had the Alsatian with him, an animal Rachman had purchased for security but allowed employees to look after so he did not have to burden himself with its welfare.

'Final word in all arguments about late rent,' Everso said, giving the mutt a sharp tug on its thick lead. It growled. Rachman would allow Fred to take it home that night.

Rachman did not share the disregard for the schwartzers that many Londoners had, and not just in that he'd happily rent them rooms (that was a simple case of profiteering, and he would do that at the expense of anyone). Like him, the West Indians were outsiders arrived from faraway lands, struggling to make London their home.

He considered Everso.

In many ways, he had natural advantages over Rachman. Michael Manly was a more English name (although Perec Rachman was not so bad, had not needed too many sharp Polish edges sanded off). He had spoken English from birth, while Rachman had needed to teach himself (though he took to languages very quickly, and could get by in German, Russian and Italian also). He was born in the Commonwealth and had the unquestioned right to travel to Britain, while Rachman had only been allowed to after his country was destroyed. And he was Christian, while Rachman's Jewishness had made him an outsider even among his own Polish people.

Rachman had one thing going for him that the schwartzers did not, though. He was white. That allowed the English, if only for the most fleeting of moments here and there, to allow themselves to believe he was not so different after all. Not even for a second could they pretend Michael 'Everso' Manly was one of them.

He also had the skill of conversation. Rachman could talk to anyone about anything in any place. Everso sat in sullen silence. He bothered himself only with the rhythms of the Grove, and mocked other Jamaicans, those who had been professionals or middle class back on the island, for now having to live side by side with the likes of him. He had no wish to play cards with the Earl of Derby, but he was a useful instrument in the slums.

When Mother bounded down into the basement office, the animal just slobbered over his hand and accepted scratches behind the ears.

'How's my favourite sailor?'

'Been sitting here almost an hour,' Everso said.

'I can go and come back, leaving you sitting here another two, if you're going to be shirty about it.'

Everso muttered something but brightened up when Mother handed him an envelope with five hundred quid.

'A monkey, since you had to do the hard work.'

'I'll give you this, you know how to pay a man.'

'What was she like, anyway?'

'Fuck like a man. Fierce lashing, even if she almost as old as you.'

'Watch it.'

'We square with Billy Hill?'

'You're square with me, and that's as far as you need worry.' Mother looked at Rachman. 'What about the other thing, Papa?'

Rachman gestured for Everso to explain.

'White feller of yours, Vic, is arranging it,' Everso said. 'I give him the addresses, he goes in and speaks to the tenants, does the jobs.'

Mother nodded. 'Don't take too long with it. We need as many of these cunts out as quickly as possible. There are killings to be made with new tenants.'

23

THE MIND IS ITS OWN PLACE

For the first time, it bothered Ray that he didn't have a key.

He'd signed up for the merchant navy before mum and sister had moved from the old place on Camelford Road down to the townhouse on Princedale Road. Though he'd been back for a few spells since, the door was either on the latch or he'd grabbed the spare keys and never had a set of his own cut. This time, though, he thought he was back for good, and without a key it didn't feel like home.

The door was locked.

He dropped his bag and banged with the side of his fist.

Mum answered the door in brown whipcord trousers, knotting the collar of her blouse.

'Ray!'

Briefly dropping her ties, she hugged him warmly.

'Did we know you were coming home?'

'Surprise.'

'Well, that's . . . Peg! Ray's home.'

Upstairs, sister's voice buzzed indecipherably.

'I'm in an awful hurry, Ray. I'm at work in five minutes.'

'Still at the studio?'

'Yep.'

She noticed him looking at her trousers and cocked a hip.

'Got these in Simpson's. What do you think? I'll be up and down ladders today, so I'll not be in a skirt, thank you. Peg! You're going to be later than I am.'

'Coming.'

Mum pulled on her coat as sister clattered down the stairs, pecking Ray on the cheek as she bolted out the door, coat and hat in hand.

'We'll see you later, love,' mum said. 'I'll pick up something nice for dinner.'

Not the welcome home he was expecting, but this was what they were like. Dashers and scurriers, rushing off to their dreary jobs. A year since they'd seen him, and they were gone already. They'd be expecting him to bring it up later, regale them with his adventures from travelling the world, but they'd never ask directly.

So many years on ships, the grinding noise of them, he was unused to the ringing emptiness of the house. It set him on edge every time. He lugged his bag up two flights and dumped it in the back room on the top floor. It was a huge house, miles too big for just the two of them. Even for three with him home now. He didn't know what mum had been thinking.

A dust sheet covered the bed, but whipping it off he found it made up beneath. He tossed the sheet onto the wooden chair in the corner and sat on the bed. The room was barer than any cabin. He'd never had anything of his own there, having dumped most of his stuff from the old place when he went to sea, feeling it was time to change. Time to become a man.

He walked into sister's room next door, at the front.

Bigger.

So many clothes.

He barely knew her any more. She was older, but it felt as if they'd swapped roles in the family, that he was the older sibling. She was still stuck here in the Dale, when he had seen the world. He knew the globe. The seven seas. The great canals linking west and east and west again. The ice at the top of the world and the white midnight sun it lay beneath.

Nobody in the Dale had seen as much as he. Was as worldly.

The sun smirked in the window pane, causing him to squint. He went over and watched the street, two children down the way vaulting over the wall from a garden in Portland Road. They tore along the pavement and veered into Queensdale Road, headed for Norland Square most likely. A ramshackle patch of parkland with tennis courts kids played cricket or football on, and whose pollarded trees sprouted witchy fingers of new growth.

Ray really knew nobody. That fact suddenly crept up on him unawares. Being at sea, he had enjoyed the same fast friendships he did as a boy on the block. You were thrown together with strangers by fate and took them as they came. Just as the kids of the Dale had respected and feared him for reliably being able to not fuck up the starting of a fire, he was widely admired on board for his consummate knotsmanship, hitching of marlinspikes and deft lashing of hammocks. There was no higher praise than coveting a man's ropework.

Back in the Dale after six years, though, he had nobody to be thrown together with. Where as a boy you could run the streets and bump into kids on any corner, forming instant bonds, what opportunities did a man have for such a balm?

The Prince of Wales sat across the road.

Like any pub before opening, it was a mournful sight, darkened windows and soot-streaked gypsum face. It straddled two streets, letting out onto them both, an interzonal couloir where intractable men gathered like rockfall to talk at one another.

He unpacked his clothes and drawered them neatly, and remade his bed in the nautical fashion. A creature of habit, he planned to get into the swing of landed life. A quick stroll down to Don's store for papers – a national daily and local weekly – and some snouts, before frying two eggs and toasting thick slices under the grill, larding them with butter until they pissed the stuff. He took his time eating, reading the local rag. Petitions against violence, stemming from Colville Road area 'clubs', so obviously the coloureds; a protest by a local association in communication with extraterrestrials through deep yogic trance; some rich old duck turned a hundred and two; letters about the wasteland corner on Talbot Grove where kids were still burning mattresses and falling in broken glass.

Some things never changed.

But other things did.

Wiping up the last of his yolk with a finger, he washed his cup and plate and ran himself a bath. An indoor bathroom was an unspeakable luxury. He lounged in the tub until the water cooled, before changing into clean clothes. Early evening, he took a leisurely walk east around the fenced Ladbroke Square Garden, where the cosseted classes privatised nature (although servants were permitted). Youths appeared in the streets, nattily dressed and riding scooters. They clutched the foot-square paper bags of record shops and were busy going places, the older ones sitting outside pubs drinking. Ray ran wild in the local streets as a teen, an urchin like the rest of them. Clothes and scooters and records and the general doing of things never came into it. But these kids were spreading their wings. The city was theirs.

He pushed open the rear courtyard doors of the Prince of Wales and made his way to the lounge because it would be quieter, and because there was nothing he feared more than a room he'd never walked into before.

He was the only patron and sat with his ale at the rear window, pretending to be waiting for someone. In the street, a coalman hauled a sack off his truck and bent beneath it, carried it out of sight.

A few old-timers came in and a postman capped off his day with a pint. Two young women blew in chattily and he looked away, watching them furtively in the long wall mirror. He felt stupid. What had he been expecting, to be welcomed into the warm embrace of . . . who exactly? He didn't want to become a fixture like the geezers in the corner. It was tempting, though, to allow the beer to creep through his body, thawing something that had gone hard and cold at sea. Christ, he needed something to fill his days, but—

'Ray?'

He turned to a face familiar from somewhere.

'Vic,' the man said. 'Vic Barlow, from upstairs.'

'Jesus, Vic. Sorry, been a while.'

'Peg told me you'd gone to sail the seven seas.'

'Home for good now, I think.'

'When d'you get in?'

'This morning. House is empty, so I nipped over here.'

'Let me buy you a pint.'

'Thanks very much. Royal Toby, ta.'

He'd drunk bottled stout on the ships, but a new start was required. Opening the pack of cigarettes he'd bought that morning, he hesitated and left them in his pocket. Vic returned with two pints.

'Got a fag, Vic?'

Vic opened his pack and showed him.

'One left.'

What a gent.

'Ta very much,' Ray said, taking it.

Vic grinned and went over to the bar, where there perched a wooden fag machine, and pulled a new pack from the drawer after sliding his coins in.

'What are your plans, Ray?'

'Haven't a clue. Get some work. Find a bird. Here, you know what's on the front page of the *Kensington News*?'

'Three-piece from Barkers, eighteen guineas.'

'No. Well, yeah. But Mrs Wilson banging on about the corner round from where we lived.'

'Where you little scoundrels used to try to burn the neighbourhood down?'

'Exactly the same.' Ray shook his head. 'I swear, it's like I never left.'

'Some things are different.'

'Scooters?'

'Opportunities. Bright young lad like you, there's always something to do to earn a few bob.'

'What are you doing now?'

'You might call it property management. For a friend of your old man's.'

Ray all but spat the name. 'Nunn?'

'Yeah. There's plenty you could do for him.'

He rolled his eyes.

'I don't mean that stuff,' Vic said. 'He has legitimate concerns. Always needs a driver for his cold stores.'

'Do me a favour.'

'You're funny about him. He's always done right by me. And here, you could work for me. That's not the same as working for him. You'd be your own man, I'd hire you job by job.'

'Doing what?'

'You handy with a paintbrush?'

'You mean emulsion, or like Picasso?'

'Lots of work about. There's this letting agent, I look to some of his properties. They changed the rent laws so landlords can up the prices for new tenants. Means they can afford to do the places up. You know better than anyone what gaffs round here are like. Painting and decorating needs doing all over if you know the right people. I know the right people, and you know me.'

'Painted a ship more than once, so painting houses will be piss.'

'There you go. Get yourself some overalls or old clobber you don't care about, and I'll take care of the rest. Put a few shillings in your pocket that we don't need to trouble the taxman over.'

Ray refreshed their drinks and they clinked glasses to their new endeavours. Tentatively he broached a subject that had been worrying away at him.

'You and . . .?'

He finished his question with a nod toward the house across the road.

'Peg?' Vic grinned, shaking his head. 'She didn't tell you?'

'Never really asked.'

'Dropped me like a hot rock. Always too savvy, your sister. Still see her around, though, in here sometimes.'

That troubled Ray for some reason. They sank a few more and agreed to meet back up in a couple of hours with a different crowd. He went home and had a nap before making himself a cheese sandwich and changing into his blue denim jeans, which were just the thing. He sat at the window of sister's room and waited until he saw Vic return to the pub. Giving him a few minutes, he followed him over.

There was quite a crowd, mostly about his age. Some of them were into the whole Ted scene, with drapes over brocade waistcoats and bolos round their neck. Nobody had blue denim, though. You had to have been somewhere for that. Ray could tell some of the girls had never seen it in person before. He wouldn't point it out but would wait for them to ask.

The ale was going down easily, and probably he hadn't slept the earlier session off. He took glass after glass, but rather than thaw that thing inside him, he felt it crystallise yet become indistinct, haloed along with everything else by the nimbus of drink.

Vic introduced him as a sailor, fetching up some bold looks from the girls, and he shared some experiences, not the true ones but the stories they had become through telling and retelling, and listened to their tales, which all seemed to end in mayhem of one variety or another and he felt frogmarched from one laugh to the next, because what else do you do with people's tales?

Standing, in order to work his wallet from his pocket and also give everyone a good eyeful of denim, he stumbled, haphazardly catching his balance on the chair. People laughed and for just a flash anger thickened within him, but he knew they were laughing with him and not at him and so he tamped it down.

'Oop, mayday. Rough seas!'

More laughter.

'Aye aye, Captain,' one girl called.

'I'll get drinks,' he said, not knowing what anyone was having, reeling incautiously to the bar where he found himself at the side of the evening. At the side of his own story.

Only the kitchen light was on when he got in. He fumbled at the door with the spare keys. At the bottom of the stairs he stood crookedly, ear lifted to the darkness, wondering if anyone would come down to say hello. They didn't.

In the kitchen he found a note informing him there was a plate in the fridge, with instructions for the oven. There was a kiss at the bottom.

A refrigerator had been an aspiration of mum's for as long as he could remember, and she'd finally got one on tick. What did chilled perishables mean next to having seen the ice at the top of the world?

He crouched in the light of the fridge, bathing in its coolness, before sliding the plate out. Some kind of pie, with mash. He didn't heat it and ate standing up. The mash hung in his gullet. He hurriedly drank a pint of water to prevent impending hiccups, and picked the meat out of the pie, binning the crust.

He had thought home would come to him.

Make space for him.

No traveller deserved this.

24

WHERE THEY KEEP PEOPLE RUNNING OUT OF LUCK

That they were having such a lamentably good time could only mean a donnybrook was on the horizon.

Bernard's was a popular spot on Sundays for those who knew it was there. A social club on Canterbury Crescent, just the other side of the railway behind Coldharbour Lane, Bernard ran it out of his basement flat, sleeping in a small room at the rear. The front and middle rooms were knocked through into a comfortable space where whatever alcohol he could get wholesale was sold at a small bar in one corner.

Proximity to the police station a couple of hundred yards down the road had curtailed his ambition in regards equipment to host a sounds system, but he had a Blue Spot for spinning calypso and when he'd taken enough cups would get his scraper out and be joined by others on the pans and guitar and brass if anyone had an instrument.

At night it was mostly men, drinking and dancing inside with white women, but on Sundays they got a big pot and a grill going out in the empty plot next door, where war had stolen a few houses, and women and children sat around and played in the sun. Food was brought by all to be cooked up and shared without claim.

While waiting for her favourite curry lamb, Nees chased a boy up and down the street, playfully brandishing a stave from a broken garden trestle. The boy, a year or two older than her, had that glint of eager fear in his eyes that suggested he wasn't entirely sure whether he wanted to be caught or not. Addie and Chabon watched from the shade beneath a tree near the road on the empty lot.

'Never know she's a Rowe girl, ladylike as she is.'

Earned himself some side-eye, but his hand found hers and she squeezed.

'Stevie okay on her own?'

'Maggie's sitting with her.'

'Let me talk with Everso.'

'No.'

'Ads, I can get him to sort a couple of rooms and—'

'I don't want anything from him he can't bring himself to give. Only time I ever hear from him is through you.'

'We're going to need something. You get on into this school to do your nursing, you think you can leave Nees with Stevie?'

Addie shook her head, pressed her eyes shut.

'Then come live in the Grove. Me and Pa can look to Nees when you're away. Stevie too.'

'I know those buildings of yours, most especially that one you in now. All those men and their white women. You want Nees there?'

'Better than a bus.'

She slipped her hand from his.

'Ads . . .'

'Wait.'

She stood as four cars sped up from beneath the railway, pulling sharply to stops outside Bernard's building.

'Get Nees,' she said.

White boys in suits flooded out of the cars, cosh or rod in hand, making a beeline for the steps leading down to the club door. The basement windows were kicked in and a petrol bomb was thrown but caught up in a bush out front, which ignited biblically.

The building couldn't contain the violence.

Knots of men fell into the street, bottles and glasses clutched as weapons. A woman took a cosh round the head trying to protect the curry pot, which was kicked over into the grass.

'Hide in tin town,' Addie told Chabon.

He knew she was going for the police. 'I'll go.'

'They won't come if you ask.' She winked. 'Besides, I'm faster.'

He hissed, 'Addie!' but she was sprinting away up the road, leaving him to usher Nees behind one of the prefab huts, some of whose residents were dragging women and children to safety, others just peering from behind their curtains at the mayhem.

Hurdling flowers and vegetable patches, Addie flew through the gardens of the huts on the other side of the street, cutting through to the corner where the Canterbury Hotel stood. The pub didn't have any rules against black patrons exactly, but everyone knew where they stood. When she went out with the girls from the factory where she worked, it wasn't somewhere they could go. They weren't welcome in most local pubs. She'd been in there alone, though, and never had any problem finding someone to buy her a drink. Her hair was straight, after all.

A shower of coppers were milling about outside the Victorian police station when she trotted up, puffing slightly.

'You all right, miss?'

Addie arranged her distressed face and adopted a voice Stevie would have been proud of.

'There is such a to-do just down the road, Constable. All manner of ruffians brandishing weapons and doing havoc in the street.'

She pointed back down the road. Bernard's was out of sight round the corner, but black smoke from the burning bush purled into the sky above the rooftops.

'Blimey,' one callow constable said.

One of them rushed inside to fetch the goon squad, the others straightening their helmets and hurrying away toward the melee. Soon enough the bells were ringing and a Maria rounded the bend from

Gresham Road, the station emptying of men, who jumped into blue and white cars or took off on foot.

Addie followed the blue swarm back toward Bernard's.

Meanwhile, Nees clinging to him, Chabon hid behind a shed in the garden of an asbestos hut across the road from the club. He was as afraid of the coppers as he was the Teddy boys, who you could always belt back.

The back of the plot of temporary housing was unfenced and gave onto a stubby street of townhouses that had been further reduced by the war. If they could get down there unseen, they could loop back round to the yard where the bus was, a place of relative safety.

'Come on,' he whispered, leading Nees through a garden of tomatoes and potatoes.

They'd barely gone three steps when a neatly dressed thug appeared round the hut, armed with an iron bar and a savage grin.

'Run,' Chabon urged, pushing Nees ahead of him.

He could hear the thug's feet outpacing his own across the uneven ground – in fucking brothel creepers, for God's sake – but he had to keep between him and Nees.

'Through there,' he yelled at Nees, directing her between huts and toward the stubby road leading to the railway.

The thug could move, had done some real running in his time, and Chabon could hear his breath behind him and his shoulders itched with the anticipation of being tackled from behind or catching a swing of that iron rod. Cornering a hut like a car on two wheels, there was a horrifying cry and the thug went down. Not down like he stumbled and windmilled and toppled over. Straight down, hard with a thump.

Chabon chanced a look behind him and saw the Ted had taken hold of a rake, but then realised, no, he'd stepped on it and his foot was now impaled upon its teeth. Chabon couldn't understand where the rake had come from as neither he nor Nees had stepped over it. The Ted screamed and screamed, and then, smiling sweetly, Addie appeared from the side of the hut, where she'd been kneeling as she slid the rake into the thug's path.

'Don't think I could have swung it hard enough to bury it in his head.'

'This'll do,' Chabon said.

There were great wards of the city reserved for people running out of luck.

Addie lived in one such place, and could see few ways out of it as long as they had Stevie. At school, when she'd raised the idea of becoming a nurse, she'd been told, 'That's not for you,' but Addie had never heard much at school aimed at improving her life. A Jamaican friend of hers had left the factory to join the nursing school at St James' Hospital in Balham, and Addie planned to do the same. She just needed to figure out how that plan would work around her mother and sister.

The unfurling of life was time's parody of grace. Stevie's existence was in her bed, tending to the lode of her own loneliness, a mine from which she seldom emerged, though she was sick of what she dug up. A chronic drinker, the way she told it she was dying of anything but. There was the emphysema, the heart condition, the couple of surgeries that were just plain bad luck, and when you put it all together it was a wonder she didn't drink more to keep her mind off it.

Running into the yard now, they could smell the pot Addie had left on the bus's stove earlier. She constantly made soups, more out of necessity than for any palliative reason, as her mother didn't keep down solids. It made no difference. Stevie wasn't about to be reasonable now she'd come to the days of bargaining.

The yard was quieter now, smaller, a place fallen to its knees. The horses were long dead. In an incident of local notoriety, Grainger had shotgunned the Dobermann after it bit him.

Shaken by the violence in the street, Nees retreated to the bus, where in a box she kept a jumble of old clothes and costumes rescued from Maggie Moxon. How she dealt with anything that made her nervous was to hide in strange character costumes or cheap, gaudy evening wear, which Addie had taken in to fit her better, raising hems so she didn't trip over the skirts. Maggie had pierced her ears with a cork and much wailing, and Nees wore great hooped earrings from which she hung small trinkets that chimed gently as she moved (Addie never did enquire where the trinkets came from).

Chabon set up deckchairs outside for him and Addie. Sounds of the dying commotion faded away and they sat in the last of the day's sun. Chabon took out a fold of pound notes and slipped them to her.

'It's from—'

'Do not say Everso. That's a lie.'

'Ads—'

'One I appreciate, but a lie nonetheless. He's never been worth much as an uncle to me.'

'He pays me, so technically . . .'

'Chay, you can't keep giving me money.'

'Hey, will you marry me?'

'No.'

'Because if we were married, it wouldn't be my money. Be our money.'

In what had become a running joke that wasn't really a joke at all, he proposed to her without fail every day. The first time, when she was pretty sure he was serious from how crestfallen he looked when she said no, she kissed him and told him she wasn't going to marry anyone else either. 'But if I was, I'd definitely let you make a counter-offer.'

Now he asked every day, probably to cover for how hurt he was that first time. Turn the whole think into a lark. Addie was certain she was too young to marry yet, though at the same time she couldn't imagine a future life for herself without Chabon.

'What else am I going to do with my money? Feels like I have hilarious amounts.'

'Put it by. Save to get out of where you are.'

'I like Notting Hill.'

She jerked a thumb in the general direction of the minor riot.

'That lot were driving around the other night jumping black boys in the streets of Notting Hill.'

'I know it.'

'Well.'

'Well, let them try jumping me on the Colville, see what happen to them.'

Grainger appeared at the back of his house. He looked much older than his years.

'Why the man always vex so?' Chabon said.

'Can't visit Mum no more.'

Chabon tutted. 'You'd tell me if he tried anything.'

'You'd know from how his heart got cut out with a spoon.'

They laughed, though Addie sometimes worried whether she and Nees were vulnerable in the yard. The thought of Everso plunging a screwdriver into mad old Geronimo still popped into her head from time to time. She should have taken that sword from Mrs Harpenden, just in case. She wondered whatever became of it. Mr Gattuso, the illusionist who'd lived upstairs, had told her the old bat had passed on, when she bumped into him down Electric Avenue in the market one day a couple of years ago. Should have gone round then and pinched it.

Chabon got up, saying he better get going.

They hugged and he held her tight, then they kissed and he got into it.

'I do believe you have misbehaviour on your mind, Charles Bonamy.'

'Just need me an accomplice.'

'Uh huh.'

Maggie stepped down from the rear entrance of the bus.

'No making kids, you two.'

'No fear,' Chabon said under his breath, and Addie stood on his foot.

'How's she been?' Addie said.

Maggie shook her head. 'She's not good, Addie. I told her we should get the doctor. I think she needs to be back in hospital.'

'Good luck.'

'We may have to take the decision for her soon.'

'I know.'

'She wants to see you. Heard the palaver down the street. What was it?'

'Teds. Gang of them turned up at Bernard's.'

'Jesus. Anyone hurt?'

'No. I mean, yeah, loads. But not us. It was walking wounded round there, though. They were swinging on coppers. Craziness.'

Maggie shrugged, like that bit wasn't so baffling.

'I'll be back over to see her before I go to bed,' she said, and sashayed off to her caravan.

'I'll stay,' Chabon said.

'No, she'll only get performative. Or pretend she doesn't know who you are.'

'What about the doctor?'

'She'll refuse to let him see her.'

Her faced creased and he held her again.

'I'm scared, Chay. I don't know what we'll do if something happens to her.'

'Told you, there will always be a room for you and Nees.'

'Nees is ten. What if they don't let me keep her? We don't have other family, they might put her in some place—'

'Hey, hey, come on. It's not going to come to that.'

'You don't know that.'

'You'll be eighteen soon, and you can look after Nees. Until then, we'll muddle by. But if it comes to it, we'll take her and run. Go back to Port of Spain if we have to. I got cousins and aunties there.'

She rested her head on his shoulder and squeezed the tears back in.

'Course, we'll have to give you lessons on how to fit in, being how you walk and talk like the English.'

She jabbed him with her elbow.

Stevie called out in her hoarse voice.

Addie held him tighter and kissed him.

'I better go see her.'

'You working tomorrow?'

'On at midday.'

'I'll call the phone box at ten.'

Addie climbed aboard to see her mother. Stevie tried on a number of smiles but none of them really fitted any more. Her hands shook badly, from medication was what Maggie said, and she beckoned Addie closer with her chin.

'Police?'

Talking was an effort, a breathless whisper all she could manage.

'Botheration down the way.'

'Gangs?'

Addie nodded.

'Told you . . . about that club.'

'Yes, Mum. We'll try to hang out somewhere that isn't being fire-bombed next time.'

Stevie gave her a look. Still had those.

'Mum, we really should call the doctor.'

Stevie shook her head.

'You need—'

She raised a shaky hand. 'Nees?'

'She's fine. She's down the other end.'

Stevie said nothing until Addie went and got Nees, who was dressed for the occasion in a black evening gown with faux pearls and a feather boa. She was getting better at the make-up, complementing her dark tones.

Stevie looked at Addie.

'Better than the Indian chief with the war bonnet,' Addie said, remembering one of Nees's more exuberant get-ups.

Nees let loose an undulating war cry before kneeling on the chair beside Stevie's bed. She enjoyed sitting with her bedridden mother and listening to her prattle on. At least once a week Stevie told the story of how Nees got her nickname, and the girls would tease her about it. But that day, she didn't have the breath to talk. Nees bunched herself up beside her mother and laid her head on her shoulder. Just feeling her breath on her cheek was enough for Nees.

Stevie beckoned her in closer. She coughed. A spastic hand flittered on her chest, and as she reached out to stroke her younger daughter's face, her fingers became entangled in one of her hoop earrings and their panicked trembling ripped it from Nees's lobe.

The girl ran from the bus screaming, fleeing the yard as best she could in an old pair of Stevie's heels and clutching a torn ear, her trinkets jangling on her mother's still-shaking hand.

25

THE ONLY END TO TIME

Years passed like a dream. Were a dream.

Lander stood in front of the Scrubs and inhaled deeply.

Summer heat and malignancy.

A six stretch for wounding with intent to cause grievous bodily harm, the screws having testified that he was the aggressor. Endless fights followed, interminable periods in solitary, almost five years in total, until word got round that the bother wasn't worth the risk with Lander.

The suit he'd worn to his second trial had survived and was returned to him, along with a new one from Her Majesty, even more ridiculous than his demob clobber. Another con being released at the same time discovered his braces had perished in the intervening years and was provided with a length of twine to secure his trousers. No ticket or travel warrant, as he was remaining in London, but he was given the few quid he earned sewing sacks over the years, a twenty-shilling grant to see him through the night and a letter to the National Assistance Board for anything beyond that.

It was enough to tempt a man to hold up a shopkeeper on his way home.

Outside the prison, beneath one of the trees lining the drive to the main road, a car was parked up with a woman behind the wheel. Dark hair. About the right age. Lander allowed himself a moment's hope.

He'd pushed Claire from his mind, pushed away every other comfort from outside those walls. Six years was a lifetime, and would only
have been made longer by what-might-have-beens. But nearer his
release, he had found himself pushing the walls outward, imagining a
new life. Furnishing it with people and things. He hadn't imagined
how he might explain himself to Claire, just that she would be there,
inhabiting this new space with him. Their comfortable silences.

But the other released con made a beeline for the car. The woman
didn't get out and they didn't hug when he got in. The car moved off
and Lander was alone. He wasn't sure what he had expected. The fleeting thought arrived that perhaps he'd expected Bob Lee to be standing
there waiting for him.

His guv'nor.

His vicar.

He was surprised to find he was disappointed he wasn't, even if it
was just to question or wind him up about something. Maybe Lee
hadn't thought about him since he was sent down. A disgrace, a minor
scandal in the annals of the Met.

He was on his own, which was simultaneously liberating and con-
stricting. After almost twenty years of everyone knowing exactly
where he was – in the marines, then working for both the General and
Billy Hill, then in a cell – he could finally exist on his own terms.

Freedom had an air of surreality to it, which in turn distorted the
past. His sense of neither was reliable. It might all be happening and
have happened to someone else. For as long as he could remember, he
had been buoyed along by the traumas of life, clinging onto them and
allowing himself to be washed down the ditches and gullies of grief
carved out by the flow of time.

Breaking bread at his mother's table with the dead coppers of his
family. Haunting the dusty mausoleum that had become of the flat he
once shared in anticipation with his wife. Content to drift, rather than
pull himself out and battle through the thorny briar of making choices
for himself.

Six years away had unmoored him from those old unsinkable sor-
rows, though. His freedom was about to begin, and he was certain it
would hurt. Unless, of course, he could find himself some other intractable woe that would sweep him along. Fortunately, having spent
years confined to a cell by himself, he'd had time to think about a few
things. Such as the men who'd robbed him.

Robbed him of his share of the biggest heist in history.

Robbed him of six years of his life.

Perhaps he wouldn't have to start the distressing business of making
choices just yet.

There was no straight route home because of the railway, so he walked
down the prison road past the dog stadium and cut north to find a way
beneath the tracks and into the Dale.

Suddenly less space, less air.

People crammed into houses crammed into tight streets.

Home again, home again, jiggety-jig.

He had no real plan, other than to find digs for the night in one of
the broken-down old boarding houses that used to litter the place, and
he hoped still did. Half a mile down Latimer Road, he turned off
before the looming Victorian school, into the tumbleweed streets
tucked in close to the railway viaduct that sliced through and above
the Dale. On Lockton Road, he found what he was looking for, the
end building in a terrace of four-storey semi-basement townhouses,
built so close against the viaduct that it never escaped its shadow. A
sign in the window, *Vacancies – ask for Mrs Mortimer*.

The front door was wedged open. Tentatively he nosed his way in.
'Hello?'

A woman in her fifties came out from the back somewhere, handsome but hard edged. Kept slim on cigarettes and white spirits. Been
dealing with his sort all her life no doubt.

'Mrs Mortimer?'

She looked him up and down.

'You after a room?'

'If you have one. The sign in the window . . .'

He glanced back over his shoulder.

'How long you thinking of staying?'

'Well, I don't know. What do you—'

'Twelve shillings for the night, but I don't do night-to-night for more than three. After that we do it weekly or we don't do it at all. I'm more than reasonable. Three quid for the week, in advance. No coloureds, no pets, no returns.'

'I can pay you for tonight now, and later I should be able to pay for the week.'

She narrowed her eyes. He counted out twelve shillings.

'That's for tonight, no matter what. I pay the week's rent later, that starts tomorrow night. I don't, I sling my hook.'

She nodded. 'I don't do funny business. Rules are simple. Front door locks and bolts at midnight. You bang on it after that, it'll open only to hand you your belongings. I don't mind a drink, but I won't abide the drugs. No visitors to your room, male or female. Keeps things simple. Breakfast is seven until eight, after that you're on your own. Dinner, four shillings extra or a guinea for the week, is five until seven of an evening. After that . . .'

'I'm on my own. Understood.'

'You're at the top in the rear. Bathroom's on the half-landing. I'll show you up.'

Two flights, and the back room next to the stairwell. Like everywhere else in the house, it had once been attractively decorated but had been left to go to seed over the years, though it did have a basin and running hot and cold. The railway passed right by the window, the track obscured by the corrugated roof of the covered station platform. A train pulled in and the glass in the window rattled thrillingly.

'You get used to that,' she said.

It was the kind of room in which you could come to terms with your own mortality.

She gave him keys for the front door and his room and left him to it. He hung his spare suit in the wardrobe. He washed, and doing so in private felt like a gift. He hadn't shaved in a couple of days, which had earned him disapproving glances that would have turned into orders to groom himself if he'd been inside any longer. As it was, he wanted to let it grow out. He worried a beard would draw attention, but he also no longer wished to see his mother's face in his own. He was the sort who'd always been told he favoured his mother, ever since he was a boy. Now, he couldn't stand that.

No buses ran through the Dale. Walking beneath the viaduct, he headed east past the prefab housing and into the leafy crescents radiating out from the Notting Hill end of Ladbroke Grove. Heading north, he entered the Grove that he knew, near the railway bridge, and bought a bag of chips he couldn't finish. The pubs were opening. Feeding the remains of his chips to the wild chickens nodding out of the alley to the railway cottages, he nipped into the KPH for his first pint in six years, limiting himself to the one, lest matters got out of hand at such an early stage.

He caught the 15 outside and sat upstairs, riding it east into Bayswater. On the upper floors of an imposing mansion on Bishop's Bridge Road, he visited the law firm of his old brief, Mr Morville, who had since died tragically in a bicycling accident on a family picnic by the sea (high winds, higher cliff). Collecting a receipt for a file deposit, he went to Dalzell Conyngham, the private bank on the ground and basement floors of the same building, and retrieved an expanding case from their vault room, leaving with personal documents and nearly fifteen hundred pounds in cash.

Pocketing a couple of hundred quid, he stowed the rest in a luggage locker at Paddington station, fastening the key to the chain of his St Christopher. Crossing the railway and canal on foot, he caught a bus along the Harrow Road and up to Kensal Green Cemetery. After a quick word with a groundskeeper who seemed to know the location of each of his wards, he found his mother's grave near the canal, across from where a full gas holder squatted.

She'd died after a short illness, two years into his sentence, and he hadn't been allowed to attend the funeral. Bent coppers in segregation for snapping a fellow prisoner's fingers get no privileges. Buried a mile from his cell, now for ever unseen.

Henry, the broken widower, inherited the house. Sold it and moved to the coast, where he took up with a retired singer who used to do tea dances and worked a few seasons for a revue show but never got further than that. Now she lived in a house by the sea bought with the proceeds of Lander's mum's death. It wasn't something he dwelt on often, but when it did cross his mind, he wished cancer on the pair of them.

The stone was small and basic. An unkempt, unloved patch of earth. There'd been nobody left to visit it. He stared at the thin grass as if he might see right through the soil to what lay down there.

Old bones in old clothes.

Right beneath his feet.

There was nothing there for him, and he knew he'd never return.

He walked back through the plots – white like teeth for the newly departed, moss furred and misshapen for the long-ago gone. At the main gates he saw him, pipe hooked in his mouth, leaning against his little Austin as if they'd arranged to meet there.

His guv'nor.

His vicar.

General Bob Lee.

'Sorry you missed her service, Dave. There was a fine turnout. Lot of coppers. You'd have felt right at home.'

'Half expected you outside the Scrubs. I'm ashamed to say my heart sank when you weren't.'

'Thought you'd want to get your bearings.'

'An ambush at my mother's grave *is* more thoughtful.'

'Give you a lift.'

'Where?'

'Does it matter?'

They drove west, around the vast carriage sheds and sidings of Willesden Junction, and cut down over the railway and into Park Royal, a sprawling industrial estate that might be a town all of its own. Here was a place where things were made in factories of all kinds. The canal cut through the middle and provided pubs and cafés. There was a bank and a greyhound stadium, a chapel and cemetery, a sports ground with tennis courts. A school stood across from a sweet factory. It was bounded in the south by Acton's streets of Victorian terraces, and in the north by the suburban sprawl of Metroland.

Jobs. Families. Lives.

'This must be hell,' Lander said.

Lee pulled the car in near the canal. Lander rolled down his window, smells of water and industry gusting in. He longed for the fumes of Soho, the food and the fights and the fucking.

He considered Lee.

'You look old.'

'Retired, haven't I.'

He said this as if his own deep suspicion was that taking his pension was stepping one foot into the grave.

'Usher you toward the door, did they?'

'It was just time.'

'Two big open cases still on your books. Nobody done for Eastcastle. And then Billy pulls your pants down again with the bullion heist.'

That had been the talk of the Scrubs. Not as big as Eastcastle, but about fifty grand's worth of gold bullion was lifted from a truck outside the KLM freight depot behind Gray's Inn Field with what the papers referred to as military precision. Prison scuttlebutt was that it took twenty seconds, two cases of gold nicked, and whilst it was happening Billy Hill was in the office of Duncan Webb discussing his forthcoming memoirs, with dozens of witnesses present. The perfect alibi.

Lander chuckled. 'Not to mention laying out his thoughts on both jobs in that memoir of his. Essential reading in the Scrubs, that was.'

'You believe some of the bollocks he wrote in that?'

'A lot of it seemed plausible. That why you're here? See if I can give you Billy?'

Lee shook his head. 'Nobody will get Hill now. He's on the verge of being completely legitimate. Property and the like. Even talk of him pushing to legalise gambling. Rolls with heavy company. County Hall. Parliament.'

'I told you, didn't I? If ever a villain was going to retire fat and happy, it was Billy Hill.'

'You know a character called Peter Rachman?'

'Papa? Sure. Used to run some two-bob rental agency. Finding rooms for tarts, mostly.'

'He's come up. The biggest slum landlord in Kensington now.'

'Christ. When I left, he'd just bought the first place of his own.'

'Has half the Colville estate these days. Hundreds of houses, Shepherd's Bush to Bayswater, but mostly the Colville. Specialises in renting to West Indians. Ramps the rents up and packs them in.'

Lander saw it all. Where the cash went, why he never saw it in the spielers or nightclubs. Papa as a front, Billy buying property, using rent payments to legitimise the robbery loot.

'Smashing cash for Billy Hill, you're saying?'

'Among others. He's a front for other heavy company.'

The stench of the behemoth's tangy breath as it licked its chops.

There was no separating criminal loot from legitimate money. No isolating of the black markets from the white. You pay politicians to act, coppers to not, and they pay their rents and buy their dinners. You rob mail vans and bullion trucks, and buy houses and grow slums. Good money follows bad, by rent or dog track or nightclub or spieler. In every pocket and purse in every flat and house in the city, looted money could be found, untraceable among all the rest. No line existed between the good and the bad. The behemoth made no judgements or distinctions when it came to the provenance of cash.

'Good for Papa,' Lander said. 'But that's not something I can help you with.'

'I didn't come to ask anything of you, Dave.'

'Oh aye? You remember my date of birth?'

'I remember everything about my wards.'

'The interesting thing about that date is that it was not, in fact, yesterday.'

Lee smiled. 'Felt like we had unfinished business. Felt like I needed to see what had become of you.'

'I spend six years alone locked in a small stone room. Have a wild guess what became. I've got something to ask of you, though, since we're sitting here all cordial. Why the whole pretence with the hotel? Sending me the note.'

'I didn't send it.'

'Whoever. Someone in the Met.'

'No, I mean we didn't know anything about it. First we heard was an anonymous phone call that morning, telling us that men involved in the Eastcastle job would be at the Mount Royal, room 365, nine o'clock. Came through on the switchboard, asked for Flying Squad. Ended up leaving a message with a secretary, and it was a while before we got to it. Billy had ears everywhere then. Christ, he even had you. So I told nobody how we'd heard, just set men up on the room and told them to arrest whoever showed up, make up a reason if they had to.'

'Bullshit.'

'God's honest truth. I had detectives question everyone at the hotel. Room was booked in person on the Friday, under the name Green, paid cash. It had been busy, and the staff on the desk couldn't recall who did it. But I went back. There was a kid, spotty-faced little rat, the desk was his first real job. There was something wrong about him, so I had him checked out. He'd lied to get the job, done a stint in borstal off the back of a forged rations wheeze he had going. Didn't want to lose the desk job, so told detectives he didn't remember anything so they didn't look at him too closely. But he told me. It was a woman. Older, he described her as. Which for him, could mean anything from twenty-five to forty. Dark hair. Attractive.'

'Fucking Gyp.'

Lee shrugged. 'We couldn't prove it.'

'Fuckers bilked me, and then set me up.'

'Worse than that.'

'Worse how?'

'Saw a friend of yours last month.'

'Oh aye?'

'Benno Kosoff.'

'Benny the Jew.'

'Right.'

'Fat fucking slob. Police still keeping track of him then?'

'Not a hard man to keep track of. He's in the same place he's been for the last six years. Same place he'll be until he dies. A room in Banstead Hospital, where food hasn't passed his lips that wasn't fed to him by spoon or straw since he came off the wrong end of a prison beating.'

'And whose fault's that? You send someone to give me a warning, you send someone better than that slob.'

'I didn't send anyone.'

'Course not.'

'At the time, I thought it was personal. I'll admit, letting you stew in there a day or so, I hoped maybe you'd reconsider your position and shop Billy to me. In hindsight, I underestimated what the screws would turn a blind eye to for a few quid. Figured Kosoff thought you ratted on him for that bank job that went sideways. Wasn't like I could ask him about it. He hasn't said a single word since that day, or even thought one.'

'What are you saying?'

'Come on, Dave. Who were you always telling me had all the coppers and screws in his pocket? Who paid everyone to do his bidding? Who set Mrs Kosoff up in a new flat in Chiswick? Certainly wasn't me.'

Lander submitted to a perfect stillness, the kind of crystalline calm that only comes with unmanageable rage.

'Billy Hill.'

'You had a few incidents in those early years, even in segregation. Then they tailed off. I think Hill realised you hadn't talked to us, and weren't likely too, and decided to let things lie.'

'No thanks to you. Right jackpot you put me in.'

'You always had a way out. You could have talked to me.'

'No. I couldn't.'

'What happened to you, Dave? What was it? Did I lose you, or were you already this thing and I never had you to start with?'

'You think too much.'

'Was it the war?'

'War didn't do it. Wasn't any one thing. It's never just one thing.'

'Your wife. Her death.'

'That wasn't a death. It was an amputation. They don't call it loss for nothing. I kept waiting for things to go back to the way they were. Or the way I was. But that's the thing. Something, some part of what I was, it went for ever. It's never coming back. I am less than I was.'

Lander bought fags and a pint of Scotch and returned to the boarding house, leaving a week's rent with Mrs Mortimer and a guinea for the nosh.

In his room, he shrugged off his jacket and hung it in the wardrobe, thinking he'd need to pick up some new togs, bit of underwear. All his worldly possessions could fit in a pillowcase. What little he had wanted kept from the Kensal Town flat had been taken to his mother's, the brief had seen to that. Christ knows what had happened to any of it. He didn't trust himself not to kick old Henry to death if he ever found him to ask.

He poured himself a drink and lay on the bed, listening to the rattling window. Clothes could wait. A relaxing afternoon of nurturing the most grievous revenge stretched out before him.

26

TEDDY BOY PICNIC

Mum was down a theatre all day for work and picked up three fish suppers on her way home, which was an on-the-one-hand-but-on-the-other-hand type situation for Ray as he vehemently believed in the institution of the home-cooked tea but also loved a nice bit of fish.

Afterwards, he cleaned up and got dressed into some old bits he found in a case on top of the wardrobe. He was half certain they were dad's, and couldn't imagine what he'd been thinking when he kept them, but they'd do for a spot of painting.

'Where you going dressed like that?' sister said.

'Work.'

'This time of night?'

'Have to do it at nights, when the tenants are in.'

'Why?'

Ray wasn't certain. 'Decorating rented flats,' he offered.

'How'd you find that?'

'Vic.'

'Vic Barlow?'

'Yeah. He says hi.'

'I bet he does. Here, Mum, Ray's working for Vic.'

'With him more than for him.'

'Vic Barlow?' mum said.

'We're meeting in the Wales first. You two fancy a gin and tonic?'

'You're meeting in the pub before work?' sister said.

Ray shrugged.

'I've work in the morning,' mum said.

'It's not a session,' said Ray. 'We're working right after.'

'Who's we?' sister asked.

'Dunno. Vic and whoever else works for him, I suppose.'

'You going now?' mum said.

'Yeah.'

'I don't know. I don't think so, but perhaps I'll pop over in a bit. Peg, what do you think?'

Ray gave it a couple of minutes, listening to them sew themselves into an evening at home with the wireless, then left on his own. Vic was already at the bar.

'The Royal?'

Ray nodded. 'Cheers. Make it a half.'

Vic winked. 'Diligent.'

'Must have had it backwards my whole life. Used to doing a day's graft and then having a few jars. Not meeting up in the pub before-hand, like we're going to the match.'

Vic grinned.

'Just a quick livener. The work's easy, mate, and we can't start till we know everyone's home. Rules about liability and that. Case any-thing happens, damage or whatever.'

Sounded like bollocks, but Ray made a note of it to tell sister.

'Bend the elbow for an hour or so and we'll whizz off,' Vic said.

'Job's local?'

'Not far. We've got wheels, five-minute drive, if that. You met the chaps?'

Three of them around Ray's age, sitting at a corner table. He recog-nised one face, a fellow pyromaniac who used to run about Camelford Road.

'Ray Martin!'

'Clive, isn't it?'

Vic was busy with someone at the bar, so Ray joined them and Clive did the introductions, explaining to the others how bewitching they found starting fires on the corner as boys.

'Here, you see the front page of—'

'The *Ken News*!'

'Yeah! Good to see the kids upholding the traditions.'

'You been at this long, with Vic? The painting?'

Laughter rippled round the table.

'The painting bit is new. But we're quite used to night shifts.'

'You know where the place is?'

'Brown Town.'

Ray frowned.

'Colville.'

'Coalville,' one of the others said.

'Other side of the Portobello, all them houses on squares between Lancaster and Westbourne Grove. Slums, mate, the lot of it. Packed with coloureds. All got the boat over from Jamaica. All pimps.'

'With white birds,' someone added.

'And we're working for them?' Ray said.

Clive grinned. 'Nah, we're working for the fella owns the buildings. He knows what he's doing. Has them in there, three and four to a room. They don't mind living like that, they're used to it.'

'They're all over now, though. Paddington to Shepherd's Bush.'

Ray hadn't quite caught the other pair's names, so followed the conversation from the outside.

'See what happened over the Askew Café?'

'Well, he was asking for it.'

'We was dancing at the Carlton when we heard about it.'

'Askew Café?' Ray said.

'Coloured café down near Ravenscourt Park.'

'Les's sister.'

'Yeah, Les lives over that way now, down in the council flats, Emlyn

Gardens. His sister was telling us about it, how the place only serves spades. No English.'

'This the one on Askew Road?' Ray asked.

'Yeah, you know the Eagle?'

Ray nodded. 'Nelly Light. Who don't know it?'

The landlady of the Eagle was a right sort and not shy about showing you what she carried. Ray had had more than a few free drinks off her in the past because she took a shine to him.

'Few doors down. Right uppity type, only serving his own.'

'Les's sister's mate was lugging about this fella whose cousin works in the garage, you know Edbro Tippers, round the corner? And he was refused service in there.'

'Crazy what they think they can get away with in this day and age.'

'You go round there?' Ray said.

'Too bloody right. Whole mob of us did.'

'Les got nicked, mind.'

'Yeah, Les is a dopey twat. Him and a few others got collared over it. But it's not like they strung the old spade up. Just smashed the place. He's cowering in back with his missus, never said a dicky bird. Might have to go a bit of compo, but they won't go down for it.'

'Be an outrage they did.'

'Outrage is what happened to Georgie.'

'Georgie Marks?'

'Got himself stabbed up, didn't he.'

'Fucking hell. When?'

'The other night. Right round the corner from his gaff.'

'Who done it?'

'Pack of darkies. Come up on him in the street. Stuck him and give him a kicking for good measure when he was down.'

'Jesus. He all right?'

'No, he's not fucking all right. Had his kidney out, I heard.'

'Shit. How many kidneys can you live with?'

Vic came over and clapped his hands. 'Chop, chop, fellas.'

As if a bell had rung, they drained foamy dregs and filed out into the gorgeous evening, the departed sun leaving a magenta glow in its wake. The other three took a car, Clive driving, and Ray jumped in a van with Vic.

'You know this George Marks?' Ray asked.

Vic laughed. 'Fucking hell. What they been saying?'

'That he got knifed couple nights ago.'

'Sure. Bloodbath it was.'

'I heard he got cut so bad they had to remove his kidney.'

'Do me a favour.'

'He didn't get stabbed then?'

'With a penknife maybe. Had it in him about an inch. Bet the boys didn't go to mentioning what happened beforehand.'

Ray shook his head.

'Now, I'm not saying Georgie is a Ted, or that he's been ever so slightly put out by the fact some West Indian lads moved in next door to him, but a bunch of Teds have put a bin through the front window of the house next door, coinci-fucking-dently whilst Georgie happens to be walking by minding his own business. Rest of them have had it off a bit lively. Georgie, future brain surgeon that he is, reckons he can just hide up near them flats at the top of his road, then wander down the street behind, round the block like he's coming back from a stroll. Like he's not their neighbour and they're not going to have recognised him. They've come out and he's walked right into them and took a pasting. Fucking kidney. He's fine. Was out of the hospital same night. They've nicked the coloured lads, but there's not a chance it holds up in court. Doubt Georgie will even turn up. Here we go.'

He pulled up on Colville Terrace. A stretch of huge dilapidated townhouses with peeling paint and crumbling plasterwork, the thin end of a scraggly, poorly maintained square opposite. Nothing like the private gardens further south. The house was narrow, but stretched back a mile and climbed four storeys from the street with arched windows above the ground floor. In the basement music played and West Indian men came and went through a downstairs entrance from a rough-and-ready rum shop. Through the window Ray could see white women dancing, pictured sister years back, smoking in the street with the black boys.

Four steps up to a once elaborate porch, where Vic shook hands with a young black man who introduced himself as Kindness. They laughed and joked, speaking behind cupped hands like accomplices. Vic told Ray it was the ground-floor flat they'd be working in, a living room at the front, bedroom in the middle and a scullery out back.

The tenants were an older white couple, Agamemnon Cudsworth and his wife Gladys, both somewhat bewildered by what was happening. Vic told Ray the score and had him deal with them.

'Mr Rachman sent us,' Ray explained.

'Who's that?' Agamemnon said.

'He owns the house. Your landlord.'

'Never met him. He's never been here. We took this flat in 1933, when Mr Heath owned it. His grandfather made hats.'

'I see. Well, Mr Rachman has sent us to do a bit of decorating. Paint the walls and that.'

'We don't need painting. Need the dry rot in the windows seeing to. And the mould.'

'We'll see what we can do.'

'And the racket downstairs. Goes on for hours, doesn't it, Gladys?'

Ray nodded. The ground-floor rooms weren't isolated from the rest of the building like the basement was. Upstairs tenants were in and out by the dozen, Christ knows how many of them up there. A young woman came down, barefoot and hitching her skirt up as she descended, thighs looking like they were tied with string where her suspenders dug in. At the bottom she adjusted her clothes and slipped on heels. Ray went out onto the porch as she crossed the street into Powis Square.

'One of the wives,' Vic said.

They watched her take up a position among the other toms.

'Like the West End,' Ray said.

'More like Piccadilly than Piccadilly, what with the clamp-down.'

Another girl came back bold as you like with a fare and the old man watched her lead him upstairs.

'Always this busy?' Ray said.

Agamemnon grumbled. 'Why are you here at this time?'

'We have to work when we know people are in. So everyone knows where they stand.'

'We're always in, we're retired.'

'Well, I suppose we didn't know that. All the work is done evenings and at night.'

The other lads, slightly tipsy, made a ruckus with the ladders and laying down sheets. Clive danced to the calypso sounds, singing non-sensically in a mock-Jamaican accent. A tin of paint was kicked over, sitting like a slab of coloured glass on the hallway rug.

Agamemnon was beside himself. The lads set about clearing it up, only making things worse, and Ray went outside to see about the noise. Vic was leaning against the front wall smoking.

'It like this every night?'

Vic shrugged. 'The shebeens move. Police might raid this one and it'll pop up again in a different basement a few doors down. Or they'll turn it into a gambling den.'

'Can we get them to keep it down a bit?'

Vic laughed.

'Why?'

'That old couple don't know whether they're coming or going.'

'Going suits me just fine.'

'I don't get it. What does this Rachman character want?'

'Listen, few years ago he bought sixteen houses in a street round the corner. The state of them, he paid eight grand for the lot. Since then, he's made over thirty thousand from them. Cleared out the tenants,

chucked a bit of matchstick furniture in so he can rent them uncon-
trolled, and brought in the coloureds. He'll probably sell them on for
a hundred grand in a year or two.'

Ray looked at the three lads playing silly beggars with paintbrushes.

'And the more blacks you move in, the lower the prices of other
properties on the street.'

'Now you're thinking like a real-estate man.'

Ray got stuck into the painting, but when the others showed no
desire to get anything done with any haste, he jacked it in. Didn't
want to stick out, be the only one giving it some grease. They were there
until gone two, the Cudsworths up with them the whole time, peering
out of their living room every now and then.

Vic told them to knock off for the night, leaving all the gear in
the hallway. Agamemnon tried telling him they could come back
in the morning, but he wouldn't hear of it.

'Couldn't do that to you, sir. Ruin your plans for the day. We'll be
back same time tomorrow night.'

Sheets bundled up and dumped in the corner, paint stains on the
rug, they left as they'd arrived, like a storm making landfall. On the
way out, Vic had a word with the same black kid he saw coming in,
and money changed hands. He dropped Ray off at his front door and
palmed him a tenner.

'What's this?'

'Pay. Week up front, get you settled.'

'We were only there a few hours.'

'It's not work that's value is counted in hours, Ray. I could do with
someone to look after the others when I'm not there. You've seen what
they're like. Fine if there's someone about to tell them what to do, but
otherwise . . .'

'I probably sound like a daft one, but I thought we'd actually be
doing decorating.'

'Ray, this work isn't just one thing. The rooms need to be sorted out. When they're free, they'll need a going-over and a bit of furniture putting in them. I need someone I can trust to do that, otherwise I'm running round hundreds of rooms.'

'Yeah.'

'Housing is shark-infested waters, Ray. But it's legal. Technically.'

What other sort of legal was there? thought Ray.

27

THE HUSBANDRY OF SMALL FAVOURS

Wearing a stolen fur coat, Addie fled Brixton in a motorcar at midnight the day after her mother died, landing in Notting Hill a fugitive.

Stevie had failed to wake up the previous morning. Addie didn't think anything of it at first; it wasn't like Stevie was ever an early riser. True, she usually made herself known, but her sleeping in a few hours felt like a gift as it was still the summer holidays and Addie had to get Nees ready and packed off with her mates before she could go to work.

'Shoes are talking,' Nees said, walking in such a way to highlight her soles were flapping at the toes. Addie didn't have the money for new ones and was trying to wait until the start of term before getting them fixed. That plan looked shot.

'Have to do for the day. See if I can fix them later.'

'I could fall over crossing the road and get run over by a car.'

'You want it written down you died because your shoes were talking?'

'No.'

'No, that'd be pretty stupid. So you better be careful walking, then.'

Nees said she was going to her friend Jeanne's place to practise with their hair, but it was more likely they'd scour the building sites of the new Loughborough Estate for whatever materials they could scavenge and sell to the scrap man beneath the railway arches for pocket money.

When she finally set off, walking in great high steps to avoid tripping over her loose soles, Addie went over to Maggie Moxon's caravan to pick up some clothes to work on. When her shifts at the factory started late, she spent her mornings doing repairs and alterations for Maggie's stock. Men were always turning up in small vans at odd times, delivering unusual heaps of clothing to her. It was better not to know, was what Maggie told Addie.

The caravan was unlocked, but Maggie was out. A few things were laid out on the small table with a note. Addie perused the racks of garments that filled all the spare space. A fur coat found her fingers, dark beaver lamb with what Addie could only describe as a subtle marmalade cast. It smelled faintly of mothballs, but that only added to the glamour. Slipping it from its hanger, she tried it on, peering over racks of clothes to see herself in the full-length mirror on the front of the caravan's tiny built-in wardrobe. She was sure whatever animals were in it had been killed just for her.

When she'd done turning this way and that, she hung it back up with a small sigh and took the clothes Maggie had left out for her back to the bus. Boiling water for tea, she went to ask Stevie if she wanted a cup, and that was when she discovered something was wrong. Addie knew nothing of the human body really, but of this she was certain.

'Mum, you fancy a cup? Mum? Mummy?'

Stevie's eyes remained open with typically censorial glister, but that was all about her that shone. She had slackened, like fruit gone soft, and though she breathed still, speech was beyond her.

Addie wasn't sure who she should call.

The doctor? Maggie would have his number.

She really thought Stevie should be in the hospital, though.

Grainger had a phone, but Addie didn't want him involved. It was bad enough the way every day he indirectly reminded her of what he considered to be favours bestowed.

'A blessing, access to copious fresh water,' he'd say, spotting Addie carting a sloshing bucket from the washhouse to the bus.

'Imagine where you'd be without a roof over your head,' when she wore four layers to stave off the cold during the white snarl of winter.

God alone knew how he'd husband the granting of an urgent telephone call.

She darted across Coldharbour Lane to her phone box, the one she spoke to Chabon on. Over the river at the far end of the city stood a matching booth on Artesian Road in Colville. Chabon had made calls to her from the box outside the Duke of Cornwall, but the locals there felt his face was showing itself too often outside their window and ripped out the handset in protest of his being black and present. The Artesian Road booth was neatly tucked round the corner of an antiques shop and attracted no such unwelcome attention.

The operator told her an ambulance would be dispatched immediately. Returning to the yard, she took the tarp off the old bicycle Chabon had bought for her to ride to work, and ducked back inside the bus to wait for the ambulance. She clutched Stevie's hand, but felt nothing back. Breathing still, though unresponsive. When she was young, Addie had always thought of death as a brief visitor, calling quietly at night to swiftly usher away the peacefully departed. That wasn't the case. Death was a guest who overstayed their welcome. Death lingered for days or months or years, never cleaning up after itself, never picking up the tab. It necessitated new habits and routines. Death meant new ways of living.

The bells of the ambulance were uncommonly loud, drawing Addie out of the bus. She directed the crew inside, and they soon had Stevie on a thin stretcher and onto one of the beds in the rear of their van. Addie was consumed with logistical thinking. She gathered some of Stevie's bits together in a bag, things she would never quietly suffer the absence of, even at the end. She told the driver she'd follow them on her bike, wanting a way to get back quickly in case she needed to fetch Nees. Grainger, who'd been dodging summonses to appear at court over some issue to do with the rent he paid for the extended yard, watched all this through his nets.

Addie pedalled hard, able to stay with the Daimler in traffic as they headed for King's College Hospital up Coldharbour Lane, but as ever Stevie was a lost cause. She arrived in the throes of a seizure and went downhill precipitously, passing away before Addie could be shown in to see her. When she got to the room where Stevie lay, she dithered outside, sneaking glances through the small door-light, vacillating nervously. A sheet had been drawn up beneath her mother's chin. She didn't look at all well.

Information was being thrown at Addie like prices of fruit at market. Everything was extraordinarily vivid, and while she was soaking up the rich surroundings – the glassy shine of the floor, the porter like a workshop teacher with his thin overcoat, the quiver of the doctor's downy jowls as he spoke – crucial details, such as how exactly her mother became dead, she couldn't swear to.

'She wouldn't like that,' Addie said, interrupting.

The doctor stopped, looked through the door at Stevie.

'She wouldn't like being seen like that. Looking like that. She hasn't liked to be seen for quite some time now.'

The jowly old doctor nodded to a nurse, who went in and pulled the sheet over Stevie's head. Suddenly there were a lot of decisions to make, but very few options. She needed Chay, but they didn't have a call arranged for that morning. She wouldn't know what to do until she saw him, though. Excusing herself from the doctor, she walked hurriedly outside and found her bike. Cycling hard up the Camberwell Road and through Elephant and Castle, she crossed over the river beneath Big Ben, cutting through the parks and past the palace, making it up to Chabon's a little over an hour after she left.

She arrived in a state, tears lost in the sweat from her ride. Conrad opened the door. From his face, he knew something was wrong, but his attitude toward what he called women and their emotional turmoil was generally to take a horror, so he didn't ask, telling her Chabon was out.

'Only ran up the Lane to get some food for later. He be back in no time,' he said, steering her into Chabon's room, closing the door and returning to the sanctuary of his own.

Shortly thereafter, Chabon rolled her bike into his room, having found it on the street outside.

'I'm not saying everyone's a thief round here, but best not to—'

He stopped, finding her sitting on the floor beside his bed in floods of tears.

'Sorry about him,' he said, squeezing down beside her and wrapping a long arm round her shoulders, pulling her in close.

It took him a while to work it all out, and almost as long to persuade her to lie on the bed for a while so he could hold her. He made them sandwiches and then they rode back to Brixton, Addie on the seat behind him as he stood and worked the pedals. Whenever they stopped in traffic, she laid her head on his back and held him tight. The first stop they made was at the chemise factory where Addie worked, getting there just as her shift was due to begin. She spoke to the foreman and explained the situation. Death or no, he wasn't happy about it, but Addie was handier with the serger than most and he didn't want to lose her, so munificently he gave her the shift off unpaid.

At the hospital, Addie was more circumspect. Stevie was there somewhere – still beneath the sheet on the bed? Or had she been moved into the company of the other departed? – and beset with that knowledge she felt small and childlike and likely to flub her lines. Chabon adopted the same voice he did with any white folk in uniform and asked questions and found out what was expected of them regarding the body.

They walked back down Coldharbour Lane, Chabon wheeling the bike.

'We need the funeral people to collect her. Arrange for a burial and everything, they deal with all that.'

'There isn't any money, Chay.'

'We'll sort it out.'

'We live in a bus, and I'm not even sure how much that's going to cost me now, or whether we'll be allowed to stay. And what about Nees? She's— Oh shit!'

'What?'

'Look at the time. She said she'd be back before tea, and there'll be nobody there. And Maggie doesn't know what's going on.'

Chabon swung a leg over the bike and stood in front of the saddle.

'On you get.'

She sat behind him and he rode for home, beneath the three bridges of Loughborough Junction and zipping through light traffic where the road felt tighter than it was with looming mansion flats one side and garden trees leaning over them from the other. At speed, he glided onto Canterbury Crescent in a wide arc and slowed to turn into the yard just before the railway viaduct.

Nees was violently rattling the door to a storage shed and screaming at Grainger, who stood shell-shocked as if in the immediate aftermath of dropping a tray of priceless crystal glasses. Addie ran to her sister as she yanked the tarp off a pile of busted old furniture, shoving things aside in her search for Stevie, who clearly couldn't have been taken off in an ambulance as Grainger had helpfully told her.

Addie grabbed her and held her until she was done struggling.

'Where is she?' Nees said.

'She hasn't been well for a while.'

'But where is she?'

'They took her to see the doctors at the hospital and—'

'Addie.'

She couldn't say it. The thing most likely to happen in their lives, the least surprising thing of all, and she couldn't find how to tell her sister.

'Mr Grainger said they took her.'

'He shouldn't have said anything to you,' Addie said, glaring at him over Nees's shoulder.

Grainger took his leave, lightly stepping away and disappearing into his house.

'I looked under the bus,' Nees said. 'And in the trunk of the old car.'

'I'm sorry. I'm so sorry.'

'She's not coming back.'

'No.'

'What happens to us?'

Addie squeezed her. 'We'll make do, won't we?'

The next morning, Nees was adamant she wanted to go to the summer club.

Nannie Binns, an impossibly old Jamaican lady who kept house for the nightclub owner Gus Leslie in his big house round the corner on Gresham Road, volunteered at the church in Angell Town and ran a club twice a week through the holidays that was open to all children.

Addie wasn't sure either way. She hadn't yet informed anyone officially of Stevie's passing, though she was due to visit the town hall and see the registrar that morning. Once the wheels were in motion, she was terrified of what would happen, whether Nees would be taken from her.

'You don't have to go.'

'Told Nannie I'd be there to help her set up.'

'I can go down and explain to her about Mum.'

Nees looked mortified. 'You can't tell her.'

'Why not? She going to find out sometime.'

'When Horace Kenny's dad got kiddy stones, Nannie made everyone pray for him and Horace had to stand up, and I don't want to stand up and be prayed at.'

'Nobody needs that.'

'Will you be in when I get back today?'

'I'll be at work, but Maggie's here.'

Nees seemed happy enough with that and trotted off. There was an hour before Addie had to be at the town hall, so she put the kettle on to give herself something to do.

'Not at work?'

She jumped at the voice, Grainger's face poking in the door of the bus.

'Shift starts at noon.'

'Little one off to her club, I see.'

'What can I do for you, Mr Grainger?'

'What happened with your mother, a tragedy obviously. And there's no good time to have this conversation, but there is the matter of the rent. You see—'

'How much you want, Mr Grainger?'

'Well, it's not as simple as all that. Your mother and I had an understanding, and we hadn't revisited that understanding since you moved in. I'd have to take into account changes in the market over the years, and the new Rent Act, of course, things of that nature. Two bedrooms and a living room with stove, completely enclosed from other—'

'It's a broke-down old bus.'

'Don't think I can say fairer than three and a half guineas.'

'You must be joking. Unless you mean a month?'

'Since you're tenants of long standing, I suppose I can see my way to accepting three guineas. A week.'

'Could sleep on the street for three guineas less and not be missing much.'

'You know me to be a flexible man, Adlyn. I'm sure I could reduce the rent substantially, were we to perhaps reach our own understanding.'

Addie laughed out loud.

'You've lost your mind. Clear out of your head.'

'Three and a half guineas by tomorrow, then. For this week's rent. And then another three and a half for next week in, say, three days?'

'This week?'

'Well, your mother passed away during the week, so that really voids our understanding. I think that's only fair. More than fair, really, when you consider the particulars of my understanding with her became impractical some time ago.'

Addie stepped toward him, forcing him to stumble backwards off the step of the bus entrance.

'I'm dreadful sorry that my mother was too ill for a shag, Mr Grainger. I can see how that must have inconvenienced you. And Mrs Grainger hasn't really been available to you either for quite some time, has she?'

'Now look, I think—'

'Have you considered it might be being with you that turns these women off prick for life, Mr Grainger? That maybe just the thought provokes some crisis of the spirit in them?'

'I can see you're upset, so I'll leave until you're of a more cordial temperament. At which point I'll expect my three and a half guineas.'

Lolloping away as fast as his fleshy middle-aged legs could carry him, he was breathless by the time he reached his door.

'Three and a half guineas for what, Red?'

Addie turned to find Everso watching thoughtfully as Grainger stumbled into his house.

'Everso.'

'Sorry about Stevie. She was something fierce. Figured her to out-live us all.'

'She's been dying for years.'

Chabon was already trying to dissolve into the background, the conversation starting about as well as he'd expected it to.

'You register the death and all that yet?'

Addie shook her head. 'I'm going to the town hall in a bit.'

'I come with you.'

'I can manage myself.'

'Spoke to a man I know. He has a white-man city law firm he put me onto. And he knows a one-armed MP who's a barrister who'll have a quiet word here and there.'

'A quiet word for what?'

'Make sure you her guardian.'

'Nees?'

'Tell them you coming to live with your uncle. Roof over your head, clothes on your back. Food in your belly. No problems.'

Addie laughed.

'Understand, I'm not going to do nothing, Red. You look out for your sister. But the courts not going to put no eighteen-year-old girl in charge of a child if they got no place to live that isn't a bus. They take her away. You want that?'

She looked to Chabon.

'He's right. It's the best way to do it.'

'Michael Manly has no record,' Everso said. 'Far as they know, he's got a job and a home, and for the court that's as respectable as a black fella gets.'

'Who's paying for the lawyers?' Addie said.

'Don't worry about that,' Everso said. 'When you have one of their lawyers, you only need to use them like a weapon. The threat of them is enough.'

So it was.

Everso accompanied Addie to Lambeth Town Hall, brandishing the name of a Holborn law firm at everyone he met, and Stevie's death was officially accounted for. Nobody asked about her children or what would become of them, for the gears of the state's byzantine bureaucracy had only begun to grind. And Everso would be ready to battle them at their own particular game.

Addie worked her shift and returned home to Chabon snapping down dominoes with Nees, stewed saltfish and dasheen on the stove, and most of their belongings packed up in pillowcases and the one suitcase they owned that hadn't fallen apart. She sat beside him and laid her head on his shoulder.

'We're leaving tonight. I got a room for you, next to me and Pa. Nothing special, but it's got beds and walls made of brick.'

'All right,' Addie said, happy someone else was making decisions.

'Hungry?' he said.

She shook her head. 'Smells good, though.'

'I had two bowls,' Nees said. 'It has blue in it.'

'There's some of Stevie's stuff still in there,' Chabon said, nodding to the other end of the bus.

'Leave it,' Addie said. 'Let Grainger deal with it.'

She fought the temptation to burn the bus the ground.

'We should leave, if we want to get buses,' she said.

'Thought we'd see about getting Miss Amabel's fella to drive us.'

Everyone in Brixton knew Miss Amabel. She lived in a flat next to the bank just down from the big furniture shop on the corner of Brixton Road with her cousin Derrick, who everyone knew wasn't really her cousin. A skilled mechanic, Derrick did his own jobs in his spare time, working on cars in the cleared bomb site that had been a church. He owned a second-hand Hillman Minx, the old-fashioned shape, and operated an unofficial taxi service for locals returning from West End clubs. Chabon was hoping to catch him going in the other way at the start of his night.

They piled their luggage outside, Nees holding the pot of stew with string binding the lid tight, and had one last look around. Addie was itching to get away from the place.

'Surely not fleeing without paying the rent you owe?'

Grainger had made his way down from his house, standing hands on hips in the yard.

'What you looking for?' Chabon said, pulling money from his pocket and walking toward the older man. 'Three guineas?'

'Three and a half,' Grainger said, less sure of himself.

Chabon counted money out as he moved, walking Grainger backwards until he fell over a holey bucket and landed on his back, arms up over his head in protection. Chabon slapped his hands away and stuffed three pound notes in the man's mouth. He counted the coins out and dropped them on him one by one.

'All paid up.'

Grainger spat the notes out, coughing.

'I'll have you over for this!'

'Yes, let's call the police, shall we? Let's get them down here.'

Grainger demurred, scrambling round in the dirt for his change.

Addie, taken aback by seeing some of Everso in Chabon, laid a hand on his arm.

'Chay, let's go.'

He grabbed up the suitcase in one hand and two pillowcases of clanging pots in the other.

'Oh,' Addie said, running off suddenly to Maggie's caravan, where she whipped the fur coat from its hanger and pulled it on. She grabbed the remaining pillowcase and wheeled her bicycle out of the yard, Nees on the saddle clutching her pot of stew.

Calling on Miss Amabel, they found Derrick had not yet left for the West End. After fraught negotiations, in which Miss Amabel intervened on their behalf with a furious stare directed in Derrick's direction, he agreed to take them to the Grove for a modest fee.

With the bicycle lashed to the spare wheel on the rear, they set off, all sat in the back, with Nees, for whom cars were something new, gawping out the window. Addie sat in the middle, one hand squeezing Chabon's, the other running through her new fur coat. She believed a person developed their full range of tools according to their longings, and feeling the weight of her mother lifted, she was ready to start over somewhere else, with new longings.

She could feel her luck recharging.

She was at large.

28

THE FAT IN THE WALLS

Lander had ideas.

He picked up a ten-year-old Lambretta, easy for scooshing around traffic on. Getting used to riding the thing, he reacquainted himself with the neighbourhood.

Crumbling houses.

Boarded-up shops.

On Bramley Road, kids burned garbage in an empty lot.

Down on Holland Park Avenue, the stucco houses grew wider and were separated by greenery. He scooted east through the West End and down to Piccadilly, all buses and cabs. At St Paul's he found the first evidence of a new London, office developments springing up near the river, large cranes swinging through the air.

To the north, Cripplegate was the same wasteland he'd left behind, now almost twenty years since the bombing levelled it. A honeycomb of cellars and foundations, the weeds and bushes wilder than ever. Boys kicked a football through what had once been a basement, and another housed the small enterprise of a scrapyard.

At Smithfield, he stopped to look at the remains of the poultry market building. In prison, he'd heard about the fire that ravaged the place a few months earlier, seen a few pictures in the papers, but in person it seemed crazy. An echo of the war.

'Fat in the walls.'

A constable had sidled up, surveying the charred ruins with him. Lander glanced around quickly, wondering if this was how it happened. Every second he was free, he expected some welcome or warning from coppers or a firm, letting him know whose city it was.

'That's what they say,' the copper continued. 'So much animal fat soaked into the cork insulation over the years, when the fire broke out the whole lot went up like it'd been doused in petrol.'

'I've been away. Hadn't seen it.'

'They'll have it rebuilt in a couple of years.'

'That's what they said after the war.'

'A city can survive with fewer houses, but not less meat. They're already up and running in the temporary market there. Soon it'll be as if this little blight never happened.'

Ain't that the way with us all, Lander thought.

The constable nodded and moved on, and Lander kicked the Lambretta into action and rolled up St John Street, parking in the mouth of Peter's Lane, in the cool shadow of a warehouse. A swastika painted on the brickwork had survived someone's feeble attempt to clean it, though one of its arms bent anticlockwise. Backing the scooter up so he just poked out round the corner, he had a good view of the Kingdom Cold Storage premises.

Billy Hill might have been the boss of the underworld, might have been the man behind everything, but there was a man behind the man. Out in the wild, Mother was king. While Billy financed headline robberies and invested in property development, it was Mother running crews and cutting throats. It was Mother making them eat brass in the streets. It was Mother sending Benny the Jew into Lander's cell to get fatal.

You only kill someone if they absolutely need killing. And even then, you don't kill them.

Billy wouldn't have been within a million miles of Benno Kosoff. That would all have been Mother. And if either Billy or Mother wanted to know Lander was out, it wouldn't be difficult, the connections they had in London prisons and the police. He suspected Bob Lee was right – they didn't care any more. Lander hadn't spoken to the police, even after they'd sent Benny. Of course, he hadn't figured that for Mother's doing, but from their point of view it hadn't led to him turning rat.

Maybe they thought what was done was done.

They were wrong.

Six years of his life taken from him. Six hard years inside, known as a bent copper. That was before he even got to the money they told him had gone up in smoke. He was going to have to see someone about that.

For a couple of hours he watched vans coming and going, nothing but meat and the various appurtenances of the cold store business. He recognised nobody. Restless, he risked crossing the road to the tobacconist to get himself some snouts and a paper. While he was in there, the old Morris rolled up, waiting for traffic to pass to turn into the archway to the Kingdom. Behind the wheel sat Mother, and it harrowed Lander to his core that the man looked the same as he ever did.

Ageless, hands of the clock taking nothing from him.

The next morning, Lander followed the General's tip and set up to watch the side entrance on Monmouth Road to the basement offices of a shop on Westbourne Grove. He smoked Woodies and for breakfast ate an iced bun from the baker's opposite the shop. Not much happened in the morning. A couple of doors down on his side of the road, a father took his son into the Freeman Hardy Willis, both carrying what looked like fishing rods and a bait box. When they came out twenty minutes later, the boy was wearing a huge grin and a new pair of boots. Lander wondered where they were headed to fish. The canal? Was that possible? Perhaps there were secret London fishing spots that people like him were unaware of.

As the day wore on, he felt as if he stood out like a brickie's thumb, so crossed the road and parked the scooter up in a debris site fifty yards down the side road from the shop he was watching. It had grown wild since the war, trees maturing to dominate the small green space, and he sat in the shade of one like anyone enjoying a free afternoon in the sun.

A Rolls-Royce turned into the road, which offered no thorough-fare, rolled down to the end and turned, coming back up and parking across from the basement door. A dark, sturdy-looking chap got out from the driver's side and opened the rear door for Papa Rachman, all turned out in sharkskin with shades, looking like a gangster from a movie.

Lander choked. 'Jesus dancing Christ.'

The heavy looked up and down the road, entirely failing to notice the bearded interloper lying against a tree beside a beaten-to-shit old scooter, and followed Papa into the basement offices. Not long after, a couple of West Indian youths showed up.

In and out, Lander followed them on the scooter as they chopped north into the Colville area. Over the next few hours, he trailed them to half a dozen buildings, grand old stucco townhouses that must once have soared but were now beaten down into slums.

Rent collectors-cum-racketeers, they must have been going door to door inside, each room in the huge houses a separate dwelling, proba-bly for multiple people. Lander was beginning to put together the wheeze – Rachman had the West Indian lads collect the rent. Proba-bly farmed the job out to them; so long as they paid him a minimum fee each week, they could keep whatever else they collected. He added dirty cash Mother gave him from Billy Hill's operations, and paid it back to them as legitimate returns on property investments. The new laws allowing landlords to charge whatever they wanted, coupled with the few options available to West Indian immigrants arriving in the capital, allowed them to clear fortunes in the rental transactions. Ties that were just beginning to be forged six years earlier had obviously solidified.

Billy's money got legitimised, the West Indian gang got bundles of cash and control of the slums, Papa took fees out of both ends and got to drive round west London in a Rolls.

Everyone was happy.

Lander was going to have a marvellous time ruining everything.

The collectors looped back round to an old stucco palace south of Westbourne Grove, near a library that hadn't been there before Lander went away. The house's black tenants were outliers in their street but illustrated the sprawl of Papa Rachman's little empire. On Holland Park Road, the youths jumped on an 88 headed for Shepherd's Bush, and Lander left them to it, having seen enough.

He'd been hankering after some good Italian since he got out, but Soho was a bit of a trek for a nosh. There was Bertorelli's in Bayswater, if it was still there, but everything about his life until that moment suggested he had the kind of luck to run into Billy and Gyp there. There were probably a ton of new places down Holland Park and Church Street, but he didn't know them. He turned up Princedale Road, which stretched up along the Norland and into the Dale.

Fish supper, probably, but a pint first.

He left the scooter outside the Prince of Wales and went into the lounge. It wasn't busy, and the barman was the breviloquent type, communicating in grunts. Lander finished his drink and left. Outside, an old bone-grubber had begged a pail of water from the pub and his horse drank sloppily. His cart was scanty for a day's collecting.

Lander kicked the scooter into action and backed up off the kerb, turning to see a woman across the road holding a camera, taking a picture, hair kiting on the breeze. She lowered the camera slowly, looking at him, and he was suddenly privy to those things one only learns with the stopping of the heart.

Delaney put down the phone and Claire surreptitiously took three photographs of him, his expression hard to pin down.

'Everything all right?'

He looked at her for a long moment before answering.

'The lead actor died in a car crash last night.'

'What? Golders Green?'

He nodded. 'It was the production's last night in Liverpool, and he went off the road afterwards.'

'Oh God, how awful.'

'I know him. Knew him.'

'You said.'

'Pretty sure he got me the work. It wasn't much, but still.'

'Are they cancelling?'

'Cancelling? Good Lord, no. The stage director is taking over for the Hippodrome dates. Jesus, they'd all have to die for anyone to even consider cancelling. One of the supporting actors was in the car too. Survived, but he's in bad shape, apparently.'

They tidied away in silence. Recently they'd been working for good productions in the West End, and it was a surprise when Delaney accepted the work for the touring Broadway production's week-long stint at the Golders Green Hippodrome. He had mentioned a few times that he knew the lead actor from previous productions, and though Claire knew his name (it had shone brighter on marquees in the past than it did now), she hadn't realised they'd been close.

'He lived in Chiswick,' Delaney said, with a knowing look.

'Chiswick isn't a place. It's an idea.'

He grinned, knowing her feelings on the matter.

'You have Hammersmith and Brentford, and in between you have people with notions.'

He let her go early as there was nothing to do except wait for a truck that was collecting some scenery.

'I'm taking the camera.'

'Fine. See you tomorrow.'

She took photos of the scenery they built, both in the studio and *in situ* at theatres, where she also took portraits of actors as she was developing a bit of a name for that sort of thing. It was a pre-war folding Zeiss she worked with, something Delaney had picked up years ago.

He had a darkroom upstairs in the studio, but had no real interest in it himself and was more than happy to delegate all the photography to Claire.

What she really liked doing was walking the neighbourhood and taking pictures. The buildings, the people, the feel of the place. The glue that held it all together. Even her short walk home could yield something of interest, as it did now with a rag-and-bone man's horse and cart pulled up outside the Prince of Wales. Face like mudcracks, the man removed a glove to stroke the animal's nose, and it rubbed its head against his, feeling his breath on its nostrils and nickering contentedly.

Claire took a couple of shots. A man was getting on his scooter behind the cart, a contrast that interested her, so she snapped off a couple more before he turned and something inside her fell into a pit.

There was no doubt.

Bearded, and older than she remembered, but it was him. Her hand went to her own face as she tried to see him through the hair.

'Claire?'

'David. My God.'

He rolled the scooter across the road, standing it by the kerb.

'How are you?'

'I'm fine. When did . . . I didn't know you still lived round here.'

'They only let me out a few days ago. I've got a room in a gaff up off Bramley Road.'

'A few days ago? I thought . . .'

'There were added complications.'

She nodded.

'Copper goes to prison and . . . you know. There was a fight.'

She nodded again, for the life of her unable to dredge up the smallest of talk.

'Someone was hurt,' he persisted, though she quite had the picture. 'They gave me more time.'

'I see,' she said, as if he'd missed a bus.

Beneath his beard, his face took on a tropical burn. He leaned awkwardly on the scooter.

'Camera,' he said idiotically.

'My boss's. He lets me use it.'

'Considerate.'

He looked across at the ragman, who thankfully took hold of the reins and led the horse on, cartwheel complaining as they went. They watched it roll squeakily up the road for a full minute, one which felt as if it began sometime in the Middle Ages.

'Doesn't look like he had a particularly fruitful day,' Lander said.

One more nod or an 'I see' would set them back another excruciating minute, so Claire said the first thing she could think of.

'I like to take photographs in the street.'

'The ragman.'

'Yes. People, if I can. But buildings are good too.'

He glanced the other way down the street. 'Not much has changed in the Dale. Not as much as I thought it would have. Another television channel, though.'

'We don't have a set.'

'No, neither do I. Heard about it, is all.'

'It's good, they say. *Sunday Night at the London Palladium.*'

'Yes.'

They fell into lethal silence again, and the scooter took the opportunity to tilt precariously beneath his weight, causing him to stumble in the process of keeping it from falling. In her mind, she saw herself reaching out and taking a firm grip of the handlebars and they'd both laugh and chat easily, and then she thought of her husband, Fred.

Lander sat on the scooter.

'Can I buy you a drink? A cup of coffee?'

'I don't think so, David.'

'No. I suppose not.'

'What are you doing here?'

The idea was forming that he had tracked her down, had been waiting for her in the pub across from her house.

'I was out for a ride,' he said, pointing vaguely toward Holland Park, 'and stopped for a pint. And as I said, I live just up in the Dale. Right under the railway, really. Trains rattle the window.'

He was babbling and couldn't look her in the eyes. His bony laugh petered out into more silence.

'Claire, that night . . .'

'David—'

'What happened at the Enterprise, when you helped me home. I've always felt I should apologise.'

'For what?'

'I don't know. I didn't do anything. Things were done to me, but—'

'David, I don't care about that night. I don't now and I didn't then.'

'I had the thought you were angry with me.'

'I was. But not about that.'

He frowned, a confused little boy. A twinning rage and fear rose dangerously inside her.

'Perhaps you don't recall the night of the biggest robbery ever seen. The night my husband went missing and never came back. If you really want to apologise, maybe there's something you can tell me about that.'

Lander said nothing.

Could say nothing.

'Teddy drugged you. Beat you. Did whatever he did to you, all because he thought you were a copper. And he was right, you were a copper. And the police arrested you, and charged you, and jailed you, all because they thought you were bent. And they were right, you were bent. And in the middle of all that, you were worried about what I thought? When you knew all along what had happened to Freddie?'

'Claire, I don't—'

'The very least you can do for me is not lie.'

She didn't want to see his face. Could remember what his gaze on her felt like, what it did to her, and fastened her eyes instead on a spot in front of her feet, took a deep breath.

'Is that why you approached me in the first place? Were you working for Teddy or for the police?' She held up a hand. 'Actually, I don't want to know. I doubt even you know.'

She laughed sharply.

'Years ago, I told myself if I ever saw you again, I'd simply walk away. I've rebuilt my life and this isn't something I need. You aren't something I need.'

'You're right. I'm sorry. I just saw you and it was . . . I'm sorry.'

He kicked the lever and the Lambretta coughed into life. She didn't move as he pulled away, sped off into the Dale. Inside, she put down her bag and camera. Hands shaking. She burred with a fitful anger, prowling from room to room, seeing not the house but some inner space bursting with squalls of emotions she couldn't name. Since she lost Fred and Joe, she had quietly knitted herself a life she was very content with, very comfortable in. Now the edges were fraying.

Upstairs, she filled two laundry bags, one with whites and bedding for the bagwash, the other with clothes. She grabbed a few items from Peg's room before looking in Ray's. It was neat, what little he had squared away; years at sea had done that for him. The cupboard and drawers were well organised, but she noticed a few things poking out of his bag. A quick sniff determined they should be added to the laundry bag.

Beneath them, she found Fred's old forage cap, which she thought had been lost years ago. She smiled, glad Ray had kept it all this time. Tucked in under that was something hard and small, a mother-of-pearl handle from which snapped a stiletto blade when she pressed the button. When it came down to it, she really knew nothing of her son's life. When he was away, he occupied very few of her thoughts, but now he was home, she was worried about him. He'd always been easily led into foolishness, something the order of the merchant navy had disguised. It didn't look like stupidity, not exactly. It was something else, something harder to fathom, something more shameful. She'd never taken the time to work it out, and his involvement with Vic Barlow, who'd always been half a crook at best, was a concern. And now David pops up right outside her home. Could she believe that? Had he come looking for her?

Worry was as useless as prayer. She replaced the knife and cap and picked up the laundry bags. The walk to the baths would open up that inner space within her mind. On her way out, she grabbed the camera.

Lander battled the itch to look back as he rode away from Claire.

His thoughts of dinner gave way to a craving for something else he had missed since going away, and he headed for Ladbroke Grove, for the Elgin. No different to when he knew it years earlier, it was still home to hustlers and drifters and prostitutes and spivs. It was early, but some lifers were already in there. He ordered a swift half and gave the nod to a brunette sitting alone with an empty glass.

'G&T,' she said.

He brought their drinks over and sat down, sinking most of his in a long gulp.

'Hard day?'

'You could be Italian,' he said.

'I could be anything.'

'You got a place? Mine is no use.'

'Round the corner.'

He nodded, waiting quietly for her to finish her drink. She didn't dally. Outside, he showed her the scooter and she grinned. They buzzed round the corner onto Lancaster Road, and he chained the scooter to the railings on the porch steps.

'I'm on the top floor,' she said.

'Me too.'

Her room was neat and clean. He wasn't sure what he had expected.

She smiled and said, 'What do you know?' like she'd heard it somewhere, or in a movie perhaps.

Most of what he knew he wished he'd learned differently, or later than he did.

'You ever fished?' he said, sitting on her bed.

She laughed. 'No. I don't think so. No, never.'

'I've never fished either. I wonder what would happen if I just bought a boat and went fishing.'

'You need a boat?'

Lander didn't know. Could you even fish in the sea? He pictured the North Sea or the Channel. Fishing in those waters seemed like something for terse men with weather-hardened hands. Not dangling a rod off the side while drinking a martini. He really hadn't thought this through.

'I should move somewhere else. With a river I can fish. I wouldn't even have to catch anything.'

She laughed again, and he removed his shoes.

29

WHITE CITY, BROWN TOWN

Ray was in his element.

Saturday afternoon down Bramley Road with the chaps, following the circuit: the Feathers on Silchester and along to the Barn, before turning into Bramley and hitting the York, the Station, and rolling down to the bottom where the Arms faced off with the Trafalgar. They were in the Dale, cash in hand, and life was good.

No work on Fridays or Saturdays. Clive explained Friday was rent day, and took through to the next night for all of it to get gathered. Didn't want to be in there causing a bother when the boys were collecting, might give the tenants grounds for complaint. Not that many complained to the gunslingers who came knocking. Fucking Wild West round the Town.

Busier than usual, everyone said. Daytrippers in the Dale on the bevvy, pubs packed and spilling out into the street. A barney beneath the arches at Piggery Junction the night before, some Jamaican and his white trollop got out of hand and a few lads hanging out under the viaduct jeered them on, which in turn got a bit physical, and some of his West Indian mates had come out and there had ensued a melee. That sort of thing might go over in Brown Town, but this was the Dale.

So Bramley was lively. They'd travelled from all over, by car and motorbike, the kerbs lined like at the coast. Islington and Camden and Hampstead and some claimed to be from as far out as Reading. Ray was sitting among a crowd in the York, big old boozer just up from the railway bridge, where they'd run into some local lads and were buying them a few as the world was set to rights. Couple of them had come from down the exchange, over in Hammersmith near the Palais, and had their tales to tell.

'We're in there, drawing down what? Three, four quid at a push. And these spades come, barge into the queue like always, which . . . let's don't even get into that, and then they get seven and eight quid put in their hand. What's all that about?'

'Seen it with my own eyes.'

Gorgeous day, sun beating down, all the girls in their dresses. Ray in khakis and a short-sleeved shirt, no need for a jacket. He'd already been next door for an ice cream at Mancini's, nudging Clive that it'd be an idea to get some for the girls. Everyone knew Mancini's, mostly because the old boy's son, Alf, had been a useful welterweight, about as good as you could get without winning a strap, but also because his mother had modelled for the Queen Victoria statue on the Mall.

Then a couple of them came out of Latimer Road station, and the jeers went up outside. They knew better than to dilly-dally, on their heels up Lancaster Road and back toward the Town pronto. The singing started and everyone moved out into the street. 'Bye Bye Blackbird' and 'Ol' Man River'. Ray barely knew the words, but it didn't matter. The choruses were easy to pick up after a few renditions, and then the more imaginative drinkers started reworking the lyrics.

A garden fire sent dark wisps up over the houses and someone cried out that it had started.

'We're firebombing the darkies out.'

Laughing and cheering, arms round each other's shoulders, they sang on, and the smoke in the late sun reminded Ray of his childhood and the mattress fires on the corner.

This was what it was to be alive.

Lander sat on his scooter and watched Papa Rachman's office. Hours at it, gutter coffee and curling sandwiches from a nearby caff, fingers betraying how much he smoked. A steady stream of lowlifes and other pilgrims pouring round the corner from the main drag and in through the basement door, Fridays and Saturdays busy days, rent days, the cash accumulating.

Banks closed early and wouldn't be open Sunday, meaning Rachman would deposit it Monday. He had muscle, and an Alsatian too, but even so the behaviour surprised Lander. Pros would stay clear, knowing not to take off anything Billy Hill was involved with, unless they were looking to unnecessarily complicate their lives. But locals wouldn't know what company Rachman kept, just that he had stacks of readies come Monday.

Maybe someone had tried it once.

Maybe everyone knew better now.

Rachman left early, mid afternoon, no briefcases and no muscle. Lander decided to call it a day. He rode back east across the Lane and the Grove, things briefly getting leafier in the gardened streets of Notting Hill before Clarendon Road dropped like an axe and he was in the narrow passages of the Dale.

The Y-shaped junction where Bramley Road forked off Latimer was beset by crowds of idiots spilling out of the Arms and the Trafalgar with bottles and pint jugs. There were jeers and songs about blacks, and he heard chants go up about Little Rock.

He weaved a path through them.

Up the road, the usual gangs of local philosophers gathered in their lyceum beneath the railway arches. A couple pointedly refused to part for his scooter, as if they hadn't seen him. His knuckles whitened on the handlebars and he thought about taking the opportunity to work off a little steam.

But it was too close to home, and Mrs Mortimer wasn't one with patience to test. There were a lot of them, too, and an air of brewing menace. He gave them the psycho deathfuck stare, eyes barking, and they backed off.

Kids.

Chumps.

Give it double portions when there was a mob of them, but alone in an ill-lit room you'd find out all about them in no time. Some oohs behind his back as he lifted the scooter over the railings onto the ledge in the basement well and secured it.

Mrs Mortimer met him inside the door.

'They've been steadily building up all day, the little hooligans. There was shouting and yobbery last night under the arches, and this is set to be worse.'

'Should leave us alone. Sounds like they're after blacks, if they're after anyone.'

'I don't rent to coloureds. This is the kind of trouble they bring.'

She glanced out the door at the crowd of white youths.

'Now, I have made some stew, Mr Lander. Would you like a bowl?'

About to refuse, Lander realised he was starving. 'That'd be very nice, Mrs Mortimer.'

She hovered round the kitchen with a cup of tea as he ate, and served up rhubarb crumble for afters. Lander gratefully had seconds of both, but with the idea he was being touched up for something.

Bug-eyed Perry saw himself as an agent provocateur.

On the one hand, he worked his tasks diligently and unquestioningly for factory management, including handing out pay packets each week. On the other, he scanned the amounts in the ledger when the secretary wasn't looking and then pretended to guess the amounts from the weight of the small envelopes in his hand, often stating the number loudly on the floor, sowing disharmony among the staff.

'I'd say we were looking at over a fiver there,' he said, judging Addie's packet before handing it to her. 'Would you like me to turn my back while you count it?'

'Would you like me to turn my back while you go f—'

The factory whistle rendered her inaudible, but Perry got the gist.

It was Addie's final shift at the factory. She wasn't going to miss the journey to and from south London – three buses, two trains and a Perry (because he lived in Clapham and by *complete* coincidence had taken to bumping into her en route). She snuck out before he'd finished with the wages, jumping on a 35 to the Common, where she caught the tube to King's Cross.

By the time the Hammersmith & City was pulling into West-bourne Park, she was crackling with both excitement and anxiety. A weekend off; a party that night, her first in North Kensington; but no plan beyond Monday morning. Chabon had told her he'd pay the rent and look after her and Nees until she found work, and was encouraging her to take the opportunity to apply for nursing school. He and his father were right next door and would take care of Nees while she was away. It almost seemed too good to be true.

Back at Powis Terrace, Chabon met her at the street door, where he sat on the step of the porch talking with his cousin, Kindness, with whom he now had something threatening to be a friendship. His bullying of Chabon had stopped over the years, due to maturity of character and the four inches Chabon now had on him, which had shown themselves in a late-night incident a few years back when Kindness had, in the words of Chabon, 'become punched'.

'You boys had a hard day's graft.'

Chabon stretched his legs out. 'There was a while there just after lunch where it looked like it might rain.'

'Nees okay?'

'Yeah. She up there with Pa. Seems fine.'

Addie leaned against the stone pier at the foot of the porch steps. 'Could sleep for a week.'

'Yeah, let's do that,' Chabon said.

Kindness grinned. 'He don't want you seeing this party.'

She cocked an eyebrow. 'You not ready for me to see what you get up to when I was at the other end of the city?'

'It's not like that. See, you don't . . . These things . . . they're not for, you know . . .'

'Ladies?'

'Yeah.'

'So there'll be no women there?'

'No. Yeah. There will, but . . .'

'White women?'

'Yeah. No.' Chabon looked at Kindness. 'You going to help me out?'

'There'll be cat of all colour there.'

'Thanks,' Chabon said.

Addie stepped past them and through the front door. 'Better get dressed up, then.'

Nees was in the hallway on the top floor and greeted her with a grunt. Stevie's absence left a hole in her life she didn't understand, and she'd never been quite as exasperated at their mother as Addie. They had her enrolled in a new school already, though it didn't start until the following week, and Chabon or his father were looking after her until then. The old man had always taken more of a shine to her than he did to Addie, who he believed to be a mischief-maker.

Everso's friend Bess also lived in the building on their floor now (her previous digs on Rillington Place having been turned into Methodist meeting rooms after it turned out the grumpy white fella downstairs had been the real killer, mad old bastard murdering a whole mess of folk), and sometimes watched Nees as she shared her love of dominoes snapping on a table (albeit with rather more adherence to the rules than Nees usually suffered), and because she'd broken her foot and was laid up with little else to do.

Addie overlooked the grunt. Whenever she saw Nees, she summoned an appearance of bereavement in her face and voice and movements, in a feeble attempt at pretending she missed their mother. She was unsure whether grief was something that could be shared in the same way as an interest in dominoes or doling out cosmetics tips, and anyway she was terrible at even giving the impression.

At some point, she would be sad Stevie was gone, that was what she told herself. At some point it would dawn on her that she would never again have a conversation with her, never again hear her voice in any way. Her mum would be gone for ever. Until then, there was too much happening for her to properly consider the matter. They had moved to new surroundings, with new people, many of whom were already more closely involved in her life than anyone had been before.

Time acted up at the factory.

Days and nights didn't matter there, only shifts, early or late. Now she was done with the place, perhaps the order of her life would more closely resemble that of Nees, or of her own childhood.

She also had Chabon to resort to, who for years had been a more reliable presence than her mother, someone to hold onto who would hold back. What she felt more than anything was abandoned by her mother, and that was a sensation that had begun long before her death and verged on physical humiliation. Perhaps that was the first stage of grief, as grief was a thing never to arrive in the form you expected it to, and sometimes gatecrashed before death itself had turned up.

Washing facilities were, if anything, worse than at the bus. There was a single toilet in the house, downstairs on the upper ground floor, which had a single cold tap. There was no bathroom. Chabon had brought up a bucket so Addie didn't have to lug it three flights. He had a spirit stove in the room he shared with his dad, which he used to heat the room and to cook rice and peas because those peas, wherever they came from, had to be cooked overnight. He heated some of the water and mixed it back into the bucket to give Addie something tepid to wash with.

Couple of times a week, she dragged Nees out into the small yard downstairs at the rear, and they used the stove to warm up buckets of water to slosh over each other in their underwear as they washed. Regular trips to the baths would have to become part of their routine.

Addie dressed for unexpected events, which was to say though it was a balmy summer's night, she could have gone to church. Chabon slipped her fur coat back off her shoulders with a roll of his eyes. She'd wear the thing everywhere if she could.

Nees was already clacking cards in Bess's room when they left, Chabon and Addie walking behind Everso and Kindness. The Town was loud and alive, and sometimes it was too much, but others, like that night, it was just fine. There were girls on the bash and the odd spark of cold violence between the boys, but there was music and laughter thickening the air. The power that made the place alluring came from the clothes, the weed, the thumping basements, and after a long last day at work those were the things Addie wanted to swim through.

They walked the length of Lancaster Road, over to Blechynden and a three-storey townhouse in the little stub of the street sandwiched between the railway viaduct and Bramley Road. This was the Dale, not the Grove. White City, not Brown Town. The streets were busy, and the raucous chanting from the York carried across Bramley but turned into a low buzz beneath the sounds system playing in the basement.

Everso covered them all on the door, conspicuous with his cash as if he was inviting someone to try it. Inside, he was drawn to the man playing the tunes, the huge boxes and stereo he had. This was what he aspired to, as his own club nights were still run off a Blaupunkt. Chabon found drinks for him and Addie, and they floated round the fringe in those early moments before the vibe caught and people started dancing.

There was weed and white women, but it wasn't the Gomorrah Addie had been teased about. It was people finding what joy they could, a fleeting happiness honed off the sharp edge of despair. People wore it in their hips and in their feet, and in the hair and sweat and dizziness that filled the dim space.

They found Everso in the back room, where it was quieter and men stood around talking. He introduced them to Clovis, owner of a tailor's on Blenheim Crescent, who took Addie to be Chabon's white girlfriend, and was mortified when he discovered the truth. Impeccably turned out, he found humour in everything and was possessed of a deep and slow head-back *ack-ack-ack* laugh that threatened never to stop. When he spoke, he bit at the air around him.

With a surprising note of familial pride, Everso explained that Addie could sew and was skilled with a serger, and Clovis laughed his laugh and said it must be serendipity as he needed someone to work in the shop with him. She thought he was covering his embarrassment over his previous faux pas, but he insisted she come in Monday morning and they'd see what was what.

The small courtyard garden was dense with smoke and party refuse.

'What about the nursing?' she asked Chabon.

'Options are good. You don't know how long it could take to get on a course. Or what it'll be like when you get there. Clovis is a good man, important in the community.'

'I'd like to learn more stuff, not on the machine.'

Chabon tugged his lapels. 'All his suits are hand made.'

She touched him lightly on his chest. 'They fit you all right.'

His warm eyes, she didn't want to be anywhere other than under their gaze. There were worlds she hadn't dared dream of that suddenly seemed within reach. The danger of possibility.

'Something happening,' Everso said, head poking out the back door.

'Something?' Chabon asked.

'Out front.'

Everso disappeared back inside. Chabon took Addie's hand and followed him in. Nothing had slowed, the music and laughter continued, but there was something beneath it or beyond it. An imperilling buzz.

In the bay window, Everso looked up through the railings to the street above.

'Trouble.'

He took the stairs two at a time up to the ground floor. Chabon pressed Addie into a corner and squeezed between revellers to the window, trying to get a look, peering into the dark outside. Under the music, the glass smashed silently, Chabon twisting away and covering his face as shards flew. A milk bottle hit against the wall and showered him in white.

'Chay!'

He ran from the bay, hooking an arm round Addie and dragging her into the hall and onto the stairs. Feet barely troubling the floor as he swept her up, hectically she checked his face and head for cuts, but found only milk, already smelling spilt.

The upstairs front door was ajar, Everso watching out the crack. A howling whirr rose above the music, occasionally reaching a scream, the noise you might imagine the wind making as it passed through holes in your body, and was then pierced by night-splitting cracks.

'Chains,' he said.

Addie ducked down and looked out under his arm. A Teddy boy swung a chain above his head as a cowboy might a lasso, slamming it into the road and dragging it, gouging up the bitumen surface. Asphalt dust from beneath misted across the street.

A dozen or so coppers milled around on the pavement between the crowd and the house, but were woefully outnumbered, twenty or thirty to one as the mob swelled and filled the street.

'Keep Britain white!' came the cry, and a brick crashed through the ground-floor bay window.

As the day drew on, Bramley Road became a gauntlet.

Both sides lined by gangs of increasingly belligerent drinkers and the spectators who'd brought an expectation of mayhem. A heady air of exuberant pride mixed with swelling outrage as they egged themselves on. From the Station pub they drifted under the arches of the viaduct and lay in wait for West Indians getting off at Latimer Road station from work. They yelled and catcalled, picking on their clothes and hats, commenting on their walk, their beards or hair, and ultimately just their blackness. An unceasing roar of abuse and laughter, punctuated occasionally by the hollers of a fight as someone was jostled or punched, chased off into side streets with milk bottles or pub glasses crashing around them.

Ray felt the welcome tingle of fear he had sometimes at sea, surrounded by something bigger than he, so vast and powerful that it couldn't be controlled. There was both terror and exhilaration in that.

A man on a scooter wended his way up the road, slowing for no one, too old for the Lambretta he rode. Ray wondered what his game was. He had a full beard and wore a T-shirt and was surely an eccentric, if not a certified lunatic. Turning into the mouth of the arch to access the street beyond, he all but chased people out of the road.

A few hung around in front of him, but his glare shifted them.

They called after him, 'Fuck off out of it, you nutter,' but not loudly.

The mob drew itself closed across the street again, young men telling each other they'd have given him a right kicking if only he'd stepped off his scooter. Wouldn't have known what he was getting into if he'd started something.

Ray knew that he did know, though.

Some men you could just tell, the way they carried themselves. He'd seen it on ships. There was no point fooling around with that kind as they had no sense of humour. Incapable of taking a joke. It was a deficiency in some men who'd never let themselves get on in the world.

A fire started for real.

Fingers pointed at the sky, thick black smoke, not leaves being burned.

Couple of streets up, other side of the viaduct, and a mob was on the move, loud and magnetic, drawn to the mayhem. Word went round, the white woman from the previous night, the black man's trollop, had been causing scenes again.

Nothing a petrol bomb through her window hadn't solved.

Police had arrested her for her own good after someone gave her a taste of an iron bar.

Coppers hurried along the pavement, too few of them strung out along the road to do much about the crowd, just hoping to keep up, willing reinforcements to arrive.

The dense mass of people, almost entirely young men, surged into Blechynden Street, across from the York, gathering numbers as it went.

The dull thump of their music.

Stale stink of their hemp.

Blacks in the street, on the steps down to a basement party.

Constables placing themselves between the crowd and the house, nervous, frayed looking. They didn't want to be there. They wanted to be with the mob, wanted to be part of the solution.

The soft purring of chains on the night air and the clang of them raking the blacktop. Cheers went up as a milk bottle flew through the basement window, leaving a sharp hole and guillotine pieces hanging in the frame.

The police closed ranks, the few of them they had, and everyone laughed.

Coppers love the darkies!

Coppers love the darkies!

More bottles were gathered, and iron railings pulled from fences. Ray helped Clive putting the boot to a loosened front wall, freeing the bricks for more righteous ends.

He coursed with it.

This was how they'd scrub clean the bitterness and boredom and disappointment, the dullness of their lot, of lives spent working with their hands, at machines, in the steaming heat and freezing cold. Now it was almost within their grasp.

A purpose.

A joyous fury.

A living thing connecting them, unifying them.

Keep Britain white!

Chabon took Addie's hand and they ran up the stairs higher into the house. Rented rooms, just like theirs at home, most of them locked.

Tenants probably in the party downstairs. The front room on the top floor was open. Two beds, clothes strewn everywhere. She flicked the light on, but he quickly shut it off.

Slowly drew the curtains closed and stood at their edge, spying through a thin gap. The mob stoked its own flames with chants and songs, and then everything tipped off the edge all at once. They rushed forward, pinning the coppers back against the railings out front, and bricks and bottles flew from deeper in the crowd.

Iron bars thrown like javelins shattered windows.

Men climbed the steps to the porch and boots thudded against the front door.

Partygoers who had been on the steps down into the downstairs light well had taken shelter inside, but all the basement windows were smashed now in a hail of scavenged missiles.

A bottle crashed against the wall outside near Chabon's head.

'Christ!'

He drew back and half a brick came hurtling through the window pane, getting caught up in the curtains. Addie screamed and Chabon gathered her up, his back to the window to give her cover. Ushering her out of the room and down the hall, he looked out the rear window.

'We can get out into the yard and go over the wall.'

'What?'

'Come on.'

On the upper ground floor, Everso and two others were trying to hold the front door, which was threatening to come off its hinges. There was yelling and screaming downstairs as a few Teds forced their way in and fights broke out.

The hallway window at the back was painted shut. A rickety old dining chair sat in the corner, and Chabon took it by the stiles and smashed the legs through the glass, clearing all the fragments from around the frame. From the sill, he stepped over onto the roof of next door's scullery, which angled across the back of the party house. He helped Addie out and lowered her into the garden, jumping down after her.

A ragged fence the length of the garden gave onto a strip of over-grown alley beside the railway arches, the viaduct slashing across the Dale. They hustled along to the road, peeking out around the end of the fence into Blechynden.

Coppers had tenuous control of the situation, the mob backed off but braying still. Every window of the house was put in, the front door hanging from the frame at an angle like the aftermath of an explosion.

Constables led the black revellers up from the basement, escorting them along the road.

Everso stood on the porch, refusing to go.

'Why we the ones being taken away? Arrest them, they smash up the place.'

Laughter and jeers.

Coppers love the darkies!

Keep Britain white!

Chabon and Addie joined the straggling caravan of partygoers heading away from the basement, the police steering them up Lancaster Road, Everso's voice fading in the background.

Lander woke, some noise he couldn't reconstruct.

He lay still, listened to the dark. Voices and yelling outside, worse than earlier.

Cold feet on the floor, he crept gingerly to the window, but could see only the corrugated iron of the railway station roof. The knock at the door gave him a start.

'Yeah, hold on.'

He pulled on trousers and turned the latch.

'Mrs Mortimer.'

She was fully dressed, all made up. Had she not gone to bed, or had she taken the time? He couldn't remember what she'd been wearing before.

'Mr Lander, I was hoping you were awake.'

'Thank that lot,' he said, jerking a thumb toward the window.

'I wonder if you might come downstairs. I'm worried about what's happening.'

He nodded. 'Let me find a shirt and shoes. I'll be right down.'

She was standing just away from the window in the living-cum-dining room in the dark, the lights off. When it wasn't mealtimes, the leaves on the table were dropped and it was pushed aside, there also being two thin settees and a wireless in the room.

'Couldn't find anything on the BBC,' she said. 'I listened to what happened in Nottingham and never thought it could happen here.'

Lander wondered what Dale she lived in. His whole life, mayhem was just what they called a Tuesday in North Ken.

'Oh my.'

She took another step back as a young black man, not more than a teenager, came belting into the road from under the arches with beetroot-faced Teds in pursuit. One clipped his heels and they pounced, laying into him. Mrs Mortimer glanced at Lander, who didn't move.

'What do you expect me to do?'

The kid didn't roll into a ball and take a pasting, though, throwing a wild flurry of kicks and punches and breaking free to streak off round the corner. It was little more than an advance hunting party. A rumble of feet and voices turned into a mob of hundreds pouring through the arches, waving sticks and coshes, chains flying.

'Mr Lander . . .'

'We'll just let them pass.'

A mob's first instinct would be to march down the main road, so his fear was they had been turned back by police from somewhere else and would now be spoiling for trouble with any prey they might come across. A fear that was borne out when they started putting in the shopfront windows across the road.

'Hmm,' he said, and then a bicycle – God knows where that had come from – came crashing though the basement window below them.

'Oh, poor Mr Enright!'

He laid a hand on her shoulder.

'Might be better if you stay in the kitchen, Mrs Mortimer,' he said, leading her through to the back of the house.

Lander went down into the basement and knocked on the door to the front room. A bewildered-looking Mr Enright opened, still in his striped pyjamas. Behind him, the bike stood upside down against the side of his bed, back wheel slowly spinning with a squeak. He'd pulled aside the thick curtains that had caught it, and the nets kited on the night air.

'I can't find my spectacles.'

Lander was about to address the issue of priorities when a petrol bomb smashed the remaining glass from the frame and ignited the curtains.

'Christ.'

He tore the curtains from their rail and smothered them with Mr Enright's blankets, stomping on the heap of smoking sheets to put out the flames. The bomb had been little more than petrol-soaked rags in a milk bottle, but a few more of them would present a problem.

All the little devils hung over the iron railings, leering and chanting indecipherable obscenities. Then, as suddenly as they had attacked, they were gone, the rabble sweeping down the street to a ritornelle of smashing glass and rallying cries.

Mr Enright sat on his bed, the squeaking wheel come almost to a stop, and reached down to the floor to retrieve his spectacles, looking back up at a fractured Lander through a cracked eye.

Everso and Clovis eventually came up Lancaster Road with the sounds system fellas, each of them carrying a big box speaker or piece of stereo equipment.

'Policemen wouldn't let us stay, and wouldn't guard it themselves,' Everso said. 'House opened up to the elements now and white vandals in for a bit of thieving.'

Clovis spat. 'More likely the policeman put his big size elevens through the boxes than those young Teds. Nobody smash up more sounds system than the policeman. Every party I ever seen them raid, they kick in the boxes.'

The fugitive party crowd had taken refuge in another basement, near the junction with Ladbroke Grove, but the vibe had been dampened by the night's events and people were leaving early in dribs and drabs. Chabon helped the others haul the equipment into a room above the party, before suggesting to Addie they go home. He could see her heart wasn't in staying.

The mob was sloshing through the streets of the Dale and hadn't ventured east toward the Grove yet, but the frisson of danger hung across the district. Addie clung to Chabon's arm as they walked back to the Town, everyone on the streets a suspect now.

Joy had died.

For the first time in her life, Addie was really afraid of the place where she lived.

30

HUSTLERS SEE NO COLOUR

Day after next, Monday morning, Lander was out and about at sparrow's.

Boarded-up windows, glass swept from the gutters, he rode the Lambretta through the Grove and out to Whiteley's department store, where he was first inside, stalking into the musky environs of the perfume section and confusing the counter girl by sorting through bottles for their atomisers rather than their scent, ultimately picking the one with the most powerful spray.

Back on the Lane, he dropped into a grocer's and picked up a cheesecloth. A couple of doors down in Carpenter's, the hardware store, he got some rope and a knife to cut it. He wasn't alone. A couple of Jamaicans were buying up hacksaws, knives, choppers, hammers.

'Home improvements,' one of them said.

Lander shrugged and showed him his rope and blade. 'I'm going to rob my old boss.'

The Jamaicans laughed and he laughed with them. The Teds were going to have a surprising night if they returned.

Sunday night had been much like Saturday, gangs of teenagers loitering at Piggery Junction beneath the arches, armed with coshes and railings and whatever they could find in the streets. They numbered three or four hundred by eight o'clock, and at the thirty or so coppers who kept an eye on them they chanted, 'We'll kill the black bastards,' and 'Why don't you send them home?'

When the West Indians didn't come out to play, they marauded the streets and clashed with the coppers, dragging one from a car and giving him a good kicking, another getting his head opened up with a bottle. Arrests were made, and the mobs chanted.

Only whites get pinched!

Coppers love the darkies!

Lander had spent the morning watching Papa Rachman's offices on Westbourne Grove, but nobody turned up, probably avoiding the area after the trouble. In the afternoon, he'd helped Mr Enright board up his window and then raided Mrs Mortimer's kitchen for cayenne pepper, mustard powder and rubbing alcohol. In the first aid box, he found some olive oil, presumably kept for ears. Mixing together a concoction, he'd let it settle overnight and transferred it to a thermos.

He'd gone to bed around midnight, when the running battles with the police were petering out and only the hardcore hooligans remained, their lonely calls for lynchings thinning on the night breeze.

Now Lander was in the street lavs at the top of Westbourne Grove, standing at the basin straining his concoction through the cheesecloth and into the perfume atomiser, the original contents of which he had poured down the drain. He tested the mixture through the spray, and it was up to scratch.

On Monmouth Road, he waited near the side door to Papa's basement office, pretending to fiddle with his scooter. It didn't take long for Rachman to arrive. Beside him, dragging along an Alsatian, was a barrel-chested goon with a pencil moustache whom Lander recognised as sometime pro-wrestler sometime stick-up man Mad Fred Rondel.

He let them open the door and get inside. A door just down the hall to the right was a bathroom, which had been kept surprisingly clean when Lander did a few rails off the top of the vanity cabinet many years ago.

He gave them a count of five and charged through the door. As far as muscle went, Rondel was useless. Wrestling wasn't fighting, and Lander threw a sharp elbow that knocked him into a senseless heap. The dog's leash was still gripped in his fist when Lander sprayed his concoction from the atomiser into the Alsatian's face, dousing its eyes and snout.

Working the leash free, he dragged the animal, which was in a blind rabid frenzy, jaws snapping and eyes rolling over white, down the hall and hurled it into the bathroom, shutting the door.

Rachman stood perfectly calm.

'Good afternoon, Dave. It has been quite some time.'

'Papa.'

'This does not seem to be a social visit.'

'No.'

'Not after a flat, I do not suppose.'

'No.'

'Would you mind checking that Norbert is still breathing?'

Lander kicked Rondel in the ribs, eliciting a groan.

'He's fine.'

Straightening the grappler out, he bound his arms behind his back, and then roped his ankles together. He stood up and considered what to do next. In the bathroom, the dog was going apeshit.

'In my mind, I'd pictured putting him in a chair and tying him to that, but I don't think I'd ever get him up onto one.'

'It is the size of him that usually discourages recalcitrance by itself. Perhaps I should reassess my security in light of this.'

'Don't be too hard on him, Papa. He'll frighten off most of the gunslingers from the Grove, and any true pros wouldn't dare step on Billy Hill's toes.'

'You are an amateur, then, Dave?'

'I'm something else entirely. Open the safe, Papa.'

'I do not think so.'

Casually Lander knelt beside Rondel, who was beginning to come round, murmuring to himself. He rolled the big man onto his belly. The dog was bouncing off the walls in the small bathroom, barking like mad and sending things flying. Lander took hold of one of Rondel's fingers and snapped it with a moist crack.

The man screamed and passed out.

The dog howled like it was moon simple.

Lander gripped another finger.

'When he runs out, I'm going to have to find new fingers, Papa.'

'This is how it is?'

'This is how it is.'

Rachman shrugged stoically and rolled aside a small filing cabinet, a safe in the wall behind it. He spun the wheel and the door clunked open. Lander directed him to sit in the chair at his desk.

'Hands on the top, and restrain yourself from doing anything hasty.'

'Have you ever known me to be hasty, Dave?'

Lander smiled. He knelt at the safe and pulled out a money sack, a couple of ledgers, and a soft leather satchel that had been squeezed in.

'This the rent?' he said, holding up the sack.

Rachman nodded.

Lander began to count.

'Two thousand five hundred,' Rachman said. 'And some change.'

'Not bad, Papa.'

'I could probably get more, but I want to be less hands-on these days. I have development projects progressing.'

'Make the money work for you.'

Lander opened the satchel, which was filled with envelopes as thick as paperbacks. In each one was a stack of banknotes, mostly the new double-sided blue fivers that he'd never seen before.

'Papa, how much—'

'Thirty thousand, a little more.'

There were documents with each stack of notes, mortgage papers. Lander gave them a cursory read, noticing many of the addresses were the same. It was a neat scam. Buying up old houses cheap because they were on short leases, mostly in Bayswater, and then splitting them into as many separate tenements as possible and remortgaging the individual units at vastly inflated prices, the payments for which were easily covered by the rents they accrued, leaving the cash value of the new mortgages as pure profit.

'You do these every week?'

Rachman made a face. 'This has been a particularly busy week. Friend of mine has a building society, and he put them through. Now, Dave, you mentioned Billy earlier, and it has not been my experience that you are a foolish man, so I assume this is your plan.'

'To steal from Bill? Absolutely.'

'I am also to assume you are no longer in the employ of Mr Nunn, then.'

'Not since we had a small difference of opinion regarding someone he sent to kill me in prison.'

'Ah. Someone who was not up to the task.'

The Alsatian threw itself against the bathroom door over and over. Lander slipped all the rent money into the leather satchel and tucked it under his arm. He pointed toward the bathroom.

'Let the help redeem himself. Leave that mad bastard to him, Papa.'

'It is good to see you, Dave.'

'Give Mother my love.'

They had them on the run, barely a black face to be seen in the streets.

If they knew what was good for them, they'd keep in hiding. From Shepherd's Bush to the Town, and over the Harrow Road, any West Indians seen were getting the treatment. Buses from Hampstead and Camden were packed out with friends come to help. Hundreds were there to watch, grab an ice cream from Mancini's and line the kerbs like at the Coronation.

The Labour MP, George Rogers, who was on their side and was already on the case of coloured vice, drove the streets in a loudspeaker van calling for common sense, decency and tolerance, but they all knew what that meant.

Gangs roved the area with table legs and broken bottles. One man snapped a great whip and it could be heard all along Bramley Road. At Latimer Road station, a Jamaican student was jumped and beaten. He fled into a grocer's, where the woman running the place locked the door and stood outside scolding the boys.

They weren't there for her, though.

Plus, her dad was well known. A former pro welterweight of no great shakes, but lacing up was lacing up. The shop's windows remained intact.

Vic told the chaps there was no work for a few days, so Ray had a few halves in the York. By eight, a good crowd had amassed outside the station and the local Union Movement evangelist was on a crate banging on to what must have been five or six hundred rapt listeners. He had a measured, confident tone and knew his stuff. Ray thought he made a lot of sense.

'Nobody wants violence, let us be clear on that point. Like any community left to fend for themselves in the face of provocation, violence is only ever a last resort here in Notting Dale. The well-to-do in their Knightsbridge flats or Berkshire estates would call us ill mannered. The parlour socialists of the suburbs would call us distasteful, and pull a face.

'But they're not here, are they?

'They don't know what we know.

'That the coloured problem is not the fault of the coloureds. No, it is not, my friends, it is not. They were made promises by governments of both stripes, just as the hard-working white Christian families of the Dale were. Promises of jobs and housing and better standards of living. Governments of both stripes who shipped the coloureds in from islands half a world away in record numbers.

'And look where we are now.

'Had we not too few houses available to us after the war anyway?

'Had we not too few opportunities for jobs and living and raising our families in comfort and peace?

'And now we see them, oh yes, we see them, my friends, packed into rooms, fifteen or twenty to a single house. No way to live, not for them and not for us. Playing their music till all hours. Their women walking our streets. Crime is rife.

'North Kensington has become a crucible of penury and prostitution.

'A cauldron of iniquity where you dare not leave your homes.'

Only the bullhorn made him heard over the roaring crowd, spittle across his chin by that point, moving beyond a carnival barker to a snake-handling preacher.

'GET.

'RID.

'OF.

'THEM!'

They wouldn't be stopped. Hundreds of feet stomping the roads heading east sounded like thunder rolling over the Town. Worked up into a frenzy by rhetoric and fistfuls of slimming pills, they were crazed but clear of purpose, howling with a single voice. The police were powerless, overrun in seconds. A torrent of white anger rushing along Blenheim Crescent, filling the road from railing to railing, sweeping up anyone in its path.

At the Dale end, where the road curved in a great sweep around the gardens of Notting Hill to the south, the buildings were home largely to whites. Cackling women hung out of top-floor windows and called down their support.

'Go on, boys, get yourselves some blacks!'

Across Kensington Park Road, those houses turned to shops, some black owned or run. Usually on a bank holiday it would be brimming with people ducking in and out of cafés, visiting the upstairs gamble houses and downstairs clubs. But the street was empty. Shutters down. Lights off.

Should have expected they'd barricade themselves away rather than meet them in the street. It was in their nature to run. Not that it mattered.

Everyone knew the target.

The Fortress.

Totobags Caribbean café was a social centre for newly arrived Jamaicans. Fresh off the boat, there was a room upstairs they could crash for a night or two until they got themselves aligned with their new reality in London. If there were going to be blacks anywhere, that was where they'd be. Playing their music and slapping their dominoes and smoking their hemp.

Even there the lights were off.

Ray had collected a broken brick along the way, clutched in his fist as he bobbed from foot to foot, somewhere a window just begging to receive it. He was across the road from the café but had a good view. The mob thronged round the stubby end of Blenheim between Kensington Park Road and the Lane, banging on doors and shopfronts, a coruscating wave of iron rods and lit rags.

For a moment it seemed as if, having not been met by a similar gang of West Indians up for a battle, nobody quite knew what to do next, where to direct their pent-up rage. Then a voice at the front bellowed.

'Burn the niggers out!'

Ray hurled his brick like a cricket ball from the rope, but it clonked harmlessly off the brickwork beside the second-floor window, which, as if they'd practised the timing, promptly opened and a shower of milk bottles rained down on the mob, followed by jarred cocktails of sand and petrol that sparked alight as they dashed on the road amongst the scattering crowd.

The door to the Fortress flew open and a crew of furious Jamaicans rushed out swinging what might have been swords or machetes. Everyone scarpered, fleeing back the way they had come, or down Kensington Park Road into the relative tranquillity of Notting Hill.

Ray never ran so fast in his life.

Behind him he heard one of them shout.

'Go back where you came from!'

Everso, Clovis, Kindness and a few others Addie knew only by sight or reputation entered the house as returning heroes, bursting with the glories of chasing off the white man.

'And then I tell them, and this is my favourite bit, I yell after them, "Get back to where you come from!" and swish the chopper round my head.'

Everso and Clovis fell into each other, eyes wet with laughter. Bess's room on the top floor had become their sanctuary during the trouble, Addie and Nees holing up in there when the boys were out in the streets, Conrad joining them. He did his bit pouring out fortitudinous rums and keeping the stoves in the hallway going to feed everyone.

The Town had been quiet all day, everyone agreeing it was best to stay indoors. Most bright sunny days, all the sporting girls would be sitting on their window ledges as soon as they were awake, blue feet kicking in the air to attract business. But curtains had been drawn since lunch. The pavements were clear, the Colville squares deserted.

Chabon sat by the window sulking, having been told to stay home and make sure everyone was all right in case the white gangs deployed flanking manoeuvres and the like, getting round the outposts of Toto-bags and the Calypso to attack the Town when the men were away. Now he was the only one without a good tale to tell about courageous encounters with the enemy, and kept a keen eye over the street below, wishing someone would come and have a go.

'Now, we need to talk about getting me fresh digs.'

This was Helmut Butler, a growling Trini calypsonian of some local note who performed in local cafés and bars under the moniker Boysee Sing, and had primarily agreed to take up arms with Everso on the promise of finding his way out of the room above a café on the Dale end of Lancaster Road that he was sharing with four other men.

'And I can't be sharing with no more kiss-me-arse Jamaicans.'

'Watch out now,' said Everso.

'You're in a roomful of Jamaicans,' Bess said.

'I ain't Jamaican,' said Chabon.

'Nor me,' chirped Kindness.

'You've been listening to the white fella too long,' Helmut said. 'Anyone from the islands must be Jamaican. Must be fifty million Jamaicans here.'

He dodged a shoe from Bess's direction.

'You Jamaicans don't like us Trinidadians,' he went on, 'because we're much too nice with the fine clothes and that. You know my threads.'

'You bought your suit from me!' cried Clovis. 'Where you think I come from, Czechoslovakia?'

'And I might work on your next suit, and I'm Jamaican,' said Addie.

Helmut and Everso looked at one another and then creased up laughing.

'You're no Jamaican,' Helmut said.

'Am too. Dad was Jamaican.'

'Yeah, but your ma was the Queen of England,' Everso said.

Helmut shook his head, chuckling. 'Jamaican. You're half a white cat. Red Cat! I'm going to call you Red Cat.'

Addie scowled, Everso laughing so hard he didn't know what to do with himself.

'Dunno what you're laughing at,' Helmut said.

Everso raised his hands in mock fear.

'Now, we all know that no Trinidadian is afraid of a Jamaican.'

'Always come back on to this,' Clovis said.

'You all know about Weatherman.'

'Who's Weatherman?' Addie asked.

'Biggest Jamaican devil up in the Grove,' said Helmut. 'Man was a stone-cold pirate until he got stabbed right in the head. Chopper in the middle of his skull. And who did him like that? A Trinidadian.'

Clovis put a hand on Helmut's arm. 'Listen, we was getting slapped about all round the Dale last couple of days until all those boys come up today from Coldharbour Lane, so you want to be grateful to your Jamaican brothers.'

'Maybe I'll teach them how to dress as a reward.'

'Things livening up,' Chabon said, looking down out the window.

'Trouble?' Everso said.

Chabon shrugged. 'Looks like those Brixton and Earls Court boys.'

Everso grinned. 'They've come looking for it.'

Chabon stood suddenly. 'Yeah, here we are.'

There was yelling and hooting below them, and somewhere glass smashed. Everso sent the boys room to room and they gathered all the men in the stairwell.

'What we need is some weapons and some organisation,' Everso told them. 'We got iron bars. We got knives. Get whatever you have in your rooms. Pull up the floorboards if you have to. We got Molotovs. We got bottles. We'll give them all the trouble they like. We'll make them think long and hard before they come round the Town again.'

There was pitched battle in the street.

Molotov flames skated across the macadam, and roving gangs of whites and blacks ran through smoke drifts, launching projectiles. Chabon, confined to the house again, held Bess's belt as she leaned out the window throwing bottles at passing white thugs, shrieking as they danced away from the dashed glass.

A burning car was used as a vanguard and rolled down the road, chasing the white boys out of Powis Terrace and back onto Talbot Road, where they were met by more tooled-up Jamaicans and hounded across the railway to the east.

At the end of the road, a black matriarch stood at the heart of the junction swinging an axe at a group of white teenagers and screaming, 'I'll murder you for this!'

She was believed.

Ray ran from the scene at Totobags until his lungs and throat burned. Ran the length of Blenheim, round the bend into Clarendon, a quarter-mile flat out that took almost everything he had. Separated from Clive and the chaps, he kept up a ragged jog, arms like string beside him, until he reached Princedale Road and the sight of mum's house.

He let himself in with the spare keys.

'Ray?'

'Yeah.'

'Thank God, it's all over the wireless how bad things are out there.'

Mum and sister were in the dining room, candles lit on the table.

'They're unhinged.'

'The BBC?'

'The coloureds. Mad. Throwing petrol bombs, waving swords about.'

He stared at the candles. 'What's this about?'

'We thought it best to keep the place looking dark, just in case the trouble came this way. The news said they were smashing windows indiscriminately.'

'Yeah. Animals.'

'I think they meant the Teds,' sister said.

'Smashing the windows of those coloureds causing all the bother.'

'Anyway,' mum said, 'I'm glad you're home.'

'Have to go back out.'

'What? Why?'

'Vic and Clive and that are out there. Got to make sure they're all right.'

'Ray, you can't go back out there.'

'Going to change.'

'Ray—'

'Leave him, Mum,' sister said.

Ray stripped off, his clothes sopping with sweat. Towelling himself down quickly, he dressed and headed back downstairs.

'I'll be back,' he called, leaving without waiting for a response.

Outside, he took the steps down into the basement well and unlocked the door to the vault. Inside he found a paraffin work lamp, which he filled up and put in a burlap sack. Making his way through the heart of

Notting Hill, he used the streets to the south of the Colville area to skirt round the trouble and come up on the Town along Ledbury Road.

The Duke of Cornwall was closed, lights out, landlord praying for his windows. Ray chanced a look round into Talbot Road. Small groups ranged the streets, bricking front windows or smashing car lights with coshes. Waiting for a quiet moment, he ran across the street and hunkered down in the porch of one of the big townhouses, behind an overflowing tin dustbin leaking juice down the steps.

Problem was, he was having difficulty finding the right one as they all looked the same to him. Wherever the basement club was, it wasn't open for business that night, and the old Cudsworths on the ground floor had their lights out like everyone else. It was either the second or the third one in from the end. He tried to picture arriving with Vic and the chaps, carrying in the ladders and paint.

Footsteps slapping along the street made him duck, and two white teenagers whizzed round the corner with a pack of blacks on their tail. Ray pressed his face into the stucco column of the porch and waited for their feet to fade away down the road.

The houses were arranged with their front doors to the right of their window bays as you looked at them. He cupped his hands to the dark glass of the window of the house the porch he was on belonged to. Nothing. He leaned over to do the same next door, but the curtains were pulled.

Old people pulled curtains.

The basements looked identical, but the curtains were the kicker.

Inside the burlap sack, he lit the paraffin lamp. Heaving the dustbin up against his shoulder, he tossed it down at the basement sash. It smashed the top pane and fell into the well, and he followed it quickly with the lamp, which crashed against a table inside and ignited.

About to run, he saw half a dozen Teds fall into the street from clambering over the iron gates to the tabernacle in the middle of the block and come his way. He retreated into the porch, kneeling down with his back against the door, no bin to hide behind.

Men in the basement were beating the flames with blankets. The door opened and a black woman in her fifties maybe, stout as an oak, climbed the steps with an axe in her hands.

'You do this?' she said to the youths, who froze like searchlights had found them.

She drew the axe back over her shoulder and the Teds scattered in all different directions.

'I'll murder you for this!' she cried, chasing two of them down the street.

Terrified, Ray rapped lightly on the door, hoping whoever lived there might let him in.

Through the letter box, he whispered, 'Help me, please.'

He made out movement behind the etched glass of the door lights and whispered again, with more urgency. 'Please, they're attacking everyone.'

The door opened a crack and Agamemnon Cudsworth looked down at him. Ray blinked. He'd bombed the wrong building, but pivoted quickly from that realisation.

'Do you remember me? Ray? I thought I should check on you, make sure you and your wife were all right, but a gang chased me. They threw a petrol bomb into next door.'

The old man's eyes flicked out into the street, where his neighbour still stood brandishing her axe.

'You better come in,' he said.

Gratefully Ray scurried inside and Agamemnon locked the door behind him.

'We're in the scullery,' he said, pointing through to the rear.

Ray stepped past the ladders and folded-up dust sheets, the pots of paint stacked in the corner, embarrassed now for his part in it. Gladys stood from the small table in the kitchen and touched her hand to the cosied teapot.

'Have a cup, Ray?'

'Don't want to be any bother, Mrs Cudsworth. Really just wanted to see that you weren't having any trouble.'

'There's a fire next door, Gladys,' Agamemnon said, coming in and closing the door to the hallway. The pair of them never left a door open, given the communal nature of the hall, and had keys for them all.

'Oh dear.'

'Windows are broken.'

Gladys poured Ray a cup. 'Could you stay, Ray? If you don't have to get back to check on anyone else?'

'Well, I suppose a while longer won't do any harm. With the bedlam out there, honestly I'd feel bad leaving you.'

Agamemnon raised a finger as if he'd struck upon an idea and pottered out of the room. The old boy returned momentarily with several rolls of gummed paper.

'Always kept some in after that last palaver, in case Jerry tried it on again.'

Ray didn't fancy going near the front windows, but he also didn't think much of his chances out on the streets, so quickly helped Agamemnon tape the windows in the old diagonal pattern to prevent shards flying everywhere if they were broken. Agamemnon drew the curtains shut, which Ray considered better late than never, and they withdrew to the scullery once more, where their light wouldn't be seen by rioters and vandals.

'I've made soup,' Gladys said. 'Boiled from the bone. Chicken is so reasonable these days.'

'I spoke with your Mr Rachman,' Agamemnon said. 'He pointed us in the direction of a flat in Maida Vale. We're minded to take it.'

Ray inhaled deeply over the bowl of rich chicken soup Gladys placed before him.

'Probably for the best,' he said.

Morning, thin smoke trails knitted into the sky from dying fires.

Addie stood at Bess's window and surveyed the street. The smouldering wreck of a car, bumped up against a lamp post. Nets blowing out through empty windows. Debris strewn along the road. Crumbling stucco piles splashed darkly with blood. It was like a battlefield.

There was a fuss on the porch steps below. Raising the sash to lean out, she could see Everso and Kindness remonstrating with two white men. She wasn't struck with the same threat of violence as the previous few nights, but Kindness swung a boot at one of their arses as they chased them off.

Everso climbed the three flights to the top floor.

'Who were they?' Addie asked.

'Looking for the gamble house downstairs.'

'They serious?'

'Yeah. We're not opening up today, though. Wait and see how tonight goes.'

'But they were white. What were they thinking?'

'They say they weren't involved. Weren't me, boss, was those other ones. Yeah, but you just sat and watched, eh?' He shrugged. 'Hustlers see no colour.'

31

THE LONG WHITE VIOLENCE

Clutching the satchel of stolen cash and a can of petrol, Lander skulked in a doorway on St John Street.

Fleeing Rachman's office the day before, he'd wheeled the scooter into the Paddington Basin, watching it sink, and got himself a room for the night in a boarding house near the wharfs.

He'd passed the day writing a letter, a confession of all his crimes from dumping his wife's killer in the Thames to the Eastcastle job to Little Phil's murder. He stashed it along with the two and a half grand in stolen rent money in his locker in Paddington station before dropping the key and his St Christopher into an envelope and posting it to the only person he trusted.

The letter cleared everything up. It wouldn't be enough to put Billy and Mother on the hook for Eastcastle, but there was enough in there about their operations, the nightclubs and spielers and rental properties, that any good copper would be able to pin them down on something. And enough cash in the locker with it for someone to leave the city and start over comfortably.

Before dawn, he'd cleared out of the boarding house. At the garage near Marylebone station, he purchased a can of petrol, explaining that his wife had run the tank empty. From there he got a taxi, using the same wife story to much mirth from the driver, getting dropped off near Farringdon station. Cutting through the workshops and distilleries of Clerkenwell, he made his way to St John Street and his ultimate destination.

The Kingdom Cold Storage Company.

They were winding down after the night market, porters seeing the last trucks off, bummerees wheeling empty trolleys. It was nothing for him to slip through the arched entrance off the main road and into the covered yard behind the building. He pulled up, sliding neatly behind a stack of discarded wooden crates.

The old crone, Mrs Cruik, a dab hand with sausages, was brushing down the bloodied cobbles. He waited for her to return to her shed before sneaking into the unloading hall, dashing past the elevators to the stairwell leading down to the refrigerated level.

Boxes of meat.

Racks of uncut carcasses.

Icy pipes snaked back and forth above him. The weather had been so riot friendly all weekend that Lander had forgotten it would be cold down there. His breath hung on the air and his skin goosed.

The walls of the cavernous cellar were wood lined. Where a rotting board had worked itself loose, the cork insulation and tar paper plastered over the brickwork were showing through. Lander recalled what the copper at Smithfield had told him, that the place went up like kindling in the fire because the wood and cork in the cold storage were soaked with years of animal fat and grease.

He pulled away some more loose boards.

A plan came to him and he got to work.

By the time he finished, he was cold to the bone and considering a foray upstairs to see if he could steal a coat from somewhere. That was when the elevator kicked into life. He got out of sight behind a heap of frosted beef, rubbing his arms and fighting the chatter of his teeth.

The lift came to a halt and the wire door was slid aside.

Mother.

He'd become no less bald in the intervening years. As hairless as he was pitiless. He'd barely stepped into the cellar when he stopped and sniffed, nose twitching like a vicar's wife. Lander knew he could smell it, and thought his plan was blown before it was even under way, but before Mother could investigate further, the door from the stairwell clattered open against the wooden wall.

A young man, his face familiar.

Someone from a long time ago.

Mother smirked. 'Young Raymond, returned to the fold.'

Shit. It was Claire's son. Paranoia seeped into Lander's thinking. What were these two doing together?

'Had Vic at the door, six this morning, saying you wanted to see me. Had the whole house up.'

'Very sorry to hear that, Raymond. How is your mother?'

'That what you wanted to see me about?'

'No. It was a conversational gambit, Ray. A way of easing into the tougher end of our chat.'

'Let's just skip to that.'

Mother stiffened. A tight smile.

'All grown up and back from the sea. Enjoy the palaver last couple of days, did we?'

'Doing what we have to. Sort out the Dale.'

'Yeah. Sure.'

'Place is a state.'

'Fucking hell, Ray. It used to be brick kilns and piggeries, populated by gypsies and Irish, and you think it's a state now?'

'Don't feel like home any more.'

'Does anywhere? That place you firebombed last night, that was one of ours.'

'I didn't—'

Mother raised a hand. 'Spare me the amateur dramatics. You were seen. Then holed up with that nice old couple you're supposed to be evicting, as it all went off outside. Tea and bickies, was there?'

'I spoke with them. They're moving. Maida Vale.'

'Oh, thank you very much, Ray. Must have been that silver tongue of yours.'

'So, what then?'

'So use your noggin next time. You want to firebomb out the spades, fine. But make sure you torch a place that doesn't put bread on the fucking table.'

'You should be throwing them out.'

'Why on earth would I want to do something as silly as that?'

'There are working-class white families whose lives are made a living hell round there.'

'So what? I've been making the lives of working-class white families a living hell for years. I'm in the living hell business, son.'

'It was always all right when I was growing up there, but since they started shipping in all the darkies—'

'You been bending an ear to them Union Movement cunts? *Mosley*. Look, what you do in your spare time is your affair. Frankly, stirring up a little trouble with the West Indians is good for us. Ghettoes are good for us. Long as your good hard-working working-class white families don't like any black in their street, then we can charge what we like for rooms in the Colville slums. But the houses have to be standing for us to make money, Ray, so the Rachman places are off limits for your little sorties.'

'That all you care about?'

'Grow up. We can get six quid a week from a single room. Some of those gaffs have over a dozen rooms. Think about how many houses we have a stake in. And it's not just the rental they bring in, it's the other money that a cash operation that large lets you hide. Until they're dumb enough to legalise gambling, this is the laundry we use for our best whites.'

'Jesus, this country is going to the dogs and you're selling it off.'

'There is no country, Ray. There's just business. And trust me when I tell you that this city has seen much, much worse days.'

'Nothing's changed in the Dale since I left. It's like the war only just ended. Nothing rebuilt, less housing, more coloured, no jobs. The place is a pit. Christ, dad went to France to—'

'Oh, do me a favour and leave out the my-old-man-went-to-war routine. I was in France too, thirty years before your dad. If all you want is to get rid of the blacks, Christ, you should have told him not to bother. You'd have been better off with that other one winning. There will always be rich cunts telling thick cunts to blame black cunts for being poor cunts. *My old man went to war.* The things I could tell you about Freddie.'

'Yeah? How about where his body is. Can you tell me that?'

Mother nodded. He moved toward a stack of wooden trays filled with cuts of pork and lifted the top one.

'Out of respect for your old man, the friendship we had for years before you were even born, and for the esteem in which I hold your mother, I'm prepared to pretend I never heard that.'

He carried the tray over to a shorter pile across the hall.

'What respect did you ever show dad? And as for mum, creeping round the place after he was gone, turning up all hours. Fucking weirdo, that's what she thought of you. Offering her a job, Jesus.'

'You should probably push off now, son. Before you say something that can't be unsaid.'

Mother stood with his hands on his hips.

'I think probably I haven't said enough. I bet there are still those who'd listen to what I have to say. Yeah, I could start with what happened the day of the Eastcastle Street robbery. How my dad went missing that day. How he'd become best buddies again with his old mate, some prick called Teddy Nunn.'

'Young Raymond Martin. Balls finally dropped, have they? No longer that boy cowering behind the banisters in his mum's house. Or maybe you are.'

'My uncle always saw you for what you was. He weren't afraid of you. And you're right, I ain't that boy no more. I ain't afraid of you either.'

'You should be.'

'Why? Because you're this big man? This villain?'

'No. Because I'm standing between you and the only way out of this cellar.'

Mother had outmanoeuvred the boy without him even realising it was happening. He was an idiot, quick mouth and slow eyes.

But he was Claire's son, and he deserved better than this.

Deserved better than disappearing into the food chain in a Clerkenwell cellar.

Deserved better than his father.

He could do this for Claire, give her son a second chance. A chance to do something with his life. He pushed himself up into a crouch, legs stiff and numb with cold. It had to be timed just right. The boy looked panicked, rooted to the spot, eyes fixed on Mother, who for his part was reaching into his belt for something.

He never went anywhere without a blade.

Lander exploded out from behind the meat and slammed into him, lifting him clear off his feet and smashing into a stack of crates. They landed in a heap, rocks of icy flesh falling on them. Scrambling to his feet, Lander pushed Ray toward the door.

'Run. RUN!'

The boy kicked into gear and sprinted for the stairs, soles like gunshots on the stone.

Mother picked himself up.

'Been expecting you, Dave. Since your little visit to Papa.'

'Thought we should catch up.'

'See, I thought we had an unspoken agreement. You were out of prison, and we'd leave you alone if you left us alone.'

'That what Benny the Jew was? Leaving me alone?'

'Now I don't mind admitting when I'm in the wrong, Davey Boy, and it might have been a tad rash sending Benny after you. But that was years ago. Bygones be bygones. I truly thought we were past that.'

'What made you think that fat twat would get it done?'

'Benny usually wasn't the hands-on type. We'd had him do a few things for us inside, and he was more of a middleman, farming that sort of work out. Guess I underestimated how much of a cunt he thought you were.'

'Heard he eats nothing but soup.'

'Yeah, he's a drooly little goon now. Top prize for that, Dave.'

'You owe me.'

'This what you're here for? Bash my brains in so I'm a straw-sucker too? Seems a little cheap, even for you.'

'I'm not talking about what happened with Benny. I'm talking about Eastcastle. I'm talking about six years of my life.'

'You were paid for doing a day's work, Dave, and—'

'Paid? Paid what? A few hundred quid. I didn't even get my cut.'

'Well, you were in prison by the time the cash was clean. And who were we supposed to leave it with? You lived alone in that mausoleum of a flat. Your good old mum made breakfast for half the Flying Squad every day. What did you expect?'

'I'll tell you what I didn't expect. In the first instance, I didn't expect to be lied to about how much the blag was really worth, being fed a load of bollocks about having to burn a hundred grand of it.'

'We never did get round to chatting about that, did we?'

'No, we did not. And in the second instance, I didn't expect to be shopped and end up inside for six years.'

'Shopped? By who? Not us. You walked into a Sweeney special at that hotel, and off the yield of the search from that arrest, you got fucked.'

'Nah. The police had no idea what was happening at the hotel. Someone told them to be there.'

'Dave, I tried to kill you *because* you were banged up. Why would I have tried to organise it in the first place if I was going to do that? I'd have just killed you out here.'

'I have an eyewitness.'

'To what?'

'To who booked the room at the hotel. A woman. A woman with dark hair. And it was a bird who called up the Flying Squad telling them to be there.'

Mother thought about this.

'And you thought, what? That it must have been Gyp?'

He roared with laughter.

'What's so funny?'

'Amazing to me how dumb you can be, Davey Boy. What other woman do we know, a brunette who might bear a grudge against you? Say, for being involved in the disappearance of her husband? And whose son you just chased off.'

In that simple truth, Lander felt gravity lose sway over his guts. It was the kind of realisation that you know in your core is true the second you hear it, slotting into place like you'd been reserving space in your mind for it to occupy.

'Fuck.'

'You soft cunt. She did you up proper. Tell you what, though, six years ain't nothing. My understanding, you never told your former Met taskmasters any of the really juicy stuff. Stood strong even after we tried to do the dirty on you. That's not to be scoffed at. We can chalk this up as a misunderstanding between old friends, call it evens if you tell me where my fucking money is.'

Lander glanced over to a pile of dead cattle, stripped and gutted. Mother squinted and saw the cash in little piles on top of it. He wagged a finger.

'That there is quite clearly the beginnings of some foolishness. You might want to rethink whatever you've got planned.'

'I was once told about a bonfire of the banknotes. Seems only fair that's what we finally get.'

Mother looked about him, the petrol smell he'd caught a whiff of earlier now making sense.

'Davey Boy, do not—'

Lander produced from his pocket a lighter, flicking the flame into life, but got no more than a step toward the petrol-doused meat and cash before Mother drew a pistol and gut-shot him. He wasn't knocked off his feet, he didn't fly backwards. It was as if someone simply switched off his legs and he collapsed in a heap where he was standing, but in agonising pain.

'What did you think, that I was just waiting politely for you to turn up after you knocked over Papa's? I don't usually carry a tool, but I knew you'd have something stupid planned. Couldn't just fuck off with your money and be a winner. You'd have some point to make. Idiot.'

Tears in his eyes from the pain, Lander managed to squeeze out a laugh.

'God fuck you, Teddy Nunn.'

Lighter still aflame and in his grip, he touched it to the trail of petrol he'd earlier spilled across the floor. Flames rushed in both directions, toward the meat piled with cash and to the grease-drenched wall, which went up like dry wood in a forest fire. Everything was engulfed as it danced across the ceiling and over the walls, and Lander was suddenly hot and cold at the same time.

The insulation in the walls fell in fiery lumps. Wooden beams splintered with surprising haste and collapsed in the heat, the network of cooling pipes they supported bursting and coming down atop them. It was as if the old building had been waiting for the fire all along and now fed itself to it with alarming zeal.

About the many ways in which death could come, he understood all too well. For every unspeakably mundane passing by failure of heart or lung, there was a tragedy less ordinary, by murder or chance. For every violent deliverer with bad intentions, there was a bringer who did not especially seek its arrival upon a dully innocent bystander.

A machinist's mishap, say.

Or a drunken driver mounting a kerb to meet a woman waiting to be a mother.

Then there were those who sought death out themselves, and as often as not were taken aback by what they found.

But David Lander got exactly what he had come for, and was not at all surprised.

From somewhere, he thought he heard the Lord's Prayer recited, the words fading into the bone-cracks of the fire. Dark oily smoke poured off the burning walls, passing over him as a cortège of screams that filled his eyes and lungs like seawater. He had never before noticed the screaming, though it had begun long before his birth and would continue unbroken long after his death.

The screaming of the world. The long white violence.

It had always been there, and that was why he could not tell it from the laughter of birds or the chatter of babes or the howling of cats in heat.

Why he could not tell it from the silence.

32

THE KINGDOM, THE POWER AND THE GLORY

His reputation manufactured solitude, even in the busiest places.

Who would come sit with Billy Hill uninvited? One day maybe someone would, but they wouldn't be looking for a how-are-you-doing or a nice cup of tea. He and Gyp sat at a table near the window overlooking the track in White City Stadium. Frankie was around somewhere, keeping an eye out. He'd make himself conspicuous if he felt something was brewing.

'Here,' Gyp said. 'This one.'

Across the restaurant, in front of the fish tank where you could pick your own dinner, walked a serious-looking gent in a not inexpensive suit.

'He has two arms,' Billy said. 'I told you, William only has the one. That's how you'll tell it's him, from the one fucking arm. When have you ever been in a room with two poor sods missing one?'

'He might have one of them fake ones.'

'He doesn't. He likes you to know.'

'There might be a group or something. A club.'

'A club? You've gotten ahead of me again, what are we on now?'

'For one-armed sods. A club, you'd see more'n one of them in a room together.'

'This is what you're selling me, a club for one-armed gentlemen?'

'How'd he lose it?'

'War. Some business with a tank and something else.'

'Well, there you are. Stands to reason.'

'What reason?'

'Must have been loads of them came back from the war short an arm or two.'

'None that I've ever met, other than William.'

'Probably meet up in whatchamacallems, reunions.'

Billy lit another cigarette. 'You want one?'

'No. Was it his good one?'

'Huh?'

'The arm he lost. Was it his good one, like his writing one?'

'Don't know.'

'Which one is it, right or left?'

'Don't know.'

'What do you mean? He's your mate, how do you not—'

'Right. It's his right. Shaking hands is a whole thing with his other hand. Like you're taking a princess's paw or something, because you always go with your right hand and have to turn it over. Frankly, it's embarrassing. He should keep it in his pocket until everyone's clear there's no shaking occurring. Course, most of the time he has his case in his hand anyway, so then you've half reached and you have to pull it back.'

'All right, don't get worked up about it.'

'Jesus.'

'Anyway— Oh, here he is. Unless there's a meeting of the club.'

'Yeah, that's him.' He waved. 'William.'

William Rees-Davies waved back and steered their way. He was in a double-breasted suit, the right sleeve pinned neatly just below the shoulder where it wasn't encumbered by a limb.

'No case,' Gyp whispered.

She reached for Rees-Davies's hand with both of hers, somehow making the shake seem natural, so that Billy felt compelled to do the same but ended up attempting an armbar.

'William, this is Gyp, my . . . my Gyp.'

'This is a spot of fun,' Rees-Davies said. He looked down toward the tote at trackside. 'How do we have a flutter from here?'

'You don't have to move,' Billy said. 'They'll come round and take your money off you.'

'Just the three of us?'

'No, Councillor Boys is coming. I don't know where he is. For a man who lives on the tit, his timekeeping could do with a polish.'

'You know who is here, at a table over there,' Gyp said.

'I know,' Billy said. 'I've deliberately not been looking at him since we arrived. You make eye contact and he does this eyebrow thing until you invite him over.'

'Who's this?' Rees-Davies said, twisting round in his chair to see.

'Al Burnett,' said Gyp.

'That rascal promised me dinner with Ava Gardner,' Rees-Davies said. 'Came to nothing, needless to say.'

'He barters in Hollywood stars but never coughs up. "Guess who was in my club the other night, you'll never get it, go on have a go." The one time he does deliver, it'll be Mickey fucking Rooney.'

'Here's Boys,' Gyp said, getting up and moving to the end of the table so the councillor could sit with the other men.

'You seen the fishes?' Boys said, smiling like a kid at his first Christmas.

'What fishes are they, Councillor?' said Billy.

'You can pick them for your plate.'

'You might have to give me a hand grabbing hold of one,' Rees-Davies said.

Boys laughed, not getting it yet.

Billy did the introductions.

'Councillor, this is our honourable and learned member for the Isle of Thanet.'

Boys held out his hand for a shake.

It took him a moment.

'Oh gosh.'

Rees-Davies nodded. 'Yes, that's what I said.'

'Oh my, I'm so sorry.'

'Not half as much as I was. Was looking forward to resuming a glorious career as a right-hand medium pacer for Kent after the war. Loved a good wobbler.'

Flustered, Boys didn't quite know how to leave it alone.

'France, was it?'

'Oh goodness, no. Never got near the place. Salisbury Plain, '43. On manoeuvres with the chaps and . . . Well, it doesn't really matter now.'

Tiring of the back and forth, Billy sat, the others following suit.

'I heard about your man,' Boys said.

'Teddy? Silly sod.'

'What's this?' Rees-Davies said.

'That fire at the cold storage place last week, the man they pulled out was a friend of Billy's,' said Boys.

'Fire? Terrible business. Badly hurt, was he?'

'Not great,' Billy said. 'Burns over most of his body. They've got him on something the whole time, so he's not really been awake yet. They're not sure about his lungs, so forth. Infection is a real threat.'

'I heard the man who died was shot first,' Boys said.

'With his own weapon,' Gyp said.

Billy nodded. 'Yeah, they reckon he was trying to rob the place. Apparently he'd tried it somewhere on Westbourne Grove the day before but didn't get away with anything.'

'Do we know who he was?' Rees-Davies said.

'No idea. Couple of porters seen him going in the place. Scruffy fella, beard and messy clothes. Probably another one fallen prey to the drugs.'

'That's a problem that'll only get worse,' Boys said.

'Whatever happened to good old boozing and betting?' said Rees-Davies.

Billy leaned in conspiratorially. 'Speaking of which.'

'I've got some good people drafting a private members' bill,' Rees-Davies said. 'Regulation of gaming houses, legalisation of small games on private property, just like we discussed.'

'Gambling?' Boys said.

'It'll take a while,' Rees-Davies said. 'Westminster is glacial. I won't introduce the bill until next year, but in the meantime we're going to be shoring up support. Ideally, by the time I look to bring it to the house, a few ministers will be supporting it and the government might take it over. Be lovely to have the Home Secretary introduce it instead. Then it'll sail through. I've got in a few ears and the reaction is promising. I've told them it's funding half the organised crime in the city.'

'And so it is,' Billy said. 'But now I need it to clean that money.'

'I won't go mentioning that to them. You've got the rent game to tide you over, haven't you?'

'Such a palaver. Keeping track of thirty or so companies. We're at arm's length from the street collections, thank God. The mortgages are a good wheeze, but that won't last. Too good to be true. I'll be glad to be out of it. A nicely furnished private casino is more my style. I tried to talk John Aspinall into letting me sit at one of his games, but he wouldn't hear of it.'

'Old Aspers is on the right track,' Rees-Davies said. 'He won't be able to charge a house percentage when we're done, but he has all the connections for a solid membership roll.'

'Yeah, he wants me to help him set up a proper club when the law goes through. Told him I had a few ideas about making up for his lost share of the winnings, and he was enthusiastic.'

'It's his mother, Lady Osborne, who's the real grifter. Good Lord, it's in her blood. You know, their being acquitted for running a gaming house was the best thing that could have happened. It shone a light on the issue in Westminster. His brief questioning the police's attitude to

John's games versus their complete indifference to money changing hands every night over the bridge tables in gentlemen's clubs across the city got a lot of the old boys worried.'

A girl came round and they placed their bets along with the order for their fish, and Billy covered it all.

'Nothing like winning on someone else's money.'

'Very good of you, Billy,' Boys said.

'It's not like I'm doing it out of the kindness of my heart. What's the score with the Ringway?'

Boys laid out the latest plans for the long-term development of a motorway box around inner London. Of particular interest to Billy was how the centre of the city was going to connect to this orbital road.

'Way the engineering bods see it, we'll run an elevated trunk road off the end of the Marylebone Road out to the western arm of the ringway. Roughly, this will follow the course of existing railways – both the trunk road, running alongside the Great Western Main Line and the Hammersmith & City, and the western arm of the ringway, which will head south along the West London Railway.'

'Compulsory purchase?'

'There will be some, though a lot of the land they're looking at is either industrial or used by the rail companies. The LCC has already purchased the slums around Westbourne Square from the borough and the Church Commissioners. Everything between the Harrow Road and the canal, going to raze the entire patch and rebuild.'

'We want to look lively then,' Billy said. 'Before they grab all the pork for themselves.'

'The interesting bit is in Notting Dale. They need a large round-about junction so the new road won't gently curve to the south with the Hammersmith & City railway but will form a right angle to the north-west of that bend where the junction will be built. That entire northern section of the Dale will go. All of it flattened. The road built. New housing developments put in. Compulsory purchases.

Demolition contracts. Construction jobs. Fifteen years from now, you won't recognise the place.'

Billy raised his glass in a toast.

'Gentlemen, White City becomes Fat City.'

Guilt was a thickly scented woods you couldn't see for the trees.

Ray obsessively read the story in the paper. He went out and bought several more papers, sat in the Prince of Wales for a couple of hours reading them. The stories were all the same, details thin on the ground.

Blaze at cold storage company.

One dead.

One critically ill.

Edward Nunn, the papers all said he was an independent driver, was fighting for his life at St Bartholomew's Hospital. The body recovered was yet to be identified.

Ray was certain he knew the man, couldn't put a name to him, though. Mum would know. It took everything he had not to bring it up with her when he got home, not to ask her outright. He desperately needed to talk about it with someone, to form the words and release them into the world before he burst.

He left the paper folded open at that page.

Knew she'd find it herself.

'My God.'

'What's that?'

'Edward Nunn, it says. Can't be.'

'Fella you used to work for?'

'There was a fire at a cold storage company.'

'Oh aye, that's him. Kingdom Cold Storage.'

She stared at him. Ray had this part all ready, had rehearsed it in his head to sound casual. Could recite it like poetry.

'Vic works for him, his day job. I met him over there for a chat about some work, saw that Nunn character.'

'It says here he was a driver.'

'Because the whole thing was a bit sus. He owned it, but not on paper. Something like that. Vic explained it but I wasn't listening.'

'An unnamed victim died. How awful.'

'It was that copper.'

'What copper?'

'One you knew. Give you a lift home sometimes, way back. When you worked with Nunn at that pub after dad went. Then he got banged up and it all came out he was some type of copper.'

'David?'

Ray shrugged. 'Dunno his name.'

'No. Never. How do you know? The paper doesn't seem to know who he was.'

'Told you. I was there seeing Vic.'

'What, when the fire was?'

'Yeah. No. The same day, but I was there earlier. Didn't know about any fire until later. But when I was hanging about out the front, I seen this bloke go in, and I swear it was him.'

'David?'

'Yeah. He looked different. Scruffier. Bit of a state, if I'm honest. Clothes were shabby, and he had a full-on beard.'

Mum's hand went to her face. 'He just got out of prison.'

'Thought he only got a few months?'

'Something happened.'

'Something always does. Reckon he was there to kill Nunn.'

'What on earth makes you say that?'

'Something I heard one of the meat porters say. That he thought Nunn had shopped him, got him put away.'

'I see.'

Ray went away feeling a lot better, like something had been

straightened out by verbalising it. This new reality, the one he had moulded and told mum, would amber in his mind and become the memory he relied on in the future. The mind was funny like that. You could rely on it being unreliable.

Claire muttered something about tea and fled to the kitchen to take stock.

David was dead.

Teddy might as well have been.

She couldn't remember, was this what she had wanted? The edges of her fury were foggy and indistinct now. It all felt like so long ago, as the past always was when it popped back up unbidden, the remnants of something immense that in hindsight looked like mad parody.

Surely nobody could connect her with these events, but even in her own mind she would have to handle them with kid gloves. Maintain the utmost politeness in their presence, wear a missionary's smile at all times.

The balance of life was tipping. Her husband, Freddie, now David and Teddy. All the men of her life dead or dying, she was surrounded now by as many ghosts as living.

What were Ray's chances?

A muddy inheritance.

She filled the kettle. Her thoughts were untidy and so she swept them up and deposited them in a dim attic along with the rest of it she hoarded but had no use for.

33

FOR EVER AND EVER

Nees begrudged her mouthy shoes.

As she pointedly walked up and down the hall in them, Addie could hear their lips smack where the sole had pulled away once more.

'They coming apart again already?'

'I didn't do nothing to them.'

'I know. I know.'

'Going to be flapping by the end of the day.'

'Well I can't do much right now, so take them off till you need them. No point making them worse.'

Nees sat in the middle of the hall and pulled them off. Conrad craned his head out of his door.

'I made too many accras for breakfast. Who's going to help me get rid of them?'

'Me!' Nees yelled, scampering down the hall in her socks.

Chabon loved an English fish supper from the chip shop, and Conrad always made good use of the copious leftovers, frying up something resembling fritters over the paraffin stove. He left Nees scoffing a plate of the things and knocked on Addie's door.

'Come in.'

He slid in sideways, keeping his eyes averted.

'I'm dressed, Con.'

'All the same.'

'Thanks for the breakfast.'

'She's the most enthusiastic about my cooking. Them shoes coming apart again.'

'Yeah. I was hoping to get a little longer out of them.'

'I know you're saving every penny you can for this nursing school of yours.'

'I'll have to get her a pair.'

'There's a fella over the way in one of the rooms. He's minded to mend most things, and owes me a favour. I'll speak to him later.'

'That'd be great, Con.'

'Tonight, I'm around if anyone needed to watch over Nees.'

'I don't think I'll be working late tonight. Clovis promised me something resembling a normal day today.'

'Well, himself will be wanting a word, so bear it in mind.'

Addie frowned. Footsteps on the stairs told her Chabon was coming, his fast stride down the hall.

'Have a word?' he said.

Conrad winked and disappeared off to see to Nees.

'It'll have to be quick, I'm going to be late.'

He pulled the door closed and snaked an arm round her waist.

'I can be quick,' he said, kissing her.

She leaned her head into his chest.

'What's this word, then?'

'It's three words. I love you. And I'm proud of you, working with Clovis as well as making plans for nursing and all. And I can get Nees a pair of shoes.'

'I love you too. And I know you can. I wanted to stretch it out until she grew out of them before buying a new pair, but looks like she's worn them through.'

'And you a little bit proud to take stuff from me.'

'Little bit that.'

'Even though we known each other for ever.'

'Even though.'

'Even though when we married, everything I have going to be yours too anyway.'

She looked up at him.

'I know, I know. No marriage talk.'

'When d'you picture doing it?'

'The shoes?'

'The wedding, dummy. Summer? Spring?'

'You serious? What are you . . .? This is you saying yes, or what's happening now?'

'This is me saying we're talking about it. Which we are.'

'This is London. Better than even chance it rain no matter what season you wait for, but I'd be happy waiting in the snow for you.'

'Well I wouldn't.' She stretched up and kissed him. 'But I love that you would.'

'You got to go.'

'Yeah.'

'See a film tonight?'

'What's on?'

'Uh . . . there's an Elizabeth Taylor?'

'Is there now. Surprise surprise.'

'In Technicolor.'

'Well, who am I to stand between you and a Technicolor Liz Taylor.'

Chabon loved the cinema. Often, when she was at work and he was free from whatever nebulous business he got up to with Everso and Kindness and that, he'd wander over to the Bughole on Portobello Road, where collapsed seating had been replaced with kitchen chairs and ratty armchairs, nick a couple of apples off a stall outside and sit in the dark hall watching the programmes all day, a dream world flickering over him.

'You got laundry?' he said.

'You offering?'

'Maybe.'

She nodded back over her shoulder. 'Bag on the floor beside the bed.'

DOMINIC NOLAN

'I'll ring you at Clovis's later, see what's happening.'
'All right.'

Chabon worked with Con for a few hours through the houses. Anything that would cost money wasn't going to get fixed, but they did what they could for leaks and blockages. Patched up broken windows with cardboard. There were sixteen houses, facing off across the thin road in almost identical terraces. Each was five storeys high and four rooms deep. While some tenants had their own room, other shared with as many as five others, sleeping in shifts in three beds depending on their work patterns.

A thousand people living in an area half the size of a football pitch.

Each of them had problems and complaints and Chabon got to hear them all. None of the houses had bathrooms, and the only guarantee that could be made about the solitary toilet in each was that they would never all be working at the same time. The public baths were a fifteen-minute walk.

When he was done, he had to get out of the place for an hour or so. There was no fresh air to talk of, the area hemmed in by railways and factories. Hyde Park was a mile away but felt like an alien planet. He walked along Talbot Road, got himself a coffee and chatted with a few people. A tenant found him and told him the skylight on the top floor of number seven was cracked. Chabon said he'd look to it.

At home, he collected up the dirty clothes in a sack and slung it over his shoulder. Mile to the baths where the laundry was. Got a few looks going in. He'd been refused entry once and made a fuss, thinking it was because he was black, and the attendant told him no men were allowed in, and two local white women came out and told the attendant more men should be bringing laundry to the place and he was let in because of them. The women were always warmer than the men, though not all of them.

He decided to use the new machines they had there. Addie would go spare if she knew, thought they were a waste of money. They did cost double compared to doing it by hand, but took half the time, so Chabon figured it balanced out in the end.

The sack was twice as heavy carrying home as the clothes were damp. At the centre of the house was a void, providing what passed for natural light to the middle rooms. At the bottom lay years of junk tossed out of windows. Broken chairs, an old wireless, a pram with no wheels or hood. Lines were strung across it, and he hung the washing to dry. What didn't fit, he hung on a drier in his room over the paraffin heater.

Everso and Kindness were drinking in the Apollo with Moses. A group of tenants from the houses were there and Everso was telling them how to arrange hearings with the rent tribunal. Chabon sat with them when he was done.

'You work for the man,' Chabon said.

'Yeah.'

'And you're agitating against him.'

'Not hardly. I'm happy with my situation. But these folk think they're being treated unfairly, and this is Britain so fair's fair. I tell them the best way I know to go about addressing that.'

'Against Mr Rachman.'

'Look, I got no quarrel with Rachman myself. I collect the rent and give him the portion he want each week, and we do all right out of the rest, yeah? And without him, where would we be living? All them people out there renting rooms with No Blacks on the signs, that's the ones who create the situation allows someone like Rachman to flourish. He's just doing his thing. Hell, he loves a black man. We keep his pockets stuffed. You had a few more out there like him, willing to rent a room to us, then he wouldn't be able to charge what he does. On the other hand, I'm not owned by the man. I do a job and I get paid for that. I earn that money fair and square. Anything else is a different matter. These are my people too, and any advice I can give them is separate to my situation with Rachman.'

Moses laughed. 'That's you. Back and front and black all over.'

'It's a funny way of looking at things,' Chabon agreed.

'That funny way puts money in everyone's pocket, am I wrong?'

'You're not wrong.'

'Then I'll keep looking funny.'

Early evening, Chabon went across to the phone box opposite the Apollo and called Clovis's shop.

'You walking her home?' Clovis wanted to know. Everyone was still on edge after the trouble.

'What I was calling to ask.'

Clovis put Addie on.

'What time's the show?'

'About an hour, I think.'

'Not sure I'll make it. I should be out of here pretty soon, but I need to bring my fur coat to be cleaned. There's a dry cleaner's open late tonight in Kensal Town.'

'You and that fur coat.'

'It has a bit of a musk to it.'

'I can do that. Where's this cleaner's?'

'You know the pub does the music?'

'Addie, that's an industrial cleaner or something there. I can't just walk in with a coat.'

'No, the other way. Back toward the canal. There's a dry cleaner's on the corner.'

'All right. I'll drop it off now and come meet you. We can go straight to the picture house.'

'Meet me at the house. I want to change.'

'You be okay walking home?'

'Chay, it's round the corner.'

'Yeah, all right.'

Back at the Apollo, he told the boys he was heading off.

'Where you going?' Moses said. 'You going the pictures?'

'I fancy the pictures,' said Kindness.

'Why not?' said Everso. 'Where you going? You're not taking her to the Bughole. Royalty then. Royalty tonight, boys?'

'Sure I've seen you three there in the back row before.'

They jeered him out the door and he hurried back to their rooms to grab Addie's fur coat. Kensal Town was across the two railways, the footbridge over the Hammersmith & City and the iron bridge over the mainline trunk, four tracks whisking people away to the glamorous uplands of Reading and Swindon.

He was still wary on the streets anywhere outside the Town or the Grove, and even that close to home he had eyes in the back of his head. He wished he had gone to meet Addie. Still, it wasn't dark yet.

He'd see her soon.

Clovis held her coat up for her to slip her arms into.

'I can walk you back.'

She looked over her shoulder at him.

'I know that look,' he said. 'It says be careful, or I might pull my shoe off and beat you with it.'

'Women take their satisfaction in more subtle ways, Clovis.'

He laughed, *ack ack ack*, like he welcomed the idea, having in his life withstood far more spiteful scrutinies than hers. Addie left work with an unfamiliar sensation – happy that she'd spent the day there. She could talk and laugh with Clovis as they worked, and felt freer there than she ever had at the chemise factory. Felt like she was growing into herself and had further room still to expand.

'I'll be fine,' she said. 'There haven't been gangs on the streets since last week. Not round here. They'll stick to their usual haunts in the Dale or Bayswater.'

Clovis waved her off. 'I'll see you tomorrow.'

Going out the door, she was still buttoning up her jacket, eyes not on the pavement, and bumped into someone as she moved off.

'Oh, excuse me.'

The Prince of Wales was deserted.

Ray stood Vic and Clive a couple of drinks, still elated from his narrow brush with Teddy Nunn that nobody else knew about. Everyone was talking about it, though. Vic had been to see the bloke who sorted the houses for Mother, some Pole, and he'd told them to carry on with what they were doing. They spent the last few days removing the slates from a roof to convince the tenants it wasn't worth staying.

'I heard the one who died was shot,' Clive said. 'That Nunn shot him with his own gun. Reckon he was trying to rob him?'

'Can't imagine Nunn giving anyone reason to want him dead, fucking prince that he is,' Ray said.

He'd taken to doing this, commentary on Mother's character. Making a point of not worshipping the bigshot villain. He was spoiling for a row, but nobody gave him it.

Vic said he knew someone who was hosting a house party and they sloped off in that direction. At the station, they met a friend of his who'd come in from the West End, where he'd picked up some bottles of two per cent lager and handed them round. May as well have been drinking gutter water.

Ray was jittery.

He didn't appreciate being on the move, wanted them to settle somewhere he was comfortable, where he could drink and float in and out of the conversation. He was beginning to think about going back to sea again. Missed the newness and the sameness of it. Different ports, different cities, but always the same ship to return to. He did better when he was in a system he could see and understood.

He thrived when he was circumstanced.

Sitting on the staircase in the house of someone he didn't know with a bottle of piss-weak beer wasn't doing much for him. He went out into the front garden for a snout. Some young bird was sitting on the scruffy lawn, leaning back against the precarious wooden fence, something she'd taken having disagreed with her. A gas holder loomed in the distance. Smokestacks from the paint works and biscuit factory belched on, even at that time of the day.

Ray longed for the salty air of the sea.

He heard someone coming out behind him and knew it was the others.

'Gis a smoke,' Clive said.

Ray shook out his pack.

'She looks like she's had enough.'

'Know how she feels,' Ray said.

'What's with you?'

'Nothing.'

'You've been a prick all night,' Vic said.

'Fuck off.'

'When it's just us, you want to say something about Teddy Nunn, that's fine. But when there's others around—'

'Fuck Teddy Nunn. Got what he asked for.'

'That's the sort of thing I'm talking about.'

'Just because you wanted to tug his prick.'

'Hey, fuck's your problem? Not everyone shared your opinion of Teddy.'

'Probably on account of him not killing their dads.'

Vic looked around to make sure nobody was listening in the house.

'It's stuff like that you don't want to be saying.'

'Shut up. I'll say what I like.'

He bumped Vic with his shoulder going out the gate into the street. Vic followed him, grabbing his arm.

'Look—'

Ray shoved him hard, Vic stumbling off the kerb.

'You want to watch it,' Vic said.

Ray had his stiletto in his hand, down by his side, but he took half a step toward Vic.

Vic grinned.

'I ain't scared of you, you silly twat. Some of these others, who thought you were a headcase when you were kids, they might be. But I know what you are. How you were two, three years older than them. Scared of the bigger kids so you pushed around the younger ones who didn't know no better. I know you don't have it to put that knife in me.'

Ray was breathing hard, fist clenched to the white around the blade handle.

Vic moved in close enough that Ray could feel his words.

'Put the knife away before I take it off you and show you how it's used, and let's go have a real drink back in the Dale.'

Ray slid the knife into his pocket.

'Fucking hell, Raymond,' Vic laughed.

Clive laughed with him, slapping Ray on the back.

'Jesus, Ray. Thought you were going psycho for a moment.'

It was a soft retreat from a hard situation. Ray forced himself to crack a smile. Impotent rage inside him like a malignancy, blocking arteries, choking off his heart.

'Must be this two per cent shite,' he said.

He missed the sea. Out there, you buoyed yourself with thoughts of home, but not the home you knew. The home you conjured with your shipmates, a melange of things you missed, things you made up. Here, now, it was as strange to him as the rickety cities of the East, where he'd spend nights among sharp-hipped boys and was sometimes robbed, among other things.

Would he stay here in the Dale? Who knew. The great thing about the sea was it would always be there waiting for him if he needed to get away. It was his true home now.

They walked past the church and the Catholic club where there occasionally were dances, and round to where the shops were. Ray was quiet, trying to let whatever it was making his chest a cave of swarming bats work its way out of his system. Coming round the corner, he blindly bumped into someone.

'Watch where you're going.'

A West Indian, with a fancy fur coat over his arm. Head down, he tried to move on around them. Ray put a hand on his chest.

'How about an apology.'

'Where you going you expect to wear that?' Clive said, laughing.

Ray reached down toward the fur coat and the lad slapped his hand away, and before anyone had time to weigh the situation up, Ray had stuck him through the ribs with the stiletto.

'Black bastard.'

He stumbled backwards, slid down the wall of the dry cleaner's he had been headed for.

Vic pulled Ray away.

'Let's go.'

Ray stood where he was. Down the road a ways two more West Indians were taking an interest.

'Come on, Ray, there are people.'

Ray followed him down a side street and they took off running. Ray veered round another corner, making for the iron bridge back over the railway.

'Where you going?' Vic said breathlessly.

'Home?'

'What about that?'

Ray looked at the bloody knife in his hand.

'Under the floorboards?'

'In your place? Don't be daft. Come on.'

They ran toward the canal, through the narrow streets to the towpath. Following it east beneath the road bridge, they ran alongside the goods sheds in the railway yard, passing the hospital on the other side. When they reached the lock bridge at the Harrow Road, they slowed to a walk and carried on going up to a bend in the canal where the sawmill and timber yard were, and tossed the knife in. They got back onto the streets where a footbridge was and walked through the Westbourne Square slums toward Notting Hill.

Everything was a heady rush.

Nobody had stopped them.

Nobody had stopped him.

He wanted desperately to laugh manically, a hyena's cackle, but concentrated hard on keeping it in. Mustn't get stopped now.

Chabon sat against the wall, winded.

His legs weren't answering him.

Two men, Jamaican from their voices, ran up and knelt beside him.

'We seen them. You okay?'

Chabon nodded. He winced.

The one nearest him held his lapel, tried to open his jacket.

Chabon fended him off with a stern look and strong thoughts.

'I'm not robbing you,' the man said.

He found Chabon's wallet, the picture inside. Together with Addie and Nees at Bernard's one Sunday in Brixton. Bernard had taken it himself with his new camera, took pictures of everyone and gave them out the next week. There was a scrap of paper with Clovis's number on it.

'Clovis? That someone you know?'

Chabon nodded. Felt like it was all he could do. A car pulled up, the driver was black.

'He hurt?'

'Yeah, I think they mugged him. Looked like one of them punched him.'

They tried to get him to his feet and that was when they got wind of the blood leaking out of him.

'Get him in the back,' the driver said. 'We take him to St Charles.'

They lifted him into the back, Chabon crying out in agony. Felt like they were tearing him in two. He reached wildly for the photo of

Addie. One of the men gave him the fur coat and Chabon looked at him helplessly.

'The picture,' the other one said.

Gathering up his wallet and bits, they got in the back with him and the driver made off at haste for the hospital. Chabon clutched the picture, blood on it now that he tried to wipe away.

He stared at it.

He'd see her soon.

Addie almost fell over the woman with the pram. She recognised her from round the way and they chatted and cooed over the child before she headed on home. She washed in cold day-old water and changed quickly.

No sign of Chabon.

'Took that coat of yours,' Conrad said.

'He's going to be so mad I made him miss Elizabeth Taylor.'

'Boy probably sit in that theatre all day tomorrow watching the film over and over.'

Nees walked down the hall slapping her feet like a duck.

'Your shoes fix themselves?' Addie said in mock amazement.

'Con's friend did it with glue.'

'Good job you didn't get stuck to the floor.'

'I wouldn't have been able to go to school.'

'Well, your shoes wouldn't have been, anyway.'

Kindness came leaping up the stairs, Everso huffing along behind him.

'You two racing?' Conrad said.

Kindness looked at the old man, then looked to Addie.

'What is it?' she said.

'Clovis got a telephone call.'

'Right?'

'From some Jamaican boy at St Charles.'

'The hospital?' Conrad said, standing straight now.

'They took Chabon there.'

'Why?' Addie said. 'What happened?'

'Find him in the street. Said he got robbed by some white boys. They thought he got punched, but . . .'

'What happened?' Conrad said.

'Is he all right?' said Addie.

Everso laid a hand on Kindness's shoulder.

'He's dead.'

Addie tried to catch Conrad, but he was too tall, too heavy, and it was all she could do to steer him into the wall, which he slid down to the floor.

'My boy. My boy.'

Nees stood rooted to the spot, like there might be broken glass all round her. Addie gathered her up into her arms.

'My boy.'

Nobody moved to do anything.

There was a terrible stillness to shock.

34

AMEN

Coppers turned Kensal Town upside down.

Debris sites, derelict houses, rubbish tips, any slum basements they could get into. Drain covers were pulled up, the pebbles in the playground were raked through and the lavatories torn apart. The railway was picked over by men with sticks. They dredged the canal with magnets beneath Carlton Bridge and the nearby foot crossings.

Nothing.

Constables went door to door questioning everyone, getting details of the night of the murder. Notes were made of any parties, who might have been there, what sort of people they were.

Ray and Vic's names came up pretty early and they were taken to Harrow Road nick for questioning. Claire couldn't believe it. She and Peg went to the station to wait for them. A crowd of friends and other neighbours went too, gathered outside. They all returned the next day when the lads still hadn't been released.

It was an outrage.

Absolute liberty by the coppers.

That second day, Claire brought her camera and got images of everything. The coppers coming and going, the jeering crowd outside, the boys with their fists raised in victory when they were finally released after thirty-six hours. It was electric. She shot five rolls of film. It felt like something she could do with her life, make a photographic record of coppers throughout the city.

The idea fizzed with peril.

That night, she let herself into the studio where she worked and developed the rolls, along with a few she'd shot the previous week. Kids playing. Buildings rotting. The Dale in action.

Her memories of her war years on the farm with Fred's family were thick with golden pastoral sunlight, rainless and merry days. If she had shot any, would photographs show that? Film was faithful to disappointments, unlike the brushstrokes of the mind. But faithful only to the fugitive moment they captured, existing without past or future.

Agitating the final print from the old roll in developing fluid, the image emerged out of acetate nothingness.

The ragman's horse and cart.

David astride his scooter.

The papers had named him now as the victim of the fire at Kingdom Cold Storage, doubtless after some confrontation with Teddy. Chances were this was the last picture ever taken of him.

He must have moved as she took it, his face washed out in a blur, as if someone had smudged it with their finger. A twilight mask.

No past.

No future.

The second time Ray and Vic were brought in by the police, Claire began to think.

The way Ray was.

Whatever had happened that day with Teddy and David and the fire, Ray having been there. Things he had said over the years. And Peg had heard stories about the riots, about Ray and his friends. He'd come home the night things were worst and gone back out again.

She hadn't wanted to think about it, for the same reason she would never share her mounting suspicions with anyone. She was ashamed. Ashamed he had come from her, ashamed she had raised him. Ashamed she had failed him in some way, perhaps after Freddie disappeared. Not given him enough of herself.

She would conceal her doubts about him.

The shame would be too much to carry publicly.

There was no crowd outside the station the second time. He walked home from the Harrow Road, arriving sullen and withdrawn. She'd made dinner and he quickly turned angry at the table.

'Do we need to think about getting a brief?' Claire said.

'What for? I wasn't arrested.'

'No, but they wouldn't let you have one before. If we talk to someone, then if you get pulled in again we can get them down the station.'

'For what? I just tell them the truth. How can I get in trouble doing that?'

'All right, it was a suggestion is all.'

'Can't believe they've had me and Vic in twice, just because we were at a party and we're white. Everyone there saw us turn up in a larger group, and they're looking for two or three blokes. Stabbing people up? That's their game, not ours. That Georgie Marks, last month, stabbed round the corner from his own home in Shepherd's Bush. Nearly had his kidney out. They're more likely to be stabbing each other up. Nah, knives are their thing.'

'What about that stiletto you have?'

The question popped out before Claire could think about it, the knife she'd found sorting through his washing in his room.

'What stiletto?'

She looked at him.

'I don't know what you're talking about. I don't have a knife. Christ, I think signing up for the ships again is what I'll do. This place is beyond the pale. Gone to the dogs.'

'All right, Ray.'

'I don't own a knife.'

'I believe you.'

'Because we can search my room. Right now, if you want.'

He slammed his cutlery down, rattling the table.

'Ray—'

'I mean, Jesus Christ. What do you think I am? An animal?'

As soon as she opened the envelope, Claire knew who it was from, knew it was his St Christopher.

The key was a mystery, a locker at Paddington.

Some game of his, sent to her just before he died.

What could be in the locker that she would want? What could he have offered her other than further trauma?

She put it back in the envelope and slid the blurred photograph of him in alongside.

Then she threw it in the fire. Watched until the paper burned away, the key falling into the ash.

Lost days.

A limbo between death and burial, the cold remains of Chabon held at the morgue for the increasingly vandalised police investigation. They didn't want to find what they didn't want to find; on the heels of the riots, an unsolved mugging-gone-wrong was the best result all round as far as the coppers were concerned.

Conrad wasn't much for talking about it. The detectives were one hundred per cent living up to his expectations of them, and he ignored them as best he could. Retreated into his caretaking duties, working all hours fixing any little thing that needed looking to on Powis Terrace. Everyone in the buildings knew what had happened. The women gave him food they could barely afford for themselves, often just basics, flour or bread or milk. From the men he received nods and looks, the occasional handshake or shoulder pat.

Wolf howls of shared grief.

When he returned to his room, he rarely went out to the downstairs gamble houses or rum shops. Making good use of the heaps of food people offered, he cooked up plates and shared them round. Addie and Nees had never eaten so good. They'd get fat on the rind of loss.

Addie kept a close eye on Nees, saw her watching everyone else, figuring out how to act to meet their expectations of how sad she should be. Trying to make sense of it in her young mind, even though she'd already had enough people leave her for a whole lifetime.

Reggie.

Stevie.

Chabon.

And now Addie always talking about going off to learn her nursing.

The day she turned eighteen, Addie let the occasion pass without comment. Everso had his white lawyers working on her guardianship of Nees, who shruggingly accepted the situation like she didn't know what alternatives people thought there might be. She didn't talk about Stevie or Chabon, but one night Addie awoke to her crying quietly. She got up and slipped into her sister's bed, and Nees let her hold her. For years, Addie had dreamed of her own bed, nobody poking and kicking and leaping on her, but now she couldn't imagine wanting to be anywhere else.

Bitter nights.

She couldn't say of what she dreamed, but took it to be Chabon as she awoke nauseous and empty, everything uncoiled and slid out of her. As though in sleep she had nestled in the scent of home, but awake could no longer catch any trace of it.

She ached with want.

She prayed this was grief, because she couldn't bear for there to be worse yet to come. If these were the rewards for life, then of what value was virtue? She should run wild, find those who had wronged her and burn down their homes with them in their beds.

Detectives returned the blood-soaked fur coat, presenting it to Addie as if doing her a favour. Perhaps it was what the attackers were trying to steal. Perhaps if he hadn't been flaunting it on the streets. Addie smiled and accepted it.

'Why, thank you so much.'

She told herself she knew the only thing they had wanted to take was Chabon's life, yet she kept the coat. More than once, she walked to the dry cleaner's in Kensal Town, carrying it over her arm, but never took it in. She looped the streets up there hoping to bump into those responsible, to what end she didn't know. She felt exposed, as if no matter what she wore, all people would see was her decked out in pleated grief and furred guilt.

Ashamed of her grief, she tried to hide it, but could no more do so than she could hide the moon. And like the moon, over the coming years it would at times blink out of sight, and at others hang fat and low, invading the blue skies of day.

She returned the fur coat to her wardrobe, where she'd see it every morning.

A dead thing itself, evidence of her shame.

Witness to this death of her love.

Hundreds turned up for the funeral, a thousand perhaps.

The congregation of a local church had been particularly kind, especially as neither Conrad nor Chabon had ever set foot in the place. He was buried in Kensal Green Cemetery, and Conrad insisted she stood beside him at the grave. Bess had stayed behind to look after Nees, who was happy for a day of dominoes.

The place was packed with stone needles and gothic sarcophagi, and as Addie watched him lowered into the earth beneath which he would rot in a box, earth that was as indifferent as the sun or the rain, she wished she could bury him someplace else where he could feed the soil and things would grow wildly above him. No neatly rolled lawns or dour stone.

'Thinking I might take a walk up to that church next Sunday,' Conrad said, when it was only the two of them left. 'Used to go every week down in Brixton, but lost the habit in this place. Be nice to find people.'

'Maybe I'll come too,' Addie said.

He smiled. She'd never thought godwardly in any fashion, and had no intentions of starting now, but she'd go with Conrad and pray for his son, the boy she loved. What possible harm could come from that? It would be nice to find people.

Out of nowhere, her breath jumped in her chest and she felt her eyes tear up. Conrad's arm stretched across her shoulders.

'Can't cry about this, what can you cry about?'

'What do I need with a fur coat? Just pride. My pride and he ends up here, in the ground.'

'None of that now. My boy didn't die because he was taking a coat to be cleaned. Only one person responsible for what happened, and that's not you. You seen them trying to burn us out of our houses. Attacking people on the street. What got him killed was the same thing.'

Tears rolled down her face freely now. 'Wish I'd just let him pick me up from work and gone straight to the cinema.'

'All that boy talked about was you. All I ever remember him talking about since you was both charging about my waist. How he was going to marry you and look after you and that sister of yours. But first, you was going to become a nurse and he was going to look to Nees while you was doing that. And I was going to help him. That's still going to be the case. He had some money set by. Not much, but however that helps you go to this school, that's what we're going to do with it. He'd have wanted that.'

People were waiting at the Greek-looking chapel, and they walked in a procession back down Ladbroke Grove, gradually thinning out as they went, until there was only those who lived in the Colville slums and they returned to their homes. The basement rum shop was open in Chabon's honour, but Addie couldn't face it and told Conrad that she needed a walk, that she'd see him later.

When she returned to the flat, she carried beneath her arm a stack of boxes that she presented to Nees.

'For me?'

'Uh huh. Present.'

'I won most of the games with Bess,' she said, opening the first box.

'Especially the ones where the rules needed changing in strange and arbitrary ways,' Bess said.

'New shoes!' Nees said, holding aloft a pair of black buckled shoes.

'There's more.'

She tore into the other boxes and found a pair of sandals and some plimsolls.

'Ready for all weather now,' Addie said.

Nees took her old glued and nailed pair off and slipped on the shiny new ones, sticking a plimsoll on each fist, and ran down the hall to show Conrad, who'd returned from the basement for a nap.

'Three pairs weren't cheap,' he said, as Nees danced up and down the hall.

'I'm staying with Clovis. I'm not going to nursing school.'

'I told you we'd all help out, Addie.'

'It's not that. It really isn't. I love working with Clovis. I'm learning things, and I think I could have my own shop one day. And I can't leave Nees. I don't want to.'

Addie had always thought of Nees being present in her life with the dismal insistence of the sea's edge rolling onto the shore. But she was wrong. That had never been the case. One day, Nees would be older, or would live somewhere of her own, and there would be days they would not see each other, turning perhaps to weeks or months or whatever might happen in life. And suddenly she didn't want Nees to age. She wanted her there always, tugging at her sleeve or moaning or ignoring her or anything she wanted so long as she was just there.

Stevie said people were what they loved. She loved the bottle.

Addie loved her father, a gone man who had never quite existed in the way she thought he had. Gone now like her mother. Gone like the past and the future. Life took so much, but it also gave; the sorrow leavened the joy.

She would find her father in other things. In Conrad and in Everso and in Bess and in Nees; the community would be her father. The streets of Colville and the Grove would be her father.

The darkness left by the departed would be her father, and into it she would bear light.

Credits

Dominic Nolan would like to thank everyone involved in the production of White City

Editorial
Toby Jones
Isabel Martin

Copy editor
Jane Selley

Proof reading
Helen Norris

Audio
Ellie Wheeldon

Design
Patrick Insole
Jack Smyth

Production
Tina Paul

Marketing
Joe Yule

Publicity
Rosie Margesson

Sales
Becky Bader
Georgina Cutler
Sinead White
Izzy Smith

Legal
Kirsty Howarth

Contracts
Helen Windrath

Special thanks are extended to: N Barr, my advocate, my friend, and my first and best eyes; Emma Lagarde, Aminah Amjad, Victoria Capello, Jenny Bent and everyone at The Bent Agency for their tireless work; Corinne Marotte and everyone at Marotte et compaigne for spreading the word; Valentin Baillehache, Jeanne Guyon, Alain Deroudilhe, Thierry Corvoisier, Mahaut Delcourt and everyone at Rivages for making a dream come true; thankpologies to everyone subjected to early reads of this thing, I was grateful for all your thoughts.

Completing this book was a bright spot in an otherwise dreadful year, and I'm particularly grateful to Nic, Toby, Si, Victoria, Heather, Harriet, Rachael and Lou for their support, and to Jo, Adam, Liz, Fliss, Elle, Barry, Kate, Niki, Polly, Susie, Simon, Rob, and Tim for daily morale boosting malarky.